The Devil Inside

'You've a lot to learn, Alexa, such a lot. You're a sensualist, that's obvious. Your responses are amazing ... but you need educating. Opening up. Sex is much more than simply fucking your boyfriend on a regular basis. Or fucking mine for that matter.' She laughed richly. 'Sex is a state of mind. A way of life. So much more than just penis and vagina. Cock and quim. Prick and cunt. it's beyond gender, even. Do you understand what I mean?'

Alexa was shocked by the raw language, but she did understand. Even as she'd listened it had all seemed so clear. A month ago, she would have thought Beatrice's pronouncements gratuitously obscene – but now she could feel wisdom at work.

There was a new world – worlds! – of sex waiting for her, but her voyage of discovery was already well under way. She'd begun the second stage on the doorstep of this house ...

By the same author:

Gemini Heat
The Tutor
Gothic Blue
Continuum
The Stranger
Hotbed
Shadowplay
Entertaining Mr Stone

The Devil Inside
Portia De Costa

BLACK LACE

Black Lace books contain sexual fantasies.
In real life, always practise safe sex.

This edition published in 2006 by
Black Lace
Thames Wharf Studios
Rainville Road
London W6 9HA

Originally published 1995

Typeset by SetSystems Ltd, Saffron Walden, Essex
Printed and bound by Mackays of Chatham PLC

ISBN 0 352 32993 9
ISBN 9 780352 329936

Contents

Dedicated to Cyrian,
who sets the standard...

Chapter One

A New Woman

One morning, in May, on the sunlit island of Barbados, Alexa Lavelle woke up a new woman. To describe it that way was a truism, she knew, but it did sum up what she felt. She just wasn't the same woman she'd been yesterday.

The world around her seemed different, too. Colours were brighter; sounds were clearer; smells assaulted her nostrils so pungently that their richness made her feel almost giddy. Lying still between the crisp cotton sheets of her wide hotel bed, Alexa experienced the weirdest sensation, a kind of buoyant rising-up that enthralled her and turned her head like sweet island rum.

The thought of spirits made her wonder if she was genuinely drunk. She remembered having headaches in the night, but felt nothing now. On the contrary, she couldn't recall ever having felt more healthy. She felt like running or skipping or jumping in the air. Her limbs were tingling with a great excess of energy, and her skin felt soft as silk and smoothly glowing.

Still trying to discover what had happened to her, she thought back to the previous day. Her memories were one complete, seamless flow, yet at the same time, it

1

was as if she was seeing the action through a filter. Today, she had a whole new set of perceptions that suddenly made yesterday seem drab.

Taking in a deep breath of the ocean-scented air, Alexa stretched, then made another discovery. Although completely alone, and so celibate since the start of her holiday that she'd hardly even thought about sex, she was suddenly aware of being aroused.

Alexa had always enjoyed lovemaking – sometimes so much so that it scared her – but right now she felt a jolt of sharp desire. The physical symptoms were real and unmistakable, and so intense they left no room for doubt.

Between her legs, and in the pit of her belly, she had a fierce urge to be filled by a man. No particular man, just a man in the abstract. One that was strong, hard, and enduring; and alive with a lust that matched her own.

What the devil's happened to me? she wondered, stirring and stretching luxuriously, then waiting for some kind of payback. She could remember why she'd had the headaches now, but it still didn't account for everything else.

Two days ago, after falling on slippery rocks and bumping her head, Alexa had spent a couple of hours in the island's main medical centre. The staff there had examined her thoroughly, done various scans and tests, but found nothing at all untoward. She'd been unconscious a second or two after the bump, but not, they said, suffered true concussion. When her fitness to leave had been pronounced, she'd been sent back to the hotel with the simple instruction to 'take things nice and easy' – which wasn't difficult at the St James's Cove Refuge.

But last night things had not been nice and easy. Half awake and half asleep, Alexa had just lain in her bed and endured, her dozy, pain-fuddled mind imagining demons jabbing spears inside her temples. Too enervated to move, she'd promised herself she'd seek help

2

in the morning. But when morning finally came, both the headaches and the demons were gone, and she'd woken up to sunlight and the soothing island heat.

And this unignorable craving for sex . . .

Stretching her fingertips slowly towards the white, stuccoed ceiling, Alexa sat up and looked around her. All her familiar possessions were here in the room with her: her clothes, her toiletries, her souvenirs and knick-knacks. And yet somehow, they didn't seem to be hers any more. Her pink sundress, draped over a woven-backed chair, looked irritatingly prim and 'covered-up'. Likewise her shapeless towelling dressing gown. She remembered loving the robe when she'd bought it, and enjoying its soft, cosy comfort; but now she suddenly wished it was sleek and frivolous instead. Something exotic in flimsy, watered silk. Red, with a fire-breathing dragon on the back.

Now where did I get that from? she thought, re-examining the sensuous image, then realising it was one she'd really seen. Her new friend Doctor Quine – the woman from the next cabana – had a scarlet robe with a dragon. Alexa remembered seeing it draped half on and half off Beatrice's near-naked body as they'd lazed together yesterday by the pool. The doctor had an incredible shape, slim yet thoroughly sumptuous, and she had a habit of displaying almost all of it. She would stretch out like a graven idol on her lounger – in the shade because her skin was very pale – and let her handsome young 'companion' read her poetry, in French, from a small, white leather-covered book. Alexa's French wasn't marvellous, but she could tell from the odd word or two, and more so from Drew's deep, velvet-brown voice, that the verse was deliciously obscene.

Flinging aside the single top sheet, then peeling off her white cotton nightie, Alexa made a long, puzzled study of her body. Like her mind, it was nominally the same as yesterday, but even so, she seemed to see changes. Her shapely, firm-fleshed thighs seemed to

3

invite her touch, as did the softly haired triangle of her sex. She felt her neat, dark pubis demanding something of her, something she'd mostly always done with a slight, childish guilt, but which now she anticipated eagerly. Her crisp black curls had a springy new lustre this morning, an opulence that encouraged exploration.

Her breasts looked different, too. More rounded, more voluptuous. Alexa knew it was a trick of the mind, but they seemed to thrust upwards and insolently outwards, and challenge her to fondle and caress them.

Experimentally, she placed the pad of one finger against the lightly tanned curve of her abdomen; then gasped aloud in surprise. A clear, silvery sensation seemed to shoot from the point of contact, just beneath her navel, and attack the very heart of her sex. The urge to follow its path with her fingers was so strong and compelling that she bit down on her lip in pure shock. It felt as if a man had kissed her belly, sucked it long and moistly, then pressed his hand into the crease of her vulva.

On the bedside table stood her fiancé's photograph, but his smiling face offered no answers. It wasn't Thomas who'd initiated the thrill. Alexa had tried to think about him during the holiday, and she even tried now, but there seemed far more than just glass – and an ocean – between them.

Oh Tom, I'm sorry, she thought confusedly, wanting desperately to connect with the photo.

But as she failed, utterly, another image formed instead; one so clear and wickedly erotic that it made her face burn, and her limbs quiver crazily.

She was nude and sweating on this very bed, pinned and spread beneath a strong, faceless man. They were writhing and struggling in a furious bout of sex, and the stranger had his penis deep inside her. For her own part, Alexa could see that her knees were bent and legs wrapped around him, and her heels were thumping hard against his rump.

But the image involved more than just sight. As

4

clearly as she could see the empty white room around her, she could feel the unknown man pounding into her. His pulsing shaft was stretching and massaging her, and he felt massive in the cradle of her thighs. With each new thrust, he drove in even further and ravished her at her soft, molten core.

Hot yearning washed through Alexa, and, pressing her hand to where her dream man laboured, she found a well of mercurial slickness. The groove of her sex was fluid and slippery and her labia were puffy and engorged. She felt alive in every part of her with a heavy, tropic power, yet at the same time felt so light she could fly.

Uttering a loud cry, Alexa smothered her last inhibitions, and gave in to the devil in her belly. Her legs flexing, she kicked out wildly, then arched back against the twisted white sheets. As her fingers danced, she made a final effort to look towards Thomas, but his picture seemed almost transparent. In her mind there was just 'man' – an immense, all-consuming presence that possessed her without revealing his face.

Rubbing faster, her bottom writhing against the mattress, Alexa crooned joyfully as orgasm bloomed. The pleasure made her legs wave, her loins clench and her hands claw savagely at the linen. For a moment, as madness gripped her, she imagined she could see faces: all around, faces that should have meant nothing to her, yet which suddenly had a breathtaking impact as bodies joined the torrid inner scene. She saw handsome, tanned men from the hotel; smiling black houseboys, their thin white trousers gaping open; total strangers all primed and ready to serve her. She even saw her new friend Doctor Quine. A woman . . . but naked and red-mouthed with desire.

What the devil's happening to me? thought Alexa Lavelle again, as she struggled for control of her senses.

What's happening and why is it so good?

Chapter Two

Tending the Fires

*A*lexa spent a long, long time in the shower that morning. First with hot water, using lots of soap, shampoo and shower gel to cleanse her body of the night's perspiration; and afterwards with cold water, as icy cold as she could bear it, to try to cool the strange heat that burned inside her.

It didn't, of course, and as she strolled out on to the veranda, where her breakfast was waiting on the table, she felt overwhelmed by the power of her hunger. Her craving not for food, but for life itself. And life in the specific form of sex.

The island, too, seemed to be conspiring against her. The rich scents of the greenery all around; the gentle breeze that tickled her oversensitive skin; the wild, singing blue of the ocean at the bottom of her garden. Even the sly lapping of the waves against the pearly sand reminded her of flesh slapping sweatily against flesh.

As she sat down on her white-painted chair and poured coffee, Alexa realised that her new sensual awareness was going to be difficult, nay impossible, to fight. Already, and without knowing how, she could sense things: almost hear them, see them and feel them. She could detect minds very close to her that were thinking about sex, and bodies that were stirring and embracing.

Were Beatrice and Drew making love now? she wondered, thinking that in her present state, she could not have had worse – or better – neighbours. With the gloriously overstated Doctor Quine around, it was impossible not to think about sex, even if you weren't normally all that interested. But when you *were* interested, and you had a kind of subtle, erotic antenna that was constantly scanning for stimulation, having Beatrice near could well be pure torment.

Even so, Alexa looked forward to the experience; if not for the doctor herself, then at least for the presence of Drew. He really was gorgeous, she accepted fatalistically; one of the most impressive looking men she'd ever met.

Thinking back, she recalled the moment she'd first seen him, just a few hours after she'd arrived at the Refuge. Even then he'd had an effect on her, and a sexual one, and that was *before* these weird changes she'd felt.

She'd been strolling around the pool, wondering what the hell she was doing there, spending money she couldn't afford, some of which wasn't even hers – and suddenly she'd seen a holy vision. A man emerging up the ladder at the deep end, water streaming off muscle and smooth, tanned skin; a perfume-seller's super-model cliché, yet real and boyish somehow. She'd taken a swift eyeful of long, solid thighs and the skimpiest of black thong-like swimtrunks then forced herself to look the other way. It was bad enough leaving Thomas behind and illicitly using his money, without mentally undressing the first stereotypical hunk she set eyes on.

Taking a long sip of the hotel's excellent coffee, Alexa tried not to think of Drew Kendrick, and instead considered the effect her new condition – or whatever it was – might have on her fiancé, Thomas.

They'd always had a pretty good sex life, although it wasn't what she would have called the hub of their relationship. What had brought them together, and still kept them together, was their work, their shared business; the small, occasionally struggling, occasionally thriving computer consultancy that she'd joined about eighteen months ago. Tom had just set it up then, and she was the first programmer/analyst he'd taken on, but they'd instantly formed a rapport. Within six weeks they'd been sleeping together; within ten, he'd offered her a partnership; and within three months, he'd suggested an engagement. Alexa had spent several days debating whether she was in love enough for a commitment, but eventually she'd given him a 'yes'. She hadn't been sure then that she'd done the right thing, and she still wasn't sure of it now. Especially now . . .

The fact she could happily blow a huge chunk of money on a holiday without him was a bad sign. Tom hadn't complained. He liked to think of himself as a bit of a new man, all for women's equality and all that, and he'd told her he accepted her right to spend her windfall in any way she wished. Barbados had always been her dream since she'd first seen it as a film location, and, though Tom couldn't get away then and there, he'd talked of taking her back there for their honeymoon.

If there is one, thought Alexa wryly, remembering how she'd topped up Aunt Julia's bequest. She'd had to sneak a little more of KL Systems' money than she'd anticipated, and it was only the fact that she'd designed the accounting system – Tom's main speciality was databases – that had kept her deception from his notice.

Lost in her ruminations, she was shocked by the sound of nearby voices; then, almost immediately, felt the resonance that went with them.

It's happening again, the sex thing, she thought as her mind filled with wild erotic images. Of the two people she could hear speaking, one had a deep and very male voice that was gentle, reasonable and even, while the other speaker's tone was far lighter, although also still husky and deliciously provocative.

'Oh no, baby . . . I can't get up yet,' she heard Beatrice protest from beyond the windbreak that divided the cabanas. 'You've worn me out, you greedy thing. I need more sleep so I can get back my strength.' Drew and Beatrice obviously had their bedroom window open – and the breeze must coming from that direction – because Alexa could have sworn she heard the rustle of sheets against bodies, and the small, playful sounds of a tussle.

'But Beatrice, this is the best part of the day and you always waste it.' Drew sounded faintly irritated now. 'And you did say you'd get up early and go exploring. You could do with some exercise, you know. All you've done since we got here is lie about on your backside, and make love.'

'But that's a form of exercise,' replied Beatrice laconically. 'Excellent for the heart-rate and circulation, as well as a good all-round toner.'

'You're hopeless!' pronounced Drew, but Alexa could hear the affection that tempered his annoyance. Sometimes the couple next door seemed a total mismatch, but at the heart of things she could tell they were devoted. Even though Beatrice was probably twice her handsome partner's young age.

'Yes, I know. Come here and kiss me,' said the doctor, her lovely voice thickened by emotion. 'Kiss me properly!' she commanded, after presumably getting only a swift peck, 'Then you can go out and play with Alexa. And make sure she's suffering no delayed ill-effects from that bump.'

Alexa was shaken by the sound of her own name, then felt even more unnerved by the silence that followed. It was a long, intriguing hiatus, devoid of sound, yet dynamic all the same.

She'd seen Drew kiss Beatrice – and vice versa – on many occasions while she'd been at the Refuge, and just to watch them was a way of having sex. The pair

9

were so unalike, the contrast was stunning. Drew was all finely developed muscle, tanned flesh and neatly cut straight black hair; while his mistress, the Pre-Raphaelite love goddess, had a slender, yet richly curved shape, milky-pale skin, and a waist-length cascade of red waves.

Alexa could clearly imagine Beatrice arching up from the bed, her body naked and flushed rosy from sleep. Her sculpted, deeply bowed lips would be fastened on to Drew's in a kiss both devouring and beneficent. Her fingertips would be searching his body, leaving no part unexplored, and she might even be stroking his sex. Alexa remembered seeing Beatrice fondle her companion like that the other day – when they'd all been together on the sun-deck – and she also recalled her own excitement. Drew's obvious embarrassment had been a potent turn-on, and so had his visible arousal. This again before her bump on the head, she now realised.

And would Beatrice now be taking Drew's hand, then placing it on her own naked skin? Alexa could almost see those long, creamy thighs lolling apart and making space for her lover's dark touch. Drew's fingers were gentle, yet strong – he was a professional masseur, he'd told her. She imagined his thumb running across Beatrice's clitoris, then startlingly seemed to feel it on her own.

'Oh . . .' she murmured, stirring in her seat, the freshly brewed coffee forgotten. The fires that'd burned when she'd first woken up were back now, and, if anything, they were infinitely more intense. Her thin jersey shorts – chosen, she suddenly realised, because they were clinging and outlined her figure – had ridden up and slipped into her furrow. It would be a simple matter to adjust her position, and use the drawn-tight wedge of cloth to –

'Hello, Alexa. Lovely morning, isn't it?'

The jerk of sitting up almost achieved the objective. With her sex oppressed, and feeling scared that her sly attempts at pleasure were visible, Alexa straightened herself carefully in her garden chair and looked up into Drew's stylishly bespectacled, dark eyes.

'Y . . . Yes,' she muttered, acutely aware of both her own flustered predicament and Drew's fresh-scented, glowing near-nakedness, 'It's lovely. Really beautiful.'

'May I join you?' he asked, looking longingly at her coffee. 'You know what Beatrice is like. She won't be getting up until midday, and frankly I could do with some company.'

'Oh. Yes, please do,' Alexa urged, wishing she didn't have to sound so eager. But in all honesty, he was a true 'thing of beauty', and with the benefit of her brand-new awareness, she could appreciate him far better than before.

'Thanks, you're a star,' murmured Drew, taking a second cup from the tray and pouring himself a steaming black brew. Alexa shifted surreptitiously in the chair again, her roused body almost calling out for his.

Drew Kendrick looked even more magnificent than usual this morning, clad only in his sky-blue swim-trunks. Studying him as discreetly as she could, Alexa wondered if he used a sunbed to keep up that deep, caramel tan, or whether he often accompanied Beatrice to the tropics. Either way, his bronzed skin was exceptional.

Once again, Alexa found his groin the object of her interest. The Lycra of his trunks was both light-coloured and thin, and, with half horror and half delight, she realised she could clearly see the outline of his penis. A feature that appeared to be just as big, sturdy and beautiful as the rest of him. It was no wonder Beatrice moaned so in the night.

Alexa's hands flew to her face, and she turned away sharply, blushing. Those goddamned thoughts again. She could feel the blood rushing pell-mell through her body, and her mind playing its salacious little tricks. It was almost as if her special sense had a separate existence of its own now. She could feel it flexing and pushing at its boundaries, trying to reach out and read Drew's hidden sexual thoughts. Unable to stop herself, she tried to divine whether he wanted her or not; then a second later, she consciously willed it, and pictured his hand stroking her body instead of Beatrice's.

'Are you OK,' asked Drew, unwittingly breaking into her fugue. 'You look flushed, a bit out of sorts. Would you like me to get Bea to check you over? There might still be some residual effects from that knock you took.'

'No. Thank you. I'm all right, really. I just didn't sleep very well, that's all.' Yes, I spent half the night feeling as if I'd an icepick in my skull, she thought, then I woke up full of dreams of rampant sex!

'Are you sure?' Drew's grey eyes narrowed, then he adjusted the position of his glasses, something she'd often seen him do when deep in thought.

'Yes, I'm sure. I'm just a bit tense that's all. It'll soon pass. I'm in the best place on earth to relax, aren't I?' She gestured vaguely at the the five-star resort that surrounded them, and, beyond that, the Eden-like island.

'Let me give you a massage,' said Drew suddenly, leaping to his feet in a quick, lithe movement. 'It's what I do, you know. And I can guarantee it'll relax you.'

It'll do much more than relax you, something impish in his eyes seemed to hint, and Alexa guessed that, too, was guaranteed.

She swallowed, understanding the subliminal message, but felt alarmed in case somehow she'd generated it herself. She saw a momentary image of Tom, then found herself on her feet, looking towards the cool, white interior of her cabana. It will have to be in there, she supposed, if Beatrice was still slumbering next door.

'Yes, I'd like that,' she said, accepting the implications and feeling them flood through her veins like voodoo punch. 'Do you need a – ' She faltered, caught again by the male symmetry of Drew's body as he stood, lightly poised, before her. 'A bed or something?'

'Stay here,' said Drew, suddenly commanding. His

firm voice and decisive action were a glimpse of the man who sometimes defied his idiosyncratic mistress. Then, with a quick smile, he turned away and walked swifly towards his own cabana, providing Alexa wth something equally compelling – a superb view of his hard male rump as it moved powerfully beneath sheer nylon fabric.

I *have* gone mad, Alexa decided. Definitely. Standing on the stone-flagged veranda, she felt lost, confused and impatient. I want this man, and I'm going to get him. I'm going to let him touch me all over – and everything that promises. Why can't I stop myself, and think about Tom?

Stuff Tom! said the newly born wanton inside her as Drew emerged around the corner of the windbreak, a thick, rolled mat tucked under his arm and a hessian holdall slung casually over his shoulder.

'Come here,' he said, still controlling her. 'Around the side, by the windbreak. That way we can be outdoors, but hidden from the path.'

'Outside?'

'Yes, why not?' His eyes and his white teeth twinkled. 'A massage is more beneficial in the fresh air. Balmy breezes on the skin and all that. Especially in a climate like this.' He nodded towards the designated spot, tucked away between the two cabanas and close to the white, openwork bricks of the windbreak. 'You're not scared of me, are you, Alex?'

The question was so much like something Beatrice might have asked that Alexa felt her mettle start to rise. 'Certainly not,' she answered, smiling what she hoped was a nonchalant smile. 'In fact I'm looking forward to this. Let's get to it!'

'With pleasure,' he said, first stepping forward and flipping out the mat with a flourish, then just standing there, eyeing her intently. 'You're going to have to take your clothes off, you know,' he continued, a vestigial smile curving the corners of his mouth – as if he were trying to play it straight, but not doing very well.

13

'I know that.' Alexa's answer was crisp, but her nerve endings were a-quiver, now the crunch had come and she had to take her clothes off and bare all.

You want this, remember? she told herself, tugging at her T-shirt, and feeling Drew's dark grey eyes steadily watching. And it's not that much different to wearing a skimpy bikini, is it? In fact it's more honest. More natural. Even so, she fumbled with the fastening of her bra, getting hot and bothered as the tiny clasp defied her. She could sense Drew challenging her, and silently calling her bluff. You daren't do it, dare you? his voice inside her mind seemed to say.

'Let me,' he said softly, around behind her in the blink of an eye, his fingers working deftly on the fastening. Alexa gasped involuntarily as the garment swung away from her breasts; her nipples were hard, and very evidently so, plummy studs in twin circles of dark pink. She expected that at any instant Drew would reach around and touch them, but instead he stepped away and to the front of her again.

'And the rest?' he queried, cocking his head on one side, still challenging.

I must! I must! thought Alexa, dithering and frozen.

'Would it help if I stripped off?' he asked, his slight smile widening to a wide, killer-white one. When Alexa didn't – couldn't – answer he seemed to take it as a 'yes' and slid his thumbs into the waistband of his trunks.

Alexa had a sudden, bizarre sense of her vision acting like a computerised targeting system. It literally homed in, there was no other word for it, and Drew's crotch was at the centre of the cross-hairs.

Like the rest of him, his cock was impressive. Long, thick and meaty, it wasn't fully erect yet, just tumescing ever so slightly. He was clearly on the way to arousal, but seemed either unware of his condition, or simply used to it. Her mouth dry, Alexa wondered if he'd had to develop a certain detachment for his job. After all, he probably had his hands on women's naked bodies every day, and those who were beautiful must surely affect him.

'See, that didn't hurt,' he observed cheerfully, and in a quick, graceful movement, stepped out of his trunks and kicked them away across the tiles. 'Now you,' he said, then paused and almost seemed to strike a pose. Almost, but not quite. 'Don't worry, Alex, women's bodies are my business. You haven't got anything I haven't seen or touched before.'

'That's all right then,' she returned tartly, scrabbling her way clumsily out of her shorts, and pulling her panties off with them in a bunch. 'I feel so much better knowing my unremarkable body doesn't impress you!'

'I didn't say that,' murmured Drew, reaching down to scoop up her clothing and toss it in a heap with his swimtrunks. 'Your body's making quite a big impression on me. It has been all week.' He glanced down quickly at his thickening sex, then grinned without apology or shame.

Alexa pretended to ignore what was happening, in spite of the fact it was impossible. She was standing stark naked beside the handsomest man on the island, who was also naked – apart from his glasses – and making a substantial impression of his own upon the acutely reactive membranes of her sex. It was as if he'd fondled her before the massage had even started.

He does want me, thought Alexa as she stepped tentatively towards the mat, and considered how best, and most elegantly, to lie down. Even if she hadn't been able to see his rising penis, she could 'feel' his desire hitting her like a ray. There were none of the 'Is he/isn't he? Does he/doesn't he?' doubts that usually plagued her. She knew – with absolute certainty – that Drew wanted to make love to her. She could almost see the fantasies in his head, and read the way he planned to make them real.

Without speaking, he put out a hand like a stark-naked gallant, and assisted her courteously on to the mat. Alexa lay face down; partly because it seemed the

15

natural position in which to receive a massage, but mainly because it hid a little more of her. Her nipples were so stiff and puckered they were embarrassing. Drew wouldn't need special powers to deduce whether she was aroused or not; her body was screaming out the message.

Lying very still, and every bit as tense as she described, Alexa listened to Drew's preparations. She heard his bag rustle as he removed things from it, then the sound of objects being placed methodically on the tiles.

'I'm going to tie your hair out of the way of the oil,' he told her after a moment.

Alexa was glad of the warning, because otherwise she was sure that she would have flinched. As it was, she trembled very finely, and prayed that Drew wouldn't notice it. His touch was efficient and strangely impersonal, and in a couple of seconds she had a tiny little ponytail.

Trying to imagine what Drew would be seeing, Alexa suddenly wished her hair could look different. More distinctive, perhaps . . . She'd been happy with it mid-length until a moment ago, but now it seemed unimaginative and plain. The colour was good – jet black, just like Drew's – but she felt annoyed that she'd never done more with it. For a moment, she coveted Beatrice's hair – a waist-kissing fall that rippled like a crimped satin cloak – then imagined a very short style instead. She pictured herself with a crop of some kind, cut well to crisp up her natural curl.

Drew's hair, she thought dreamily, was as perfect and healthy as the rest of him. Thick, straight and shiny, it tended to dangle across his forehead in a love-lick. Was it dangling now? she wondered, as he bent over her and studied her naked rump.

'I'm going to touch you now,' he said, warning her again, but still causing her to tremble. She nearly jumped out of her skin when his fingers made contact, settling lightly on the nape of her neck. 'Relax, Alex, give it up,' he purred, as his thumbs began to circle against her spine. 'Why are you so tense? You're on your holidays. The sun should make you mellow and loose.'

'Some people just don't get "mellow",' she replied, trying for sarcasm in an effort to be impersonal. Drew's hands managed to be both firm and floating in one motion, and the pressure was electric against her skin. He was doing big, kneading sort of shapes on her shoulderblades, and though it should have been professional and innocuous, the sensations were shooting straight to her sex. She almost choked with desire when he made a small, impatient sound, then threw his thigh across her body and straddled her.

'You're so wound up, Alex, I need more leverage,' he said, by way of excuse, as his penis brushed the crease of her bottom. As his hard penis brushed the crease of her bottom . . .

'You've got to help me, you know,' he continued, as if his erection and its resting place meant nothing. 'You've got to let yourself go loose, and stop fighting me. Let your muscles give, and tell me as soon as it feels good.' He'd returned to the muscles of her neck now, his fingertips working determinedly on the stubborn tension spots.

It feels good now! she thought savagely at him, unable to prevent herself clenching her bottom. Did it feel as if she was gripping him, she wondered, but discerned no change in the rhythm of the massage.

'Alexa?' he prompted, lifting one of her arms and shaking it gently.

'Look,' she gasped, as he pressed against a patch of skin on the inside of her elbow that she'd never even realised was sensitive. 'This is your job, you're a masseur. Don't you know when you're doing it right?'

'Yes, of course I do,' he said, pressing again and making her groan this time. 'But it's much better when there's feedback.'

'Better for whom?'

17

At that, Drew simply laughed and scooted down her body, his penis bouncing, then sliding silkily down her thigh. Alexa could feel warm moisture trailing from it, and not oil – because so far he'd only applied that to her shoulders.

After a second or two of adjustment, he settled into a crouch, his bottom right down against her heels. Alexa could feel his balls pressed against the backs of her ankles, their firm oval shapes slightly hairy. As he began to massage her buttocks, the movements of his body slid his testicles against her, making them roll in their loose, crinkly pouch.

The massage itself was more forceful now, and Drew's grip on her far more intrusive. She could feel his thumbs working deeply, digging into the muscles of her bottom-cheeks and moulding them with a concentrated precision. The action was so strong it should have hurt her, but he was so skilful, so almost uncannily attuned to her anatomy, that the pressure he imparted was sublime. She squirmed and crooned with pleasure when he stretched her anal furrow, then felt mortified at revealing how she felt.

'Good, huh?' enquired Drew, suddenly closer, his breath warm and fragant on her back. 'Do you want more? Tell me, Alexa. Go on, tell me.'

'Yes. No. I don't know!' she gasped, shocked when his hands abruptly left her bottom. 'You're talking at me again. You're confusing me.' As she spoke, she felt Drew on the move again, slipping from astride her with lightness and agility, then sliding an oily hand down beneath her ribs. With a neat, negligent wrist action, he flipped her over, then repositioned her, like a cook turning a tender cut of meat.

'Don't you like to talk?' he enquired, making a tiny, mouth-zipping action with his finger and thumb.

'I'm not used to conversation at times like this,' she said, fighting an urge to cover her breasts and her pubis.

'Well, I didn't used to be – ' Drew turned away, the

muscles in his back and shoulders stretching as he reached for another shot of oil. 'But Beatrice insists on it. She talks all the time. Especially during sex. Whispering this, demanding that . . . and promising one helluva lot of the other.' He grinned at his small joke, then flexed and pulled at his long, tapered fingers. 'She wheedles, she praises, she tells me what to do.'

'Don't you find it distracting?' Alexa's voice was faint, and, to her own ears, very distracted.

'Sometimes,' he murmured, laying hands on her again, 'but there's an easy way to shut her up.'

'What way is that?' It was difficult to talk, but she managed.

'Work it out, Alex.' Drew laughed softly, and Alexa realised it wasn't at all by accident that his erection was rubbing to and fro against her thigh. Closing her eyes, she imagined Beatrice effectively silenced, her exquisite red lips folded firmly around his stiff wand of flesh. Drew's big hand would be cupping his mistress's jaw, holding her still, and, for once, in his control.

Now I'd like to see that, thought Alexa suddenly. She'd surmised already that the fabulous Beatrice rarely kowtowed to anyone, least of all to this paragon who served her.

All at once, Drew's manipulation of Alexa's shoulders ceased, and he ran a fingertip along the curve of her brow. Automatically, she opened her eyes, then gasped again. His face was just inches from her own; his breathing so light she'd never felt it, and his eyes like polished slate behind his spectacles.

She tried to turn from him, but the fingertip was persistent and slid instantly to her jaw to still her.

'Why are you resisting me?' he enquired. As he spoke, Alexa smelt the sweet, minty tang of his toothpaste. 'Is it the headaches? Or your boyfriend? Or is it just me?'

'No!'

'"No what?"' he persisted, his body moving subtly as he tilted his head with the question. He was com-

19

pletely erect now; and, to her horror, Alexa found herself still avoiding his eyes, this time by staring down between their bellies.

To his credit, Drew said nothing, and didn't even smirk; although it was obvious he enjoyed her scrutiny, because his penis seemed to twitch in response.

'No, I don't have a headache,' she said in a small voice, conscious of Drew studying her mouth, no doubt wondering if she could use it as cleverly as Beatrice did hers.

'Boyfriend then? Surely he doesn't disapprove of you having a therapeutic massage?'

'I don't know. I don't think so. He lets me do more or less what I want.'

'Hmmm . . .' Drew seemed to consider this most seriously, his parted lips only inches from hers. 'Must be me then?'

Alexa wanted to look away again, but even though Drew had removed the restraining finger, and now had both hands on the mat, at either side of her head, she still couldn't tear her gaze from his face.

'Yes! Yes, it is you!' she said belligerently, fighting herself far more than she fought him. She wanted him now, like life itself, but her pride made her resist appearing easy. 'First you keep nagging me to talk to you while you're doing the most intimate things to me, and now you won't stop staring!. It's all too intense, Drew, I'm not used to it.'

She sensed him speculating, imagining what her sex life might be like. She wanted to tell him to mind his own business, but that would mean telling him she could 'read' him. And she didn't even understand her new ability herself, much less know how to describe it to a man.

As his mouth moved above her, she stiffened, expecting some comment about Tom, but all Drew said was, 'Would it help you if I took off my glasses?'

'Can you see without them?' she asked, saying the first thing that came into her head.

'Yes, perfectly,' he said, without hesitating.

'Then why the hell do you wear them?' she demanded, beginning to wriggle beneath him, and feeling his cock roll against her, its warm tip dripping satin fluid.

'In the vain hope that people will take me seriously,' he said, sounding serious. And as he lowered his body a little further, his grey eyes seemed to glower behind their cosmetic glass discs. 'Oh, I know what you think. That I'm just Beatrice's toyboy. A body without a brain.' This last was said with some vehemence, as Drew sat up suddenly, pulled off his glasses, and slid them away across the tiles with scant regard for their expensive designer frames, not to mention the fragile glass lenses.

He looked troubled, deeply thoughtful for a moment, his gravity at odds with his waving erection, which still reared up in splendour from his groin.

'Are you?' Alexa asked, wanting to plumb the secrets of the odd, but handsome couple who'd made such an impact on her holiday. 'Are you Beatrice's toyboy?'

'Sometimes,' he murmured, hesitating. Then, as he spoke again, he let his hand drop blatantly to his cock. 'I do have the right qualifications.'

'What do you mean "sometimes"?'

'I mean "not always". I have a life. I make choices.'

'What choices?' Alexa was pushing, and she knew it.

'Well.' He paused again, then moved in close again, bracketing her head with his hands as he looked directly into her eyes, his own far brighter without their filters. 'I can have sex with you if I choose to.'

'Is that a fact, you arrogant pig?' raged Alexa, beginning to thrash beneath him but getting nowhere as he pressed his weight – and his sex – down upon her.

Ignoring her protest, Drew continued to stare down at her, his straight black brows raised questioningly. 'What about you, Alex?' he whispered, 'Do you make choices? And if you do, what do you choose?'

It was a pivotal moment, but Alexa's body had already made her decision. With a noise that was half a sigh, half a growl – a noise that on her own lips astounded her – she lifted her arms from where they lay upon the mat and wound them around Drew's perspiring back.

'I choose what you choose,' she told him, then pressed her mouth against his for a kiss, and took his soft laugh of triumph from its source.

As his tongue moved immediately between her teeth, probing audaciously, it seemed to bring with it a dark lode of images.

All the sexual fantasies of her waking now returned to her. The man above her assumed a myriad of roles, not just the one of a new, insolent, but basically benign lover. She seemed to see a man in a black mask leering salaciously as he fingered her body. Then it was the same man, fucking her urgently as Beatrice looked on, with her breasts unclothed. The doctor was watching, watching, watching – but she was also being loved herself, too. A young woman, hooded in leather, was sucking at one nipple and pinching at the other with her fingers.

It was all bizarre and dreamlike, but Alexa suddenly fell back into reality. Drew's body had shifted above her, and he'd put his hand between her thighs to touch her sex. In an instant he was stroking her clitoris, very delicately, just as she'd imagined he would, the contact like a moth's fluttering wing.

She groaned, and he made a sound in response that seemed to vibrate inside her mouth and her mind. His fingertip floated again, then danced down to her moist vaginal entrance while he lifted his lips away from hers.

'Yes,' he said, his deep voice smug. 'You do chose me, don't you? At least your body does. You're wet through down here, Alex. And all for me.'

'Do you get all this from her?' Alexa demanded, her voice shaking as her legs waved and her buttocks beat the mat. He was spearing her now, pushing a single long finger inside her.

'All what?' he asked, grinning as he pumped her

22

slowly. 'All this?' He pulled out the finger, glistening, and held it between them, before her eyes, so close she could almost taste her own juice.

'No!' she squeaked as he reinserted the digit with a shocking efficiency. 'Not that . . . The way you are . . . so bloody clever, So gloating. Oh! Oh God!' His thumb settled squarely on her clitoris, and in a heartbeat she was throbbing and contracting, her flesh gripping him and jumping like a pulse.

'Beatrice is a good teacher,' he whispered, his lips worrying her throat as she came. 'It's difficult not to emulate her sometimes.'

Alexa was no longer listening. Her loins were dissolving. Her mouth was open and she was gasping. She needed air, oxygen to breathe, but it was being consumed by the flames between her legs.

'Please,' she hissed out, then grunted, deprived, as Drew's finger slid clear of her sex.

'Your wish,' he sighed, then nipped wickedly at the soft place between her neck and her shoulder as his prick forged easily into her, 'is my command.' he finished, shimmying his hips to bed his flesh even deeper.

Alexa didn't come again straight away, although she half believed she should have done. Instead, she trembled on the very brink of it, her clitoris quivering as she explored her strange insight, her understanding of what Drew was feeling, too. With each thrust, each stroke of his fascinating rhythm, she felt his pleasure in tandem with her own. He was pure power inside her: dominant, supreme – and revelling profoundly in the experience.

This peculiar transcendentalism didn't last for more than a few seconds, and when a new orgasm began to simmer again, right at the very edge of her consciousness, Alexa was back in her own body with a vengeance. She felt herself being stretched, ploughed into, laid open; her clitoris tugged by the motion of Drew's cock. Moaning with relief, with fulfilment, and with

23

pure, uncomplicated happiness, she tried to arch and get him further inside her. Drew in turn seemed to be seeking some obscure, sweet spot right at the heart of her; seeking, seeking, seeking, and shouting in triumph as he found . . .

Grabbing her tight against his chest, he came in a long, hard spasm, moaning incoherently as his flesh leapt and juddered.

Well, I've done it now, haven't I? thought Alexa as Drew rolled off her, and she snuggled against him as if they'd been lovers for a lifetime.

I've done it . . . So why don't I feel guilty?

You young rogue! You don't have to enjoy it quite so much! thought the red-headed woman concealed behind the blocks of the windbreak. Her voluptuous body was clad in a soft cotton robe the colour of sandy earth, in stark contrast to her usual vivid clothes. It wasn't wise to wear bright primaries whilst spying . . .

Oh Drew, dearest, what on earth does that feel like? pondered Beatrice, watching the tensing of his firm, athletic buttocks as he drove into the young woman on the mat.

It wasn't the first time Beatrice had wondered what it was like to be a man, and longed – with all her passionate curiosity – for the chance to change sex for one day. She didn't think she'd need longer than that, because she derived great satisfaction from being female – and suspected that men, no matter how sexually proficient they were, could never reach the highs that women did.

Still admiring Drew's grace and strength, she turned her attention to the young woman who lay beneath him, the new friend she'd specifically sent him to ravish.

You're quite a prize, my dear, she told the gasping girl fondly. A shining star if you only but knew it.

Always sensitive to beauty, Beatrice had noticed Alexa Lavelle the very day she'd arrived. The girl had

24

certain tantalising qualities that seemed to cry out to her. Alexa was vulnerable, slightly unsure of herself, yet had a challenging air of wildness in her, too. A kind of suppressed daring that seemed to bubble up from time to time and wreak havoc.

But it isn't very deeply supressed, is it, sweetheart? Beatrice reflected. Not if Alexa could come away to Barbados without her fiancé, and quite blithely spend a huge amount of money.

Well done, sister, applauded Beatrice silently. She'd never believed in denying herself in any way, least of all in the disposal of income, though in her case, ample funds weren't a problem. Her practice, and certain contacts she made by way of it, kept her far more than adequately provided for.

We have a lot in common, Alexa, she told the girl who was moaning beyond the windbreak. For one thing, we both adore Drew.

Beatrice watched closely as the young woman's legs jerked and flailed, and an orgasm quite clearly overcame her. Drew's penis must be very deep now, stretching and caressing with its hot living bulk. Beatrice shuddered, remembering those same sensations as she'd felt them this morning; in the small hours, when she'd woken Drew with a kiss and a grope, then whispered a string of crude nothings in his ear. Ever willing to serve, her fine young animal had roused from sleep immediately and in seconds she'd had his cock where it mattered.

And it's where it matters, now, isn't it, my dears? thought Beatrice, her own sex aching as she saw Alexa dig her nails into Drew's back. Without a second thought, Beatrice flipped aside the floating panel of her robe, then pressed the heel of her hand against her sex.

Oh yes, Alexa, yes, she mouthed, noiselessly echoing the girl's excited cries. Rummaging through the thick crimson curls of her pubis, Beatrice sought out the raging pearl of her clitoris. Then attacked it with her lacquer-tipped finger. Engorged already, it jumped and spasmed as she pressed on it, primed and ready after just one hungry pass.

Locked into the pleasure of the couple beyond the windbreak, Beatrice felt her vulva twitch in time to their gasps. Pressing a knuckle into her mouth, she leaned heavily against the bricks, her knees almost buckling as she joined them in climax.

Half blind, and her body incandescent, she stared up into the brilliant sky above her, where it was visible in broad stripes between the palm leaves. Somewhere high in the blueness a gull was wheeling; she heard it scream thinly and cry out, as if for her.

Oh God, this is paradise, thought Beatrice, as the morning sun blessed another perfect day.

Chapter Three

Return of the Changeling

*L*ondon was a shock to the system. At least it was to one mellowed by Barbados. And by the sun, the sea and good sex . . . Most of all the sex.

Perusing her tanned body in the bathroom mirror, Alexa imagined Drew Kendrick's even browner hands moving slowly over it. She could almost believe she saw marks; brands, imprinted by his repeated caresses, that identified her clearly as an adulteress.

But is it adultery if you aren't married? she wondered, knowing she was splitting hairs to salve her twanging conscience. She would have said she felt guilty, but in her heart of hearts, she realised she didn't. Barbados had been beautiful and liberating – and Drew Kendrick the most liberating thing about it, with his perfect body and his thick unflagging prick.

You've got to forget all that now, she told herself. It'd been a fling, an aberration, a temporary blip in her relationship with Thomas. The trouble was, her body still missed its steady diet of Drew's.

And it wasn't only her body that was missing things. She kept looking around and expecting to see Beatrice sweep colourfully into view. She missed her new

27

friend's deliciously wicked confidences, her observations on life and the people all around her. The day seemed almost sterile without the prospect of sitting in a bar with Beatrice, and listening to the doctor's uninhibited speculations about the sexual preferences of strangers passing by.

The most intriguing aspect of this game had been something Alexa hadn't mentioned to her companion – the way her own peculiar new sensibility had often confirmed Beatrice's outrageous diagnoses. When the doctor had suggested that the distinguished couple at the next table might be into a spot of fairly civilised bondage, Alexa had suddenly and vividly seen it. The woman, a skinny blonde, tied to a plantation-style bed in one of the hotel's cabanas; her sinewy legs held apart, and her ankles tied to the bedposts by a pair of her own Hermès scarves. Her partner, her husband one assumed, crouched on the mattress beside her, his fingers working roughly on her sex.

Oh God! thought Alexa, returning to the present with alarm. Her reflection itself was betraying her. Her honeyed skin was flushed, and her hand had strayed instinctively to her crotch, where she was rubbing herself almost without realising it.

'Lexie? What are you doing in there? Aren't you coming to bed?'

Tom's voice made her jump. She knew she had to go back to the bedroom quickly, but somehow she didn't want to face him. It wasn't that she didn't feel attracted to him any more; quite the reverse. She wanted him a great deal tonight, as much as she'd ever done, but she couldn't stop thinking of other men, a lot of whom she didn't seem to know.

And she sensed that Tom was frightened of her. On her first night back from the island, she'd reached out to touch him, and he'd flinched away as if her skin was charged with static. He'd muttered something about 'working too hard', then just turned over and gone to sleep. It was this that had begun her fancies about being

28

'marked' somehow. Was there a vibe that only a man could detect? A resonance that told Tom she'd been unfaithful. It was almost a week now since her return from Barbados, and still they hadn't got around to making love. She hadn't even sensed any desire in him, though her own body was tense with frustration.

'Lexie?' he queried again, and Alexa felt a small plume of anger. How dare he get impatient if he didn't even want her? Reaching out towards the towel rail, she resolved to force the issue. And draped across it was the main weapon in her fight.

She'd bought this royal-blue teddy the day she'd decided to accept Tom's proposal; and later, given him herself, wrapped in it, as a present. Since then, she'd only worn it on special occasions, but each time their lovemaking had been memorable.

The teddy had also taught her something about their sex life in general. She knew now that her fiancé wasn't a man to make the first move, and if she wanted him, the initiative had to be hers.

Sliding the thin fabric down over her body, she savoured its cool sheen against her skin. Tonight, the rich, dense blue looked better on her body than it had ever looked, but she couldn't decide whether it was her toasty glow from Barbados or the changes in the woman beneath the tan.

As she adjusted the fit of the teddy, then snapped the poppers closed, her fingers brushed lightly against her pubis and reminded her how much she needed sex. The contact had been next to nothing, but the degree of reaction was alarming. She could feel her juices flowing, her vulva unfolding like blossom. At this rate, the teddy would be soaked between the legs before she even got as far as her lover.

Posing again, she appraised her body in the mirror. Her figure was good, and even better after a week in which her appetite for food had been displaced by a different kind of hunger.

Facially, too, it would be false modesty not to say she

was attractive. Pretty even. But her features seemed swamped by her hair at the moment, and its unstructured curliness displeased her, just as it had when Drew had tied it back. On impulse, she found a soft elastic tie and some pins, then returned to the mirror. Combing through her hair with her fingers, she drew it up and away from her face, then secured it in a compact little knot.

What the looking glass now offered was the impression of a short, elfin style – which she liked. That's it! To the hairdressers we go, she said silently, already vivified by yet another change.

Not wanting to hear Tom call out again, she gave the teddy a last little tug, and the mirror a final swift check. 'Irresistible,' she whispered, but was it true? There was only one way to find out.

When she walked into the bedroom, her fiancé didn't look up at first, but continued to peer at the screen of his laptop, which was perched – as it often was at bedtime – across his knees. Alexa watched him make several rapid keystrokes, then frown slightly and stab at the spacebar.

'All work and no play, love,' she said softly as she drew nearer.

Tom's eyes widened as he looked up at her.

'L . . . Lexie,' he stammered, as if genuinely stunned. His 'lappie' slid ever so slightly sideways.

In the few seconds before she· actually reached the bed and climbed on to it, Alexa felt another rush of insight. It was stronger this time, the strongest it had ever been. Her mind seemed illuminated like a high-resolution monitor, and Tom's confusion scrolled vividly across it.

Oh, he wanted her all right – she needn't have worried about that – but he was nervous, too. Strangely scared of her, just as she'd suspected.

His awe only exacerbated her lust. She felt powerful in a way that was new to her. She felt unstoppable, confident, alluring. She was a huntress, and this man was her prey.

'I don't think we need this, do we?' she said as she scooted across the bed and knelt beside Thomas. She saw a flash of annoyance in his eyes when she placed his beloved laptop on the bedside cabinet, but she quashed it with a fierce look of her own. Then, before he could speak, to protest or otherwise, she came up on her knees, looming over him, and pressed her mouth down aggressively on his.

He yielded instantly, lifting his hands to try and caress her, but desisting when she captured his wrists. Pressing his hands back against the headboard, on either side of him, she worked her lips hungrily against his to subdue him. Feeling him acquiesce, she jabbed her tongue into his mouth.

The thrill of being in control was both astonishing and astonishingly arousing. What had been a glow between her legs was instantly an inferno, and she wanted sex in just the same way she had in Barbados. Sharply. Desperately. Dangerously. With any man, it didn't matter who . . .

Her hands around Tom's wrists seemed to immobilise him, even though he was no wimp and could have easily shaken her off. He didn't dare shake her off, she sensed with excitement. Almost growling, she intensified the kiss.

Probing with her tongue, she let it slip moistly over his teeth and his palate and sipped his saliva as a bee would sip nectar. She could feel him trying to push up from the bed, and rub his penis against her body through his pyjamas, but smiling inwardly she denied him the contact. Her mouth alone she permitted him. That, and the very tips of her lace-covered breasts.

'Lexie, please,' she felt him trying to say, around her tongue, but instead of freeing him, she kissed him even harder. Her body felt as hot and stirred as it would have done with his prick deep inside her, and she kept on kissing until her jaw began to ache.

31

When she pulled away, both he and she were gasping.

'There, isn't that better than work?' she enquired, stroking his chin with her fingers as she sat back. The skin of his face was trembling where she touched it, as if he'd just taken a slight electric shock.

'Oh yes . . . Oh yes.' His voice was muffled, heavy with desire and the after-effects of the kiss, and, as she released his hands, he pushed his fingers through his hair. 'Oh God, Lexie, you're so beautiful,' he gasped, reaching out, then almost sobbing when she quickly backed away.

'If I'm so gorgeous, why didn't you want me when I got home?' she enquired, the question only half teasing.

'I . . . um . . . I thought you might be tired from the flight and everything.' He looked down for a second, shamefaced. 'I wasn't sure if you were interested.'

Bullshit! said a voice in Alexa's mind, while her body told her not to pick a fight.

'I'm interested,' she said crisply, then reached out for the tie of his pyjamas. 'So get these off, then kiss me properly. I want you naked. I want to see and feel you.'

Visibly shaking, Tom complied, struggling clumsily out of his pyjamas in his haste. As she knelt back on her heels, Alexa watched him, and for some reason found this ungainliness appealing, despite its total contrast with Drew's fluid grace.

I've been spoiled, she thought, feeling suddenly wistful. In Barbados, she'd been made love to by a perfect male animal, a paragon, a man whose whole purpose in life was to please women. There weren't many of those in real life.

When Tom was fully naked, she brightened. His cock wasn't quite as magnificent as Drew Kendrick's, but it was willing and it was hard just for her. With new energy, she launched herself against him, pushing his back against the mattress with her weight and momentum.

This too, was new. Alexa wasn't used to being on top

with Tom. Out of habit, they usually ended up in the missionary position; which – though mostly satisfying, and sometimes wonderful – most certainly wasn't the dynamic she needed now.

Pressing him down, she felt almost like a vampire. She attacked his mouth again – taking, taking, taking – and stretched her body out full length over his. She kissed. She nibbled. She bit into his defenceless lower lip, delicately at first, then more hungrily, and his lack of protest empowered her even more. She circled her hips very slowly and teasingly to rub the lace of her teddy against his cock.

But suddenly simple rubbing wasn't enough. She wanted direct contact against her skin, and direct stimulation of her sex. Making a harsh throaty sound of impatience, she released Tom's mouth, arched backwards from his body, then ripped at the teddy's fragile bodice. With two quick wrenches, she snapped the shoestring straps, then peeled down the lacy blue fabric and bared the honeyed smoothness of her breasts. She saw Tom's eyes flash as he took in the evenness of her tan and the hardness of her nipples, then she smiled defiantly to silence his questions. When his mouth seemed about to open, she swooped down again and crushed it with hers. Still kissing, she reached down and groped for the fastenings of the teddy, then parted them in a single ragged tug.

Her sex free, she slithered sideways, then parted her legs and pushed her body against Tom's. A couple of wiggles, a twist this way, then that, and she felt herself opening and spreading until her whole vulva was pressed flush against his thigh.

Cool it. Stay still. Make it last, she told herself sternly. Every part of her felt swollen and volcanic. Her clitoris fluttered against the twitching mass of muscle beneath it. She could come now, violently, from one jerk of her hips, while Tom remained agonised and waiting.

Go on, just do it! urged the devil inside, the wild erotic imp who'd been born during a headache in

Barbados. Take him! Have him! Use him! He's yours now. He's easy. Come! Come! Come!

Slowly, almost scared to do it, she moved, but then stilled again as a more generous urge filled her.

Tom deserved more than this, she realised. He hadn't hurt or cheated her. She'd taken from him; betrayed him physically, and deceived him over money. His only crime was to be himself, and as she looked down on him, taut and sweating beneath her, she realised that wasn't such a bad thing. He was a workaholic sometimes – most times – but he was also intelligent, quietly handsome, and faithful. His willing body was firm-fleshed against her, and if she used him, she had to please them both – or sully the very point of making love.

Smiling, she sat up, her sex still divided by his thigh. Tom stared up at her yearningly, his eyes dark and unfocused, his bruised mouth a smudge of pure desire.

'Please, Lexie,' he whispered again, his voice a trembling thread.

'What do you want, Tom?' she asked, knowing the answer full well. Somewhere at the back of her mind she almost felt like laughing, in spite of their intimate situation. They were locked in a drama, a comedy almost. It was a game, one they were playing for the very first time, but she doubted whether Tom would see that. His mind seemed focused solely on penetration.

'Please, love, let me have you,' he pleaded.

'"Have"?' she mocked. 'You want to "have" me, do you?'

'Y . . . yes,' he said, his voice smaller than ever, 'Oh Lexie. please!'

'Then you shall have me,' she murmured soft and low, aware of how thickened her voice sounded.

Moving with a grace and economy she hadn't realised she possessed, Alexa swung herself upwards and straddled Tom's pelvis. She felt tension cord her thighs as she held herself above him, but contrarily she didn't sink down. Instead she hovered, and heard him groan as his penis bobbed and bounced against her, trying in vain to find her entrance and slide in.

'Wait,' she hissed, her voice even more determined. She'd never felt so completely in charge . . .

Tom's face seemed to crumple, and for a few seconds he tossed his head from side to side on the pillow. Alexa smiled inside; felt a soft, wet quivering in her vagina, then plunged down on him without any warning, pitching forward to absorb his shout with her mouth.

'Yes! Yes!,' she crowed, suppressing his sound with her own as the membranes of her sex fluttered wildly. 'Yes!' she gasped, as blind rapture rose through her like a fountain, then seemed to bubble in her fingers and her toes.

Straightening up and throwing back her head, she almost screamed with exultation when, beneath her, Tom began to jerk and writhe.

He was coming. She was coming. And within the pleasure was a certain sense of wonder.

There had been plenty of orgasms in the months they'd been together. There had never been an episode without them. He'd come, then he'd caress her afterwards until it happened for her, too; or she'd come, and he'd follow on a moment later as she calmed. Whichever, there'd always been a climax for them both.

But this was the first time they'd ever achieved it simultaneously. It was the first time they'd ever reached the peak as one.

35

Chapter Four

The Devil Demands

*I*t had been like priming an engine.

Alexa was glad that Tom had to set off early the next morning, on his way to see a client up north, because she didn't really know how to face him. Their silent pact of celibacy had been broken now, with a vengeance, by a night whose excesses made her blush.

Once had most definitely not been enough.

Although Tom had – initially – gone to sleep, not long after their first bout of lovemaking, Alexa had pressed him into service a second time. Lying in the darkness, she'd felt her body grow restless again, and tension build in her belly, and between her thighs. The delights of what had just happened, and the novelty of their mutual climax, had seemed more like a goad than satisfaction. Her head had filled with images again, pictures of dark acts and pleasures; and even though she'd tried, very quietly, to masturbate, her body had demanded a man's touch.

'Wha . . . What?' Tom had burbled as she'd pulled his fingers, then placed them between her legs. He'd still seemed half asleep, but he'd rubbed her.

And so it'd gone on, until deep into the morning's

early hours. Once he'd woken, Tom had responded with more enthusiasm, but towards the end she'd sensed – in spite of his erections, and his obvious pleasure – that he was faintly horrified by her enormous need for sex. When the time had come for him to get up, Alexa had hidden her face in the pillow, and pretended to be sleeping. She'd told herself she was a hopeless, spineless coward, but she couldn't face the questions or what she'd most likely see in Tom's eyes.

'You're going to have to put a lid on this,' she murmured to herself as she parked her car in the underground car park beneath the building that housed KL Systems.

Their premises were in an excellent location, but were far better than they could comfortably afford. Which was another thing that stoked Alexa's guilt. She'd pushed for this move when Tom had counselled caution, and now, instead of working hard and running a tight operation, she was throwing money away hand over fist. And hiding the fact from Tom. Her fiancé was still oblivious to her unauthorised spending, but unfortunately Quentin, their young programmer, wasn't. Alexa wondered why the boy hadn't said anything yet.

At least she had been wondering. Yesterday, she'd discovered the reason for his silence, and the revelation had both appalled and thrilled her.

Their number-crunching wizard was infatuated with her. He'd hidden his feelings magnificently until yesterday – probably because he was equally infatuated with algorithms and C++ code – when her new senses had finally diagnosed them. Proximity had shown her his libido.

He'd been standing looking over her shoulder as they'd struggled with a macro conversion error; and, borne on a waft of fresh, pine-scented cologne and nervous male sweat had come an image that had made her almost delete a file.

Staring at the screen, she'd suddenly seen what Quentin was imagining. Herself, pressed against the desk, keyboard and printouts pushed hither and thither as he penetrated her roughly from behind. He'd had her half naked, and she'd been squeezing her own breasts . . .

God, another one I daren't face, she thought now as she travelled upwards in the lift, then gave herself a sound mental shaking.

Studying herself in the mirrored wall of the cab, she ticked off the reasons why Quentin might be enamoured. And as the tally mounted, her confidence soared.

She hadn't had her hair cut yet, but even without that it was obvious she'd changed. She looked brighter, more vivid, and larger than life somehow. It could have been the new make-up she'd tried, or just the tan, but every instinct said the radiance went deeper.

It was about sex, this new look of hers. The glow of animal sensuality. Thomas, she suspected, was choosing to ignore it, but in young Quentin it had clearly struck a nerve.

Now then, Quent, what about this? she thought mischievously, casting a glance at her impressive reflection. She'd chosen a short, tight black skirt – Tom said it made her look tarty – and teamed it with a sleeveless black silk top, and a boxy, big-shouldered crimson jacket. It was power-dressing, and not very subtle, but the strong colours enhanced her gypsy colouring far better than safe neutrals would have done.

I should have been wearing this stuff all along, she thought, stepping out of the lift. And heels too! Her slim, high-heeled shoes tapped provocatively as she strode along the corridor, and gave her walk a slight hip-swinging lilt. The back suede courts had been at the back of her wardrobe for a long time – for 'best' – and the old Alexa would never have worn them by day. The new one, however, had stepped into them without a second thought, because they looked brilliant with her five-denier black stockings.

'Morning, Quent,' she called out breezily as she

walked into the office – again following the new Alexa's proclivities. There was no use, or fun, in avoiding the issue, so she might as well face Quentin head on.

'You haven't been here all night again, have you?' she enquired, taking note of her young colleague's red-rimmed eyes and the way his short brown hair was standing up in spikes as if he'd repeatedly run his fingers through it.

'Well, yes, I have,' said Quentin sheepishly. 'I wanted to debug that comms program for Cornell Associates. You know they're screaming for it.'

'Yeah, I know.' It was so difficult to focus on the punters and their demands at the moment, but with an effort Alexa tried to concentrate. A major media client like Cornell shouldn't be kept waiting, and if she'd had her mind properly on the job, she would have been pushing the work ahead personally, instead of relying on Quentin's conscientiousness and skill. The lad was a star, truly, and suddenly she saw him in a new light.

'You're a sound man, Quent,' she said, unable to keep the warmth from her voice, and seeing an answering flash of heat in his eyes. 'I don't know what we'd do without you.' She moved closer, catching the faint odour of his unwashed muskiness and finding it subversively stirring. 'Did you suss it?'

'Yes . . . yes, I did,' he said, his pride in his work and his natural shyness fighting their usual guerrilla war across his face, 'It's sweet as a nut . . . We can install any time.'

Unable to catch herself in time, Alexa stepped forward and kissed him. She felt him flinch when she made contact, as if she'd hurt him, and beneath her lips, his stubbly cheek was burning hot.

'Bless you,' she said softly, pulling away, shaken herself and finding it difficult to hide it. 'You saved the ship again, Wesley,' she told him, her hand on his arm as she tried to redirect the awkward moment. Quentin was a major *Star Trek* fan, and referring to him as the

39

Starship Enterprise's precocious 'child prodigy' was a special running joke that they shared.

'I wish you wouldn't patronise me,' he said, his chin lifting, his eyes pained.

Alexa was aghast. Not so much by having offended him, but because his moody rebelliousness made her insides melt and quiver. Until yesterday, she'd never considered Quentin sexually, but now she realised she'd been making a mistake. He was strangely good-looking in a mournful, skinny rabbit sort of way, and his young body was lean, but seemed strong.

'I'm sorry, Quentin,' she said quietly, 'We take you for granted, and we shouldn't. You're an enormous asset to us, and I'm going to see Tom about an increase in your pay.'

Quentin's odd look seemed to suggest 'what with?', and reminded her of her tricks with the accounts.

'Look, I'll make us some coffee,' she said quickly. 'And you look as if you could splash cold water on your face or something.'

'Yeah, I will. Thanks,' he muttered, then moved away in the direction of the corridor that led to the staff restroom. 'I'm sorry I snapped,' he said as he paused in the doorway, 'It was uncalled for. Forgive me. I'm just tired.'

Alexa said nothing. But as he turned, she smiled at his narrow boyish back.

In the tiny office kitchen, Alexa set about making the coffee, but her mind wasn't really on the task. All she could see was the anger in Quentin's pale face, and the lurid visions that she'd dipped into yesterday.

I wonder what he's like as a lover? she mused, dismayed at how easy it was to consider. I'm going crazy here, she thought, as an image of herself and Quentin phased quickly into view. Crazier, she amended, remembering last night and the demands she'd made on Tom.

Her hand shook and ground coffee went all over the worktop. It was insane but she was aroused, on fire,

40

suddenly prickling in every sexual nerve. After last night's performance, a normal woman would be sated for a month. But I'm not normal any more, she thought, closing her eyes and pressing her pelvis against the edge of the fitted unit. And young Quentin is so close and so sweet . . .

Don't do this, she told herself, walking towards the door. Mixing work with relationships was dicey at the best of times, even when you were engaged and presumably 'settled'. But what she was about to do now was perfect lunacy, the worst possible thing. Yet somehow, she couldn't halt her steps.

Go for it! urged another voice inside her – the one that had sent her after Tom last night. Again and again until the pair of them were exhausted. It'll be so easy, the voice said. And you need it. How are you going to get through the day feeling like this?

'This' meant the sudden engorgement between her legs. The terrible hardness of her nipples. The rush of fluid across the folds of her sex. The sensations goaded her as surely as the voice.

At the door of the staff washroom, she paused and listened to the silence, and the last hopeless complaints of common sense. To enter now could well mean disaster in a dozen different forms, but ignoring all of them, she reached for the door handle.

Inside though, Quentin was slumped forward across the sink, his eyes closed, and the side of his face pressed up against the mirror. He appeared to be seeking comfort from its cool, glass surface. Alexa sensed that he was fighting the same demons that she battled, but that his conscience was trying somewhat harder.

Her own demons were winning, hands down. Especially at the sight of Quentin's back. He'd taken off his shirt, presumably so he could wash, and his wiry body was naked to the waist. The young programmer didn't have the godlike physique of Drew, or even the compact muscularity of Tom, but his arms and shoulders were far from unattractive.

As he detected her presence, Quentin's eyes snapped open, then met hers through their reflection in the mirror.

'Alexa,' he gasped, jerking away from the basin and turning around, his face a mask of indecision and desire. He'd been thinking of her – lusting after her, that was obvious – and she could feel that her presence made things worse. Or better.

'I – ' he began, lifting his narrow hands towards her in a gesture of confusion.

Alexa had never felt her new 'gift' more strongly. It was almost true mind-reading now, and she could taste the colour of her colleague's raging need. His thoughts and his libido were transparently accessible, and showed terror, and hope, in equal parts. He wanted her to have come for the reason she had come, but he was also deeply afraid of being mistaken.

As if she'd done it a thousand times, Alexa moved smoothly towards him, then halted as her prey squirmed in his trap. Between her body and the basin, there was no safe place to run, and Quentin's mouth – a soft and very kissable mouth, she noticed now – opened helplessly, yet uttered no sound.

'Don't say a word,' Alexa whispered, placing a finger across his lips, then running it slowly to and fro across the lower one. Almost automatically, the young man's mouth opened and he sucked in the questing digit, his dark eyes fluttering closed in stolen bliss.

Taken aback by the sudden sensuality of Quentin's reaction, Alexa let her body fall against him. Between her legs she felt a wetness and a weakening, and her clitoris quivered as if Quentin's lips were there instead of wrapped around her finger. Without conscious thought, she reached down, hiked up her skirt, and let her thighs part so she could rub herself against him. Rocking slowly, and hissing with pleasure, she felt the hard bulge of his sex against her leg.

Sliding her finger from his mouth, she put both her arms around him, then kissed him, pushing her tongue between his moist and yielding lips. His whole mouth and tongue were pliant; as she worked him, she experienced a rising sense of victory.

It was just like last night. She could control him as effortlessly as she had Tom. She could have him, do anything, exploit him in any way she pleased. His hard cock was completely at her disposal, and that thought made her clitoris throb and swell.

Suddenly, she could think of nothing but her own amorous flesh. Her sex seemed to cry out, its voice both beguiling and demanding, and alive with the need to be touched. She wanted to be naked. Exposed. Rocking against Quentin, she abandoned her hold on him and reached down and started tugging at her clothes.

The moves were awkward because her partner was so stunned; but after a few seconds, she had her skirt around her waist.

'Help me, Quent,' she hissed at him, barely recognising her own voice. 'Take my pants down. I want you to touch me.'

As his fumbling fingers grappled with her underwear, and his eyes went round with amazement, Alexa wished her panties had been a bit more glamorous. They were pretty – white with a tiny pink flower design – but to be in character, they should have been racy. A scrap of black lace and satin, or maybe a semi-transparent crimson G-string?

Quentin, however, seemed enchanted. He got the white cotton garment as far as her knees, then seemed to freeze, transfixed by her triangle of silky hair.

It was far enough for Alexa, too. Taking Quentin's hand in her own, she pressed it unceremoniously between her legs.

'Rub me, Quent,' she ordered softly. 'Rub me hard and make me come. I need it.'

'But Alexa – ' he gasped again, but got no further when her mouth silenced his.

While his fingertips worked clumsily through her soft pubic bush, Alexa closed her eyes and focused on her hunger. It had been born in the heat of Barbados, yet it still flourished in these far cooler climes. Subduing Quentin's tongue, she groaned into his mouth as he found her sweetest spot. His touch was untried, almost rough, but its very lack of finesse was what she wanted. Beating her pelvis furiously, she lost contact with his finger, but got a sharp thrill from reaching down to guide him.

After a few moments, Quentin – always quick to learn in everything – seemed to find just the rhythm she needed. The flat pad of his middle finger settled squarely on the button of her clitoris and nudged it blindly to and fro and back and forth. The caress was crude, and unsubtle, but its effect was instantaneous. With no warning, and no build-up, Alexa felt climax overwhelm her. Parted in pleasure, her lips slid messily off Quentin's as she slumped forward against him and the sink.

Still pulsing, and softly gasping, she felt him enfold her in his arms and support her. Somewhere at the back of her mind, she made a note of his tenderness. His consideration, despite the lust he was feeling . . .

'Oh, Quent, you're a jewel,' she whispered. She should have felt ashamed of what she'd done, but instead she was almost proud. She'd seen what she wanted, and she'd taken it. Remorse might – and probably would – come later, but for now she didn't feel a trace of it.

And Quentin wanted her. Probing with her peculiar perception, she felt his chaotic blend of horror, desperation, and an arousal so profound that just the edge of it seemed to reach out and sear her. For a moment, she could almost imagine she was him, and that she had a cock, and it was aching for release. She sensed his anger, too; his suppressed fury at her taking and not giving, that she'd led him on and not allowed him to fuck her.

A picture filled her mind again, the same as yester-day, yet relocated to this room. She was over the sink, her face close to the taps, her cheek against the porcelain, while Quentin took her powerfully from the rear. He was humiliating her, growling coarse words into her ear as he used her, but every fibre of her being was in ecstasy.

Smiling, and knowing exactly what to do, she pulled away from him, turned neatly on her heels, then lay forward – against the sink – with her chin resting on her folded arms. Adjusting the spread of her feet, she parted her thighs – within the constraint imposed by her dangling knickers – and pushed her bottom back lewdly towards Quentin.

'Well,' she purred as he hesitated. 'It's what you want, isn't it?'

His answer was halfway between a sob and a hiccup, but the jingle of his belt and the rasp of his zip were reassuring. Freeing one arm and reaching behind her, Alexa encountered what she sought. Her fingers curled around a thick, velvety shaft, a penis that felt unexpectedly substantial given the slender proportions of its owner. Tugging gently on its bare, sticky tip, she guided it quickly towards her, then flexed her muscles in an attempt to draw it in.

'Do it, Quent,' she hissed, feeling the hard, slippery thing that lay against her nudge infinitesimally into the niche that desired it. 'Yes, sweetheart, yes!' she crowed, as he finally took the initiative and pushed.

All-conquering now, she pushed backwards – and bit down on a harsh cry of triumph as her vagina seemed to sigh, then admit him.

Oh God, what have I done? she asked herself, looking up into the mirror and her own face. She was flushed, she was sweating, and her eyes were wide and dark. Her bright lipstick was smudged around her mouth.

I look like a cheap slut, she thought, and I'm doing it with Quentin. He's only twenty-one and he works for my fiancé and me. Do I really need trouble like this?

Of course you do, whispered the dark, dark voice

inside her. You love it! You bloody love it! Now stop whinging and enjoy him. He's lovely . . .

Gasping, she craned up, looked into her own eyes again, and saw mischief in their brilliant green depths. She churned her body, and Quentin groaned in response, the sound like a clarion call to arms. Clenching the muscles of her sex, she caressed his penis as it throbbed inside her, and his head lifted as if he'd heard a silent order. Their eyes locked immediately in the mirror.

'Alexa,' he breathed, looking at her; yet, she sensed, not seeing her. Quentin's eyes were wide, too, but unfocused, their pupils dilated near-black. He was her creature now, just as Tom had been last night, and the feeling was so heady she almost laughed.

Smiling a slow, slight smile that for an instant seemed to penetrate his stupor, she lowered her head again, laid her cheek against her arm, and thrust out her bared bottom against him. Serve me, the gesture said. Give me pleasure. Give me everything you have.

Obediently, Quentin began to move, his lips murmuring broken nothings in her ear. His strokes were shaky and undisciplined, but the angle was perfect and the depth quite sublime. Alexa felt his long-fingered hands curve hungrily on her thighs, gripping hard so he could plunge even deeper. Between her labia her clitoris tingled violently, as if protesting, and, shifting her legs a little, she reached down to stroke it. The tiny bud felt hard, and glassy with her juices, and though it was difficult to maintain a pressure beneath Quentin's wild plunges, she persisted and continued with her rubbing.

Quentin came quickly, but Alexa matched him effortlessly, her climax exploding beneath the tip of her own finger. She felt Quentin's flesh kick inside her, somewhere in the centre of a closing ring of heat, and his hoarse cry rang out across the washroom, echoing strangely in the bell-like acoustics. She herself remained silent, her mouth moving spasmodically against the immaculate white tiling, and her lipstick smearing over it like blood. It suddenly seemed important to keep the whole experience inside her, and not to appear vulnerable to the man across her back.

That she could still reason whilst in climax appalled her. Maybe I am possessed by the Devil? she thought blearily. The changes. The hunger. The sexual ruthlessness . . . Something's taken me over, she decided, there's no other explanation. And as her poor wrung-out victim slid away from her and backwards, she, too, eased her weary body to the floor.

Things had been awkward as they'd picked themselves up and begun to set their clothing to rights.

'Go home, Quent,' Alexa had urged, after she'd pulled up her pants, tidied her lipstick and then wiped the long scarlet smears of it off the tiles. Several feet away – a safe distance, perhaps? – the young programmer was struggling with the buttons on his crumpled white shirt, an expression of pure shell-shock on his face. He looked as if he'd been hit by a steam hammer, or abducted by aliens, and seemed to have lost the ability to co-ordinate his movements. Alexa was quite frightened at how 'normal' she felt beside him.

'You're tired,' she said gently. 'Take the rest of the day off. I'll sort out what needs to be dealt with.'

'But – ' he began.

Alexa cut him off.

'Quent. Go home.'

'But what about . . . What about what just happened?' he persisted, showing a flash of spirit that she found curiously exciting.

No! Not again! she thought in horror. We've only just . . .

'I don't know what just happened, Quentin,' she said, her voice a sham of level, reasoned calm, while her body was already reigniting. 'I'm feeling very odd at the moment. I don't quite know what I'm doing half the time. I need to think things out. Find out . . . Find out things.' It sounded stupid and airy-fairy, and Quentin's dark eyes looked hurt. 'Look, Quentin, let me sort myself out. Then we'll talk about this. I promise.'

Funnily enough, he'd accepted that, and gone home as good as a lamb, leaving Alexa alone in the office and feeling just as confused as she'd tried to describe.

Sipping a belated coffee, she sent her mind winging back to Barbados, to compare waking up, that first morning, with her half-ecstatic, half-terrified condition of now. Her sex drive was an uncontrollable monster, but brought such moments of extreme and exhilarating sensation with it that her previous life seemed to have been lived in slow motion. Or in a fog.

It is marvellous, she thought, rubbing her hand unconsciously over her body: her thighs, her abdomen, her crotch. But I can't let it run away with me all the time or I'll get into trouble. Get arrested. Or worse. I've got to learn to govern it somehow. To use it. I need help. Guidance. Counselling or something. I need to talk to someone who understands.

Beatrice.

As the name bobbed up, Alexa wondered why on earth she hadn't thought of it sooner. Beatrice Quine wasn't only a doctor; she was a woman, and a sensualist herself, to boot. She'd seen this insane thing start, and Alexa had a sudden, shrewd suspicion that the doctor herself suffered from the very same malady. Or a touch of it. If it could be called a malady.

I'm sure she knows, thought Alexa. Beatrice had shown an extraordinary perceptiveness back on the island. And her knowledge, and her candour, had been frightening. Alexa could still see those radiant brown eyes . . .

But how do I approach her? she pondered, topping up her mug with the far-too-strong coffee. They'd behaved like intimate friends on holiday, but surprisingly made no formal pledge to maintain that friendship.

God, I never even arranged to see Drew again,

thought Alexa with a shudder. And I went to bed with him!

She supposed that putting her holiday liaison behind her had been a way of returning to normal, 'real' life. Or trying to. Part of her, the scared part, had convinced her that if she looked upon her fling as just a glorified fantasy – like the ones that now constantly plagued her – it would somehow become exactly that. And she could say goodbye to her last few shreds of guilt.

Sitting down in her swivel chair, Alexa eyed the screen of her personal PC and frowned at its cheerful, scrolling message. Jiggling the mouse, she cleared the saver, then clicked the icon of her personal organiser.

She'd entered Beatrice's details on her return from Barbados – downloading them from the Psion she always carried – but seriously wondered if she'd ever actually need them. Now it seemed she did.

Beatrice Quine was a doctor, in private practice, and thus, for a price, Alexa could simply 'consult' her. Half her mind asked where the money for private medical fees would come from, but the other half – the same half that'd made her virtually rape her innocent puppy of a programmer – coolly pointed out that the funds would come from the usual source. The KL Systems account. A balance that was diminishing alarmingly, quite unknown to the 'K' of the equation.

Squashing her final qualm, Alexa picked up the phone and started dialling.

'Good morning, Doctor Quine's surgery,' announced a female voice on connection.

Alexa's tongue seemed to adhere to the roof of her mouth. It was silly to have expected Beatrice to answer her own phone, but somehow she'd been hoping against hope. It would have been such a relief to hear that creamy-silk voice again, and to be soothed and cajoled into confessing.

'Hello, may I help you?' enquired the unknown woman on the phone. Almost automatically, Alexa noted that this voice, too, was extremely appealing, but crisper and more businesslike than Beatrice's sultry drawl.

'Er . . . yes . . .' stammered Alexa, wondering if she was making a complete fool of herself. 'I'd like to make an appointment to see Doctor Quine if possible?'

There was a cautious pause, and the faint sound of pages being flicked. 'Are you one of Doctor's regular patients? I'm afraid I don't recognise your voice.'

'No, no I'm not a patient. I . . . I didn't realise . . .' Alexa's voice tailed off, her hopes plummeting, disappointment like lead in her belly.

'Well, I'm afraid Doctor's list is quite full at the moment,' the young woman went on, her tone kindly, as if she were genuinely sad at letting Alexa down. 'But perhaps we can refer you to a colleague? Someone with similar specialities?'

'No, thank you. It's all right,' replied Alexa flatly. 'It's really only Doctor Quine I want to see. I met her recently, in Barbados, and she seemed like someone I could talk to.' God, this sounds so pathetic, thought Alexa as she spoke. Just like a mawkish kid . . .

'Just a moment.' There was a sudden blankness on the line, as if a mute of some kind had been employed.

'What name is it please?' The voice returned, still pleasant and helpful, but with an unexpectedly vibrant edge to it, as if the word 'Barbados' had altered all the variables.' Perhaps we can help after all.'

'Lavelle. Alexa Lavelle.'

'One moment. So sorry about this,' apologised the voice. There was another brief pause, then the young woman came back on the line again, 'Hello, Ms Lavelle, sorry to keep you waiting. Would you be able to attend at three o'clock tomorrow. Doctor has an opening then, if that's convenient?'

'Oh, yes! Yes please!' Alexa almost sobbed, feeling so grateful that tears pricked her eyes. She couldn't understand what was happening to her, or why seeing Beatrice – instead of some other doctor or counsellor –

was suddenly so crucially important. 'That'd be great! Marvellous! Fine!'

'Very well. We'll book you in. Do you know how to find us?'

'No.' She'd no idea! 'But it's OK. I have the address. I'll get a taxi. No problem.'

'Good, that's settled then. We look forward to seeing you tomorrow. Goodbye, Ms Lavelle.'

'Goodbye,' murmured Alexa as the line went dead. Goodbye, whoever you are.

Alexa felt almost drunk with elation. She wanted to jump up and down and shout. She felt as excited, almost, as she had done earlier with Quentin, but she still didn't understand the reaction.

Until now, she'd always hated going to the doctor's.

And I've never made so many preparations for a doctor's appointment before, either, she thought the next day, after a night of poor sleep and frantic masturbation.

With Tom away she'd had the flat to herself, and the tenor of her thoughts had been uneasy. The changes at the heart of her were growing and strengthening, and her mind seemed filled constantly with sex.

Sex with Quentin. Sex with Drew. Sex with a whole cadre of new men whose faces were all unknown to her, just as they had been in her Caribbean fantasies.

It was only occasionally – to her chagrin – that Tom seemed to figure in these dreams. So very occasionally that she had to ask herself if she'd ever really fancied him. She'd believed she had . . . Last night she definitely had. But now? And as for loving him . . . She hardly dare think about that one.

She occupied herself for the early part of the evening by trying to catch up on work she'd forgotten during the day. After her dismissal of Quentin, she'd lost interest in all the projects she was supposed to be chasing – including the critical Cornell account – and simply locked the office and left everything hanging. It was completely irresponsible, but somehow she hadn't been able to help herself. The afternoon, she'd spent shopping like an airhead, and spent even more money she didn't possess. Buying an outfit – more correctly, a selection of outfits – that she could wear for her appointment with Beatrice.

Since when was it necessary to have new clothes to visit the doctor? she asked herself. Since now, whispered the demon who'd entirely taken her over.

In an attempt to bolster her flagging credibility as a serious professional, Alexa had bought a new suit. The excuse was that it would be just as appropriate for seeing prospective clients as it would be for visiting voluptuous, teasing-eyed doctors.

Made from ruinously expensive pure wool gabardine, the grey pinstripe ensemble had a severity that was also profoundly sexy. Especially with just a camisole beneath it. Which was another deliberate extravagance. From a chain store, she could have got something pretty enough for a few pounds at most, but in South Molton Street it made her Visa card scream.

You! she'd thought accusingly, seeing her urge to spend as a physical entity. Are you a relation of the other one? That devil that makes me want sex all the time. The one that makes me fantasise, then do stupid things when I really should know better.

Last night, after several restless hours and resorting to her usually dependable sleep-inducer – a mug of Horlicks and ten minutes with the manual of a newly released tax management program – she'd suddenly begun to feel uncomfortably warm. Her skin had seemed to itch. Not tangibly – there was no rash or irritation to put a cream on – but internally and far more alarmingly. She'd felt a slow, diffuse heat building somewhere beneath her skin, like an exasperating tickle that she couldn't reach to scratch.

Flinging aside the manual in annoyance, she'd seemed to hear Quentin's broken cry of 'Alexa!', then immediately after that the lapping waves of Barbados.

Drew Kendrick's deep voice had whispered wickedness against her ear lobe, and she'd almost felt his fingers between her legs.

After that there had been just one possible course of action; and after an extended string of climaxes, she'd finally slept.

This morning, waking early, she'd resisted the same urge but was now regretting it. And a phone call from Tom had only complicated matters, serving to remind her how little she was thinking of him. She'd tried to show enthusiasm for the project he'd described – *really* tried – but even to her own ears, her interest had sounded hollow. Fortunately Tom hadn't seemed to notice anything amiss, and had broken the connection with a cheerful 'Love you, Lex!'

When she reached the office, Quentin's eyes were accusing. She didn't know what he was expecting, but he'd clearly made some kind of effort with himself, based on yesterday's experience. He was wearing a smart new jacket that Alexa hadn't seen before, and he had gel on his usually floppy hair. He stared at her for a count of ten, then opened his mouth and shut it again. On his second attempt, Alexa raised her hand for silence.

'Please, Quent,' she said, hoping her smile wasn't too sweet. Too false. 'Don't say anything. We'll talk soon, I promise.'

The young programmer seemed to accept this. With a shrug of his narrow shoulders, and a hint of resignation in his voice, he launched straight into the business of the day.

Oh, nice one, Lavelle, thought Alexa, only listening with half her attention. It would have been much better to sort this thing out, but naturally you know better . . .

The worst of it was that Quentin's small efforts with grooming had made quite a difference. He was a handsome lad, really; it was just that she'd never really noticed the fact. And beneath his shyness lurked a mind of true brilliance.

Please! Oh no! thought Alexa, as yesterday resurfaced. What Quentin had lacked in sexual finesse, he'd more than made up for in almost delirious desperation. She tried not to get too close to him, but as he showed her a new help screen he'd written for a specialised project-planning program, she couldn't avoid catching a heady drift of scent from him.

Like his jacket, his cologne was new, but it only reminded her of how he'd smelt when he was in her. That male musk, that slight sharp tang of sweat, its very pungency inciting her to madness. She watched the dance of his fingers as they flew across the keyboard, but instead saw their pale tips on her body.

No!

Muttering something vaguely complimentary about the help screen, she shot away across the room to her own machine.

It was insanity to foster any kind of liaison with Quentin. He wasn't what she really wanted, and she knew that, he was just a tempting titbit. A plaything. A boy, for God's sake!

But who did she want?

Tom? It didn't seem so – more and more it didn't seem so.

Drew Kendrick?

Possibly? Probably. Yet somehow, even he wasn't all of it. She wanted to see him again – to have him again, yes indeedy! – but he wasn't the whole answer to her problem.

Yet she hadn't the faintest idea who truly was.

Chapter Five

Circe

With Quentin dispatched on a system installation, and various waiting clients fobbed off with excuses, Alexa left the office.

Her attitude towards KL Systems had changed, she realised with some guilt. Within a few days she'd gone from almost desperate concern at her own lack of interest to a sort of mildly hysterical laissez-faire. She was letting Tom's precious enterprise slide right down the pan, but she couldn't seem to make herself care any more. She wanted to care, and she was sure a little part of her did care, but it was becoming lost in a high tide of sex.

Beatrice will help, thought Alexa, striding out of the building that oppressed her. She'll know what to do.

The trouble was, going to Beatrice might produce even more problems. The good doctor might not even think Alexa needed curing, she might simply prescribe more of the same.

After a taxi ride she couldn't quite remember, Alexa found herself in one of London's most prestigious shopping streets.

What am I doing here again? she thought, feeling the

onset of a familiar, vulnerable daze. Any minute now, lulled by the traffic and the jostling of the passing tourists and shoppers, she'd slip into some luxurious store, seek out the 'designer' section and find herself trying on clothes she couldn't afford.

'For pity's sake, pull yourself together, woman!' she said aloud on the pavement, drawing a stare from a passing young man. His handsome face split in a grin, and, without thinking, Alexa smiled back. His hair was straw blond, and he looked fit and virile. She felt a familiar tug of desire, then spun abruptly on her heel and walked off in the opposite direction, her nipples stiffening and her entire body shaking.

Oh God, it's happening again! Total strangers . . . Blond hunks on the street . . . I could easily have gone off with him. To a hotel. A parked car even. Let him kiss me, and slip his hand in my pants.

Weaving her way quickly among the crowds, with no direction in mind, Alexa turned down a side-street, a narrow, more select-looking thoroughfare that she couldn't recall passing along before.

The shops here were all small, understated and exclusive-looking, and Alexa got a shock when she paused and stared into a window.

The wares of this particular boutique were displayed with a deceptive carelessness. Across a bolt of flesh-coloured silk were strewn a selection of what at first appeared to be randomly chosen garments. Nothing matched, they weren't on models and dummies of any kind, and the arrangement seemed totally haphazard. And yet, anyone shopping in this particular emporium would probably have a definite and very circumscribed agenda. The shop – proclaimed as 'Circe' in narrow black script on a plain white hoarding – sold lingerie designed purely for seduction.

Alexa could only gape at the beauty before her; and at the sheerness and the breathtaking brevity . . . Made from nylon, or viscose, things like this would be the sleaziest of tat, but in this window there was nothing cheap or nasty. The silks were pure, the lace French, and the stitching so delicate and almost invisible it could only have been hand-done. There were no price tags in sight, nothing so vulgar, but everything about these fripperies shouted money. Alexa guessed that the white basque in the centre of the display, trimmed with lace and crystal beads, could easily cost more than her new suit.

Oh no you don't, she thought, planting her feet firmly on the pavement. She could feel her soul gravitating towards the glass-panelled door, and the tantalising items beyond it, but she knew her spending spree had gone far enough already. Good clothes for work, like the suit she had on, were just about acceptable. But supertax underwear? No way!

Even so, she couldn't help looking.

The basque wasn't the only glorious thing in the window. What about that black pierced satin bra? Or that tiny G-string in dove-grey lace? If either were under a hundred pounds, she might be able to justify –

Suddenly, as she battled with her conscience and fingered her bag with her credit cards inside it, she felt a familiar blast of feverish sensation.

Confused, knowing the feeling had come from without not within, Alexa looked quickly around her. A man and woman were just entering the shop together, arm in arm with their laughing faces close, and she realised that *they* were the ones pumping out the heat.

Dear Lord, whatever next? thought Alexa, realising she'd sensed the couple's desire before she'd even set eyes on them. Without hesitation, she followed their trail into the shop.

The tiny jangling of a bell greeted her entry. The boutique was bigger than it appeared from the street, and the lovers were already at the far end of the room, in conversation with the woman who appeared to be in charge. The sales assistant nodded amenably in Alexa's direction, mouthed 'Be with you in a minute', then returned her attention to the man and woman. Relieved at being left alone – she hated the 'high-pressure' sales pitch – Alexa began idly scanning a rack of delicious silk skimpies, each suspended on its own tiny hanger from a long, gleaming bar of polished chrome. Picking up a pair of lemon-coloured briefs roughly the size of a floppy disk, she studied her quarry discreetly from behind them.

They were certainly worth anyone's attention, and Alexa couldn't decide which of them was the most striking. The man – the husband, she amended, seeing a fine glint of gold on both their marriage fingers – was tall, swarthy and distinguished, with a glint of serious mischief in his dark chocolate eyes, and hands that constantly touched his lovely wife. The woman was like a creature out of a fairy tale: a slender, smiling aristocrat with a temptress's body and a sleek bob of Cleopatra-like black hair.

Just my colour, observed Alexa, thinking for a minute of the other appointment she'd made yesterday. It's no use you wanting a bob, Lavelle, your hair's too wild and too curly, she told herself. Then, aware that she was staring too intently at the woman and her husband, she returned her attention to the undies before her.

The first ensemble she picked up was rose pink. Not a shade she usually chose, but in this case an exquisite temptation. The bra was very soft and delicate, its shot-silk cups cleverly cut on the bias, and beautifully shaped without wiring or padding. It would feel gorgeous against the skin, she thought dreamily, imagining the wafer-thin fabric pressed tight against each breast, held in place by a man's encircling hand. And the high-cut briefs were more of an incitement than a covering. Knowing it was fatal, she took a glance at the price tag, and the damage was as bad as she'd expected. Not quite as expensive as her tailored grey suit, but even so, not all that much cheaper.

While she was still wincing at the amount of money she was now almost certainly going to spend, a low, seductive giggle caught her attention. The slender, black-haired woman was inclining towards her husband, listening closely to something whispered, and clearly very detailed.

'No, Julian, please. Not again!' Alexa heard 'Cleo' say as her husband winked and touched her bottom, then turned away to study a half-slip of pewter lace.

'Is everything OK?'

A husky and strangely familiar voice from just beside her made Alexa almost drop the pink silk knickers.

'Oh . . . yes,' she answered, turning to the sales assistant who was standing just a yard away. 'Everything's lovely. It's difficult to know what to choose.' She smiled at the young woman, really seeing her for the first time now, and realising that she was far from the unctuous, super-groomed figure that usually peopled shops like this. And it wasn't only the voice that was familiar.

There was something about the girl's bone structure, and the reddish shine of her fiercely cropped hair, and, in an eye's blink, Alexa had it.

Why didn't I see it straight away? she thought. It's so obvious. The hair was far shorter, the face was younger, and a little harder, and the clothes – a fetishy get-up of vinyl jeans and body-hugging top – were totally wrong, but she could suddenly see Beatrice Quine in front of her. Or a Doctor Quine into Rocky Horror, or punk . . .

Beatrice's look-alike wasn't fazed in the slightest by being stared at. 'Yes, there's some great stuff, isn't there?' she replied easily, then nodded towards a row of curtained booths at the far end of the shop. 'You can try some of the items on, if you like.'

'Thanks. Yes. I might,' answered Alexa woodenly. The young woman made her extremely nervous this close, and it was almost a relief when she walked away, then sat down by the till, to read a magazine.

Weird, thought Alexa, resuming her browsing. Was the resemblance all in her mind, or did a punkette sales assistant in a fancy West End knicker shop really look so much like a top people's doctor?

By the time she'd worked her way to the end of the rack, the question still perplexed her, and she had a handful of garments to try on, all of which she couldn't afford. Holding them up in turn, she eyed each beautiful creation regretfully, and she was just trying to talk herself out of the last one when she saw movement in the periphery of her vision. With a thick sheaf of robes, negligées and teddies over his arm, 'Mr Handsome' was just guiding his wife into a cubicle.

Driven by forces she barely understood, Alexa snatched up the rose-pink bra and pants, plus a couple of other things, and fairly shot across the room towards the changing area.

'I'll try these,' she called over her shoulder to the sales assistant, who looked up from her reading and smiled.

It was a smile that nearly brought Alexa's rush to a halt. It was full of knowingness, complicity, permission, almost; as if the young woman knew exactly what the couple were up to, and, equally, why Alexa was following them.

Even more like Beatrice, thought Alexa, shaking as she drew the heavy curtain.

The changing cubicle was smallish, but luxurious, with a white-painted wooden partition to either side, and a full-length mirror hanging on the back wall. The thick, poppy-coloured carpeting seemed to fondle her toes when she slipped off her shoes, and both the lining of the curtain and the brocade-covered reproduction chair in the corner were co-ordinated in precisely the same shade. Under other circumstances, Alexa might have taken her time in there, and relaxed as she tried on her choices, but it was the action beyond the thin white division to her right that concerned her, not a few scraps of silk she couldn't afford.

Almost immediately she heard another giggle, then the distinctive sound of a zip going down, and then the rustle of hastily shed clothing. Holding her breath, Alexa decided that her own side of the partition must be sounding suspiciously quiet, so – as the two voices beyond began a teasing, indistinct banter – she started unfastening her own clothes.

As she slipped off her jacket, then her camisole, it wasn't herself she seemed to see in the mirror. Instead of her own breasts, as she slid off her simple cotton bra, she saw the elegant white orbs of 'Cleopatra', their dark nipples being pinched and caressed. The dark man's touch was possessive and familiar, almost insulting. He'd staked his claim in full on his wife's slender body, and her beauty was his to command.

Bastard! thought Alexa, leaning forward, and fitting her breasts into the soft, rose-pink brassière. In her mind's eye, she now fancied she saw the woman next door teetering naked on her high heels, her hands on her head, while her husband continued to handle every part of her. He seemed intent on controlling her and teasing her, and pushing her to her limits; making her cry out when she ought to stay silent. One hand was spread crudely against her vulva, moving in a brisk, sawing action, fingers between her legs and thumb pressed upwards against her mons, while the other was at work on her bottom. The woman rose on her toes, biting her lips and shimmying, as a finger pushed slowly into her anus.

'Ju! Oh God, no!' Alexa heard the woman say, and felt her own knees go weak at the thought of what was happening so close to her. She had no doubt that her 'vision' was quite real.

'Oh, please, love. Not that!' The voice was broken now, rough with ecstasy. The woman was being lifted higher. She was dancing and weaving. She was being rocked on the intrusion in her bottom.

'You love it,' hissed the man called Ju, then he murmured something else that Alexa couldn't hear, although in her mind she could see what he'd ordered. 'Cleo' was tugging her own nipples now, twisting and twirling them in her fingers, while her husband attacked her clitoris and her rear.

Alexa's hands trembled as she fastened the clasp on the pink-silk bra. The cups were as light as thistledown, but her breasts were aching furiously inside them. She looked down at the rest of the ensemble and knew it would be ridiculous to try any more items on now, but still began unfastening her skirt. Somehow it was all a part of the wickedness. She wanted to be wearing hundreds of pounds worth of silk lingerie that didn't yet belong to her; she wanted it on her body as she listened; she wanted it to get wet with her juices.

In the mirror, she saw her tanned chest flushed with excitement and her nipples hard beneath the fabric of the bra. As quietly as she could, she slid down her plain white knickers and stepped out of them. When she unclipped the pink panties from their tiny hanger, she faltered, and almost dropped them . . . as a loud groan rang out from next door.

What's he doing? What the hell is he doing to her? she thought, momentarily losing her focus. A dozen lurid scenarios flashed through her mind as she wiggled into the costly silk briefs, which were her size, but incredibly tiny. The delicately stitched gusset was sticking to her within seconds. I'll have to buy them now, she reflected vaguely, feeling her fluid anoint the fine cotton lining.

'Relax,' whispered the seductive male voice next door. 'Open up to me, darling. Do it now; like that. Hold steady.'

The voice was so warm and so urgent that, without thinking, Alexa clutched herself and rubbed the wisp-like panties. He's taking her somehow, she thought, He's having her, and for some reason it's not easy.

'Oh, Ju . . . Oh God! Oh! Oh! Oh!' The cries were forced, exhaling grunts, tiny expressions of pleasure and distress.

'That's it, my darling,' the violator purred. 'A little more. Wriggle on to me. Let me in . . . Oh God, Celeste, you're so hot!'

'Oh dear Lord!' breathed Alexa almost silently, as at last she seemed to 'see' what he'd done.

They couldn't be. He couldn't . . . How could she let him do it in a nearly public place?

Alexa could see them quite clearly in her mind now, this 'Ju' and his wife, 'Celeste'. The beautiful woman was bent forward at the waist, draped across the back of a chair, and her husband's penis was buried deep inside her bottom. She was completely nude – apart from her shoes – and he was clothed; and in an act of both love and humiliation he was sodomising her and manhandling her breasts.

Alexa's own rear seemed to be tingling now, and her clitoris was on fire beneath her fingers. Biting her lip, she scrubbed at her vulva through the thin wispy panties, and jerked roughly at the hub of her passion. Slumping forward, mirroring the unknown Celeste, she longed, for one moment, to be her. To be deliciously shamed by a mysterious dark lover; to be abused, and be made to submit. She'd been loved as an equal by Drew Kendrick, and she'd wiped the floor with both Tom and young Quentin, but right now she wanted the flip side, the passive role. She wanted to be the object of a man's deep depravity.

Or maybe it didn't have to be a man's?

For a moment she seemed to see the sales assistant, her pale face stern and forbidding. What if she were to throw back the curtain, and see what was happening to Circe's exclusive merchandise before it'd even been paid for? The rosy-coloured pants were sticky now, soiled and fragrant. Surely that was just cause for a humbling if ever there was one?

It was as plain as day. The striking, punkish young woman would lay hands on Alexa, then force her into a state of indignity . . . Perhaps make her strip naked in the centre of the shop itself? Show her bare buttocks to any customers that entered. Make her part her own cheeks. Expose her anus, and invite some kind of entry . . .

Sliding down noiselessly to the carpet, Alexa leaned against the chair and surrendered to her fantasies. To the sound of unashamed moans from the booth beside her, she saw herself, braced against a long rack of lingerie, while the unknown Ju probed her bottom – first with his fingers and then with his prick. As he possessed her, moving fiendishly in and out of her rectum, both his wife and the salesgirl stood by: both reaching boldly beneath Alexa's body, one towards her breasts, and the other her sex.

'Oh no . . . Oh no . . .' she whispered, as orgasm gripped her, like a pincer between her legs. It took an effort of will not to flap about crazily and let her feet slide out beneath the curtain. Taut in every nerve, she crushed her clitoris beneath her thumb, and almost pushed a portion of the panties inside herself as she used her fingers to excite her pulsing entrance.

The climax seemed to go on for minutes on end, and several times she almost shouted aloud; but finally Alexa regained control.

What the devil am I doing? she thought, struggling to her feet. In the mirror, her reflection was shocking. Her dishevelled hair was all over the place, her chest and throat were mottled with crimson splodges of blush, and the fragile lingerie was twisted on her body, showing one breast and her black pubic curls.

I look like a slut again, she decided grimly, trying not to listen to the commotion a few feet away. Celeste and Ju were still performing, that was obvious. And if she could hear their gasping, and the rhythmic jerk-jerk-jerk, it must be clearly audible in the shop. As yet there'd been no enquiry of any kind from the sales assistant, but Alexa had a feeling such goings on might all be part and parcel of the job.

Is that why she hasn't challenged me either? she wondered, trying to set her hair and her new under-clothes to rights. Do people masturbate every day in these cubicles?

It took several minutes to restore an appearance of

normality, but eventually Alexa managed it. The adjacent cubicle was all quiet as she stepped out into the shop, and – on the strength of the hubbub that Mr and Mrs 'Ju' had raised – she decided to hope that her own escapade hadn't been noticed.

'I wonder if you could slip these into a bag for me,' she said as coolly as she could, holding out her own white bra and pants when she reached the till. 'I love the pink ones so much that I'd like to wear them. I hope that's all right?'

'No problem,' replied the sales assistant casually. Without turning a single, sleek auburn hair, she reached under the counter, drew out a slim, white card box and some tissue, then wrapped Alexa's plain Marks & Spencer cotton smalls just as carefully as if they'd been Circe's finest satin.

Making a show of looking for her credit card, Alexa tried to hide how much this small procedure affected her. There was something very stirring about watching another woman handle her used underwear, and the sales assistant seemed to treat the panties in particular with a peculiar sense of reverence, as if she treasured their faint female fragrance.

She's a lesbian, thought Alexa, as if a light-bulb had suddenly flicked on in her brain. Staring down at her overworked Visa, she saw a vision of the other woman's sexuality. A vision in which she played a part.

On the plain of a black silk sheet, she was looking down at her own naked body, and the 'v' of her widely spread thighs. Between them, like a pony nuzzling at a salt block, the sales assistant was licking neatly at Alexa's sex, her long rosy tongue darting and diving as she lapped up the richly pungent juices. Her strong, dextrous hands were under Alexa's bottom, and as she crouched down, her body sweetly flexed, her own bare rump was on display.

A soft clearing of the throat brought Alexa tumbling clear of her fantasy. Her 'lover' was holding out the box in one hand, and asking for the card with a discreet gesture of the other.

'I'm sorry. I was miles away,' apologised Alexa, feeling the blood rush betrayingly into her face.

'Yes, it's easy to get distracted here,' murmured the young woman, slipping the card deftly through the reader, whilst looking towards the still occupied cubicle.

Alexa's blush redoubled. Should she comment? Give some indication of what she'd heard? It was perfectly plain that the sales assistant knew exactly what was going on, and seemed to condone it. But would she want others to know she knew?

'They're regulars,' she said simply, as she handed Alexa a pen and the sales voucher to sign.

Alexa winced at the sum being debited, but accepted that in some ways it was a bargain. You'd never have had an experience like this in M & S, her inner devil pointed out, and that thought made her crack a little smile. The sales assistant smiled in return, as if she, too, perceived the added 'extra'.

'I hope we'll see you again,' she said, as Alexa took her card and receipt, then turned to leave.

The words were the bland inanities mouthed in every shop across the country a hundred times a day; but when Alexa looked up and met a pair of large, intent eyes the colour of polished slate, she realised the sentiment behind them wasn't innocent. The strange young woman was looking at her with the same frank, assessing scrutiny that Alexa had received in Barbados from Beatrice. She'd told herself she was mistaken when she'd seen it then, but now her peculiar new gift was growing stronger, she knew it and understood it, loud and clear.

She wants me! She's a lesbian and she wants me! thought Alexa bemusedly as she almost ran from Circe's perfumed confines.

And, oh God, I think I wanted her . . .

*　*　*

It was a relief that Fausto was talkative. Once Alexa had outlined what she wanted, and received her hairdresser's unqualified approval, she was able to relax while he chattered on and snipped.

Everything about the episode in Circe was astounding. What she'd done; what she'd heard being done; what she imagined might be done if she ever got to know that salesgirl better.

It's a whole new world, she thought as wet black tresses fluttered down to the floor. A world within a world. What would have happened if I'd gone there before Barbados? I might never have heard a thing. Or heard it and thought nothing of it. Just someone struggling with something too tight for them . . .

Similarly, she realised she could well have dismissed the PVC-clad sales assistant as another of those attention-seeking types that she didn't care for very much. People in kinky clothes with radical haircuts and ambiguous, affected manners.

But things had changed. She'd changed. And what she'd wanted then, and what she needed now, were two animals of an entirely different hue.

And that's what this afternoon's all about, she thought decisively. About a way of taming the beast, getting myself under control, behaving in a way that won't scare the shit out of Tom. And Quentin. Beatrice will know how to handle this, she consoled herself, twirling a strand of hair that'd fallen into her lap, then suddenly noticing how long it was. For the first time since she'd sat down, she looked, really looked, into the mirror.

Oh Lord, it was too late to change her mind now! Fausto had sliced away an amazing amount of hair, and, shorn of its straightening weight, the remainder had sprung back into crisp, glossy curls that clung fetchingly to the shape of her scalp. The style was sophisticated, yet elfin, and she looked both knowing and girlish all at once. After ten seconds, she wished she'd done it sooner. Much sooner . . .

'Is good, eh?' crowed Fausto, clearly pleased with such a major transformation.

'Yes, oh yes,' Alexa whispered, putting up her hand and tentatively fingering a curl. 'It's very good. I should have had it cut years ago.'

'Now we dry,' Fausto continued jubilantly. 'A little spray for body. A little scrunch maybe? Some movement. Yes, is good!'

The cost of the cut, however, was not good. There was a big difference between her usual light trim and a complete restyle as done by the owner of the salon. Alexa shuddered as, yet again, she handed over her credit card, then added Fausto's gratuity from her wallet.

As she stepped out of the shop, a glance at her watch gave her another shock. It was already two thirty, she hadn't had lunch, and she was due at Beatrice's surgery at three. She wasn't hungry, but she had wanted to prepare herself somehow. To work out precisely what she'd say. She'd wanted the details of what had happened to her on the tip of her tongue: everything to be as organised and logical as it was possible for it to be. But now it was doubtful that she'd physically get there on time, much less be ready, in her mind, for the meeting.

As luck would have it she got a taxi immediately, and as she sat back uneasily on the black leather seat, she tried to settle her thoughts and shape an outline of her plight.

But what in heaven's name could she say? 'Oh, Beatrice, I feel randy all the time. I can't stop having sex and I can't stop having fantasies. And when I'm not having my own fantasies I'm having someone else's!'?

It sounded preposterous, but she could only tell the truth.

Chapter Six

A Consultation

*A*lexa had never expected to find a house like this so close to the heart of the City. Located so prestigiously, Beatrice's home must be worth half a million at least, so clearly her practice was lucrative.

Built of clean, grey stone and with tall, mullioned windows, the house stood a little way back from the road, its well-kept garden surrounded by a low wall, and, within that, a vigorous yew hedge. Alexa wondered if the gardening was one of Drew's duties, then remembered that he had his own practice, or whatever it was called, as a masseur. He wasn't a kept man by any means, even though, in Barbados, Beatrice had often made it seem so.

Still, thought Alexa, it's nice to flex the truth a bit. She imagined Drew stripped to the waist, digging, with sweat standing on his broad, tanned back. It seemed like only yesterday she'd seem him naked, then felt his penis push slowly inside her. Fumbling with the catch on the gate, she seemed to feel the sensations she'd enjoyed on the island; her inner flesh yielding to the size of him while the scent of his cologne made her weak.

Good God, Alexa, pull yourself together! she thought as she stood before the black painted door. This's just what you're trying to avoid . . . It's the reason you're here. For heaven's sake, show some self-control.

Taking a deep breath, she scanned the pair of gleaming brass nameplates, each with its separate bell-push. Drew's said simply his name followed by an unfamiliar qualification, and she was sorely tempted to reach out and press it. With him, she could be sure of a warm, straightforward greeting. Simple friendship, even, despite the fact they'd had sex. They might even actually end up in bed . . .

No! Stop it! That isn't why you've come here, she told herself angrily. Her purpose now was to control the appetite, not stoke it; and, with a pang of both regret and anticipation, she pressed the other button. The one beside BEATRICE A. QUINE, MD B.Sc.

A bell trilled inside the house, some distance away, but it was a full minute before her ring was answered. Still hoping for Drew, but half-expecting Beatrice herself, Alexa was surprised – and a little let down – when the door was opened by a nurse; a tall, rather slender blonde, coolly clad in the traditional white dress.

'Hello, may I help you?' the nurse said pleasantly, her hazel eyes warm but neutral. It didn't seem as if Alexa was expected.

'I . . . I'm Alexa Lavelle. I have an appointment with Doctor Quine. I'm sort of a friend of hers. We met in Barbados.'

The nurse's steady gaze made Alexa feel suddenly hot. Somewhere far back in those intensely glowing eyes there was knowledge and a definite hint of humour.

Am I being messed about with here?

For a moment, Alexa wondered if the young woman actually knew who she was but was deliberately making her explain herself. It might be some ploy of Beatrice's perhaps? One of her devious little tests. She'd played games like that in Barbados.

'Of course. Do come in. You're expected,' said the nurse, and gave Alexa a truly lovely smile. 'Please come this way.' She stood back gracefully to let Alexa pass, then gestured in the direction of a staircase. 'Doctor's busy at the moment, but she's asked me to take extra special care of you. Follow me, the surgery's upstairs.'

Taken aback by the sudden change from query to welcome, Alexa followed the young woman up the stairs.

'I'm Camilla, by the way. Camilla Fox.' The nurse turned on the corner landing, and flashed Alexa another delicious white smile. 'Beatrice has told me all about you. I do hope you're not getting more headaches.'

'Er, no, not exactly,' replied Alexa, now thoroughly flustered. What the devil had she told Beatrice on the island? Anything incriminating? Anything embarrassing that this nurse knew, too?

As Camilla preceded her, Alexa suddenly found her face almost level with a trim, rounded bottom. The nurse's cotton dress was uncompromisingly plain but looked well cut from fine, expensive cloth. White as a cloud, it skimmed rather than clung to a shape that was exquisite; and its modest knee-length skirt showed the backs of a pair of legs that would have put many a top model to shame. Especially as they were clad in the sheerest of sheer black stockings with an arrow-straight seam up the back.

She's gorgeous, thought Alexa as she continued to follow Camilla, this time on to a wood-panelled corridor. Dotted along the walls were a number of vaguely familiar-looking paintings, and interspersed with these were what had to be Beatrice's collection of diplomas.

Where does she find these people? thought Alexa, her attention returning to the nurse. First Drew Kendrick, superman, and now this sleek blonde Camilla? Does everyone Beatrice knows have to be extraordinary?

Halfway down the corridor, Alexa was ushered into a small, cosy room furnished in creams and soft browns, and a proliferation of William Morris-style prints. It seemed to be a waiting room of sorts, although it had nothing at all in common with the grim characterless areas so favoured by the NHS.

Camilla's next words gave Alexa a shock.

'Would you like to undress now, please?' she said, reaching out to take Alexa's bag and briefcase.

'Undress?'

'Yes, of course.' Camilla smiled as if she were explaining something elementary to a particularly dim child. 'We can't examine you still in your clothes, can we?'

Oh God, it is a game! thought Alexa wildly, as – for the first time since she'd stepped across Beatrice's threshold – her special gift clicked into action. As Camilla's fingers touched hers, in the course of taking her bags, she sensed a field of radiant sexual interest. The clinically pure nurse wasn't as pure as she seemed, and beneath that stark, unsullied whiteness lay dark desire.

She's a lesbian. Like the woman in Circe.

As the thought crystallised, Alexa knew that Camilla wasn't going to leave the room and let her undress in private. This was part of the game, too, maybe the nurse's own variation. And sure enough, as she began unbuttoning the jacket of her suit, and wishing she'd had a chance to change since this morning's mad caper in Circe, Alexa saw Camilla reach for a clipboard, that lay to one side on a Victorian desk, and begin jotting down notes on a form.

'How's your health in general, Miss Lavelle?' she enquired, as Alexa struggled with her silk camisole, then burst off the round pearl button that fastened it and sent it flying away towards the carpet. Not sure whether to bend down and try to find the thing, or just ignore it, Alexa muttered that she 'felt OK'. Then she blushed, vividly, because the nurse was staring at her rose-pink silk bra; almost as if she'd been there in the shop this morning, and seen the events that had led to its purchase.

72

'This's lovely,' Camilla commented, and in a movement so swift Alexa hardly registered it, she was around behind her, and unfastening the bra's clasp. As it came open, she reached forward – under Alexa's arms – and eased the soft cups from her breasts.

'Lovely,' Camilla whispered again as Alexa looked down to see alien and very female hands momentarily holding her, then sliding away out of view. 'It really suits you. You have the most beautiful breasts. They're just as the doctor described them.'

Doctor? Described?

Still looking down, and watching with an almost remote fascination as her nipples puckered and hardened, Alexa desperately cast her mind back to Barbados.

Drew had seen her breasts. Drew had stroked them and kissed them. But hadn't she always kept her bikini top on when Beatrice was around? She remembered a kind of fear, a formless shyness that was now becoming clearer. It had been her innocent response to a woman's subtle overtures, she'd covered up because she'd been scared of being wanted. Beatrice had lain around topless – and generally bottomless, too – for a lot of the time, but Alexa had kept herself hidden. Concealing a response she'd been unable to accept . . .

'Now the rest, please,' murmured Camilla, moving around to Alexa's front again, her clipboard once more in her hands. 'Mustn't keep Doctor Quine waiting, must we?'

'I suppose not,' replied Alexa, turning her attention to her skirt.

She's bloody well loving this! she thought savagely, watching Camilla's neat but arcane notations. I wonder if she'd be so smug if she knew that I could 'read' her? And that I know how much she's attracted to me?

But am I attracted to her?

The question followed quite naturally. So much so that she came within a breath of voicing it aloud. What do I feel? What do I feel? she pondered, sliding her skirt down her thighs on its lining. Am I a lesbian, too? she asked herself as she kicked the garment away slightly, and almost automatically, Camilla paused in her jottings to reach down, pick it up, then fold it carefully and lie it across a chair.

I suppose I must be one, she thought, remembering her fantasies about the sales assistant in Circe, and the nascent urges she'd ignored back on the island.

But what about Drew? And Tom? And Quentin? I must be bisexual then, she thought, seeing a sudden graphic picture of a man's naked penis, but not knowing, or somehow even caring, whose it was.

The image, and the ideas behind it made her blush furiously, and she looked down and saw the redness crawling up across her chest. She wished again that she'd had the foresight to go home and get changed. What'd happened in the changing cubicle at Circe had made her sticky, and her thin, pink pants still bore the evidence. Something else Camilla would probably note down on her blessed clipboard in due course!

Standing in her shoes, hold-up stockings and knickers, Alexa felt like a tawdry but inexperienced stripper. The fact that her heels were new and very high, that her stockings had lace welts, and that her panties were so thin they were almost transparent didn't help matters either. She'd never felt more exposed in her life, and she had a feeling that when she finally and inevitably took everything off, she wouldn't feel nearly as bare as she felt now.

In contrast, Camilla seemed even more hygienic and unruffled. She looked up at Alexa once, twice, three times, and after each glance returned scrupulously to her notes. Alexa could still sense the other woman's arousal, but the lack of visible evidence of it was unnerving. Camilla's slightly tanned skin was smooth and cool-looking, and the crisp, white bodice of her regulation dress moved only gently with an even respiration. Everything about her was imperturbably spotless; from the tips of her polished black shoes, to the

crown of her beautifully coiffed head of golden hair
beneath its primly starched, saucer-sized cap.

'I think that's enough for the time being,' said the
nurse looking up from her board. 'If you'd like to sit
down over there, I'll run through the first part of the
examination.'

Alexa had a million protests, but felt so disorientated
that she didn't utter any of them. As she sat down on a
deeply upholstered sofa, however, and felt the kiss of
soft velour against her thighs, the questions rang
monotonously in her mind.

Why am I having a complete physical if I only came
here for a chat? Why have I been made to undress in
the waiting room? And why the hell, if it's Beatrice I'm
consulting, is it her nurse who's going to examine me?
I know she wants to examine me, every last bit of me,
but isn't it all just a teeny bit unethical?

After a moment or two, Camilla came across and sat
beside her, placing a few, small necessary implements
on the low, polished table close by. Alexa had never
noticed her don it, but the nurse was now wearing a
stethoscope, with its earpieces hooked around her neck.

The first part of the examination was disappointingly
impersonal. With no explanation as to why she was
doing it, and not her employer, Camilla performed a
series of routine and unthreatening procedures. She
looked into Alexa's eyes, ears and mouth with a variety
of gadgets, then took her blood pressure, temperature
and pulse.

From time to time the nurse's soft fingertips lingered
on Alexa's skin, and when it happened there was a tiny
shooting thrill. Camilla's touch was very light, hardly
like touching at all, but even so it imparted real
pleasure. Alexa wondered what she'd be like as a
lover . . .

Capable, most certainly, and clever; full of subtlety
and effortless technique. In a flash of her special new
vision, she saw Camilla crouched elegantly between
Beatrice's long, pale thighs, and then lowering her

75

moist, rosy tongue into the doctor's open cleft. With no doubt in her mind whatsoever, Alexa knew that this had happened fairly recently, and would happen again soon, probably before the day was out. But when the next flash showed Camilla between her own legs, she shivered. It was too much, and she tried to close it out.

'I'm sorry, are my hands cold?' enquired the nurse, her eyes twinkling.

'No . . . No, they're fine.'

'Well, that's all right, then, because I have to listen to your chest now.'

Alexa held herself as still as she could while her lungs were sounded, her back gently tapped, and she was asked to cough; but she couldn't remain still for the thing that happened next.

With no warning, and what looked like a faint grin, Camilla examined her patient's breasts.

It started as the sort of ordinary check-over that Alexa was used to – but then seemed to continue. And continue . . . When the first firm palpation was over, Camilla began a series of more delicate strokes, her fingertips gliding in ever-closing circles until she was caressing – there was no other word for it – the very nipples themselves.

'You're very sensitive, aren't you?' murmured the nurse, flicking a thumb-pad across each swollen crest.

'Y . . . Yes,' gasped Alexa, her body moving and swaying of its own accord, her breathing uneven and shallow.

'That's good,' said Camilla, her thumbs still dancing. 'The doctor will be very pleased with that.'

The examination was becoming increasingly unusual. Camilla's practised hands were moving over other areas now; cruising lightly over the slope of Alexa's taut belly then skipping across the narrow pink divide of her panties to touch the bare skin of her thigh above her stocking. Alexa had a sudden strong sense that the other woman wanted what she wanted, but was prevented by some prior embargo.

Beatrice, you bitch! thought Alexa angrily. She was fully aroused now, fired-up, the area between her legs hot and yearning. And she wanted the hands of this cool white nurse to minister to that yearning. To touch her sex. She no longer cared at all that those hands were female; the first women's hands – bar her own – that would stroke her and bring her to pleasure. She wanted, no profoundly needed, Camilla to touch her clitoris, but understood that Beatrice – for some reason best known to herself – had forbidden it.

As her fingers walked towards Alexa's groin, Camilla seemed suddenly to remember herself, and withdrew her hand rather sharply. Tut-tutting under her breath, she retrieved her clipboard and signed what she'd written with a flourish.

'Let's take you to the doctor now, shall we?' she said briskly, then stood up in one neat, fluid motion. 'Come along,' she chided, as Alexa struggled to get her wits into gear. 'Doctor's busy and we mustn't keep her waiting.'

Alexa felt confused and aggravated. She was blushing as pink as a peony and nearly naked, and between her legs her sex felt uncomfortable – and now she was to be dragged to somewhere else in this goddamned house; all without the offer of a robe!

'Excuse me,' she said, finding her tongue at last, 'but shouldn't I have a gown or something?'

'Oh, you don't need a robe. Don't be silly!' said Camilla in her even, patience-with-the-patient voice. 'Doctor's examination room is only down the corridor, and the house is perfectly warm.'

Again, Alexa demurred. 'I suppose you're right,' she muttered, rising to her feet and following Camilla. The nurse smiled and held open the door, ushering Alexa back out into the corridor, but this time gesturing in the opposite direction to the one from which they'd come.

This place is a maze, thought Alexa, and as she passed close to her white-clad companion, she caught a sudden sharp wave of fragrance. It seemed to cut like a blade through the pervasive background odours of lavender wax, wood and pot-pourri with an edge that was relentlessly green. It was fresh and light, yet strong, too. Stunningly clean. If a perfume could signify personality, then Camilla's could not have been more fitting.

The next room Alexa entered was as much like the nurse as her scent was. White, stark, and shining, it was the total opposite of the cosy, chintzy waiting room, and not at all what Alexa had expected.

Shuddering, she took in a vista of scrubbed surfaces and ultra-pure hygiene. It appeared to be more of an operating theatre than a consulting room, and the couch at its centre was terrifying; fitted as it was with a variety of stainless steel projections, and a set of dangling cuffs that looked horribly like restraints. The couch was currently covered by a spotless white sheet and had a single flat pillow at one end.

An altar. And I'm the sacrificial victim, thought Alexa, as hysteria bubbled around the edge of her mind. They're going to initiate me there on that table, strap me down and . . . and relieve me of a kind of virginity, I suppose.

There was no sign of the High Priestess, however. The room was filled with a variety of disquieting paraphernalia, but there was no sign of Beatrice herself. Is she even here today? Alexa wondered. Or is this delay just another of her ploys?

'Don't be alarmed,' said Camilla kindly as she bustled to and fro, rearranging things that already seemed in apple-pie order. 'There's not long to wait now. Doctor will be with you very soon.'

At a loss, Alexa just stood there, her eyes drawn irresistibly to the couch.

'Yes, that's a good idea. Lie down and relax,' Camilla encouraged, following the look. 'But I don't think we need this, do we?'

As she spoke, she flicked away the covering white sheet and began folding it up like a flag.

Alexa gulped. The couch beneath the sheet wasn't upholstered in the fawn or tan she'd been expecting; the leather that covered it was a livid blood red, almost obscene in such a sanitised setting. It looked like a lush, glossy mouth in a white-skinned face, and made Alexa think instantly of Beatrice. Was the choice of colour intentional?

'Come on, let's have you up then.' Putting aside the sheet, Camilla helped Alexa up on to the sanguineous couch, a process which seemed to require a lot of patting and guiding with the hands. Alexa tensed initially, but after a moment the feeling fled, leaving her pliant and passive beneath the nurse's calm touch.

Camilla's last act was to slide off Alexa's shoes, then, still holding them, she retrieved the folded sheet and made her way quickly to the door.

'Just relax, Alexa,' she said again very softly. 'Only a few minutes now.' And with that she slid soundlessly from the room.

What now? thought Alexa, shifting her back against the opulent red leather. Is the rest of me to be examined? She touched her fingers to the fine pink fabric that covered her pubis, and instantly regretted it. The momentary contact was electric. Through silk, through the glossy mesh of her own hair, she could almost feel the pressure of her fingertip as it bore lightly downwards towards her core. She wanted to press harder, to slide her fingers into her groove and masturbate, but if she did that, she knew Beatrice would appear.

But it would illustrate the problem, she reasoned dreamily, letting her finger rest lightly where it lay. I'm on fire all the time. I want more; more sex than Tom can give me, and more than I can possibly provide for myself. And I can't stop thinking about it because it's all around me all the time – like a radio I can't switch off or tune out.

And the 'broadcast' was all around her in this room, she realised, despite its white utilitarian purity. The couch wasn't just a mouth, it was a woman's vulva:

79

naked, glistening and exposed. Not for the first time, Alexa wondered exactly what Beatrice Quine's speciality was. The leather, the padding beneath her, seemed to resonate with pleasure, as if it had been used, time and time again, to satisfy the doctor's lusty appetites. Alexa imagined Beatrice herself on the couch, her long legs spread wide as Drew did his duty between them. With her eyes half closed, she seemed to see his muscular form moving; thrusting slowly and majestically as his mistress growled profanities in encouragement. For the purposes of fantasy, Camilla was looking on with sharp interest. The nurse was naked, and her beautiful, pertly rounded bottom was perched neatly on a high, chromed stool. As she watched her mistress, her pointed breasts were shaking, and between her legs her slim hand was at work. Bizarrely, she still wore her white cap.

What am I doing? What am I doing? thought Alexa, sitting up and gasping for breath. I can't stop it! Sex, all the time! I can't stop thinking about it, even if I try!

And I shouldn't have come here. This is the last place on earth for me. This is a palace of sex, not a place to forget it. I'm only going to want it more and more.

Confused, and tense in every nerve, Alexa lay down again. She seemed to understand her new self less and less by the minute. Did she want to stop thinking erotic thoughts altogether, or to just be able to manage her new libido as it was? She enjoyed the power, and loved the exhilaration, but the sheer size of her need was alarming. Not to mention inconvenient. She thought bitterly of Camilla's urgings to 'relax'. It was impossible here; even the leather of the couch seemed to stimulate her, absorbing the heat of her body as she lay on it.

Closing her eyes, Alexa listened for sounds in the house around her. Somewhere, at a distance, she fancied she could hear voices, but couldn't be sure whether they were real or imagined. The room she was in had only one window, partly open, and through it drifted a snatch of faint bird-song, and with it the whirr of a sprinkler. If she went to the window now, she could probably look down on the gardens at the back of the house, and perhaps wave to Drew, in the garden, then lean outwards, exposing her breasts . . .

No! No! No! Gouging the leather beneath her, she stirred uneasily, feeling lust coil like a serpent in her belly.

I mustn't! I mustn't! she thought, tossing her head from side to side on the pillow. She could almost hear her own flesh calling out to her, the soft, hot niche of her vulva crying out that her fingers explore it. I mustn't start. I mustn't do it . . . Because if I do, I will be caught for sure.

But what if all this is bona fide? What if I was imagining that Camilla wanted me? Making more of a simple examination than ever really existed?

Bullshit! she told herself, giving in and clasping her fingers to her breasts as a compromise. You know what you know. Since you cracked your head on that rock, you know when someone desires you.

Squeezing her nipples furiously, Alexa panted. Then held her breath as – out in the corridor – there came the sound of nimble, determined footsteps. Her hands flew to her sides just in time, it seemed, because a second later the door swung open, and Beatrice swept into the room, all smiles.

'Alexa! Your hair! It's wonderful!' she cried, crossing the space between them in a few light strides, and, before Alexa could even stir, kissing her firmly on the cheek.

'Let me look at you,' she continued, sliding her arm possessively beneath Alexa's naked back and helping her up into a sitting position. 'It seems an age since Barbados. I've missed you.'

To the bemused Alexa, Barbados was just yesterday. It seemed only hours since she'd been lying on a patio, in the sun, watching this woman being massaged by her lover. By their lover . . .

Beatrice was fully clothed today, but somehow still

managed to look sexual. Her remarkable hair was wound in a twisted crown around her head, and her beautiful body clad in sleek maroon silk – a loose but elegant pyjama suit with wide-legged trousers and an embroidered Nehru top. Over this, negligently it seemed, she wore a white cotton coat as crisp and pristine as Camilla's snowy dress. The nurse herself, Alexa noticed, had also slid discreetly into the room.

'This is so gamine.' Beatrice ruffled Alexa's new curls. 'So distinctive . . . It really suits you.'

'Thanks,' murmured Alexa, thrown off balance.

I'd forgotten about Beatrice, she thought as the doctor's fingertips trailed delicately along her jaw. The woman was overpowering, like a whirlwind, a hot breeze from somewhere wild and exotic. She was also always about six inches closer than a person ought to be, yet the invasion felt provocative and thrilling. Her floral perfume seemed intense enough to touch.

'Well,' said the doctor briskly, stepping back a pace, then reaching out to stroke Alexa's naked hip, 'At the risk of sounding clichéd, what seems to be the trouble?' Her brilliant eyes narrowed appraisingly, 'You certainly look well enough. In fact you're in superb condition.' As if to confirm her diagnosis, Beatrice ran the backs of her fingers right up Alexa's body until she reached her bare breast. With a nod, she flicked lightly at the nipple. 'No, nothing wrong there,' she observed almost reflectively as the rosy little bud visibly stiffened.

How to describe it? Her 'trouble', or whatever it was . . . She couldn't even begin to try when her heart was pounding and her breast was tingling. Alexa was struck quite dumb by the smiling, brown-eyed doctor, and when she opened her mouth, then glanced swiftly towards the silent Camilla, Beatrice gave a soft peal of laughter.

'Oh, you mustn't worry about Sly,' she said confidentially. 'We don't have secrets here, you know.' Her smiled broadened, and she tapped the side of her strong, straight nose. 'It's a confessional. All girls together.'

Who's 'Sly'? wondered Alexa numbly, and her confusion must have shown, because the doctor turned briefly towards her nurse.

'You've met my Camilla already, haven't you?' she enquired archly. 'My nurse. My sly Ms Fox.'

Alexa nodded at the nurse, who smiled a small, indulging smile, then ever so slightly rolled her eyes; as if she found her employer delightful in the main but sometimes just a little bit embarrassing.

'Of course, she's examined you. Silly me,' continued Beatrice blithely. 'Now perhaps I think I should examine you, too, and maybe then we can discover what your problem is?' Her eyes still intently on Alexa, she snapped her fingers, then held out her hand, and into it Camilla – Sly – put the stethoscope.

A number of the procedures the nurse had carried out were now repeated by the doctor. Alexa wondered whether she should point this out, but the march of Beatrice's fingers kept her silent. Like Sly before her, the doctor didn't confine her explorations to purely clinical matters. Every touch seemed to linger a good deal longer than it should have done. Every pressure was a little stronger than it should have been, and not exactly in the place one would have expected.

As she ran through her assessments and her soundings, Beatrice asked a great many superficially very ordinary questions. She enquired about Alexa's appetite, weight, and menstruation in a completely routine way, yet somehow managed to imbue each enquiry with a suggestive new meaning. It was almost a relief, while she was palpating Alexa's quivering breasts, when she suddenly demanded, straight out, 'And how's your sex life?'

'I . . . I . . .' stammered Alexa, embarrassed that the examination of her nipples was making her wriggle and breathe heavily. Beatrice was gentler, and if anything more circumspect than her nurse, but what was happening was still blatantly erotic.

'Ah, so it's that kind of problem,' observed Beatrice archly, letting her pink, pointed tongue dart out for a second and touch the centre of her sculpted lower lip. 'Well, in that case, we'll do a complete examination.'

She's taking advantage of me, thought Alexa dizzily as Sly encouraged her to lie back on the couch. It's almost as if she isn't even a doctor at all, but just a predatory lesbian who's found a clever way to trap her female victims, and get her hands on every inch of their bodies.

The thought was preposterous, and Alexa knew it. There were qualifications on Beatrice's nameplate, citations on her walls; she'd even been treated by her before, in Barbados just after she'd fallen.

My mind's playing tricks again, she thought. It's me that's making this sexual. It's just a perfectly standard physical examination, and I'm turning it into a complex and protracted seduction.

And yet . . .

'Now, let's have these off, shall we?' said Beatrice briskly, touching her fingers to Alexa's filmy panties. 'Sly, if you please?'

All businesslike seriousness now, Beatrice stepped away from the table and began to study the contents of Sly's clipboard. In the meantime, the nurse had moved forward, and, sliding her fingers efficiently beneath the elastic of Alexa's briefs, she began easing them down over her hips.

'Hup,' she encouraged softly, and Alexa lifted her bottom meekly, her face blushing crimson when she caught sight of her panties. The fabric of the crotch was clearly wet.

She nearly sobbed aloud with shame – and astonishment – when Sly held out the offending garment to Beatrice, her fingers spreading the shining stain for inspection.

'Perfectly normal,' commented Beatrice levelly, then

added a note to Sly's hand-written list. Alexa wanted to turn over and hide her burning face in the pillow, but, as she twisted, the nurse gently prevented her, then tidied the curls that clung sweatily to her brow.

'It's nothing to worry about, sweetheart,' she said cheerfully. Then she put her pink lips to Alexa's ear and whispered, 'And I must admit that I'm a little wet myself.'

It's true! Oh God, it's all true! thought a stunned Alexa. They are seducing me! I was right all along.

She began to struggle, but in a flash she was being gently shushed and settled.

'Easy . . . Easy, my dear,' said Beatrice, her voice kind as she returned to the couch. To Alexa's abject horror, she was pulling on a pair of translucently thin rubber gloves. 'Just a simple examination. It won't hurt a bit. In fact, you should find it quite pleasant.' She pushed the menacing latex smoothly down one finger. 'Sly, would you do the honours, please? I need a little more – ' She hesitated again, as if for effect. ' – room to manoeuvre.'

Alexa could hardly breathe, and her belly seemed to beat with something that wasn't quite fear, but was certainly its close relation. She felt like a doe trapped by a pair of scheming huntresses as the nurse positioned her. Sly's hands were cool and dry, and though her fingertips exerted barely any pressure, Alexa couldn't help but obey them, bending her knees and opening her thighs.

'Shall I remove the stockings, Doctor?' Sly enquired, touching the sheer grey nylon that covered Alexa's ankle.

'No, I don't think so.' Beatrice cocked her head appraisingly on one side. 'They're so pretty; I'd rather they stayed on.'

Help me! thought Alexa, feeling arousal pool low in her belly. Both doctor and nurse seemed to be playing their charade unremittingly straight, but the action was becoming more and more surreal.

They were infernal, the pair of them. They were arranging her body exactly how it suited them, with her legs wide apart for their perverse titillation. She was being spread, laid open, every whorl of soft flesh made accessible. The very thought made her sex drip and ripple.

'I think we're ready now,' said Beatrice matter-of-factly, snapping the thin rubber at her wrists. 'Would you pop a little cushion beneath her, Sly?'

Sly, too, wore rubber gloves, and just the sight of them made Alexa's heart race. She felt limp, helpless, utterly without will, and the nurse – showing an extra-ordinary strength for one so slender – eased Alexa's body a little way down the couch, then lifted her hips and placed a cushion beneath her buttocks.

Raised up like this, Alexa discovered that the whole angle of her pelvis had altered. As she'd suspected – and hoped? – the whole length of her womanhood, every delicate, glistening secret, was completely and unremittingly displayed, her smoky stockings making the sight all the lewder.

The waiting was almost unbearable, and Alexa found she couldn't help struggling. She could taste the other women's excitement, and it seemed to blend like an explosive with her own.

'Very quiet now, Alexa,' said Beatrice, her voice low and charged and almost trembling, 'Can you stay still, or shall I have Sly hold you?'

Alexa was aware that she was making sounds, low grunts and groans, but couldn't seem to shape sentences or words. She closed her eyes and felt Sly's rubber-covered fingers grip her shoulders; then she arched, moaning loudly, as another finger – also sheathed in latex – rested lightly on the in-slope of her thigh.

By the time it touched her vulva, she'd come.

Chapter Seven

An Intriguing Prognosis

'Most intriguing,' murmured Beatrice, looking at Alexa over the rim of her glass, 'You're the first patient I've ever had to present symptoms quite like those. I wonder if I ought to write a paper?'

She's not playing any more, thought Alexa, sipping her own wine. She's had what she wanted and now she's reverted to really being a doctor.

The two women were sitting on an overstuffed moquette-covered sofa in yet another room of Beatrice's huge house. Judging by the long-faced clock in the corner of the room, Alexa guessed it was a good two hours since she'd had her examination, but just thirty minutes or so since she'd woken up on the red leather couch.

Looking back over the 'consultation' seemed like remembering a long, blurred dream. She recalled slender, rubber-clad fingers; sliding over her, touching her, travelling teasingly over intimate terrain. She'd been probed, caressed; brought to peak after peak of sensation and her responses always noted and observed. Not once had the pretence of a genuine examination been dropped, but her special sense – when she could think sufficiently clearly to analyse it – had told her the whole thing was a sham. A beautifully rehearsed masquerade. Beatrice Quine had provided her with therapy, but not in the conventional sense. She'd simply ignored Alexa's fears and confusion, and given her exactly what her body had been crying for – pleasure in Dionysian abundance!

She'd begged to be left alone – because she just couldn't take any more – and she'd been kissed, very gently, by both women, then wrapped in a blanket to rest.

Some time later, after Alexa had slept for a while, Sly had returned bringing towels and – finally! – a robe. Still feeling slightly dopey, Alexa had let herself be led to an old-fashioned but well-appointed bathroom, and then enjoyed a warm, scented bath.

As she'd wallowed, she'd allowed herself to speculate. What had been happening while she was dozing? Had her two seducers carried on their game of 'doctor'? Sly had looked as imperturbable as ever when she'd brought the towels, but, even in her relaxed and drowsy state, Alexa had noticed that the third button from the top on the nurse's snowy dress had somehow mysteriously come unfastened. What was more, when she'd finished bathing, and found her way to Beatrice's cosy, over-decorated parlour, Alexa had discovered the physician herself with a creamy, faraway expression on her face – and with her elaborately coiffed hair now unbound. The long, red waves that had been wound around Beatrice's head like a diadem were now loose and tumbling down over her shoulders. The whole mass of hair shimmered like a mat of silken flame, and from time to time the doctor toyed with a strand of it, as she listened intently to what Alexa had to say.

Her predicament seemed more difficult to describe than ever after what had taken place in the consulting room. Editing what she said stringently, she stumbled and dried up several times, and eventually, Beatrice had shaken her head slightly, then risen and crossed to the sideboard, only to return with a decanter of sherry and two glasses on a tray. Alexa had sipped the rich wine and felt its glow warm her belly, and after that it'd been easier to go on.

She brushed – with some care – over her interlude between the cabanas with Drew, yet sensed that Beatrice wasn't fooled. The doctor's luminous brown eyes narrowed shrewdly at the mention of her companion, and a delicate half smile curved its way around her lips.

Alexa found herself trying to play down the degree of her affliction, too. What she'd done so far had felt wonderful at the time, but described now, as cold facts, her actions would sound gross and unthinkable. Seductions. Casual sex with mere boys. Masturbation in public places. Not to mention a score of weird new urges that someone of Beatrice's persuasion would probably interpret as a challenge, if not an out and out come-on.

Shifting slightly on the sofa, and struggling to project a degree of detachment, Alexa folded the borrowed robe around her legs. It was towelling, luxuriously thick-piled and fluffy, and felt sublime against her freshly bathed skin.

'Now, let's review this. Get the big picture clear in our minds.' Beatrice sipped thoughtfully at her sherry, then reached for the cut-glass decanter.

Should she really be drinking? thought Alexa suddenly. After all, this was supposed to be a visit to Beatrice in her professional capacity. It seemed a bit off-the-wall, somehow, that a doctor should be drinking on the job. Not that Beatrice was like any doctor Alexa had ever met before, a fact that had been obvious as far back as Barbados.

'Right. You took a blow to the head at St James's Cove. You lost consciousness momentarily, but all the write-ups and X-rays indicated no concussion and no evidence of physical trauma.' Beatrice paused, and picked up what appeared to be Sly's red clipboard, which now – mysteriously – had a slim wodge of medical documentation attached to it, and looked suspiciously like the notes that had been made at the island's clinic.

How the Devil did she get those? thought Alexa, shaking slightly. I only phoned yesterday. Those forms couldn't even have got here by Express Courier in that time.

'And I examined you myself at the time, too,' the doctor when on, running a long, perfectly manicured fingertip over the data. No scarlet nail varnish today, however. 'You were perfectly fit. A little shaken, but nothing more drastic. Why didn't you tell me about these headaches?'

'They were gone before I had a chance. And then I had other things on my mind,' replied Alexa sheepishly, knowing the crux of the matter was approaching.

'Ah, yes,' said Beatrice roundly. 'You had your libido, and my Drew, to distract you.'

Alexa had just taken a sip of sherry, and she spluttered as it went down the wrong way. In an instant Beatrice was right next to her, slapping her back with just the perfect degree of force, and saying 'there, there', in a soothing, very medical voice. When the minor pandemonium was over, she nodded in the direction of the decanter, and Alexa gratefully accepted another drink.

'I . . .' she began, feeling pinned by Beatrice's brilliant eyes – which were almost the same shade as the sherry.

What can I say? Alexa agonised. I slept with her boyfriend. Several times. And it was my choice all the way along. I could have stopped it at any time, but I didn't.

'You don't think I didn't know?' said Beatrice, her voice strangely kind. 'I sent him, sweetheart. It was obvious you were in need of a man. And there aren't many who are more of man than Drew, be honest.'

'But he's your . . .' Alexa felt even more confused. What was Drew to Beatrice? She still hadn't worked it out. Was he her boyfriend? Toyboy? Lover? Companion? He seemed to be all these and more, yet the relationship had a flavour of compulsion. As if Drew's service wasn't entirely of his own free will.

Beatrice thought for a moment, as if considering Alexa's unheard list. 'My companion?' she enquired finally, with a lift of her perfectly plucked brows. 'Of course he is. But he's a free agent, too. We both are.' She hesitated again, then gave Alexa a slow, narrow grin. 'That's not quite true. I'm a free agent. But Drew? Well, he's a slightly different case. But our sexual relationship isn't mutually exclusive. I don't mind him having other women. Especially ones . . .'

Suddenly, Alexa was watching what seemed to be a impressive show of self-control, one she envied and wished she could emulate. Beatrice's eyes fluttered closed for a millisecond, then she reached for the clipboard again and returned her attention, with obvious difficulty, to the notes.

'Back to business,' the doctor said, with a half sigh. 'I mustn't get ahead of myself, must I?'

Thoroughly unnerved by what she was sensing from Beatrice, Alexa waited for the next round of questions.

'So. It seems you need more sex – or whatever – now than you ever did before? Is that correct?'

Alexa nodded.

'And you . . . how shall we say . . . sense the eroticism in others, too?'

Another nod.

Beatrice picked up a slim black pen, capped in silver, and made a swift note that Alexa couldn't read from where she was sitting.

'And that's a problem?' enquired the physician with an impish grin. 'If the accident had decreased your desire, there'd be cause for concern. But in a healthy young woman like you, a high sex drive is an asset, not a malady. The only thing I can really recommend is that you make the most of it.' She laid aside the clipboard, and reached out to take Alexa's hand in her own warm and very soft one. 'And, as for the increased "aware-

91

ness" . . . What I wouldn't give for such a blessing! Professionally and personally. With a gift like that I could always have the upper hand. Even when I'm playing the submissive.'

Again, the doctor's words were puzzling, but hinted much. Alexa couldn't seem to imagine a time when Beatrice wouldn't be in charge of things, her dominant aura demanded it, yet she'd uttered the word 'submissive' with an edge in her voice. As if it were something that excited her, a thrilling mask that she loved to assume.

'But I – ' Alexa began, about to list her problems with her new state of being. She felt her lips frame words, or try to, but nothing came out. She could only feel the heat of Beatrice's hand where it gently stroked hers.

'Don't worry, my sweet,' said the doctor quietly. 'You'll soon get used to it. I'm sure it must be frightening right now . . .'

'Oh God, yes it is!' gasped Alexa, in the second before she almost fell into Beatrice's arms. Suddenly she was crying, bawling like a baby, but with sweet relief, instead of fear and distress.

She felt Beatrice stroking her back through the robe, and knew it was all right. It felt as if something had tilted inside her mind; like an abstract painting, being turned through forty-five degrees, and suddenly making perfect, representational sense. She was blessed not damned; perhaps all she needed was to keep the right company?

'You're right,' she hiccuped to Beatrice, as the cleansing tears finally dried up. 'I am scared, but I think I'll be OK once I get used to it. I'm just not used to having so much sex!' She grinned and rubbed her eyes, glad that she'd cleaned off her make-up before her bath, and that she hadn't turned herself into a panda-eyed, streak-faced freak. 'I feel so ignorant. I don't know much. I keep having urges I don't understand. Yet . . .'

'It'll come,' said Beatrice, her wicked smile just inches

from Alexa's damp face, 'before you realise it. You just need a bit of guidance, that's all.'

Snuggled against Beatrice's lovely breasts, Alexa knew exactly where that guidance would come from – but just as that thought began, another one dashed the hope completely. She pulled away, pushing off her comforter's white hands.

'Oh God, I'm sorry. Y . . . You're my doctor, now, I suppose,' she stuttered, the truth like ashes. 'What am I thinking of? My appointment must have ended ages ago.' A new horror occurred. 'You don't charge by the hour, do you?'

'I could do,' said Beatrice, leaning back into the seat, and eyeing Alexa from beneath long, masking lashes. 'It depends . . .'

Alexa felt like a small, furry animal trapped in the gaze of a hunter. A huntress . . . She was being played with, toyed with, just as surely as she had been in the consulting room. Beatrice Quine was an unashamed predator, a connoisseuse of bodies and pleasure, and she'd just bagged her quarry with total ease.

The robe was warm, but Alexa shivered. The only way out of this was to bluff, to try – belatedly – to play things straight and cool. She could pay Beatrice's fee, mutter some excuse about seeing everything more clearly now, and walk out, free and unobligated.

Her feet both metaphorically and physically cold, she attempted nonchalance. 'Just what are your fees, by the way? I forgot to ask.'

Beatrice reached for her sherry, took a minute sip, then named a sum that was truly unthinkable – especially to those in debt already.

Alexa could feel herself blanching, and with a shaking hand, she took her glass, refilled, from Beatrice.

'Can't you afford me?' the doctor teased, and Alexa experienced another momentary flashback to Barbados. Hadn't she been confiding in this woman even then? She remembered one balmy night, with the rum punch flowing freely, when she'd gigglingly disclosed all her wild ways with money.

'I think I can find the cash from somewhere,' she now said quickly, wondering how much more spending she could bury in the accounts program.

'But life would be a lot easier if you didn't have to,' observed Beatrice drily.

'Yes.'

It was no use trying to hide things. Whether it was financial fibs, or sexual indiscretions, Beatrice Quine seemed to see through them all. Aren't I supposed to be the one with 'powers', thought Alexa suddenly, looking up into the other woman's seemingly all-seeing eyes. And knowing that Beatrice knew everything . . .

'Actually, there are some things you could do for me.' Beatrice's tone was deceptively light.

Here it comes, thought Alexa, her mouth dry despite the sherry. The sting. The main event. The real reason I got my appointment.

The worst, and the best, of it was that there was no doubt. No wondering. No 'does she/doesn't she?' No question about what Beatrice was after. With her senses so receptive, Alexa felt as if every hailing frequency was wide, wide open; and the message was 'Alexa, I want you.'

But what about my signals? thought Alexa, feeling hot when a second ago she'd been cold. What do I want? Without conscious effort, she remembered the feel of Beatrice's touch. Long, tapered fingertips gliding across her skin, dipping into her sex. It'd been beautiful. Amazing. As good as anything a man had ever done.

And it wasn't as if the feelings weren't reciprocal. Alexa cast her thoughts back to Barbados, and saw everything with a new illumination. Beatrice was delectable, and her body near-perfect. Alexa thought of the other woman's nakedness and admitted she'd desired it. At the time, in her naiveté, she'd misinterpreted what she'd felt. She'd thought the responses – the stirrings and the wetness – had been solely for Drew.

'It's all right. I didn't mean right now,' said Beatrice, amused.

Alexa took another gulp of sherry, realising she'd automatically been pulling at the sash of her robe; making ready to give her body all over again . . .

'And it isn't quite what you're thinking.' The doctor's eyebrows again. 'Well, it is what you're thinking, because if you really can sense my sexuality, you know that already. But there's something else that I'd like from you, too. A way you can help me work something out.' She shrugged, and her rounded breasts shook sensuously beneath the satin of her top. 'You're not the only one who's beholden to someone, Alexa. I too have certain . . . obligations.' She shrugged again, then licked her red lips.

Curiosity had always got Alexa into trouble, and it rose up now, like a hound sniffing the air.

What's this? she thought, feeling an intense sexual frisson: a cocktail of fear, excitement and a yearning that was both irresistible and dark.

It's a man. Someone in Beatrice's life. He's important, and she's scared of him. But it's more than that. Alexa looked at the doctor, and for a moment, saw her shield come down. Beatrice seemed locked in some kind of delicious, erotic weakness. A state that thrilled her. It was a condition of control totally lost, and it aroused Alexa as much as it did Beatrice.

'Who is it?' she asked impulsively, knowing that to get involved was probably lunacy, but still craving it already, with all her heart.

'A man, of course,' said Beatrice, her vibrant eyes meeting Alexa's square-on. 'Someone exciting, but impossible to handle. He's beautiful, but he demands . . . everything. He's helped me, and now he wants total service in return.'

'Service?'

'Well, maybe that's not the right word,' mused Beatrice, lifting a frond of her hair and twirling it between her fingers. It was the first time Alexa had seen her nervous. 'It's more . . . "amusement". Stimulation. His tastes are discriminating. Specialised. I could offer myself – ' She paused delicately, and her lashes flicked downward while her body visibly shuddered. 'But he's already got me. He wants more.'

Good God, she's a procuress! A female pimp! thought Alexa, horrified by the way her sex quickened at the idea. There was an immensely powerful man in Beatrice Quine's life, and the doctor was trying to please him, find him new playmates and new bodies to enjoy. What was required were young women like herself. Green, relatively innocent, but sensualised. She should have protested immediately, voiced revulsion in no uncertain terms, but her body was crying out just the opposite. She was on fire with a raging 'need to know'.

'And do you think he'd like me?' she said quietly, squeezing her thighs together and feeling herself flow.

'He'll love you,' said. Beatrice fiercely. 'Who wouldn't?' she added, her lips parted, moist and betraying. 'But at the moment he's too rich for your blood, sweetheart.' Her long, white hand snaked out, relieved Alexa of her forgotten sherry, then clasped her fingers in a passionate grip. 'You've a lot to learn, Alexa, such a lot. You're a sensualist, that's obvious. Your responses are amazing.' It was her first overt reference to the stimulation she'd given in the consulting room, and she had the grace to blush very slightly. 'But you need educating. Opening up. Sex is so much more than simply fucking your boyfriend on a regular basis. Or fucking mine for that matter.' She laughed richly. 'Sex is a state of mind. A way of life. So much more than just penis and vagina. Cock and quim. Prick and cunt. It's beyond gender, even. Do you understand what I mean?'

Alexa was shocked by the raw language, but she did understand. Even as she'd listened it had all seemed so clear. A month ago, she would have thought Beatrice's pronouncements gratuitously obscene – but now she could feel wisdom at work.

There was a new world – worlds! – of sex waiting for her, but her voyage of discovery was already well under way. She'd begun the second stage on the doorstep of this house . . .

As the heavy front door snicked shut, Beatrice whirled and leaned happily against it.

'Yes!' she cried, thinking triumphantly of the girl who'd just left.

Alexa Lavelle, eh? Beautiful, beautiful Alexa. Her raven-haired nymph from Barbados; oh God, how she'd longed to see that sweet bod once again!

Oh Bea, you're such a bad thing, so greedy, she admonished herself, pressing the flat of her hand against the silk across her crotch. She's so innocent. She knows nothing. How luscious it will be to corrupt her.

Squeezing her pubis briefly, then abandoning it, Beatrice straightened up and moved forward from the door. 'Corrupt' wasn't precisely the word for what she meant, she knew that, but 'educate' sounded so dry, so formal, so inapplicable to the juice-filled Alexa.

As she bounded down the stairs to the basement, Beatrice was intensely aware of her own body. She was aroused again just thinking about her delightful new friend. The sight of Alexa, bare and defenceless on the examining table, had affected her far more than she'd expected. Far more than it was wise to reveal. It was the girl's freshness that undid one so, Beatrice supposed, that fact that she was gorgeous but untried, and quite unaware of her own huge potential. To not take advantage of her had been impossible; a pussy as lovely and as running wet as Alexa's had simple screamed out for a hand to caress it.

'And she knows about you, Quine, you do realise that, don't you?' she muttered to herself, thinking of Alexa's weird and miraculous gift. Had it been a shock when she'd discovered how much she was desired? By another woman. 'She knows you're a disgracefully lecherous old pervert. It's such a relief that you don't have to tell her!'

That's the best of it, really, thought Beatrice as she let herself silently into Drew's part of the premises. Alexa knew the score already, or at least some of it, and she'd seemed to be intrigued, not repulsed. Beatrice couldn't wait to tell Drew.

The door to the treatment room – where her associate performed his magically relaxing massages – was ever so slightly ajar, and Beatrice paused outside it. She could hear noises of movement from the area beyond, but not – to her joy – the sound of voices. Drew must have seen his last client for the day, and be alone now, tidying his equipment.

Why do I need to do this? thought Beatrice as she pushed the door with her toe. I've had my fun, with Sly, and lots of it; it's pure greed to want more. Especially when he's probably still sweet on Alexa.

'Come in, Bea,' said Drew even before the door was fully open. 'I was wondering when you'd show your face.'

Her companion was folding some towels when she entered, and he looked up, his expressive brows raised.

'How so?' queried Beatrice, sidling forward.

Drew looked vaguely cross about something, and flattened his pile of towels with an unexpectedly vehement slap.

Oh Drew, you're so beautiful when you're angry, thought Beatrice inconsequentially, crossing the room to inspect his collection of massage oils. She was fully acquainted with the blends that he used – in fact she often prescribed aromatherapy herself – but she gave him the impression that she was concentrating intently on his bottles and his potions.

'I saw Alexa Lavelle coming up the path about three hours ago, and I notice she's only just left,' said Drew after a moment. It was obvious he hadn't been duped.

'Did you speak to her?' enquired Beatrice, feeling a dart of jealousy. It wasn't fair, Drew had had Alexa to himself on holiday, while she herself had only got as far as a little fondling in the guise of a physical examination.

'No. I didn't let her see me.' Drew's beautiful grey eyes went narrow. 'She had such a befuddled expression on her face as she left, that I thought she probably had quite enough on her plate already. She was unfaithful to her fiancé with me, in Barbados, if you remember? I didn't want to compound her guilt.' He frowned. 'It's a pity *you* don't have the same qualms, Bea.'

'*Moi?*' Beatrice feigned outrage, loving his righteous indignation. 'What on earth could I do to make her feel guilty?'

Drew's handsome mouth thinned. 'You wanted her in Barbados, but I had to stop you from rushing things. I assume you've done the deed now?'

'And what deed would that be?' asked Beatrice, sidling up behind him. She could smell the strong sweat of his recent exertions, and see it black on black in the cotton of his vest. There was a stain lower down, too, in the crease of his buttocks, where his marl track-pants embraced his firm rump. Almost delirious, Beatrice imagined easing down the soft, grey fabric and licking away that sweat, using her tongue on his bottom and anus. He loved that, she knew full well, and it would be a way of defusing his irritation. Her fingers were just flexing, anticipating the action, when he whirled around, his eyes darkly flashing behind his glasses.

'Don't pussyfoot around with me, Bea,' he said, whipping out a hand and grabbing her wrist. 'By "deed", I mean seduction. Have you had her yet? Stripped her? Had your sticky little hands between her legs . . .?'

'There's no need to be so coarse,' Beatrice murmured primly, feeling his anger stir the devil in her groin. 'I've examined her, naturally, but in case you've forgotten . . . I *am* a doctor!'

Drew ignored this. 'You can't just keep using people,

Bea. We're not your toys. I owe you, but Alexa Lavelle doesn't. You can't manipulate her life just for your own amusement.'

He was pulling her closer as he spoke, and their eyes were within inches of each other. She could see he was furious, she could see he almost hated her, but his pupils were enormous, like black coins behind his glasses, and below, his erection brushed her thigh.

'I don't mean her any harm,' she whispered, almost choking with desire.

'I know that,' he murmured, less hotly, 'But you are going to change her life, aren't you?'

'It's changed already,' answered Beatrice, knowing now was not the time to explain Alexa Lavelle's special powers. Drew was all hers now, and discussing Alexa too much would distract him.

'You're the Devil, you know that, don't you?' accused Drew, as their bodies slid close, then moulded, like mercury, to each other. Beatrice could feel his sweat soaking through the rich satin of her tunic and trousers, probably ruining it, but with a moan in her throat, she pushed closer, seeking out his hard mouth with her own. 'You're indecent. You're a user.' he continued, smearing the words against her face as he kissed her and ground his cock against her mons.

Beatrice felt her belly seem to melt, and her sex ooze lasciviously in her thin silk panties. Drew was mauling her neck with his lips and his teeth, and, for a moment, she turned her face aside, grinning and thinking – distractedly – of something Alexa had described to her. Something that her own ruined knickers had reminded her of.

How strange that Alexa should find Circe by herself. It was almost as if some arcane, sensual force had controlled her. Sweeping her pelvis in a circle against Drew's bulging crotch, Beatrice thought of her new friend's halting description of what had happened amongst the lingerie. Of her uncannily clear description of the punkish assistant. Of the remembered response

100

she'd tried so hard to hide, but which had been so sublimely transparent.

If only you knew, Alexa Lavelle, Beatrice thought exultantly. If only you knew what lies just ahead of you. And not only 'what', but 'who' . . .

'You shouldn't be allowed to get away with this!' hissed Drew as Beatrice reached down to touch his cock. Dashing her hand away, he then grabbed it, and hooked the other hand in the same grip. With both her wrists pinioned in one large hand, he used the other to reach for her trousers.

In one swift, economical movement, he wrenched the loose silk pants down as far as her knees, then followed them with the knickers beneath.

'Oh no you don't!' he snarled as Beatrice tried to rub the curls of her pubis against him. 'Not this time!'

Beatrice felt very close to fainting, blown away by an ecstasy of desire. Drew was so strong. So focused, yet so animal at times like these. And it brought out the weakness in her. She loved his anger; she loved his tightly leashed power. She loved the way that he sometimes expressed it, letting rip when she pushed him too far.

'Oh, Drew, please,' she moaned, begging for something she was sure she'd soon get. As she swayed, still trying to rub him with her body, she felt his free hand rummage roughly at her sex.

'You whore,' he said softly, the word affectionate. 'You sleazy little bitch,' he purred, stirring negligently at her juiciness and making her whimper as he pulled away his fingers. 'You're not getting what you want. Not this time . . . Or at least, not yet.'

'No,' she gasped, meaning 'yes', as he dragged her across the room with him. With her trousers and her underwear hobbling her, she could only shuffle and gracelessly hop, but somehow even that turned her on. The ignominy. The humiliation. The awareness of her fluids already seeping heavily down her thighs.

It took Drew just a second or two to locate what he

101

wanted – a Victorian chair that stood in the corner, with a tall back and a leather-covered seat. Grasping it in one hand, and still holding Beatrice with the other, he dragged them both to centre of the room, and set the chair down a few feet from his massage table.

'You can't keep doing it, Beatrice,' he half gasped as he sat down. 'You can't keep manipulating people,' he said, his voice cracking again – with excitement – as he pulled her face down across the spread of his knees.

In an agony of anticipation, Beatrice moved restlessly on his lap, testing the force of the hand that still held her, clasping her own hands at the small of her back. She could almost see her own bare white bottom, its pallor an irresistible lure that always worked like a spell on her captor. Beneath her belly, his erection poked her rudely, and, above, she could almost feel the condemnation in his eyes.

'You're despicable, Bea,' he said softly, leaning over her, his mouth near her ear and the trailing mass of her hair. 'You're unprincipled, immoral, and I ought to hate you. Utterly.' His strong hand squeezed her wrists almost painfully. 'And the worst of it is, even if I could pay you back what I owed, I still wouldn't be free, would I?'

Beatrice kept still, her half-naked body his answer, her head light with power and affection. She felt fingers settle delicately on her bottom, exploring her cheeks, her furrow, her dark anal niche. Any second now he was going to spank her and hurt her, but right now it was only pleasure he gave. She felt her juice trickle down on to his thigh.

'Do it then,' she said through gritted teeth, her desire so intense it was killing. 'I deserve it. I admit it. But I don't care . . .'

'You should!' he cried as the first smack landed, and Beatrice's bottom seemed to explode in soft pain.

The glow of the impact dissipated almost instantly, then reformed in the cleft of her sex. She could feel her whole quim pulsing, almost gasping, and imagined what it would look like to Drew. Pink, intimate flesh in reflex motion, the shimmer of wetness and lust. The image dissolved as he hit her again.

'Oh no! No-o-o-o!' she crooned as the blows pelted down, and the skin of her behind seemed to sizzle. His hand was so big, and so merciless; honed for pleasure, yet proficient with pain. Heat streamed from her mal-treated buttocks and sank into her vagina and the bud of her clitoris. He wasn't touching her sex – not at all – but his angry spirit was reaching out to inflame it. As a much harder slap fell, she convulsed into an orgasm so rich and intense it was blinding. Thrashing on his lap, she seemed to hover up in a ball of golden lightness that was circled all about with red, her floating hair and the sweet fires of pain.

'Yes!' she shrieked, changing her tune and offering her haunches up for more.

'You devil!' he growled, returning to his first insult as his hand crashed down and down and down. 'How the hell can I hurt you when you love it! You bitch! You bitch! I hate you! You always have to win!'

If Beatrice hadn't been hurting so much, she would have laughed herself giddy in triumph. Drew's voice sounded so tortured, so desperate, and the beauty of it was that he was right. The pain in her bottom was turning her on and on, piling pleasure on top of pleasure on top of pleasure. She felt transfigured, exalted, adrift on a stinging wave of bliss. With a loud groan she pushed her bottom upwards, in a frenzy to receive the next blow.

But instead of striking, Drew's hand came down almost claw-like and grabbed at her glowing left cheek.

Beatrice howled as he squeezed and manhandled her, then came again as his fingertips dug and gouged. Still coming, her vulva still fluttering, she slid half off his lap, then tippled over and slid to the floor. With one hand crushed against the folds of her sex, she scrabbled at his track-pants with the other, tugging the grey cloth clear of his crotch with a strength borne of blind desperation.

As she knelt up, then dived for his genitals, she felt him lift his bottom and help her set him free. He was completely nude beneath his fleece-lined pants and in a flash she had his stiff cock in her mouth.

Beatrice sighed at the sight of Drew's sturdy member. He tasted salt and fine and quintessentially male, and when she flicked the tip of her tongue across his swollen, weeping glans, he cried out, and thrust strongly with his hips.

'Beatrice! Oh Beatrice!' he gasped, unable to keep still as she plagued him with her repertoire of tricks. Reaching inwards, between his thighs, she played delicately with his balls in their velvet soft pouch, then passed a single finger across his perineum, scratching the skin there with the tip of her nail. When she felt him edge forward, parting his legs to give her access, she sucked hard, pushed her tongue at his love-eye, then slid a finger over the crinkle of his anus and circled it tantalisingly around the tiny hole.

'Yes! Oh God! Yes, Yes!'

Even with her mouth full, Beatrice smiled.

How easily a man can be conquered, she thought indulgently. Drew had smacked her bottom, and she could still feel the pain of it, but he was the helpless one now. The one losing control as he climaxed. His hands – deep in the crimson of her hair – were spasming and grabbing, and his cock was trying to dive down her throat.

Oh my darling, darling boy, thought Beatrice with great fondness as she swallowed and enjoyed his pungent taste.

Don't you know you'll never get the better of me? she teased wordlessly, then let his softening flesh slide out between her lips.

You were right, my sweet, I will always win, she told him silently as her cheek brushed his thigh. You'll never break free because you wouldn't want to if you could!

Chapter Eight

Let's Get Loose

*A*lexa studied the small black plastic card, and wondered what the devil she was doing.

'Lucretia Quine', it said in silver letters, with the words Photography, Film and Video beneath, followed by a W10 address, with phone, fax and e-mail numbers.

Beatrice's cousin, thought Alexa, tracing the incised lettering with her finger. But why am I going to see her? I can't remember. What on earth have I got myself into?

'I'll introduce you to a few people,' Beatrice had said. 'People who can help. I can't do it all myself for you, sweetheart, and somehow I don't think you're quite ready for me yet.'

What help? All what? Alexa was scared to find out, but couldn't wait to begin. She only wished it didn't disrupt her work so.

Yesterday had been lost, and today hadn't even begun. On the phone, she'd glibly assured Tom all was well; then, in almost the next breath, she'd been calling Quentin to tell him she'd be late. If Tom checked back with the office and actually spoke to Quent, there'd be trouble of course, but somehow, no matter how much she tried, Alexa couldn't make herself care.

Standing where the taxi dropped her, she reflected that this wasn't her best day, really, to be visiting a photographer. Last night, she'd hardly got to sleep at all, her mind full of first Circe, then Sly and Beatrice and that blood-red couch. In the mirror her face had looked peaky beneath her tan, and there were a matched pair of dark shadows beneath her eyes. And no wonder . . . At some time in the small hours, she'd succumbed, with resignation, to the lure of her own fingers and slicked her tired flesh into a long string of orgasms. Only then had she slept, her doze light and fitful, before morning had arrived far too soon. And she could remember a dream about red leather . . .

It hadn't been an ordinary examination, no way! With hindsight that was easy to see. She'd just lain there, like a ninny, and let a pair of blatant lesbians make free with her. And the worst of it was, she adored it.

And this Lucretia? she thought, fingering the ridiculously pretentious business card. I suppose she's a lesbian, too. Or a bisexual at least. There was no doubt that Beatrice was into men at least as much as she was women, and Alexa sensed that exquisitely clinical Sly swung both ways, too. So the odds were that this Quine cousin also took her pleasure with both sexes.

'What is it with this family anyway?' muttered Alexa as she reached towards the button on the entry-phone. The names, for Christ's sake! 'Beatrice' was unusual enough, but, as she'd made her way to the sitting room, Alexa had taken a glance at one of the good doctor's diplomas – trying to decide whether it was pukka or not – and had discovered that the 'A' in the middle was 'Astarte'.

Good grief, it was like waking up in a Gothic fairy-tale! And as for 'Lucretia'? That was worse! Alexa had always considered her own first name a bit fanciful, but it seemed perfectly plain and unremarkable when compared to the extravagantly named Quines.

The entry-phone buzzed in another part of the tall,

grey-fronted building, and a second later a voice said, 'Yo?'

'I . . . um . . . Are you Lucretia Quine,' stammered Alexa, taken aback. The single syllable had sounded strangely familiar, as if she'd heard that husky voice somewhere before. Very recently.

'The same. And you?'

Again the familiarity.

Her voice is like Beatrice's, you twit, Alexa told herself. That's it. That's where you've heard it. And yet the explanation didn't fit somehow. There was another element in there, something she'd heard in the last day or so.

'My name's Alexa Lavelle. Your cousin, Beatrice, sent me. She said I'd be expected.'

'It's news to me,' said the distant Lucretia crisply. 'But never mind, come on up! She probably just forgot to ring. She's like that.'

The door clicked, then swung open as a spring-loaded catch was released.

Come up, the woman had said, but it took Alexa longer than she'd expected to reach the stairs. The hall where she found herself was painted stark white, with plain boards beneath her feet. The walls were covered with amazing images; huge A1-sized monochrome prints that Alexa suspected would never see commercial publication, their content being quite graphically obscene.

The first showed a black man's crotch rising from the waves of some foamy sea, his erection as stiff and gleaming as if carved from a block of solid ebony. Every fine detail of his genital anatomy was high-lighted by a white and relentless illumination: his glans, the tiny eye, the thick bulging veins that wound their way towards the mat of black hair at his groin. There was no face to be seen, and very little body, apart from the hips. Alexa wondered if the poor man had been drowning, or maybe he'd been too aroused to care?

The black penis was probably the tamest of the

107

pictures. The next showed a pale, thin young man – if that was what he was? – who seemed to have not only a prick and testicles, but also a substantial pair of breasts. His face was painted quite perfectly, and around his substantial male waist was laced an elaborate corset made from pierced and sequinned white brocade.

Alexa didn't look at any more pictures; not because she'd didn't find them thrilling, but because if she lingered any longer, Lucretia Quine might think she'd got lost.

At the top of the stairs was a panelled, black-painted door, with a brass knocker in the shape of a skull. Nice, thought Alexa, reaching out – with some reluctance – to touch it.

She was saved from her squeamishness, however, when the door swung spontaneously open, with the same smoothness as the one on the ground floor.

The figure in the opening was one that Alexa immediately recognised; the punk assistant who'd served her in Circe.

'You!' they both said, in unison. Then Alexa giggled, and Lucretia grinned wryly.

'Small world,' she said, then stepped back to let Alexa into her apartment beyond. 'I thought I recognised the name just now. I remember checking it on your card yesterday.'

'Yes . . . I . . . I'd forgotten about that,' replied Alexa, not really knowing where to look first: at the long, unrelentingly white room before her, or the woman who obviously both worked and lived in it.

Lucretia Quine wore no vinyl today, but her black denim jeans were so tight they appeared to be bonded to her. Her loose cotton top – white, and decorated with black skulls and crossbones – was so thin, and so gaping in the armholes, that, as she turned and led the way, she gave Alexa a perfectly clear view of one breast. With a nipple that was as hard as a peach pit . . .

Against her will, Alexa felt a flare of excitement; the same sudden, almost horrifying tug that she'd felt seeing Beatrice only yesterday. Breathing deeply, determined not to be a helpless victim this time, she offered her hand when Lucretia turned around.

'We haven't been formally introduced,' she said, aware of how stilted and unnatural she sounded. 'My name's Alexa, and I . . . er . . . met your cousin in Barbados. She's . . . She's . . .' What could she say? What was it that Beatrice was doing?

'Yes, she is, isn't she?' replied Lucretia, quirking her finely pencilled brows ironically, as if she knew exactly what Beatrice was up to, and was used to nervous young women arriving on her doorstep like this. 'I'm Lucretia Quine, but people usually call me Loosie.' She paused, waggled her eyebrows again. 'That's with a double "o" and an "s", for obvious reasons.'

The reasons weren't obvious to Alexa, but she had a feeling she might discern them soon.

'Oh. Right.'

'Drink?' enquired Loosie Quine, as if Alexa were a regular visitor with business that was clearly defined.

'Yes, please!'

It was early, but a drink sounded wonderful. It might loosen me up, thought Alexa, then grimaced at the unforced little pun. Already standing at a drinks cabinet that seemed to be made from a packing case, her companion grinned back, as if she'd interpreted the smile as for her.

'Gordon's OK?' she enquired, lifting the eponymous dark-green bottle.

Not a gin drinker, Alexa still said 'Yes,' then felt cross that she hadn't asked for something different. She'd only been here a couple of minutes at most, and already she was losing the initiative, and letting this strange woman take the upper hand.

'Try it with this,' said Loosie, gesturing with another bottle, a tall, narrow one filled with yellow liquid. There was something floating inside it that looked suspiciously like weeds of some kind. 'It's a herbal distillation. Something of Beatrice's actually. You'll be surprised how pleasant it tastes.'

'Er, yes. Great,' replied Alexa doubtfully, as Loosie slooshed in a generous shot of gin and another of the dubious golden potion. 'I'm game for anything.'

'Hope so,' said Loosie lightly as she brought their two drinks across the room and nodded to a squashy leather sofa with cushions the colour of peppermints.

'So,' she continued as they both sat down, and Alexa took her discoloured gin, 'what brings you to me, Alexa Lavelle? What does Bea think I can do for you?'

Alexa sipped her drink, then coughed. The taste of the spirit was fierce, but after a second or so, the accompaniment filtered through, too. The herbal concoction made the gin taste quite pleasant, imparting a flowery, almost perfumed tang that had a sweetness that wasn't sugary or sickly. Encouraged, Alexa took another small sip, then a bigger one. She needed something to help her frame an answer.

In the strange, extended seconds it took to find words that were suitable, Alexa observed that Loosie Quine was as beautiful in her own way as her cousin. The photographer was younger, possibly by as much as a decade, yet, in a certain superficial way, she also seemed older. She was hard and very cool-looking, as sleek and impenetrable as lacquer. Her hair was short and gelled, and her eyes were ringed with sooty blackness. Her jeans and her calf-boots were uncompromisingly mannish, and it was only her painted lips, and her breasts, so delicate and round and almost visible, that clearly conceded her gender.

A butch dyke, thought Alexa solemnly, preparing to speak. It was coming through loud and clear now; Loosie was both lesbian, and strongly dominant. In every sense, she wore the trousers.

Drinking again from her gin, Alexa suddenly felt calmer. She knew where she stood now; she had an advantage. Her secret antennae had decoded the signals, and the alcohol was dealing with her shyness.

'I don't know,' she said finally. 'I've really no idea why I'm here. I don't know why I told Beatrice that I'd come, because I'd no intention, at the time, of doing what she said.'

It was the truth, and her companion seemed quite untroubled by the statement. Loosie swirled her drink in her glass, then lifted it to her lips and drained it in one swallow.

'Another?' she queried.

Alexa nodded, thinking of the effects on a breakfast-less stomach, but – as she already felt them – liking them too much to really worry.

Loosie returned with two more, slightly fuller meas-ures. 'Well, Alexa,' she said. 'I don't know why you're here either, but it's just the sort of thing Bea would do.' She drank more gin, then licked a droplet from her darkly painted lips. 'I suppose you realise that she plays with people?' Alexa nodded. It was true, she was a pawn already, that was obvious. 'She likes to ever so gently tip people off-balance . . . and when they're teetering, she just reels them in like trout.' Loosie studied her glass as if it were the contents of her cousin's devious mind. 'The trouble is, I don't know quite who she's trying to unsettle here. You or me?'

For several moments, the photographer continued to stare into her glass, and though Alexa was gradually feeling more mellow, she felt obliged to relaunch the conversation.

'What were you doing in Circe?' she asked. 'Obviously you're a successful photographer. Why do you have to work in a shop?'

Loosie laughed. 'I'm nowhere near as successful as I'd like,' she said amiably. 'Too much of a specialist, I suppose.' She shrugged, making her breasts float beneath the cloth of her top. 'I know the owner of Circe, so I help out there for a bit of extra cash.' She looked up and pinned Alexa with her piercingly dark eyes, which were as grey and shiny as gun-metal. 'And I meet interesting people there. People who'll be photographed. Exhibitionists. I suppose you noticed it's that kind of shop.'

'And how,' murmured Alexa with feeling, thinking of Mr Handsome and Cleo in the cubicle. He'd been buggering her, she knew that now. Right there, behind a single curtain, taking his wife both illegally and with force. Alexa took a big mouthful of gin as her own deepest urges overwhelmed her. She wished it had been her in the next cubicle, being abused by some ravishingly and mysterious stranger.

When she surfaced from her fantasy, Loosie was regarding her intently, her bright, steely eyes slightly narrowed. Without thinking, Alexa let her own eyes slide down the other woman's body to where her nipples were standing out against her top.

'Have you ever been photographed, Alexa?' she said, cocking her head on one side, as if she were blocking out a shot. 'I need a model. Today. I was going to phone someone, but you'd be much better. If you fancy trying something different, that is?'

The question dangled suggestively; for a moment Alexa felt as if she'd lost the thread of the conversation somehow, or let it get washed out of her grasp by the drink.

Whatever it was that Beatrice had sent her here for, she didn't think it was photographic modelling.

Or was it? Beatrice had talked enthusiastically of Alexa 'expanding her horizons', and 'loosening up'. Remembering this last expression, Alexa giggled, realising how Beatrice had prefigured her own pun.

'So?' prompted Loosie, her tongue flicking out between her teeth for a second, like a killer lizard sizing up its prey.

'Why not?' cried Alexa, feeling reckless. At least she had something to 'do' now. Her purposeless visit had a purpose.

'Excellent!' Loosie sprang lithely to her feet, her small breasts jostling as she did so. 'I think you'll need a bit of face make-up. You look a wee tad pinched about the eyes . . . But if your body's this colour all over – ' She dipped forward and touched Alexa's knee, 'I think the rest of you will do fine as it is.'

Shakily, Alexa stood up, too. She'd not expected the first touch to feel so good.

I am 'bi' then, she thought as Loosie led her to one side of the long, open-plan room, where there was an antique lacquered screen and a mirror. I like it when women touch me. I liked it yesterday, with Beatrice and Sly. And I like it today, with Loosie; even if it's only my knee.

But she wanted more.

Even as the photographer's fingers rested lightly on her back, through the cotton of her jacket and blouse, the skin beneath registered a caress. Alexa felt her mind begin to float, buoyed up by gin and herbs, and she looked down on two women who were opposites. Herself, in her trim suit, with her curls and high heels, looking completely feminine; and Loosie, all toughness, attitude and angles. They couldn't have been more dissimilar if they'd consciously tried, and yet, for her part, she felt the attraction like a magnet. Her 'aware-ness' told her Loosie felt it, too.

'You can undress here,' Loosie said, matter-of-fact-ness belying the vibes. 'I've some costumes . . . You get started, and I'll bring them.'

Standing alone behind the screen, Alexa realised she was still clutching her drink. Shrugging her shoulders, she tossed it quickly down her throat, and pulled a face at its strong, silvery kick.

I'm always undressing for the Quines, she thought, suppressing a titter as she started on her jacket. It's getting to be a habit. I'm addicted. And it seemed easier than it had done yesterday; in barely thirty seconds she was down to her undies, still white cotton but with a delicate trim of lace.

'Very nice,' said Loosie, popping her head over the top of the screen and wolf-whistling.

Alexa let out a squeak of surprise. She'd never heard the woman approach.

'But try this – ' Loosie tossed a garment over, 'and some more of this – ' She lifted up the bottle of gin.

Alexa held out her glass.

'Come on. Chop chop. I'm almost ready out here,' the photographer said briskly, then turned and walked away, her bottom moving trimly beneath her jeans.

'This' – the confection Loosie had left for her – made Alexa drink her gin rather quickly. It was a corset of some kind, possibly from Circe, but it seemed to be only part of an outfit. Made of silk-lined crimson velvet, it looked like the bustier component of some sumptuous Renaissance court gown; but there was no skirt or underdress to go with it. If she put it on, her breasts and midriff would be covered, just, but her belly and her pubis would be naked.

Very, very dubiously, Alexa removed her bra, her suspender belt and her stockings, then studied the logistics of the corset. Over the head, or step in? Either way she'd have to loosen off the laces – which fortunately were situated at the front – and either way it was going to be a squeeze. Breathing in, she lifted the thing above her, then slid it on over her head and down her body.

The satin lining felt exquisitely sensuous, like a giant, soft-skinned hand caressing her. Alexa sighed aloud, then bit her lip, wondering what on earth Loosie would think she was doing.

She probably wants me to be touching myself, she thought, fitting the basque to the shape of her torso. She's probably imagining me masturbating right now. Bringing myself off as I try on her kinky basque.

Oh dear Lord, I'm drunk, Alexa observed blearily. Two – or was it three? – gins in quick succession. A recipe for disaster – and moral downfall.

But was it just alcohol that was intoxicating her? There was a delicate, dreamlike clarity to her feelings. She was totally in touch, still in control, miraculously;

still herself in a way she never ever was when she was tipsy.

It's Beatrice's herbal jungle juice! she thought suddenly, beginning her attack on the fastenings of the corset. All part of the scheme, she decided, taking in the lacing's slack. She grinned. All Loosie's claims about 'knowing nothing' were baloney. The cousins Quine were in cahoots, that was obvious, and Loosie had been briefed to expect, then seduce, a new victim.

But I'm not a victim! I'm here because I want to be, Alexa told herself. And I'm staying because Loosie . . . Well, I like her. I want her. Even if I don't exactly know what to do about it yet.

Whirling, she turned towards the mirror, and renewed her efforts with the corset and the laces.

The red velvet was beautiful, and almost obscenely lush, and, though there was comparatively little of it, it looked stunning with her colouring. Its richness seemed to demand that her hair be black, and that her skin be honeyed gold from the Caribbean sun.

And it wasn't only the colour of her body. From somewhere, she seemed to have acquired a new voluptuousness. Sexy curves that seemed expressly designed to fit the corset's waspy shape. The only wrong note was the chaste white expanse of her panties; but, though she wanted to, she couldn't quite bring herself to shed them. They were the last element of the Alexa of a month ago – the unawakened Alexa – but even though that woman was almost gone now, she was reluctant to expunge her entirely.

'Ready?' called Loosie from over the other side of the room where, by the sound of her, she'd been arranging her equipment.

'Almost,' Alexa responded, twitching the basque a little further down, then hitching it up again. There was no way, when the panties came off, that she could hope to maintain her decency. With her heart thundering, she stepped back into her heels.

Loosie said nothing as Alexa emerged. Instead, and

115

already with a couple of cameras slung around her neck, she moved towards what looked like a music centre, and pressed a touch pad in the middle of the console.

Expecting a subdued classic, Alexa got a shock when she heard dance music instead. It was fast, thundering, unremittingly techno, but somehow its clinical, computer-driven rhythm had a stark sexiness that couldn't be denied.

'Come here,' said Loosie huskily.

Alexa obeyed, feeling hopelessly vulnerable, and embarrassed by the presence of her panties. She wished to God she'd had the guts to take them off, and felt more naked than ever because of them.

When she stood directly before the photographer, Alexa felt her body quiver finely. There was a smoky look in Loosie's eyes, an expression both dreamy yet assessing, where desire and professionalism seemed to blend.

'Lovely. Very lovely,' she murmured. 'But I think there's something wrong with this picture . . . Don't you?'

Shyly, Alexa reached downwards, and slid her thumbs into the waistband of the pants.

'Allow me,' said Loosie, darting forward, and dashing roughly at Alexa's hands.

The photographer's fingers were surprisingly cool as they slid beneath the elastic, then flicked the offending panties downward. Alexa could feel the pads of those fingertips touching her skin, all the way, as Loosie peeled the garment from her body.

'Step,' the photographer instructed when the panties were around Alexa's ankles. 'Again,' she prompted when Alexa obeyed and they were off one foot.

'That's better,' said Loosie. And then, almost before Alexa could analyse what was happening, her pubic hair was being fluffed and finger-combed. 'Your pussy's too pretty to hide, sweetheart. You should go without panties more often.'

116

Alexa stayed still, frozen, holding her breath. Loosie's fingers were still resting on her pubis, almost rubbing against the meeting of her labia. At any second, the woman could increase the pressure, slide a digit in between the soft lips and start caressing the swollen clitoris within. Alexa knew that if she made even the slightest of movements, Loosie would consider the way clear, and the rules of their game would reconfigure. It was what they both wanted, that was true, but some shred of Alexa's inhibitions still lingered.

Loosie didn't force the issue. With a crooked grin, she withdrew, then gestured towards a low, white-covered bed that was surrounded by a selection of lighting paraphernalia.

'Over there, sweetie, that's where the action is. But first you need a little more make-up.'

Loosie's make-up table was another packing case, or more correctly two, with a slab of white plastic plonked across them and large swivel mirror on top of it. Stored in what looked like office filing trays, was every conceivable colour of lipstick, pencil, eye-shadow and face make-up, along with every brush and sponge required to apply them. Alexa, who'd always kept things subtle, frowned at the multicoloured selection, but Loosie just smiled, pulled up first one straight-backed kitchen chair, then another, and nodded that her new model should sit.

'Don't worry, I won't make you look silly,' she said almost gently. 'And you'll be wearing a mask with it anyway.'

When Alexa was seated, Loosie took the other chair and faced her, then reached for a pot of foundation.

It was daunting, but exciting to be sitting face to face with an undeniably beautiful – and bisexual – woman; especially when she was clothed and powerful, and you were exposed and confused. Alexa felt an insane urge to shuffle, and an even madder urge to reach down and touch herself. The urge flared exponentially when

117

Loosie began smoothing her face with a soft tinted cream, in strokes that were both flowing and evocative.

Alexa had to close her eyes. Loosie's gaze was intense and concentrated, and not all of it focused on the make-up. She was smiling slightly as she worked, and whistling beneath her breath to the music. It was obvious she was thoroughly enjoying herself.

'Why do I have to wear a mask?' enquired Alexa suddenly, as her eyes were being defined with a carefully smudged, slate-grey outline.

'Well, you don't have to wear one,' replied Loosie, pausing to sharpen the pencil, then blunting the point with her finger. 'Eyes closed again please,' she instructed, then resumed her task, 'But these photographs are a commission. Someone's going to buy them, and see them. I thought, under the circumstances – ' she glanced down at Alexa's bare sex, ' – that you'd prefer to remain incognito.'

'I didn't realise . . . I . . .'

What had she thought? That the photography was simply part of the seduction?

'I – ' she began again, half protesting, then felt Loosie's cool finger on her lips.

'Shush, I have to do your lips now,' said the photographer, then she set to work again with pencil and brush.

Having lost the initiative, Alexa suddenly didn't feel like fighting any more. She was in it now. She was a porno model, even though the shutter hadn't even clicked yet. It was fate. She was defenceless. She wanted it.

'There,' said Loosie with a flourish, taking Alexa gently by the chin, and turning her to face the mirror. 'Aren't you beautiful?'

Alexa didn't know what to say. Loosie had applied relatively little make-up but the effect it had produced was profound. Alexa saw a face that was her own, but dramatic and vibrant, almost threatening in its sultry sexuality. Dark, smudged eyes; red lips, densely coloured and matte. She was a temptress. A harlot. A vamp. Her face as erotic as her uncovered crotch.

Reaching amongst the clutter on the plastic worktop, Loosie picked up a mask, as promised, and, watching Alexa's face in the mirror, she laid it precisely across her freshly painted eyes, then tied its trailing ribbons behind her head.

'Lovely,' purred the photographer, reaching for Alexa's hand and urging her to rise. 'Now come along, my sweet; let's get to work.'

At the white-sheeted bed, Alexa lost her nerve, and as she stood there, masked, basqued and exposed, her knees trembled and her teeth began to chatter.

'Oh baby, don't worry,' said Loosie kindly, her sharp eyes missing nothing. 'You'll be all right,' she whispered in Alexa's ear and enclosed her in a warm, gentle hug. 'I'd love to kiss you, sweetheart,' she murmured, dipping down and pressing her mouth to Alexa's quivering throat, 'but I've done far too good a job on your lips.'

Alexa's knees buckled, but Loosie's cradling arms held her up. The photographer was obviously far stronger than her lean frame suggested, and she was able to support Alexa's weight with little outward effort. With a smile, she lowered her burden towards the bed.

Lying back gratefully, Alexa closed her eyes behind the mask. 'Relax,' she heard Loosie say.

'I'll be back in a minute,' the photographer continued, then strode quickly away across the room.

Alexa lay in an ungraceful heap for a moment, then tried, with difficulty, to compose herself. There was no mirror nearby but she tried to imagine what she looked like; an exotic masked figure clad only in a basque, and showing the dark curls of her pubis beneath it.

'Drink this. You need it,' said Loosie when she returned, slid her arm beneath Alexa and held another strong drink against her lips. The mix was more herbal this time, and the taste so subversive that Alexa downed it all in one, then let Loosie lower her back on to the pillows.

'That's it, baby. No tension now. Let your legs fall apart, there's just one more little job to do.'

Closing her eyes again, Alexa was beyond caring. Her sex rippled as her thighs sagged open.

'Gorgeous,' whispered Loosie, from very, very close. 'We almost don't need this at all.'

Suddenly, Alexa felt an exquisite tickling sensation begin in the membranes of her quim. It was fine, mysterious, featherlight, and so tantalising that she moaned out aloud. When she looked down, Loosie was crouched between her legs, wielding a delicately pointed brush and painting her sex with something transparent and sticky.

'What's that? What's it for?'

'It's glycerine, sweetheart,' said Loosie, still daubing, and making Alexa wriggle and squirm. 'You've got to look wet. Aroused. And this just creates the illusion. Although, in your case, we hardly need to bother. You're as runny as honey already.'

As the brush moved quickly and cleverly over her, Alexa could barely contain herself. Loosie was right, she was wet through, almost swimming, and every part of her sex felt inflamed. The tiny brush strokes were driving her crazy. It was all she could do not to grab Loosie's wrist, and make her drop the pointed brush, so she could put her clever hand to better use.

'I . . . I want – ,' murmured Alexa, reaching down blindly and feeling Loosie knock her gently away.

'Not yet, little greedy. We'll get to that. We've got to take some photographs first!'

The very second Loosie stopped applying the glycerine and took up her camera, Alexa was already masturbating. The gleaming cosmetic created a fabulous slickness, and her fingers almost flew across her clitoris; first rubbing furiously, then flicking and pinching. From across a great distance – an echoing chasm – she could hear the insistent click and whirr of the shutter, and her closed eyes registered a brightly flashing light. Within a very few seconds she was climaxing massively, her painted lips contorting in a snarl.

In the sharp, very lucid part of her mind that was detached from her pleasure, she could clearly see the pictures being taken. She supposed she was almost seeing things through Loosie's eyes – and through her lens – because she could sense a yearning hunger all around her. A woman's urge for a woman's sex, the need to touch, to fondle and to kiss. Stimulated beyond measure by the awareness of being wanted, Alexa writhed and redoubled her efforts, feeling her sex convulse in a procession of orgasms.

Against the backing of white, and to the driving techno music, Alexa astounded herself with her boldness. Almost without any prompting at all, she found herself taking up the lewdest of poses. Spreading herself. Penetrating herself with her fingers. Slipping a breast from the top of her corset, and rolling her engorged nipple with her fingers.

She lay on her back, drawing up her knees, to show the entire length of her sex and her anus. She pulled apart her own bottom cheeks. And when Loosie handed her a dildo – a great, thick penis shaped monster – she plunged it immediately and deeply into her vagina, then splayed her legs again to show herself, stretched.

It wasn't for quite some time that Alexa realised the flashing and the shutter's whirr had stopped. She'd been so lost in her own lascivious dream-world – full of watching men, unknown faces leering, and lovers of both sexes masturbating furiously with her – that she hadn't noticed the photoshoot was over. When she opened her eyes, she saw that Loosie was sitting on one of the straight chairs, motionless and watching, with one long leg crossed casually over the other, booted ankle on denim-clad knee.

Alexa knew she should have been embarrassed, but found she wasn't. She was aware of Loosie's storm-dark eyes staring intently at her vulva and, the dildo, and in a slow gesture that was almost imperious, she reached down, rocked the thing inside herself, then moaned at the spasm it created.

'Do it again,' said Loosie, her voice thick. 'Do it again, you dirty little cat.'

Alexa obliged, swivelling her bottom on the sheet this time, then bringing her knees up and lifting her hips.

'Oh God,' the photographer gasped. Then, in a flash she was down on the mattress, her slim hand knocking Alexa's aside.

'Play with yourself,' ordered Loosie, beginning a slow pumping action with the dildo. 'Touch yourself . . . Touch your clitoris. Your nipples.'

Alexa obeyed, pinching her clitoris with the fingers of her right hand, while with the left she cupped a breast and flicked at her nipple with her thumb. She felt Loosie's free hand slide beneath her bottom, the middle finger in search of the portal.

All the pleasure, all the stimulation, seemed to meet somewhere around her middle, and coalesce into a white ball of bliss. She was wriggling, shuffling, heaving her body around on the bed, but neither she nor the photographer lost contact with her body, even though Loosie hissed repeatedly, 'Keep still!'

Alexa had her eyes tight shut, and her mouth wide open as she panted for air. She could smell Loosie's perfume, fresh and green, and the other woman's sex-musk, just as pungent as her own. She felt a mouth close tightly on her unattended nipple, and a finger push into her anus; then she squealed when it was suddenly too much, and the orgasm so intense it almost hurt.

After a while, Alexa became aware of small movements – the rustle of clothes, the click of a belt – and when she looked up again, Loosie was naked. The photographer's body was slender and athletic, and her skin almost white, like her cousin's. With her closely cropped haircut, she looked like a wood nymph, a sensuous pixie whose actions were gracefully limber.

122

As she crouched on the mattress, Loosie's breast pressed against Alexa's arm. She knelt forward, kissed Alexa's lips, then murmured in her ear, her voice a low rasp. 'Will you do something for me now, baby?' she asked cajolingly, snaking out her tongue and licking Alexa's neck. 'Nothing much. Just for a minute . . . It won't take long.'

'Of course,' replied Alexa through parched lips, shifting her body and feeling the dildo dance and jostle. Another round of pleasure was beginning.

'You darling,' crowed Loosie, and before Alexa could register her intentions, she was already scooting forward on the bed.

Alexa got the impression of an almost balletic agility, and then Loosie had turned around completely – so her bottom was towards the top end of the bed – thrown her leg across Alexa's head, and was squatting directly over her.

'Just lick me, sweetheart,' she instructed very softly, then lowered her sex on to Alexa's open mouth.

Lucretia Quine felt happier than she had done in a long time. Sipping her camomile tea, she looked down at the black-and-white prints spread out over her worktable and considered the kindness and the beauty of women, and thought what a benison her own sex were to her.

The kindness came primarily from her cousin. There was no reason on earth why Bea was obliged to send her such a gift, to share such a delicious new treasure – but she had. Beatrice was usually the most selfish, self-indulgent creature that Loosie had ever met; and yet, instead of being greedy, she'd been generous to her cousin. A cousin who was still smarting from a bastard who'd hurt her, and who needed something nice in her life.

Something, or somebody, really nice: the girl whose beauty, and whose nascent but alarming sexuality, was celebrated in these dozens of pictures.

Oh Alexa, thought Loosie, abandoning her tea, and picking up one of the choicest of the shots.

In it, Alexa Lavelle looked totally wanton. Her long thighs were as wide apart as it was possible to be, and between them was the protruding white dildo. Alexa's expression was mindless, almost savage, and her fingers were curled into fists. Behind the mask, her eyes were open, but rolled up to show the whites. Her mouth was distorted in a snarl. From the red basque a single breast had escaped and was naked, and the nipple stood up like a dark stud. Even now, the photograph made Loosie want to touch herself, and she pressed her pubis through the silk of her robe.

She'd enjoyed herself so much with Beatrice's pretty new friend, and, oh boy, how she'd loved that nimble tongue. Once Alexa had adjusted her mindset – and understood it was perfectly OK to make love with another woman – she'd taken to everything with voracious enthusiasm. Loosie had been surprised, when they'd talked quietly afterwards, to find that her cousin hadn't already initiated Alexa, although it sounded as if it hadn't been far off. Loosie was fully aware of what an 'examination' by Beatrice might entail.

Now that's something I would like to have seen, thought Loosie, flipping aside her robe and rummaging for her clitoris. Quickly and efficiently, she brought herself to a climax, imagining Beatrice with her fingers inside Alexa, while Sly – all pure and pristine in white – looked on, with her hand at her groin.

'Too much!' murmured Loosie, getting her breath back as she let her mannish silk dressing gown slither closed. With a sigh, she looked down at the photos, then, sorting through them, she selected a dozen of the best. The most sublimely outrageous shots, she slid into a cardboard-backed envelope. Scowling at the taste, she licked the flap and sealed it, wishing someone would have the good sense to make the glue taste nicer. She thought longingly of the delicious flavour she'd encountered earlier – when she'd laid her tongue across something far more exciting than an envelope!

After writing a label, Loosie picked up her mobile phone, flipped it open and pressed the short code for an often used number. She heard a ring at the other end, then another, but almost immediately after that it was picked up: as if the party had been anxiously – or maybe greedily – waiting.

'Hello, Bea,' said Lucretia Quine to her cousin. 'I've got exactly what you wanted. I'll have them biked round to you. Enjoy, then let me know what you think.'

As she snapped the phone shut, she was smiling . . . and still thinking of Alexa Lavelle.

Chapter Nine

Party Animal

G ENERAL PROTECTION FAULT
Shit! That was what happened when you day-
dreamed around an untried program.

Alexa pushed her fingers through her hair, making it
more tousled than it already was, and admitted her
mind wasn't on the job. She was making elementary
mistakes, stabbing at solutions before she'd thought
them out. She was thinking about sex, not computers.

Guilt had brought her back to the office after her
meeting with Loosie, but unfortunately it hadn't set her
brain into gear. She was supposed to be debugging a
program for an important new client, but all she was
doing was repeatedly crashing.

Quentin had been eyeing her nervously all afternoon.
She could sense the repeated glances emanating from
his cubby-hole in the corner, and she had the distinct
impression he was waiting to be pounced on. She could
sense his excitement. And she could sense that he
wanted her. Quite desperately. But although she
couldn't stop thinking about sex, she had little remaining energy for action. Which was probably a blessing in
disguise. Things were bad enough at KL system

already: to foster a relationship with Quent would be disastrous.

Studying the dismally locked screen, she stifled a yawn. What had happened on Loosie's white daybed seemed to have drained her somehow, yet its very strangeness demanded an analysis. Serious thought, but after a serious night's sleep.

Wearily she rebooted the computer, sipped from a cup of cold black coffee and did the best of a bad job with the program. There were still several minor glitches, but they'd have to wait until tomorrow. Or sometime. It was after six and she was dog-tired and confused.

'Night, Quent,' she called out, feeling guilty, as she always did, at leaving him to lock up, tidy up and generally pick up the pieces for her irresponsibility. He looked exhausted, too, she realised. There were dark, purplish shadows beneath his eyes, and the skin across his cheekbones looked tight.

Alexa paused on the threshold, watching him. It was odd, but his signs of fatigue were quite attractive. His chin was stubbly, too, and it made him look older and engagingly dissipated. She remembered his hands on her, and how frantic yet gentle he'd been. She took a step back towards him, her inner devil stirring; then shook her head as she understood what was happening.

'See you tomorrow,' she called out in a strangled voice, then almost threw herself out on to the landing, slamming the door behind her as she went.

You nearly did it again, you fool! she accused herself all the way home. Even after what had happened with Loosie Quine, and all those orgasms, poor Quentin had started looking like a possibility again.

At home, she tried to distract herself with television, but every programme she switched to was banal. She took a long bath, and while she soaked she tried to do the crossword to keep her mind occupied; but the ill-

127

fated paper only ended up as pulp when she dropped it and it went beneath the water.

In bed, with a mug of Horlicks, she tried hard to take in an article on networking, but, after reading the first sentence for the seventeenth time, she threw the journal off the bed in disgust.

Reaching for her Psion, she called up the number of the hotel where Tom was staying, then cancelled it and summoned Beatrice's number instead. She remembered when she'd entered it – what seemed like a century ago in Barbados – and how amused the doctor had been by an electronic address book instead of a paper one.

She picked up the phone, started dialling, then put it down again. What could she say? I went to your cousin's and we made love. Was that what Beatrice had intended? What if it wasn't? And anyway, it was half-past eleven at night. If Beatrice wasn't out somewhere, at some glitzy party, she was probably already in bed. And she wouldn't be alone with Horlicks and computer magazines. She'd probably have Drew between her thighs. Or Sly's pretty face. Or it could be any number of unknown other lovers of either sex, performing whatever perverted act took her fancy.

I don't know what to do next, thought Alexa perplexedly. She'd made no formal 'appointment' with Beatrice: no time, no place, nothing. She'd stumbled out of that beautiful house in a daze, really, with only Loosie's address on that glossy black card. Everything was so mixed up, so casual. The only constant in the whole thing was sex, and, as she snapped off the light, and shuffled down beneath the covers, she slid her hand between her legs for comfort.

The next morning, Alexa couldn't face Quentin, or the office, or anything; so she phoned in, said she'd work from home. Then, still in her nightie and robe, she logged on to the KL Systems LAN.

A night's sleep, even a troubled one, seemed to have done her good, and the glitched program soon yielded to her efforts. Pleased, and relieved that turning into a nymphomaniac hadn't ruined her brain altogether, she decided to celebrate with breakfast.

Halfway through an enormous bacon sandwich, a beaker of tea and a brainless chat show on morning TV, Alexa was surprised to hear the doorbell.

She was expecting no one. The post had been. Everyone she knew was at work, and would phone, not visit. Embarrassed by her scruffy dressing gown, she padded her way to the door and opened it.

A motorcycle messenger stood on the threshold, holding out an envelope.

'Alexa Lavelle?' he enquired, his voice muffled by his shiny, luridly patterned helmet.

Alexa nodded, took the envelope, and signed the chit, and was still staring at her own name, flamboyantly scrawled on white vellum, as the biker stomped away down the stairs.

The handwriting was distinctive, and she felt she ought to recognise it. Her fingers shook as she tore open the envelope, then shook more when she read the signature.

Dearest Alexa, the note began. Come to a party . . . It's just the sort of thing you'll love. Very educational. Be in the bar of the Hotel St Vincent at eight tonight, and we'll send someone to collect you. It was signed, Much love, Beatrice.

How the hell does Beatrice know what I'll love? thought Alexa crossly. She was right about Loosie, but that doesn't mean I'll go for all her kinky schemes.

Studying the note, she wondered whether to ring Beatrice and decline the invitation, but then decided not to. She didn't have to stay at the party long. She could have one cocktail and leave. She didn't have to linger to the bitter end. Especially as Tom was due home tomorrow morning.

At two in the afternoon, when Alexa was finally dressed, the doorbell trilled again.

'Now what?' she muttered, saving her work and going to the door.

It was another delivery. A box this time, brought by an express parcel service, but with the same bold writing on the label.

Me again, Beatrice had written. A friend bought me this frock, but it doesn't really fit. I'd love it if you'd wear it tonight.

This scarf, thought Alexa sarcastically, lifting the dress from its bed of folded tissue. Vibrantly dark red in colour, Beatrice's 'frock' seemed to be constructed from a collection of large raw silk handkerchiefs. Halter-necked, it was completely backless, and also fairly frontless, with a deep 'V' that plunged to the waist. The skirt was short and multilayered, and fell in jagged pixie points which would be lucky if they covered half the wearer's thigh. It was a breathtakingly beautiful dress, and a designer exclusive, but it would need a helluva lot of bottle to wear it.

A lot more bottle than I've got, Alexa thought longingly, stroking the silky fabric and almost sighing with pleasure.

But was that necessarily true? If 'bottle' equated with the 'where angels fear to tread' syndrome, then in the last few days she'd shown more than enough daring to wear the dress!

Quentin. Loosie. Beatrice herself. She'd plunged wildly into all these adventures, and not come to any real harm from them. Surely she could wear Beatrice's outrageous party frock? As long as she could find something suitable to go under it . . .

There was very little that would go under the dress. Any lingerie on her top half was right out. No bra, no camisole, no slip. And the situation below wasn't much better.

In the end, and with much trepidation, Alexa chose a black cotton G-string; one she'd bought for Barbados, but not worn. Not dared to wear. As her legs were

tanned she rejected tights and stockings, and just
slipped on her fanciest pair of shoes – a delicate pair of
Maud Frizzon courts that she'd purchased in her latest
round of splurging.

Posing before her mirror, she'd decided she looked
amazing; but, waiting for her taxi in the lobby, she
wondered if that equated with 'ridiculous'. The weather
was warm; even so, the dress was minimal, and
exposed her back, her arms, her shoulders and her
chest, and also a good expanse of her legs. She'd flung
an embroidered and fringed black shawl around her,
but still she felt horrendously uncovered, and totally
vulnerable in her flimsy silk layers.

The taxi driver had obviously driven far more out-
rageously dressed travellers in his time, because he
made no comment as he took her fare. But, in the hotel,
all eyes fell upon her. A beaming commissionaire held
the door open, and beyond that a red-faced, stammer-
ing bellboy took it upon himself to escort her to the bar.
In the softly lit, luxurious room itself, Alexa could have
sworn she heard a murmur of acknowledgement, but
the surrounding drinkers were too discrete to point and
stare.

Someone to collect you, Beatrice's note had said, but
that someone could be anyone, Alexa realised as her
stomach did a somersault. She felt unsure of herself at
the bar, and on show. To cringe in her shawl would be
the epitome of gaucherie, so she'd laid it, with her bag,
on the stool beside her and was toughing out her state
of half nakedness.

Sipping a glass of white wine, Alexa kept her eye on
the door and watched out for a face that looked anything like familiar. She half hoped Drew would be her
escort. Or perhaps Sly, who she knew less well, but
who seemed friendly, if a little self-contained.

Another thought occurred.

Maybe Loosie was going to this bash, too? She'd not
mentioned it, but then again, they hadn't exchanged
much conversation. Kisses, yes, lots of them. Alexa

blushed, remembering how many of those hadn't been on the mouth.

She was just looking at her watch for what felt like the twentieth time – after finding it was only a minute after eight – when two men appeared in the doorway of the bar. Alexa had never set eyes on either of them before, but instinctively she knew they'd come for her. She wasn't sure whether to be delighted or appalled.

Both were slender, black-haired and swarthy, and both were so toe-curlingly handsome that there was little to choose between them for raw allure. The taller one of the two had long hair, bound in a meticulous ponytail, and a soulful, almost artistic expression; his companion had short, roguish curls and a dazzling white grin. Both were perfectly dressed in pale, unstructured suits and Alexa felt a jolt of pure excitement when – as one – they began walking towards her. About to rise, she thought better of it. The short, petalled skirt was so precarious, and she was showing almost all her thighs already.

'You must be Alexa,' said the first of the strangers to reach her – the one with the naughty, twinkling smile. 'Beatrice told us to look for a beauty.' His smile widened as he reached out towards her.

Taken aback, Alexa allowed her hand to be raised to a pair of soft, warm lips, then kissed with economy and passion.

'And you are . . .?' she said, as confidently as she could, meeting first one, then another, pair of eyes.

'Yusuf,' said the taller man, as he, too, kissed her fingers.

'Siddig,' murmured his associate, nodding.

'And Beatrice has sent you two to collect me?' said Alexa, withdrawing her hand almost reluctantly. She was aware of people around her looking on with interest; the women, in particular, with envy.

'That's right,' said Siddig, clearly the spokesman. 'But the pleasure is ours, I assure you.'

Sweet-talking bastard, thought Alexa wryly, although

she couldn't deny the man's charm. Both he and his friend were obviously Middle Eastern, and fully endowed with the prerequisite glamour. Just one of these two would have overwhelmed most women, but as a team they were nothing short of devastating.

'I'm sure it is,' she said smoothly, determined to keep her head, for the time being at least. 'Do we leave straight away?' she enquired, reaching for her bag and her wrap, and seeing heat flare in both men's eyes as the movement caused her neckline to gape.

'Only if you want to,' observed Yusuf, stepping to the other side of her, while Siddig stayed where he was.

'We could have a drink here first, if you like?' offered Siddig, making it sound like an indecent suggestion.

'OK,' said Alexa, no longer quite sure of her poise. Yusuf shifted her shawl and bag to the next stool along, and then, in a manoeuvre of co-ordinated elegance, he and Siddig sat down on either side of her.

Within seconds more drinks were brought, and Alexa decided she'd better try to make conversation with these two visions who'd been sent for her pleasure.

But just as she was about to attempt her first witticism, a stunning revelation took her voice.

They're a team, she thought, the skin on the back of her neck prickling as her special awareness switched on. Always a team. They work together in the bedroom too, on one woman, and tonight they'll be working on me!

'Are you cold?' enquired Siddig, his beautiful eyes concerned as Yusuf reached out for her wrap.

'No, I'm fine,' she answered, her voice breathy, almost squeaky.

'But something made you shiver,' he persisted, his mouth an impish curve.

'It was just a sudden thought I had . . .' she faltered. 'I was wondering what everyone was thinking. About me. Here. Dressed like this. With two men.'

She turned from one to the other. Yusuf was also

smiling now, while Siddig was openly smirking, his dark eyes alight with sexual challenge.

'Does it matter what they think?' He made a tiny graceful gesture which could have signified the entire population of London. 'It's what *you* think that counts. How do you feel about being with two men?'

And it wasn't drinking with two men he was asking her about either, she realised. He was referring to the main agenda, and his question was: would she make love with two men? At the same time. In the same bed. Give herself to both of them at once?

Chickening out, Alexa reached for her glass. 'What do you think?' she murmured almost inaudibly, then sipped her wine while Siddig softly laughed.

Beatrice Quine, I'll kill you! thought Alexa in the momentary conversational hiatus. Now look what you've landed me in! I thought it'd be a couple of innocent hours, in public, at a party – and now I've got to fend off two Middle-Eastern gigolos!

The trouble was, she wasn't going to fend them off, was she? They were gorgeous, a twin feast of exotic manhood, and her body was alive with hunger. Her nipples were pointing through the thin silk of her bodice and she could feel her G-string getting wetter and wetter. To her great relief, she wasn't sitting on her skirt.

'Beatrice tells us you're a computer programmer?' said Yusuf, dispelling the charged silence.

'A systems analyst, actually,' answered Alexa, pleased to have something safe to talk about as she outlined the subtle differences between the jobs. The two men were clearly not techno-buffs, but it was obvious they weren't ignorant, either. Their questions were both intelligent and informed, and to her surprise, there were no double meanings.

'And what do you two do?' she asked eventually, after telling them a great deal about KL Systems, but virtually nothing about Thomas and Quentin.

'This and that,' said Siddig casually. 'Modelling. Film

work, as extras.' He paused and looked her candidly in the eye. 'But mainly we're escorts. We provide company for women who need it. We're professional dinner partners. Theatre companions. Party-goers . . . And whatever else our clients might ask of us.'

And I bet they ask. And ask and ask and ask, thought Alexa, feeling the warmth in his eyes sweep over her. He'd been smiling, watching her face, but on the final statement his gaze had panned downwards for a second, and seemed to rest on her breasts like a caress.

'Oh,' she said in a small voice. 'And do you always work together? Or is this a special assignment?'

'Yes, we are a team,' Siddig answered smoothly. 'A package deal, you might say. But every "assignment" is special. And some more than others.' His pink tongue emerged from his lips for a second, and seemed to emphasise the last statement like a kiss.

Again, Alexa perceived a line. More sweet talk. And cursed her maddened body for buying it hook, line and sinker. She was shaking harder than ever on the inside now, although on the outside she was managing to stay calm. Her vagina was a hot well of moisture, her flesh ready for the handsome man beside her. Either of the handsome men beside her. Or both of them; turn and turn about.

'You obviously enjoy your work,' she answered non-committally.

'So do our clients,' said Yusuf, at her other side, leaning close.

Alexa reached for her glass, but before she could grasp it, Siddig's hand had caught hers, enfolded it, then brought it gently up to his lips. Turning it over, he kissed her palm slowly and succulently, his tongue tracing the lines of its weblike print as if he were divining her destiny by taste.

'Shall we go?' he said, looking up, then nodding towards Yusuf.

Alexa walked from the bar and the hotel on a carpet of air, her arm tucked lightly in Siddig's. It was only when she reached the long black limousine awaiting them outside that she realised Yusuf had brought her belongings for her, unselfconsciously carrying her wrap and her bag like a bearer in the service of an empress.

And it was Yusuf who held back when they reached the car, too. Siddig slid neatly into the rear seat first, then drew Alexa forward to join him, guiding her with both her hands in his. Yusuf climbed into the car behind her, and as the door closed, she understood their ploy. They'd sandwiched her again, trapped her between them, but this time beneath the veil of dark seclusion.

'Do we have far to go?' she asked, as the limousine pulled away sleekly from the curb.

'Far enough,' replied Siddig as his hand settled delicately on her thigh, and another hand – not his – claimed the other one.

So this is it, she thought dreamily. They're starting on me, and we haven't even arrived at the party.

Insistently the two hands drew her legs apart, and as someone – she knew not who – flipped her skirt from beneath her, she felt the leather seat against the bare skin of her bottom. Lying back, and silently accepting them, she gave herself up to her burgeoning sensuality, and forgot both the chauffeur and the night world passing by.

As he was on her left, she deduced that it was Yusuf who began kissing her throat, while Siddig ran his fingers up her thigh. A hand slid neatly and flatly beneath the silk of her bodice, then curved to fit around her aching breast. Fingertips gripped her nipple and rolled it, and, with her body singing with desire, she groaned out loud.

'Ah yes, that's good,' purred Siddig in her ear, as one of his hands wiggled in underneath her bottom, and took a firm, possessive grip of one smooth lobe. One finger nudged aside the cord of her G-string, then pressed on – slyly – to push against her twitching anal cleft. Before she could stop him, or protest, he was

136

rubbing her, tickling at her anus while Yusuf pinched her teat.

She hardly knew what to do with her own hands; she seemed to have lost all volition and free will. Ineffectually, she tried to stroke their thighs, and find their groins, but they both laughed and eased their bodies out of reach.

'This is for you, sweet Alexa,' hissed Yusuf, nibbling her ear.

'Don't worry about us,' said Siddig, as his finger probed the portal of her bottom. 'We'll take our pleasure later, don't you worry.'

'But what about the party?' Alexa gasped, as he pushed harder, opening her a little.

'Hush! We're going there,' he said soothingly, as his other hand climbed inexorably up the front of her thigh. 'But it's not really an ordinary kind of party . . . And you need this,' his fingers found the lace edge of her G-string, 'warmed up a little first.'

Breathing in short, hurried gasps, she felt him brushing lightly, almost tentatively over the triangle of fabric that covered her, while behind he had the first joint of his finger up inside her. The sensation of having something in her bottom was horrifyingly delicious, and darts of feeling jittered up and down her spine. Half of her desperately wanted him to take his finger out, and let the dangerous agitation subside, while the other half wanted to sit down hard on it, and feel the digit slide as deep as it could go. All of her was begging that he'd touch her clitoris.

But he didn't. She started to move herself, in frustration, but Siddig remained perfectly still: his finger just a single inch inside her, while his other hand lay lightly on her mons.

Then Yusuf moved. Almost as if he'd heard some discreet command from his companion, the taller man began working on her breast.

Sliding her flimsy bodice sideways, he freed the soft globe he'd been handling, the one nearest to him, and

137

left it exposed, naked in the darkness. And as Siddig began whispering something in her ear – something beautiful but incomprehensible, in his own language – Yusuf slid one hand around her back, and one under her bare breast, then lowered his mouth to engulf her throbbing nipple.

Hot needles seemed to shoot between her breast and her sex, and between her thighs – beneath Siddig's resting hand – her flesh juddered and seemed to cry out for attention. She made a sound in her throat, as indecipherable as Siddig's subtle murmurings, yet instantly he seemed to understand.

'What is it?' he demanded. 'What do you want?'

At the sound of his friend's voice, Yusuf looked up from her bosom, his eyes enquiring in the half light.

'What do you want, Alexa?' repeated Siddig, both his hands quite still, yet somehow in violent motion.

'I want you to . . . To . . .' Her body was screaming, but her tongue seemed to clog. 'I . . .'

Siddig's finger moved infinitesimally inside her, and at the same time, Yusuf bowed his head again, his long tongue pointing out to touch her nipple.

'Go on,' urged Siddig. 'We're yours. What do you want?'

Feeling blood rush hectically into her face, Alexa turned away.

'Touch my clitoris, please,' she said, her voice so soft she didn't think he'd hear it.

'Of course,' said Siddig, almost formally, his fingers already on the move. Within seconds, he'd pushed aside the edge of her G-string, parted her silky pubic curls and found the swollen knot of flesh that seemed to sob for him. When he pressed it, then swirled it, Alexa came immediately, her ragged cries echoing loudly in the car.

Shaking, her sex pulsating, she reached out blindly for both her glorious men. Her fingers grabbed and scrabbled at their muscular thighs, her nails digging through their trousers as she spasmed.

'Oh boy,' she gasped presently, as the pleasure ebbed away and left her glowing. She was lying back in Yusuf's arms somehow now, and Siddig was gently sucking on her fingers.

'Oh boy indeed,' he said, looking up, then reaching forward to twitch her bodice and make it decent. He'd rearranged her G-string as he'd withdrawn his questing hand, and, though she was still sticky, her quim was primly covered.

'What must you think of me?' she asked, feeling the blush burn like flame beneath her tan. 'We haven't even got to the party. We're in a car, for God's sake. I'm not usually like this, really.'

As she sat up, patting and fluffing at her hair, Yusuf reached for her bag and passed it to her.

'You ought to be,' said Siddig softly. 'You're exquisite, Alexa. So beautiful and sensual. I wish all the women we have to be with were like you.'

'I feel like a bimbo. A slut,' she said despairingly, but got a pleasant surprise when she took out her pocket mirror. Her party make-up was intact and her hair still looked good; even the flush on her cheeks was flattering. 'A tart,' she added, smoothing a finger across her eyebrows. 'The way I've behaved. God, I feel so cheap!'

Siddig laughed again, and shook his head, then reached for her hand and kissed it. 'Never cheap,' he said against her skin, then looked up. 'How can you be cheap? We certainly aren't.' He gestured to himself and Yusuf.

A horrible suspicion struck Alexa. 'What do you mean by that?'

'I mean that our fees are considerable . . . The very cost of our services denies the concept of "cheapness".'

'But who's paying?' demanded Alexa, her voice rising in dismay. Good God, she was in enough trouble over finance already!

'I'm afraid we're not at liberty to disclose that,' said Siddig, his face neutral but his eyes dark and teasing.

'Is it Beatrice?'

'We can't say,' answered Yusuf, his expression the same.

'It's a matter of professional discretion,' observed Siddig. 'But don't worry; you'll find out eventually. The person in question will probably tell you.'

Gathering her will, Alexa prepared to interrogate them, but just then the car began to slow.

The distance they'd travelled was a measure of her abandonment. They were clearly well away from the centre of London now, and possibly even past suburbia, too. Outside the car's tinted glass, full night had fallen, which only added to the drama of the view. The limousine was pulling up before an imposing Palladianesque mansion whose white stone portico was illuminated by floodlights. A footman ran down the steps to greet them, and behind him were a brace of smart, but archaically clad housemaids. There was no sign of a host or hostess in the doorway, but every window in the house was ablaze with light, and moving figures were clearly visible inside.

'Whose house is this?' asked Alexa as Siddig and Yusuf helped her from the car and the footman hovered solicitously nearby.

'No one in particular's,' Siddig replied, his smile oblique. 'It's just a place where certain friends gather. Come on, let's go inside. I'm sure they're all dying to catch their first sight of you.'

'All who?' Alexa asked nervously, but her companions seemed to choose to ignore her.

Inside, the mansion was dazzling. Alexa got an impression of whiteness, marble and rococo. Gold leaf everywhere. There were quite a number of people in the huge entrance hall, all laughing over drinks, and chatting. One or two turned curiously as she entered. In another room somewhere, there was chamber music playing, but it was too distant to discern an actual melody.

Alexa knew no one. The guests she could see were all – bar none – expensively clothed and vivacious, but not one bore a face she'd seen before. When a maid brought a tray bearing flutes of champagne, she took one and sipped it gratefully. Her dress was at the right party, but inside it she'd suddenly never felt more like plain old Alexa, working girl – an interloper, a fish out of water.

'Don't worry,' said Siddig as if he'd read her mind. 'You look adorable. Everyone will love you.'

Alexa smiled, more thankful than ever for her twofold escort. With two handsome men at her side, she at least looked like part of a small group, not a singleton or someone's 'other half'.

'Come on,' encouraged Yusuf, touching her arm. 'The people who matter are upstairs.'

What do you mean, *'matter'*? Alexa wanted to ask, but as they moved towards the stairs, a sight – seen at the very edge of her vision – arrested her and made her stop dead in her tracks. At first, she thought her eyes had deceived her, but when she turned, and took a better look, she saw that the nearly impossible was real.

She'd already noticed, even in the short time she'd been in the house, that her own outfit was by no means the most daring. Every gown in the place was outrageous.

But it wasn't a stunningly dressed woman that had shocked her.

A blond, very beautiful young man was kneeling on the floor several feet away. He was wearing leather, but his eyes were downcast, and his whole demeanour cringing. Around his neck was a narrow metal collar of some kind, which was attached to a thin studded leash. The woman standing beside him was holding the other end of the leash, but otherwise completely ignoring him.

Aware that she was staring, and attracting attention herself, Alexa moved on, falling into step beside Siddig and Yusuf.

'What's happening there?' she whispered as they reached the landing and she was able to look down at the young man unobtrusively. 'Is this a fancy-dress party? Beatrice never said anything.'

More laughing guests were passing now, and Siddig drew her gently to one side. As they stood against the wall, he reached up and touched her face, and she could smell her own body on his hand. 'Sweet Alexa,' he whispered. 'You really don't know, do you?'

'Know what?' she hissed, suddenly half knowing but needing confirmation.

'He's her slave, Alexa,' said Siddig, with a smile, nodding in the general direction of downstairs. 'He has no will. He does what she wants. And she wants him on his knees and collared. Do you understand?'

Alexa nodded, thinking furiously. Ideas and images were pouring into her mind, all loosely related but still slightly jumbled. She looked up, saw another of the 'Edwardian' maids standing beside her with drinks, and exchanged her empty glass for a full one, then drank more champagne while she ruminated.

All this wasn't entirely new to her. Kinky behaviour was quite trendy now, and her own imagination had been full of it since Barbados. There were articles about bondage and sadomasochism – and especially about 'female dominance' – in the racier women's magazines almost every week, but, until now, had been something that other people did.

Or had it?

She hadn't hit anyone or put them in chains, but she had taken charge, hadn't she? Running off to the Caribbean; almost raping Thomas the other night when *she* wanted sex and he didn't; seducing innocent Quentin in the office. She'd let herself be manipulated – in every sense – by Beatrice and Sly, and Loosie; but they were women themselves. Prime examples of what she'd been reading about. Beatrice in particular fitted the 'domina' profile to a T. And wasn't Drew just a step or two from male slavery?

It all seemed to add up quite elegantly, and yet . . . What was it Beatrice had said? 'When I'm playing the

142

submissive . . .' Where on earth did *that* fit into the scenario?

'What are you thinking about, Alexa?' asked Siddig in her ear, and when she turned, both he and Yusuf were closely watching her. 'Would you like a slave?' he went on. 'It could be arranged, you know.'

'I . . . I don't know.'

It was true. The whole concept was bizarre, absolutely impossible, yet the idea was insidiously exciting. She saw a picture of that strong male throat, firmly collared and beneath her own heel, and felt lust coil like a snake in her belly.

'You will do. Soon,' said Siddig, his voice sexy and ominous. 'Come along. Let's move on. There's far more than that just ahead.'

Chapter Ten

French Ice

*A*fter so much strangeness, it was a relief, of sorts, to see someone known to her. If 'knowing' was what it could be called.

Alexa's heart started pounding, and her palms grew sweaty. Loosie Quine was standing at the other side of the room, chatting to a couple who also looked vaguely familiar. It took Alexa several seconds to realise it was Mr Handsome and his wife, from Circe, and by that time Loosie had left them, and was coming across the crowded room, smiling.

'Hi guys,' said the photographer to Siddig and Yusuf. Then, with her eyes intent and sparkling, she turned towards Alexa. 'Well, hello,' she murmured, her voice softer and loaded with meaning. 'I didn't expect to find you here.'

'Why not?' demanded Alexa, stunned into saying the first thing in her head. Loosie's very presence was enough to bemuse anybody, but what she was wearing – or wasn't wearing – took one's breath.

'Well, I got the impression you were new to the scene. That you weren't into all this.' Loosie flicked her long tapered fingers towards the room and its various eccentricities.

You look amazing, thought Alexa, wishing she could say it.

The photographer was wearing tight, black leather trousers with boots and a chunky biker's jacket. On her hands were leather gauntlets, and at her throat a studded choker, but that appeared to be the sum total of her clothing. Underneath her mannish jacket her torso was all woman, and her small, pointed breasts were proudly naked. Her nipples were erect, and looked darkened, as if they'd been fondled by someone's fingers, then dipped in rouge.

'It's so warm,' she said, laughing softly at Alexa's wide-eyed gaze. 'Feel how hot I am.' Reaching out quickly, she took Alexa's hand and pressed it to her skin beneath the leather.

'See?' she purred, leaning close, her strong fingers making Alexa caress her.

Involuntarily, Alexa squeezed. Loosie's breast was warm, and her flesh firm and scented. Voluptuous memories passed through Alexa's mind. She seemed to taste again a woman's pungent flavours – Loosie's sweat, her muskiness, her quim – and feel those slender thighs gripping at her head. She wondered if the photographer was wearing any panties beneath her leather, then imagined, if she was, that they were odorous and soaked with her juices.

It took her several seconds to remember she was still holding Loosie's breast, but when she tried to pull away, her hand was clamped. Beatrice's cousin was just as strong and wiry as her hard-line clothes suggested, and she lifted Alexa's fingers and slowly kissed them.

'See you later, lover,' she said, then released her grip. 'I've got to mingle now. Have fun!'

'What are you laughing at?' demanded Alexa, when Loosie had disappeared in a flash of black leather, and the grinning Siddig had taken her place.

'So you know our friend, the photographer, do you?'

he said, taking her elbow and leading her forward. There was a wide double doorway at the far end of the room, and there seemed to be activity in the area beyond it.

'Yes. Yes, I do,' replied Alexa, her skin feeling hot where he held her.

'Well?' queried Yusuf from the other side, innocently.

'No! Not really,' Alexa answered. It was obvious she hadn't fooled them, though; they'd both seen her fondling Loosie's breast.

The next room held an exhibition of some kind. Large white-covered panels had been set before each of the walls, and on these hung a series of massively enlarged photographs, whose style and content was disquietingly familiar . . .

They were all black and white. They were all unequivocally sexual. There was no doubt they'd been taken by Loosie Quine. And in yet another room, just beyond the first one, there appeared to be an even larger collection.

Alexa was just having the most horrible of all horrible forebodings when a voice she knew well called her name.

'Alexa! Alexa, my dear! I'm so glad you've made it.'

It was Beatrice, of course, standing by one of the giant photographs, and on the arm of a tall, perfectly dressed man with a stunning head of silver-white hair. As Alexa approached, she saw that Sly was also with them, but for some reason, the nurse was in her uniform. Or what seemed to be a uniform. On closer inspection, the dress, apron and cap were not the exquisitely plain and clinical ones she'd worn at Beatrice's surgery, but a stylised, more elaborate version, such as might have been worn in the 1940s or 1950s, complete with elasticated belt, laced up brogues and a fob watch.

It is fancy dress after all, thought Alexa, smiling nervously as she realised Beatrice was dressed as a 'roaring twenties' flapper. Her gown was a sublime,

wanted her to reveal the dress's origins, that it was important somehow, and yet dangerous.

'A friend lent it to me,' she said finally, and saw Beatrice bite her lower lip. 'She said it didn't suit her, and that I could wear it tonight.'

She'd done it now. It was clear that the dress had special meaning for D'Aronville, and it wasn't hard to deduce that he was the one who'd given it to Beatrice in the first place.

'I see,' said the Frenchman, his eyes narrowing. Slowly, almost measuredly, he reached out and took Beatrice's champagne glass from her, and, having given it to one of the ever-present maids, he took the doctor's two hands in his, turning her around to face him.

'Is this what you do with my gifts, Beatrice?' he said quietly and without a trace of vehemence. He was smiling slightly, his blue eyes glittering, and for a moment his mask seemed to slip. As if someone had given him a gift.

Beatrice, on the other hand, was staring at D'Aronville with an expression that approached adoration. She looked hazy, dewy-eyed, rapturous; nothing at all like her usual imperious self. Alexa could almost believe that the doctor was about to have a climax – simply from looking at Sacha D'Aronville; from being raked by those cold, piercing eyes.

What's he like in bed? With those eyes . . . The thought came suddenly, but Alexa realised it had been brewing since she'd first seen him, across the room. Would he still be so unmoved? So calm? Or would he change and become fire instead of ice?

'I'm waiting, Beatrice,' said D'Aronville softly, but Beatrice, looking down at her satin-clad toes, seemed unable to answer.

'A gift,' he went on, his tone still even but something in his eyes beginning to stir. 'Given in good faith, yet you pass it on to another without even a thought.'

It's all an act, thought Alexa, wanting to smile at the sudden revelation. An excuse. She sensed breath being held all around her. A tight wire of artifice stretching out between the doctor and D'Aronville.

Beatrice appeared to be the underdog here, the victim, but was she? Alexa felt a huge wash of excitement pass through her, a delicious thrill of sex that poured out of the shamefaced Beatrice and passed into everyone else. Something was going to happen here any second, Alexa realised, something incredible and beyond her experience.

'I'm sorry,' murmured Beatrice, looking up through the veil of her lashes, her face serious, but her body language smiling.

'But is that enough?' queried D'Aronville.

'No. No, it isn't.' Beatrice's answer was studiedly contrite.

'And what do you think *is* enough?' her inquisitor continued, as the assembled watchers seemed to pounce on each word.

'I . . . I think I should be punished,' replied Beatrice, her voice almost a whisper.

Alexa felt like laughing now, and she almost did, but on one level this was all deadly serious.

'Yes, perhaps you should,' observed the Frenchman lightly – as if he didn't care one bit either way.

'Please, will you punish me?' the doctor asked breathlessly. Her smooth, pale face was wildly flushed, her equilibrium obviously upset. Beatrice was aroused beyond measure, and Alexa could feel it. It was a taste on her tongue, rich and flavourful; a sheen on everything she saw. She sensed it washing through the people around her. The 'boys', Siddig and Yusuf; and Sly, wide-eyed and pink-faced herself. As Alexa watched, hardly breathing, she saw the nurse reach out and take Beatrice's hand, as if to buoy up her employer's fragile bravery. Only D'Aronville remained imperturbable, sipping his champagne, his eyes on Beatrice.

'Of course, my dear,' he said, as if she'd asked him for the correct time, or another drink. 'Camilla, would you help her?' he asked, nodding to the nurse in her snowy-white apron.

Sly nodded, and looked on the point of curtseying, then led Beatrice a little way forward, towards an upholstered Victorian side-chair. The nurse turned the chair a little – showing surprising strength in her arms and wrists – then edged Beatrice until she was standing behind the back of it, with her belly pressed rubbing against the headrest.

'Over, sweetheart,' said Sly gently, and Beatrice tipped forward on to her toes, face down over the back of the chair, gripping its seat tightly as she settled.

He's going to beat her, thought Alexa. Licking her dry lips, she breathed deeply and stared at Beatrice's bottom, trim and heart-shaped beneath her lovely antique dress.

Slowly, very decorously, Sly began to raise the hem of the shimmering beaded skirt.

Beatrice's cream-tinted stockings were rolled down halfway to her knees, and secured there with narrow, ribbon-trimmed garters. The look was authentic for a flapper, and also showed a great deal of Beatrice's slender, pearl-white thighs. Alexa's fingers tingled with a powerful urge to touch her.

As the pretty beaded skirt went higher, and Sly tucked and folded, Alexa gasped at the sight of Beatrice's lingerie. She was wearing a pair of exquisite French knickers made from mocha-coloured silk – the legs trimmed with a thick band of lighter, more silver-toned lace. The garment was so charming, so pristine, and so elegant that it came as an even greater shock to see the dark, spreading stain at Beatrice's crotch.

Alexa felt her own body responding, and her own skimpy G-string getting damper. She wanted to reach out and touch the stretched satin across Beatrice's lush bottom; to give reassurance, although of what she had no idea; to press her hand to the wet place between Beatrice's quivering legs and to make the doctor moan loudly and rub against it.

Ever the efficient one, Sly slid her fingers beneath the elastic of Beatrice's silken pants and prepared to tug, but two words from D'Aronville held her steady.

'Not yet,' he commanded, his voice as tranquil as ever.

Sly bobbed her head respectfully again, then stepped back.

'An implement, if you please, nurse,' requested D'Aronville, shrugging free of his immaculate Italian-tailored jacket.

'*Bien sûr, Monsieur le Maître,*' Sly murmured, then walked smartly across to an ornate lacquered cabinet in the corner of the room. Alexa couldn't see its contents from where she stood, but what Sly returned with made her blood run cold.

It was a thin, yellowish cane that gleamed nastily in the room's brilliant lighting. As the nurse handed it to D'Aronville, Alexa heard the low hum of voices behind her and realised a largish crowd had gathered. Poor Beatrice was to be spared no blushes . . .

By now, the self-appointed wielder of justice was in his shirtsleeves and rolling his cuffs back neatly to his elbows. Alexa marvelled at the dispassionate precision of his actions, but couldn't help glancing downwards towards his groin.

Was he aroused? she wondered.

Probably, she decided. And possibly a very great deal. Sex was the beginning, the middle and the end of what was happening here – people didn't do these things for any other reason.

When she looked up, she felt chilled and shivery. Just as she was watching D'Aronville, he was watching her, observing her observations. He nodded very slightly towards his own body, and for an instant a narrow smile curved his lips; then he looked away again and turned towards Beatrice.

'Do you require a restraint, cherie?' he asked, leaning right over her, almost kissing the nape of her neck. 'A gag, perhaps?'

'No, Monsieur le Maître,' Beatrice replied, her voice quivering with emotion. 'No, thank you,' she added, as if a lack of manners would put her deeper in jeopardy.

'Very well then, cherie. Kindly make yourself ready,' said D'Aronville gravely.

Alexa watched in fascination as Beatrice flexed her supple body and pushed her rump even higher in the air. D'Aronville took a step back, cocked his silvered head to one side, as if sighting the first blow, then let the rod rest across Beatrice's bottom. He was finding the distance, calculating the swing, and, to Alexa, the process was viscerally arousing. She wished it were her across the chair instead of Beatrice, her bottom about to be belaboured – even though she'd always been a coward about pain.

When the first stroke fell, the noises were unexpectedly loud. There was a slicing 'swish', then a horrible, solid 'crack' as the cane met Beatrice's firm cheeks. The doctor grunted, but didn't cry out, and the tensely stretched legs shook wildly.

From behind Alexa there was a quiet clamour of admiration; the audience was clearly impressed. The blow had been clean, and, even to untutored eyes, beautifully executed – and Beatrice had borne it with grace. Alexa knew that if it had been her, she would have been yelping now, sobbing her heart out, but even that didn't stop her feeling jealous. Or her quim throbbing softly with desire.

With all attention on Beatrice and her suffering bottom, Alexa wondered if she dare reach down discreetly and touch herself. Just one little rub, through her dress, and she fancied she might easily come. She felt distended, engorged, her clitoris swollen and hungering, brought to madness by the sight of a single blow of the cane. How would she feel after six? After a dozen? Or when Beatrice was inevitably ordered to bare herself? How would she feel in the good doctor's place?

After a few seconds, D'Aronville raised the cane again, cracked it down, then seemed to fall into a slow, lazy rhythm; whacking the seat of Beatrice's satin knickers with an accuracy that was supreme and unwavering. The doctor maintained her poise for about six strokes, then began to pant heavily, fighting for control. After ten blows, she was crying like a baby.

'Oh, Beatrice . . . Ma petite,' murmured D'Aronville, pausing in his labours and stepping close to the noisily weeping woman. 'How you disappoint me tonight. What has happened to your bravery? Your fortitude? The control it has cost us both so much to achieve?' He reached down, turned Beatrice's wet face towards him, and gently kissed her mouth and then both of her eyes. 'I fear we must start again, Beatrice. And more stringently.' Then, as Beatrice burst into a fresh gale of weeping, he stepped back and gestured casually towards Sly. 'Nurse. Bare her, if you please. Her bottom, and a little more thigh.'

Once again, Sly stepped forward and laid hands on her employer. Hooking her thumbs neatly into the waistband of Beatrice's knickers, the nurse skinned them quickly down to knee level, then adjusted the rolled stocking-tops to nestle against them. Beatrice was completely uncovered from the small of her back to the lower part of her thighs now, and Alexa smothered a cry of distress when she saw the furious redness that had previously been hidden.

The coffee-coloured silk had offered no protection. Beatrice's pure white buttocks were already liberally striped in an arrangement that was chillingly symmetrical. Sacha D'Aronville was clearly an artist when it came to pain.

Alexa knew her own jaw had dropped at the sight, and she was still staring open-mouthed when D'Aronville spun on his heel and pointed towards her with the cane.

'Perhaps, you would like to assist us, Alexa?' he said, his voice silkily pleasant in the way a schoolmaster might be when about to expose a poor pupil's slackness. 'Beatrice will struggle now, and try to evade the rod.

154

My blows will be all the more telling if you come here and hold her hands.' He gestured towards a spot a few inches from his victim's shaking shoulders.

Almost dreamily, Alexa moved forward and reached for Beatrice's slender white hands, where they lay, limply, on the chair seat. The doctor's skin was very warm, and her palms were sweaty, but as she looked up – from her demeaningly prone position – her tear-filled eyes were radiant.

You're loving this, aren't you? thought Alexa as her own eyes locked with Beatrice's brown ones. The doctor seemed to be silently telling her something. Trying to impart the mystery of the feeling.

But I know already! thought Alexa, flexing her power. Understanding. There was pleasure within the pain; exaltation at the heart of the debasement. How long will it be before this is me? she wondered as Beatrice's fingers tightened, and D'Aronville stepped away to arm's length.

'Are you ready, mesdames?' he enquired, setting his feet menacingly apart. Alexa got the impression that all the strokes so far had been child's play to him, and that from now on, he would be striking in earnest.

'Yes,' she said, her voice as small as Beatrice's had been.

'Yes,' said the doctor hoarsely, her hips moving slightly on the chair back, her beautifully marked bottom all aquiver.

The cane hissed down and impacted as fiercely as before. At the instant of contact, Beatrice's fingertips gouged Alexa's palms cruelly, and the doctor groaned from between tightly clenched teeth.

As the rod struck again and again, Beatrice's cries became louder and louder. She was hurting Alexa's hands with her grip now, squeezing convulsively as D'Aronville applied each livid stripe. Alexa could see a cross-hatched pattern on the other woman's bottom, vivid scarlet against purest creamy white.

'Kiss me,' gasped the doctor suddenly, and for a

moment Alexa was confused. Was Beatrice talking to her? Or Sly or D'Aronville? She hesitated, looking down into Beatrice's tight, straining face for an answer.

'Kiss me, Alexa,' she said again, then yelped as another cut fell on her bottom. 'Give me your mouth . . . Help me get through. Help me take it.'

Obediently, Alexa crouched down, aware that in her short skirt her thighs, and much more, were on show. As she leaned towards Beatrice, the doctor craned forward a little, fastening her mouth on Alexa's with near frantic hunger, her tongue plunging immediately inside.

It was the most licentious kiss Alexa had ever experienced, far more demanding and exploratory than any man's. Her mouth was pillaged, her jaw stretched and her very life-force drawn out and consumed. She felt each impact of the cane as a jerk of Beatrice's body; every time it brought a wild sense of ravishment. She was enraptured, she could hardly breathe, but just as she rallied and started kissing Beatrice back with a vengeance, the doctor whimpered and her lips slid away.

Blows of the cane were still falling, but the target area was gyrating and churning. Beatrice had gone beyond shame, it seemed, beyond pain and the tyranny of the rod. She was pounding her pelvis against the back of the chair, and circling her hips in an obscene primal rhythm. She was climaxing purely from her beating.

'And do you, too, want a taste of the rod?' enquired D'Aronville a moment later, as Alexa rose slowly to her feet and left Beatrice still jiggling and squirming and wriggling against the chair.

The Frenchman's eyes were candid and challenging, as bright and vivid as a wintry blue sky. Alexa wanted to say 'yes'. She wanted to touch herself, or touch Beatrice. Or even fall down again to kiss that crimson-streaked bottom. So much of her yearned to lie across that chair and feel the cane wreak havoc across her own

156

flesh, but still she felt a small core of fear. She hesitated;
just a moment too long . . .

'Perhaps another time?' suggested D'Aronville,
gently taunting, before he nodded to Siddig and Yusuf.
'Take her away, my friends,' he said. 'I think she has
need of your services.'

Alexa opened her mouth to protest, but already the
Frenchman had forgotten her. He'd turned away, handing his cane to Sly, and was unbuckling his thin
snakeskin belt. She felt Siddig's hand on her arm, and,
numbed, she simply went with him; aware of the stares
of those around her, yet detached from them, as if by
an impermeable membrane. The people who took time
to peer at her were nothing, just ciphers. The only ones
who mattered were Beatrice, D'Aronville and Sly. And
her companions, her two limousine lovers.

Her feet were floating, her mind still fully engaged
with visions of Beatrice's striped bottom, but she was
vaguely aware she was being led away from the assem-
bly. The 'boys' were with her, one on either side, both
escorting her and buoying her up with their strength.
Between her legs, she could feel her sex wet and
swollen, turned to yearning by the sight and sound of
pain. It was grotesque, but she couldn't deny the truth.

Turning to Siddig, she opened her mouth to ask a
question, but he shushed her with a finger on his lips.
'Soon. We'll talk . . . But I think you might prefer a
private place.'

They passed into a corridor, containing several sets
of white-painted, gold-handled double doors; without
pausing, Siddig opened the second one along.

'Here we are, Alexa,' he said cajolingly. 'We'll have
quiet in here, and all the peace you need.' Both he and
Yusuf stood back to let her enter.

The room she stepped into was like the bedroom of a
French despotic monarch. The rest of the house was
overstated, but here the luxury was almost a parody of
itself. Everywhere she looked there was gilt, mirrors,

velvet hangings and an abundance of tassels. She would have laughed if she hadn't felt so fazed.

'Is this a set-up?' she demanded of Siddig, as he closed the doors behind them. 'Don't say they always leave magnums of champagne lying around on the off chance . . .' she added, pointing to the bedside table and a bottle of wine chilling in an ice bucket.

The bed itself was immense, almost cinematic. Alexa had seen four-posters before, even slept in them, but this one was the size of a small car park, and its golden counterpane so bright it hurt her eyes.

'Ah, but they do!' exclaimed Siddig gleefully, striding across to the bottle of champagne, then flipping its cork with accomplished deftness. When he'd frothed the sparkling bubbly into a trio of slim flutes, he turned and gave Alexa an impish grin. 'People tend to want to split off into small groups at these affairs, so the bedrooms are always kept in readiness. We could have gone into any one of the rooms along this corridor, and found champagne.' He held out a twinkling flute towards her.

Alexa took it, then wandered away from him, ostensibly to study her surroundings. 'These people . . . In the small groups . . .' she began, then was caught short by her own reflection in one of the mirrors. She was pink faced and her eyes seemed twice their normal size. 'What do they do? You know; is this an orgy?'

'Oh, nothing so ordinary,' said Siddig, draining his glass, then putting it aside. As Alexa watched him warily, out of the corner of her eye, he shrugged off his pale, stylish jacket, slung it across a chair, then kicked off his Gucci loafers, too. Next, he launched himself backwards – like a naughty little boy in a school dorm – and bounced on the thickly mattressed bed.

'What then?' she persisted, turning to face him as he stretched back and folded his hands behind his head. Yusuf, she noticed, was still standing by the foot of the bed – almost to attention, it seemed – his champagne barely touched in his hand.

'There'll be some straight sex, of course,' Siddig said

airily, 'but you're more likely to find interesting variations.' He let the sentence dangle, then smiled and patted the bed beside him, 'Why don't you join me, Alexa? The bed's soft, the linen's clean and neither of us bite unless we're asked.' He nodded at Yusuf, who also nodded and grinned.

'By "interesting variations", do you mean beating people; with canes; for no proper reason?' she said, holding back and sipping at her drink in short, nervous gulps that she hardly even tasted. She'd already begun to understand what she'd seen, and why it had stirred her, but somehow the words seemed important.

'It's what she wanted, Alexa,' said Siddig, his handsome face suddenly serious. 'Probably the very reason she gave you the dress.' He paused, running his long fingers across the bright brocade cover at his side. 'The type of games D'Aronville likes to play need a structure. Some kind of formal trigger . . . It's like ritual. It needs cause and effect.'

'And do you want to beat me?' asked Alexa in a tiny voice, aware that she might be triggering a need he hadn't yet expressed.

'Only if you want it,' answered Siddig, holding out a hand towards her.

'I don't know . . . I don't know what I want.'

'Well, let's find out, shall we?' he coaxed, patting the bed again. 'Come to me, Alexa . . . Please?'

Alexa was aware that Yusuf had somehow appeared at her side, and his strong hand was pressing lightly on her back. Feeling as if she were floating again, she moved across the room towards Siddig, letting Yusuf take her glass as she reached the bed, slipped out of her shoes, and allowed Siddig to draw her down beside him.

As she shuffled sideways across the bed, following him as he made space, Alexa was aware that her gauzy skirt was rising. She was showing thighs, stocking-tops, even the bare slope of one buttock. It was nothing the two men hadn't seen before, in the car, but even so she felt nervous and embarrassed. She wished Yusuf would turn down the lights, but for some reason, she didn't dare ask. She could only watch, feeling more and more edgy, as he, too, removed his jacket and shoes and climbed on to the bed, then sat cross-legged at her feet, still and watchful.

Alexa turned again towards Siddig, and found his near-black eyes almost burning. With a slight movement, and no effort, he pressed her backwards, by her shoulders, on to the pillows.

'And so . . . our evening really begins,' he whispered almost solemnly, as his fingertips descended to her breasts.

Chapter Eleven

Duet for Three

'*B*ut . . .' Alexa protested, and was silenced by a quick, hard kiss.

'Enough already,' said Siddig, with a surprising vehemence, his mouth sliding downwards on to her throat, his white teeth nipping at the cord of her neck. She felt his hands tighten on her breasts, squeezing to a point that was almost painful. She was just about to complain, when the pressure released, and he lifted his head and looked down at her.

'You're not quite ready for pain yet, are you?' he said quietly, his dark eyes luminous.

Alexa didn't answer. She couldn't speak. She could still see D'Aronville applying his cane; see Beatrice's animal writhings; feel the heat and the rapture of their kiss.

'I don't know,' she said again, wishing she was braver, more sensual. She sensed an immense lust in both the boys now – a hunger. But they wanted 'variations', too, not the straightforward pleasures of fucking.

'No. You're not ready,' said Siddig, sitting up, shaking his head, and smiling. 'Not yet.' He glanced momentarily towards Yusuf, and, as if in answer, the taller man bent down, took one of Alexa's feet in his hands and began a slow, sensuous massage. 'We'd better leave that scene to D'Aronville. After all, he is Monsieur le Maître . . .'

'What – ' Once again, Alexa's exclamation was stifled, as Siddig covered her lips with his again, his tongue plunging instantly inside. She tried to push him off, but his slender, wiry hands held each of hers, and kept her still as he ravished her mouth. Even so, she began to struggle, and felt Yusuf extend his hold to both of her feet and apply his mouth to the arch of one instep.

What does D'Aronville want to do to me? she wondered frantically as Siddig's tongue caressed hers. The Frenchman had challenged her, it was true, so arrogantly, but it had seemed little more than an afterthought, a piquant spice to his domination of Beatrice.

I'm nothing to him, thought Alexa, probably a disappointment. Too green for him to bother with after all. She wondered briefly what Beatrice had told him about her, then squirmed again as her body seemed to light up with fresh desire. It was Siddig who was kissing her, his tongue that was nearly halfway down her throat like an exotic pleasure-giving snake; yet suddenly she imagined he was D'Aronville – kissing her with all the same savage power, yet studying her intently as he did so. His blue, blue eyes would be wide open as he tasted her, monitoring her reactions, yet remaining unmoved.

'Why would D'Aronville want me for his games?' she demanded when Siddig released her. 'He seems to have enough going with Beatrice. He's her Master or whatever, isn't he?'

'That's true,' observed Siddig, pulling her up from the bed like a rag doll, and reaching for the back of her dress, 'But he wants you, too. I thought you knew that. Beatrice owes him a favour. A big favour. Which is the very reason she got you here.' He found what he was seeking, and suddenly the minimal dress was loosening. He'd unfastened the button at the nape of her neck and now the tiny zip was sliding undone, too. 'It's time you were naked,' he continued, matter-of-factly, peeling the entire front of her frock from her body.

Alexa was almost too preoccupied to realise her breasts were uncovered. "But D'Aronville doesn't want me just because she told him about me? That's ridiculous.' Without thinking, she lifted her bottom, and let Siddig slide the dress down over her hips. Yusuf took it when it reached her ankles and laid it neatly over the footboard of the bed.

'Siddig! Answer me!' she cried, folding her arms across her breasts, and having them unfolded, immediately, by Siddig. 'How much does D'Aronville know about me? Why on earth would he want me so much?'

The two men exchanged glances, and suddenly a grotesque truth dawned on Alexa. Siddig's soft voice supplied only supplied confirmation.

'He's seen photographs of you,' he said, already reaching out for her breasts.

Oh no! Oh no, no, no!

Alexa thought of what she'd done in Loosie's studio . . . Her own insane lewdness . . . She'd been masked throughout the whole shoot, but what did that mean, when the photographer was quite happy to reveal your identity?

It was Loosie's fault. It was Beatrice's fault. They were in it together . . . As were these two handsome men who were now ogling and touching her body. It was a conspiracy to procure her for some jaded French deviant. It was their fault, but it was also her own. For wanting it – or something like it – to happen.

'But they were only taken yesterday,' she quibbled, watching her own nipples swelling beneath Siddig's experienced touch.

'There are such things as couriers, remember?' he answered, tweaking her. 'And Loosie develops all her own stuff.' He pulled her nipple, drawing her breast out like a cone and making her writhe. 'D'Aronville was looking at images of your naked masturbating body less

163

than three hours after they were taken.' Alexa closed her eyes in shame, then turned away. 'And we saw them very shortly afterwards.'

'But why?' she said, her voice tight. Siddig was playing with both breasts now, tormenting them with strokes and tiny pinches, rousing her to a state of sensual madness, and making the flesh between her thighs ache with need.

'Because you're beautiful,' said Yusuf, joining the conversation while his hands smoothed her ankles.

'That's true,' murmured Siddig, bending down to touch his tongue-tip to her left nipple, then licking it slowly and moistly. 'And he's a connoisseur of beauty. Just think of Beatrice. And Sly. And Loosie . . . He's had them all. Don't you think that you're in good company?'

'No! Yes! I don't know,' wailed Alexa, as Siddig suckled strongly, moulding her free breast with his narrow brown hand. She sensed Yusuf moving on the bed, then she panicked and stiffened. Her legs were being lifted clear of the cover, and gently bent, then her bottom and hips were raised up, too. She felt Yusuf's soft lips start roving across her, kissing her thighs and the skin behind her knees.

Alexa jerked, terrified of her own precarious position as the two men murmured and calmed her. As she stilled, she felt a fresh, hot flood of embarrassment. Yusuf now had a clear sight of her raised and naked buttocks; he could seen her anus in its deeply shaded furrow and the rude sight of her G-string's narrow thong.

She felt worse, far worse, when Siddig abandoned his efforts at her bosom, and sat back on his haunches beside his friend. Both men now each took an ankle, and hauled her up so they could get a better view.

'He'll be having Beatrice now,' said Siddig, almost wistfully.

For a moment, Alexa had almost forgotten who he was talking about, then to her horror she remembered

D'Aronville, and imagined him here in the room with them, too, his blue eyes staring coldly at her buttocks.

'He'll have her here first.' A finger worked its way slyly beneath her G-string and wiggled into the portal of her vagina. 'Then he'll have her here.' The finger was withdrawn, and then – moistened by her juices – inserted into the portal of her anus.

Alexa groaned, feeling the same powerlessness as she had in the car. The digit in her bottom seemed to weaken her, subdue her. She could have hit out with her hands, tried to knock the men away from her, but she felt shackled by fear and dark delight. She could feel her fluid welling, running down towards the impaling finger, soaking the tiny patch of cloth between her legs. As the finger crooked, she whimpered and moved her hips a little, as if controlled by the intrusion in her rear.

'Ah yes, you like it,' said Siddig, his breath wafting warmly across her bottom cheeks. 'Just as Beatrice does.' He kissed one taut globe, then rubbed his chin across her sopping cotton-clad mound. 'She'll be shouting now. Howling with bliss while Monsieur le Maître buggers her with her friends looking on.' His face withdrew, but his voice – and his finger – lingered on. 'She loves that . . . Loves being humbled. And being watched. He'll be pounding her. Crashing against the stripes from his cane and the weals from his belt. She'll be beside herself, almost wetting herself with pleasure and pain.'

'Oh please,' moaned Alexa, almost beside herself. The finger inside her, and the husky voice of Siddig made her crave . . . crave something she knew not quite what. She wanted pleasure, and she wanted orgasms. She wanted more of the strange, almost drug-induced weakness she was feeling . . . Surrender. Possession. Subjugation. She tried to imagine wanting pain, then saw Sacha D'Aronville's impassive face, and heard his voice forbidding it. For the moment . . .

'Please,' she reiterated vaguely, almost dancing on

the obstruction inside her. Her pelvis was swaying, but Siddig moved with her, his finger in her tight, forbidden channel.

'Do you want us?' he purred, pressing his mouth against her calf. 'Do you want us here?' He jogged his finger.

'Oh yes! Oh God! Please; do it!' she pleaded, as hot shivers racked her running sex.

'Then you shall have us.' He nipped the soft skin at the back of her knee, and slowly, very slowly, withdrew his teasing finger from her body. 'Won't she, Yus?'

'Oh yes,' affirmed Yusuf succinctly, rubbing the ball of her ankle with the pad of his thumb, while between them they lowered her to the bed.

When she was lying flat, her chest heaving with frustration, Yusuf took his turn to kiss her, taunting her mouth with soft, darting nibbles while Siddig removed her saturated G-string. Alexa heard him sigh, and when Yusuf stopped kissing her and knelt back, she saw that Siddig had the tiny, triangular piece of cotton pressed rapturously to his nose and mouth.

'Divine,' he whispered, then placed it almost reverently with her dress. 'And now us . . .' he went on, his eyes sparkling as his fingers flickered up the inside of her leg.

What have I done? What have I done? thought Alexa as she lay in a motionless frenzy of lust. Two beautiful men were stripping their clothes off before her, preparing for an indecent act of sex. They'd displayed her and fondled her, and whilst she'd wriggled on Siddig's long finger, she'd shamelessly begged him to bugger her. She'd begged like a shameless slut for something she'd always feared but half longed for – the feel of a man's penis in her bottom. She thought of what she'd heard in Circe, what her mind had instantly interpreted it as. A woman thrown forward; her husband shafting her obscenely; the woman climaxing.

Beginning to move uneasily, Alexa let the inner picture change. She saw Beatrice, draped across a chair in the crowded salon, her lividly caned bottom impaled on D'Aronville's stiff cock. Her legs would be flailing uncontrollably, she'd be sobbing and biting the upholstery, but her vulva would be fluttering with pleasure.

The soft jingle of a belt buckle brought Alexa back from her fantasy. Siddig and Yusuf had shed their socks, shoes and shirts, and were now both stepping from their trousers. Both men had smooth, brown, superbly toned bodies, and while Yusuf's was long and lean like a sprinter's, Siddig's was more muscular and compact. Each of them wore an ivory silk thong.

Expecting these to be whipped off flamboyantly, Alexa watched, rapt, as Siddig turned away from Yusuf. In response, the taller man leaned forward, undid the knotted cord that fastened in the small of his companion's brown back, and then – as the ties fell away – he reached around and cupped Siddig's genitals through the silk. A wanton, almost beatific expression passed across Siddig's handsome face, and he pushed his crotch into Yusuf's cradling hand.

Of course, they're bisexual, too, aren't they? thought Alexa as Yusuf withdrew his fingers and with them came the tiny white covering. Siddig's dark, circumcised cock was as well-formed as the rest of him, and pointed upwards from his groin when revealed.

The idea of the two men making love together was too fascinating to resist. Yusuf was allowing Siddig to unveil him now, but in Alexa's mind they were already several steps ahead. She saw them caressing, kissing each other's body, then finally rearranging themselves. Yusuf – the quieter, more deferential one – would bend over, reach around and spread himself, then surrender his arse willingly to his friend.

They do! Of course they do! They're lovers! Her erotic sense had been almost overloaded tonight; too many messages around her, and all of them strong. But now, here, in this quiet luxurious room, one signal had become blindingly clear.

Although Siddig and Yusuf both wanted her, they

were both equally hot for each other. What would they say if she asked them to show her what they shared?

But before she could speak, both Siddig and Yusuf were on the bed with her, their meaty cocks bouncing within her reach. It seemed the most natural thing in the world to stretch out and touch them, and first one, then the other moaned softly.

'Mmmm . . . That's good,' murmured Siddig, his hips wafting to push himself towards her. 'Are you still hungry for us?' he asked, folding his hand around hers, and with his free hand, angling her face towards his. 'No doubts? No second thoughts?' He was asking if she still dare do what she'd begged for.

'None,' she said, twisting her face to kiss his hand. 'I want you. I want you in my . . .' She felt blood pour into her face, more embarrassed by the word than the deed.

'Your *joli petit cul*?' he supplied, softening the impact by lapsing into French, but making Alexa shudder at the thought of D'Aronville. As the rest of her body blushed, she nodded.

'Well, we know a nice way, don't we, Yus?' he said, nodding to his friend, then lifting her hand from his cock to his lips. 'A gentle way . . .' He kissed her fingers lingeringly, as if sampling his own taste, then slid backwards and sat up against the bed-head. Reaching around, he stacked pillows behind his back, and when he seemed satisfied with that, he spread his legs and settled his bottom.

What am I supposed to do? thought Alexa, staring helplessly at his thick jutting cock. Just climb aboard?

As she hesitated, Siddig turned to one side, opened a drawer in the bedside cabinet, then reached in and fished something out.

It was a small oval-shaped container of some kind, that had the flat, black gleam of onyx. Siddig lifted the lid, and immediately there was a strong, but quite pleasant smell of herbs.

'Something to ease the path,' he said, then dipped

his fingers into the pot and smeared some of its contents on his cock. The ointment, or whatever it was, had no colour but made his dark flesh shine invitingly. Delving in once again, he coated himself thoroughly, then passed the black container to Yusuf. 'And now some for the lady,' he said, as his friend took the jar.

'Kneel over, sweetheart,' said Yusuf quietly, laying a hand on Alexa's shoulders, 'Put your bottom up. Let's make you nice and greasy.'

Oh God, I can't do this! thought Alexa, but nevertheless she went forward and lifted up her rump. It seemed impossible that she could let herself obey so easily, that she could display herself, but then again she'd done such things for Loosie, hadn't she? And the camera had only magnified the shamefulness of it all.

She almost cried, several times, as Yusuf slowly and methodically packed her bottom with the soft, scented cream. There was a mad churning in her bowel – a forbidden, dirty delightfulness. It made her bite into the shining golden counterpane, and almost gnawed through it, as Yusuf's fingers slid repeatedly inside her.

'There. You're ready,' he said as he finished, then dipped down to press a kiss to her back.

'Now . . . We all have to work together to make this happen,' said Siddig a little hoarsely, and as Alexa straightened up, she realised he was masturbating. His penis, poking through his fingers, looked larger than before, and Alexa felt fearful as she imagined it inside her.

'Don't be frightened,' Yusuf said, his face against the back of her neck. 'Relax. Allow us to pleasure you.' He kissed her shoulder, reassuringly. 'Turn around now, Alexa. Go loose, and leave everything to us.'

Intrigued in spite of her anxiety, Alexa swivelled round, hitched backwards, then felt Siddig take a strong, but gentle grip on her ribcage, just beneath her arms. 'Relax. Go with it,' urged Yusuf, straightening her legs, and taking a similar hold on her thighs. Then, at a silent signal, the two men lifted her effortlessly between them, supporting her body with just their powerful brown arms.

Suspended over Siddig's body, Alexa felt his cock brush her bottom. 'Reach down now, Alexa,' she heard him say. 'Reach down and hold yourself open. If you're stretched, I'll slip in more easily.'

Reaching down with both hands, feeling his gripping hands beneath her arms, Alexa gingerly cupped her own buttocks. The act of holding open her own slippery bottom cheeks was exquisitely demeaning, but as her anus met Siddig's rampant member, she cried out more in welcome than fear.

'Yes!' he hissed.

'Oh God, yes!' she gasped, as very slowly they let her descend.

Penetration was incredible. A maelstrom of sensation coursing through the nerves of her bottom, her sex, and her belly. She felt a hideous urge to defecate, that made her squirm and heave her hips, but her two lovers held on tight. They continued to lower her imperturbably on to Siddig's rigid penis, both murmuring encouragements and endearments as she fretted.

After a few seconds that seemed endless, the bad feelings faded and were replaced by a new one. It was pleasure, but it was maverick and dangerous. She was possessed, invaded, violated in the most primal of ways. She had a man's penis pushed deep inside her bottom, a baton of flesh that opened and stretched her; she wanted to weep, abase herself, praise her abuser, then make herself more abused than ever to please him.

Even as she felt the emotion, she knew she'd never be able to explain it. Yet she loved it. She sighed and purred as they let her settle down, and her buttocks pressed against Siddig's lower belly.

'Are you comfortable?' he asked, his voice tinged with irony as both he and Yusuf released their hold on her.

'Comfortable' wasn't the word Alexa would have

chosen to describe the feeling, and it was plain that Siddig knew that.

'I . . . I don't know,' she answered, then whimpered as his hips swirled and his penis jumped rudely inside her. 'I've never felt like this.'

'Is this the first time you've had a man in your arse?' His hands curved around her, and cupped her breasts almost negligently, but Alexa sensed his surge of excitement. She'd given him a virginity of sorts and it thrilled him. He and Yusuf were women's sex objects, but deep down, she realised, they still retained typical male attitudes. Such as the overweening desire to be the 'the first' . . . Alexa would have liked to debate the point – with one or both of them – but with Siddig's thick penis in her rectum it was difficult to marshal her arguments. Especially when he was squeezing her breasts in slow, heavy rhythm.

Beginning to pant, and feeling her empty vagina fill with fluid, Alexa hardly knew what to do with her hands. She was fully supported on Siddig, her back against his chest, her bottom cradled by his loins, and her legs stretched out on top of his. She didn't need to steady herself because she was perfectly balanced on his body and anchored securely by his cock. In addition, she had Yusuf's hands holding her ankles.

'Am I the first?' demanded Siddig, punctuating the question with a jerk of his hips.

Alexa cried out, her legs kicking ineffectually against Yusuf's grip, then whispered 'yes' as waves of heat boiled in her quim.

'Lovely girl,' crooned Siddig, moving her breasts in slow, powerful circles, that stopped just short of hurting her. Without thinking, Alexa moaned and grabbed her crotch, her fingers digging blindly for her clitoris.

'No need for that, my sweet,' said Yusuf, prising the hand away, then licking it clean of her wetness. 'Allow me,' he continued, giving each of her fingers a suck, then releasing them as he changed position.

Alexa watched, her pussy on fire, while he lay face

down on the bed between her legs, then scooted himself purposefully forward. Within seconds he was licking her sex.

'Oh God!' she cried, finding a use for her hands at last. Digging her fingers into Yusuf's shiny black hair she tried to pull his face closer to her body . . . even though his mouth was now jammed against her vulva and his long tongue was stabbing at her clitoris.

Orgasm came quickly, and as her sex contracted and convulsed, she was aware – in a dim, dreamy way – that she wasn't the only one groaning and squirming.

As her innards spasmed, her sphincter was squeezing Siddig's penis – and he too was being pushed far too far. He cried out harshly, something incomprehensible, in his own language. She heard the word 'Allah' and a stream of fevered exclamations, then his voice degenerated into deep, almost agonised groans and his flesh leaped tellingly inside her.

Feeling Siddig's climax seemed to push her own pleasure higher. Alexa began to fly again, her clitoris swelling and pulsing against Yusuf's industrious tongue.

'Oh God,' she cried, calling on her own deity just as Siddig had called on his. The sensations were too sublime, too rich and too strong, and though she wanted to stay with them, and reach yet another new height, she felt herself fade and black out. Her mind sank gratefully into a warm, dark well, and her body seemed to melt, then follow it.

When she came to, she was empty again, and Siddig's penis was resting against her bottom. The two men had shifted her on to her side, and she was lying between them like the filling of a sandwich, facing Yusuf and with her back towards Siddig. She could feel Siddig's face nuzzled in against her shoulder, and from the evenness of his breathing, she deduced he was dozing. Yusuf, however, was awake.

'How do you feel?' he asked, raising a hand to her sweaty forehead, and fluffing the curls that were stick-

172

ing to her skin. 'Did my brother hurt you?' He reached around and feathered a finger across her anus.

'No . . . No, I don't think so,' she whispered, feeling the ghost of possession in his touch. She wiggled her hips without thinking, and then stopped, and went quite still as her brain suddenly slipped into gear.

'Are you and Siddig brothers?' she asked, remembering the passion she'd sensed flowing between them.

Yusuf laughed and cupped the cheek of her bottom. 'Not brothers in the literal sense, just kinsmen,' he said smilingly. 'We're of the same house. The same blood.' He paused, and she felt his hand move behind her, to brush against Siddig's quiescent prick. 'We're far closer than brothers could ever be,' he finished significantly, then pressed forward, almost squashing her, and massaged his own, fully hard penis against the sweat-streaked curve of her belly.

Alexa's eyes flew open, trying to absorb the facts. Siddig and Yusuf were homosexual lovers, as she'd suspected, and Yusuf was now intensely aroused. So, was it actually her he wanted? Or the 'brother' drowsing against her back? Or – and after what'd just happened, this was a distinct possibility – was it a duet for three he desired? A decadent tangle of lips and hands and sexes . . .

'Do you make love with Siddig sometimes?' she asked in a small voice, reaching down to caress his butting cock.

'Yes, he does,' said a husky voice in her ear, and she felt a kiss against the back of her neck while another, stronger hand closed tightly over hers and intensified its grip upon Yusuf. 'Would you like to see what we do?'

Alexa couldn't speak her answer, she wanted what he was offering too much. The idea of watching these two beautiful men making love was the most delectable, irresistible temptation. She nodded. She could no sooner say 'no' than stop breathing.

'You'll have to give us some space then, my darling,'

said Siddig, giving her bottom a playful little smack as Yusuf peeled away from her front.

As the taller man went back into a kneel, then slid elegantly from the bed, his long red penis bounced and swayed. It looked fierce. Aggressive. Dominant. And Alexa suddenly realised something intriguing.

Although Siddig was the natural initiator in this partnership, it seemed he didn't always take the lead. Both literally and figuratively, he was about to roll over for his 'brother'.

Sensing Siddig on the move behind her, Alexa sat up, then rolled herself to one side out of the way. As she did so, Yusuf took a thick angora blanket out of the ottoman at the foot of the bed and draped it round her shoulders, before climbing past her and turning his attention towards Siddig.

A strange metamorphosis seemed to have taken place in Siddig. He seemed less forceful, less confident, more yielding. In the blink of an eye he'd become loose-limbed and compliant; almost melodramatically femi-nine. He was pouting quite coquettishly at Yusuf. And when the taller man lunged determinedly towards him, he whimpered and fell back against the pillows, surren-dering to his brutal, punishing kiss.

Beneath the blanket, Alexa's body came alive again. She'd thought that her appetites were thoroughly sated, but as she watched Siddig capitulating completely, and letting his mouth be raped and his body roughly fon-dled, she felt her own sex begin to burn again.

'Whore!' growled Yusuf, his hand closing cruelly on Siddig's rousing genitals and squeezing until the other man squealed.

It wasn't at all what Alexa had expected, but the sight of it made her long to take poor Siddig's place. He was sobbing now, and as Yusuf's other hand had gone around behind his bottom, she assumed he was being molested there, too. His muscular brown legs were kicking and waving, yet he clung to his tormentor like a houri.

Yusuf was talking again now, and looking down into Siddig's tearful eyes. The words were all in their own language, but the intent and the body language were clear. Siddig was being castigated, and physically demeaned, for being 'easy', promiscuous, and the masculine equivalent of a splay-legged, over-responsive trollop.

In between his moans and groans, Siddig himself was replying. He seemed to be begging forgiveness, promising to make restitution, and offering his body in the very way he was being taken to task for. It was all a psycho-drama, impossibly theatrical and ridiculously contrived, but Alexa felt her vulva start to drip. It was as exciting as watching D'Aronville cane Beatrice.

For a second, as she thought of the untouchable Frenchman, Alexa shuddered. It was almost as if he'd walked into the room and stood beside her. She looked around, half expecting to see him, but after a heartbeat, she told herself she was stupid, and returned her attention to the men on the bed.

As she watched, open-mouthed, Yusuf virtually dropped Siddig back down on to the counterpane, then, with a negligent shove against his hip, tipped him over from his back on to his front. Siddig shimmied slightly, as if specifically drawing attention to the perfection of his buttocks, and offering ecstasy in the dark groove between them.

Yusuf slapped his partner on the thigh. Very hard. Then let his hand soften into the tenderest of caresses.

He loves him, really, thought Alexa, sliding her fingertips between her thighs in search of the tiny throbbing trigger of her clitoris.

Applying a cruel pinch to Siddig's left buttock, Yusuf reached over, grabbed a couple of the pillows, then pushed them towards his hapless victim.

'Beneath your hips, slut,' he said curtly. 'I want to get into you as deeply as I can.'

Alexa shuddered, remembering what it had felt like with Siddig inside her bottom. His penis was large, but

Yusuf's, if anything, was longer. And thicker. It would feel like a cudgel. A thick, unbending club.

Mounding the pillows into position, Siddig moaned and rubbed his pelvis against them.

As Yusuf moved menacingly over him, Alexa reached for the tub of lubricant and held it out. Yusuf shook his head and waved the stuff away. Alexa knew her horror must have shown on her face, because suddenly he dropped right out of his character, and smiled.

'He likes it better this way,' he mimed, his voice silent, but his brown eyes filled with feeling.

So it's still Siddig that's in control, thought Alexa wonderingly, as she watched Yusuf spit on his fingers then smear first himself, then his partner's anus with saliva. The game was harsh because Siddig liked it harsh. It was nothing at all to do with Yusuf's wishes. He was only giving Siddig exactly what he wanted, and when he used his thumbs to pry open the bottom of the man beneath him, it was an act of love, not one of desecration.

Even so, Siddig howled when he was penetrated. Yusuf pressed into him, wiggling the tip of his cock to get a purchase, then slammed forward in an unrelenting rush, using his grip on his companion's hips to give him leverage.

As Yusuf rose and fell, rose and fell, it was clear that Siddig was in heaven. His cries were goads of encouragement, not shrieks of pain or fear, and his expression was one of total, soaring bliss. His delight was so intense, so all-consuming that it seemed to wash through Alexa's body too. She felt it like a brilliant, blinding glow in her fingers and her toes, and a soft, electric pulse-beat in her sex.

Climax claimed her again, so quick and sweet that she could hardly breathe, and for a second she felt her mind black out again. Gasping, she put out her free hand, scrabbling and searching, and found Siddig's hand where he was gouging at the bedclothes. Their fingers clasped, then laced and squeezed in silent unity

. . . just as Yusuf threw his head back and roared with joy.

'Remarkable, truly remarkable. Your young friend is insatiable, Bea. A fresh body, yet so very keen to sin.'

Beatrice looked up from between Sacha's thighs, surprised by the huskiness in his voice. Releasing the head of his cock, she smiled and then kissed it messily. It was good to know her latest plan was working, and that something, or more pertinently, somebody, had broken through her lover's cool façade.

Glancing towards the large television screen, Beatrice saw a pin sharp image of Alexa Lavelle. The young woman's body was half swathed in a blanket, but fortunately the uncovered half contained a clear view of her crotch. She was masturbating savagely, and her bare legs were jerking and scissoring, yet somehow she and Siddig were still managing to hold each other's hands. Ah, bless, she thought, then resumed her pleasant task.

'You chose well, cherie,' said Sacha presently, his tone more normal as he pushed her head aside, then substituted his own hand on his cock for her mouth. Beatrice had been sucking him intermittently while they'd watched Loosie's latest video masterpiece, but more out of habit than in an effort to make him come. The tape was the thing he found most interesting tonight, and he'd insisted that Loosie edit it, right here in his bedroom, less than an hour after the damn thing had been shot. Alexa and the boys were probably only just into their taxi when the very first splice had been performed.

'I wonder if she realised this was your bedroom?' mused Beatrice, moving in to caress her French lover's testicles, while he in turn fondled his own cock. 'She might not have been so keen if she'd realised . . .'

'You think she dislikes me?' demanded Sacha, his free hand winding into Beatrice's long red hair and forcing her to lift up her face.

'Perhaps,' answered Beatrice, conquered – as ever – by the sheer blueness of Sacha's piercing eyes. 'She probably hates us all. She's not stupid. She must realise that I'm procuring her for your use.'

'Am I to be denied by your ineptitude?' Sacha enquired, the stern words belied by his slight, indulgent smile. Beatrice groaned as he abandoned his cock and reached down to cup her naked and still-blazing bottom. His long patrician fingers dug deep into her right buttock, making the pain flare, and her quim ran so much it dripped right down her leg.

'I should beat you again,' he growled, tipping her back amongst the sheets, his grip on her backside still vicelike. 'But I have need of you.' In a quick, deft move, so typical of him, he slotted his penis inside her and pushed forward, grinding his hips so her raw bottom grazed the mattress.

Beatrice mewed like a cat, her spirit rising on a luscious crest of agony. The pain from her caning, and the lashing with Sacha's thin belt that had followed it, seemed to blend with her profound sexual hunger. Her vulva rippled in an instant, blinding orgasm. As she throbbed, flailing her legs and clawing her lover's back, she could feel him still moving his body intently, crushing her buttocks against the bed to fire her pain.

And she could hear his voice, too, cool and even as ever, mouthing fabulous threats to raise the level of her pleasure.

'You're going to suffer in France, you know,' he murmured as he pounded deep inside her. 'I'm going to keep you naked in chains. Have you service every man on the estate. I'm going to tie you to a tree in the garden with your legs spread wide open for everyone to see. You'll be stretched and gagged. I'll invite all my friends on the Côte d'Azur in to finger you and fuck you. They'll be able to do anything they want. Anything . . . And you won't be able to do a single thing about it.'

After that, he spoke no more, because Beatrice was kissing him as she came and came and came.

Chapter Twelve

Deeper and Deeper

'Where the devil has all our money gone?'

Alexa hadn't had the faintest idea how to answer that question, and she didn't think Tom would have believed her if she'd tried.

Idiot! Idiot! Idiot! she told herself. You knew damn well he could get round any password. How long did you think you could get away with it?

When Alexa had let herself into the flat, in the early hours, her fiancé's presence had brought her down to earth with a bump. Especially as he'd obviously discovered a few things.

Well, at least he didn't ask me where I'd been until three in the morning, she thought now, next day, as she sipped her coffee and nursed a slight headache. Being furiously pissed off about the missing cash, Tom seemed to have let that one slip by, and Alexa had used his anger as an excuse to race straight to the bathroom. Thank God she'd had her shawl wrapped around her.

When she'd returned to the bedroom – in a prim nightgown and with the smells of sex, male sweat and men's cologne washed off her – the room had been dark, and Tom had been curled up under the covers, his back turned stonily towards her.

'We'll discuss this in the morning,' he'd growled when she'd rocked the bed slightly climbing into it. For that, Alexa had been – and still was – profoundly grateful, and strangely enough, had then gone straight to sleep.

And she'd slept and slept and slept. She'd been completely unable to respond to the alarm and had just groaned and burrowed further beneath the covers when it had sounded.

'You're going to have to face me sometime,' she muttered, mimicking Tom's dour pronouncement when he'd left for the office on his own, without even trying to get her up.

'But what if I don't want to,' she answered herself, reaching for the coffee pot, and topping up her mug. She was still in her dressing gown, and Tom was now long gone, but somehow nothing real or mundane could seem to touch her.

I wish I could just run away, she thought, and leave this whole muddle behind. I could hop it to Barbados, it'd be easy. I could get a job there and never come back . . . Beatrice might come out again, too. And Drew. I could do a bit of programming or something at one of the hotels. Then at night, we could all –

Alexa, what the bloody hell's the matter with you? she thought wildly, sitting up with a jerk and nearly spilling her coffee down her robe. She'd sat down to try and think her way through the 'money' problem, not the 'sex' problem – and here she was fantasising again.

Wriggling in her seat, she reached down between her bottom cheeks and touched herself through her robe, trying to discern whether she felt any different down there. Whether there was evidence of what had happened last night.

You let a man you've never met before bugger you, she accused herself grimly.

Let? What was she talking about 'let' for? She encouraged him! She'd begged him! And while he'd done it, his best friend had licked her clitoris.

It had been depraved. Indecent. Against the law, for God's sake! But given half the chance she knew she'd do it again.

What is the matter with me? she thought again, feeling her body begin to rouse beneath her dressing gown. It was like being on a grand slalom. A log flume. A runaway train without brakes. Her race towards degeneracy was getting faster and faster, and she no longer felt any inclination to slow down.

You love it, don't you? she demanded. Being with Siddig and Yusuf had been beautiful. A delicious and strangely enriching experiment. And if it hadn't been them, it would have been someone else. Beatrice? Sly? The tempting, treacherous Loosie? Or perhaps even Sacha D'Aronville? Even now, she could still see those unflinchingly blue eyes, and imagine herself being caressed by – or punished at – his hands.

I'm meant for him anyway, aren't I? she thought, lining up the ever-increasing evidence. Beatrice had said as much, back at her surgery, and the commissioning of the photographs confirmed it. Loosie Quine hadn't been waiting for another model at all the other day. Alexa realised now that she herself had been the intended subject from the start. Loosie had been employed to photograph her in compromising poses, no doubt for an exorbitant fee.

'I'm just fresh meat . . . A new conquest,' said Alexa, swirling her fast-cooling coffee. 'I should be angry. Why aren't I?'

It was peculiar. She should have been furious all along. Protested vehemently when Beatrice had even begun hinting. Yet she'd let herself be used and manipulated from the very first moment. And felt a certain safety in the heart of the peril. A relief; as if some great burden of decision-making had been lifted from her shoulders. Maybe life was easier when you were caught in a log flume?

Looking down at her dressing gown, Alexa grimaced, then stood up with purpose. There was a lot to do in the real world today. Lots of decisions and chores. And placating Tom was at the top of the list.

But, just as she was about to take her shower, Alexa heard the trill of the phone. Winding herself in a towel, and sighing resignedly, she prepared for her fiancé's recriminations. It could only be him, ringing from work, saying it was about time she got herself in there . . .

'And how are you this morning?' enquired a familiar female voice when Alexa answered the call. 'Not too fagged out, I hope? I did tell the boys to go easy, but they often get carried away.'

'Beatrice!'

'Who else?' The doctor chuckled softly. 'Well, did they wear you out?'

'No! Of course, not. And ne–'

'Then why are you at home? Obviously something made you oversleep. I phoned your office and an extremely rude and grumpy-sounding man said you weren't well and hadn't come in today.'

'That'll be Tom. He came home unexpectedly. And what with me rolling in at three in the morning . . .' She paused, wishing she could slide along the phone wire and commit murder when Beatrice went 'tsk tsk'. '. . . and then him finding out how much of our money I've spent. Well, I'm not his most favourite person at the moment.'

'He sounds like a miserable tight-arse to me,' observed Beatrice pithily. 'Why don't we do lunch and you can tell me all about it?'

'Yes, I think we'd better,' replied Alexa, trying to get a grip on the conversation. 'I've a few things that I want to discuss with you, Beatrice.'

'Uh-oh, that sounds ominous,' said the doctor blithely. 'But I probably deserve everything that's coming to me. Why don't we say Selene's Kitchen at one? My treat.'

'I should think so! I'm flat broke, as I'm sure you

realise. It is partly your fault.' It was an exaggeration really, but it seemed important to try and assert herself a little. To try and steer in the stream.

'Oh, I shouldn't worry about money, Alexa,' replied Beatrice mysteriously. 'I think I may be able to help you in that department. Ta ta, I'll see you at one!'

'Beatrice! Beatrice! What do you mean?' Alexa demanded of the receiver, but it was too late. The good doctor had already rung off.

Selene's Kitchen was the sort of exclusive, overpriced restaurant that Alexa would never have chosen for herself. Not even now, when she seemed to have as little control over her spending as she did over her sexual appetites. Despite its rustic name, the Kitchen was quietly and discreetly luxurious, and filled with people whose lifestyle was probably the same. Even in one of her better suits, Alexa felt like a hobo who'd wondered in off the street; and the fact that Beatrice was late didn't help matters either. Happily, the head waiter was welcoming.

'Ah yes,' he murmured, beaming at Alexa as if she were a regular patron. 'Miss Lavelle, Doctor Quine's guest. Please come this way. I've selected a particularly nice table for you.'

Alexa felt like saying that all the tables looked the same, and as long as it had four legs and a top it'd be OK, but she restrained herself and smiled sweetly. When she was settled – at a table that really was well-situated, set in a booth in an open conservatory – she resisted alcohol and asked for a Perrier, knowing that for this lunch a clear head was essential.

As she studied the menu, Alexa suddenly had the feeling she was being watched. Looking up as unobtrusively as she could, she realised that she was indeed being studied; by several people, most of them men. A little flustered, she returned her attention to the menu, then looked up again a minute or two later. The people who'd been watching her before were eating now, but one or two other people were now looking instead.

So look! she told them silently. Take a good look! I hope you like what you see . . . I do! Feeling bolder, she smiled brilliantly at the nearest watching male.

'That's the spirit!' a voice beside her encouraged, and when Alexa looked round, she found Beatrice standing just a couple of feet away, her brandy-coloured eyes full of fun. 'Acting aloof is a waste of time, I find,' said the doctor airily, sliding around the banquette and settling next to Alexa, 'You never know . . . You could be snubbing someone totally delicious. I always like to keep my options open.' With considerable *élan*, she signalled for the waiter, but as she did, Alexa became aware of a slight uneasiness in her companion's posture, as if sitting wasn't quite as pleasant as it should be.

'So I've noticed,' observed Alexa.

And there was no need to worry about being stared at any more because Beatrice Quine was now the centre of attention.

Far from dressing like a responsible physician lunching with a patient, Beatrice seemed to have got herself up as a Victorian cricketer today; complete with blazer, cream flannels and V-necked cable-knit slip-over. The blazer was edged with a maroon satin binding, and she had a thin, silky scarf in the same rich colour wound into her hair in a complicated chignon.

'Don't judge me, Alexa,' said the doctor gently. 'I have appetites, and I feed them.' She smiled and her eyes narrowed. 'And what's more, my dear, you seem to be taking to the life quite well yourself these days. I didn't see either Siddig and Yusuf, or Loosie having to force you into anything . . . Or even Drew for that matter, back in Barbados. You're as natural a libertine as I am!'

'Oh, I think I've got a fair way to go before I catch you up, Beatrice,' Alexa answered quickly, alarmed, as ever, at how much the doctor knew about everything, yet still feeling the urge to smile. Beatrice was a profligate and a schemer, and a disgrace to her chosen profession, but for all that she was wickedly likeable.

'You're probably right there,' Beatrice replied, reaching out to touch Alexa's hand. 'Shall we have a drink?'

'I'm all right . . . I've got one,' said Alexa feeling her resolve waver. Beatrice's touch was so warm and gentle, and her smile so beguiling, that denying her anything was well nigh impossible.

'Rubbish! I mean a real drink!'

With impeccable timing, the waiter arrived immediately, and Beatrice ordered a magnum of champagne without listening to Alexa's repeated protests.

'Shouldn't you be seeing patients or something?' Alexa queried while they waited for the wine to be brought. 'I can't see how you have such a successful practice, if you're always . . .' How to put it? 'If you're always busy doing other things.'

'Don't worry, child, I do all right,' said Beatrice, sitting back on the banquette – rather gingerly, Alexa noticed – and regarding her intently. 'It's your finances we've got to worry about today. Why don't you tell me the whole sordid story?'

With some trepidation, Alexa outlined the background to her 'other' problem – the one she'd only touched upon so far. When the champagne arrived, it quickly became quite easy to describe the purloining of joint funds for the Barbados trip, the wild expenditure on clothes and lingerie, and the consequent computerised book-cooking.

'You're losing me now,' said Beatrice when, without thinking, Alexa started to describe how she'd been able to make the accounting software tell lies. 'But I get the general picture.' She drained her glass, then topped up both hers and Alexa's again. 'You've got to get rather a large amount of money from somewhere . . . Soon. Or both you and your fiancé will be bankrupt.'

'Er . . . yes. That's about the size of it,' answered

Alexa, taking a deep swallow of champagne. 'I'm up shit creek, I'm afraid to say.'

'I can help you, you know,' said Beatrice, letting her long lashes flash down, then up, for emphasis. 'I know someone who'd be prepared to invest a very considerable sum in you.'

'I know you do,' replied Alexa, feeling dizzy – not from the champagne, but from a huge dark wave of voluptuousness that seemed to flow out of Beatrice in her direction. They were talking about something powerful and forbidden. Money for sex. A selling of the body. But at the highest and most refined of levels.

Beatrice didn't answer, but her finely plucked eyebrows arched, as if to say 'Go on, then. Tell me what you know.'

'It's D'Aronville, isn't it?' demanded Alexa softly. 'He's the one you were telling me about, back at your practice. He wants me for something. Something like last night . . . What he was doing to you.'

'Yes, he may well want to cane you,' Beatrice answered calmly, as if corporal punishment for erotic titillation were perfectly commonplace. 'But that will only be one diversion amongst many, I suspect.' She paused, seemed to catch her breath, then looked for a moment almost moonstruck, her brown eyes focusing on a point somewhere a few feet behind and to the right of Alexa. 'But you can ask him about that yourself . . .'

'Ask him what?' asked a quiet, very Gallic voice.

Alexa's first instinct was to whirl around; but, finding a reserve of self-control, she took a sip of her wine, then turned slowly in her seat.

Sacha D'Aronville was standing right behind her, looking as severely elegant as he had the night before, but smiling an unexpectedly personable smile. He wore a black leather jacket and a pair of faded blue jeans, but he was still, by far, the most sophisticated male in the room. Alexa's flip greeting died a death on her lips.

'H . . . hello,' she whispered, wondering what on

earth you said to a man who was determined to buy you.

'*Bonjour, Mademoiselle*,' he answered, his blue eyes glinting as he nodded. 'Beatrice.' As he nodded again, in the doctor's direction, his chiselled mouth seemed to quirk with slight humour.

Expecting D'Aronville to sit opposite her, with Beatrice between them, Alexa was alarmed when the Frenchman didn't move. The tiniest of signals seemed to flash between him and the doctor, and then Beatrice slid carefully back around the curved banquette and patted the place where she'd just been sitting.

'Scoot over, Alexa,' she said. 'Sit between us . . . It's so much more cosy.'

Alexa thought 'foolhardy' might be a better word to describe sitting between Beatrice and Sacha, but nevertheless, she obeyed without a murmur, still bemused by the Frenchman's cool poise.

'So, Beatrice, you've obeyed me for once,' murmured Sacha as he slipped into Alexa's vacated seat, effectively trapping her. 'I half expected to arrive and find the young lady not summoned. Or maybe here, but wearing one of your dresses.'

'I've followed your instructions to the last detail, Maître,' answered Beatrice, her tone respectful, but her face a picture of yearning. 'I've primed, her but she doesn't know the details.'

'Excuse me,' piped up Alexa, suddenly infuriated. They were talking about her, not to her. 'I'm here, you know. And I'm not dumb or dense. Is there something you wanted to discuss with me, Mr D'Aronville?'

'Yes, Mademoiselle Lavelle,' he said evenly, turning to look at her, his blue eyes calm but interested. 'And I believe we should be candid.' He paused as the waiter brought a glass for him, and more champagne, and discreetly left another menu. 'We both have something that the other one wants. Or perhaps I should say "needs". I have a vast amount of money, some of which I could channel your way in the form of contracts and recommendations to ensure the continued viability of your computer consultancy.' He paused again, and sipped his champagne with obvious and genuine enjoyment, 'And you, cherie, have a beautiful face and a very fresh and seductive body which I would like to possess in a variety of ways.' He regarded her very steadily over the rim of his glass, then tipped it slightly in a toast. 'Do you think we could do business?'

It was exactly what she'd been expecting, but even so, Alexa stared at D'Aronville in horror. There were bad words for what he was proposing, but it wasn't the concept itself that appalled her, really, but her own overwhelming eagerness to accept. The knowledge that she was going to accept, without asking for conditions, or any modifications of the terms.

'I'm not a prostitute,' she said, making her final stand against the inevitable.

'If you were one, I wouldn't want you,' D'Aronville whispered. 'A moral girl is far more piquant.'

Beatrice giggled then, and the Frenchman turned swiftly towards her, his face bland, but his eyes like blue sparks. 'And I see that you will need further attention, too,' he said, placing his glass on the table before him, and running his fingers thoughtfully up and down its stem. 'Come to my apartment tonight at eight. *Sans culotte*. And bring a ruler with you; white plastic for preference.'

'But, Maître, I still hurt,' protested Beatrice, her face rapturous.

'All the better,' returned Sacha, still fondling his glass.

'Is that all you do, then?' enquired Alexa, breaking the charged silence because she too was too excited to stay quiet. 'Beat women's bare bottoms?' A passing diner gaped at her in amazement, and realising the champagne had made her loud, Alexa blushed as pink as a peony with embarrassment.

Sacha D'Aronville, however, remained unmoved; his matt, rather fine-textured skin staying as pale and unblushing as ever. 'All?' he queried pleasantly, 'Oh my dear Alexa, how little you know of *la discipline.'* He pronounced the word as a French one. 'There are a hundred variations to a simple spanked bottom, and every one of them exquisite and sublime.'

'For whom?' Alexa demanded, already believing him, but not knowing why.

'For the penitent, of course.' He smiled, his cold face suddenly quite kind. 'And for you, Alexa, if you choose to accept my proposition . . . To punish you isn't all I'll require of you, but it will most certainly be one of the elements.'

'But . . . I . . .'

He reached out and laid his hand over hers. 'Come now, Alexa. I have my sources. I know your situation. Spend a few days with me, in France, and I can save both your fiancé and your business from total ruin.'

For an instant, Alexa saw Thomas, his face filled with shock, anger and disappointment. She'd let him down in so many ways – the worst being that she'd never really loved him – and even though succumbing to D'Aronville and his schemes would probably be the greatest betrayal of all, it was at least a way of repaying the squandered money.

'I . . . I accept,' she said quickly, giving in to her own impulsiveness as much to Sacha D'Aronville.

The Frenchman smiled, his eyes a degree or two warmer than she'd ever yet seen them. 'Good,' he said quietly. 'Shall we begin straight away?'

'Here?'

'Where else?'

'But what . . . what are you going to do?' Good God, he wasn't going to ask her to bend over here in the restaurant, was he? So he could smack her bare bottom in front of an audience?

'Oh, don't worry, Alexa, it's not that,' said the Frenchman, clearly interpreting her fearful look correctly, and almost benign now he'd got his own way.

189

'We'll just conduct a simple exercise. A test of your obedience to my will.'

'What do I have to do?' asked Alexa, acutely aware of Beatrice listening raptly beside her.

'Just sit still,' Sacha said, with a faint, mocking grin. 'Sit still and enjoy your lunch. It'll be as simple and as difficult as that.' With that he nodded in Beatrice's direction, then picked up a menu and placed it before Alexa. 'Why don't you help our young friend choose, my dear,' he murmured archly to the doctor, although Alexa got the distinct impression that he had very little interest in anything they might eat.

Beatrice moved up close on the banquette to study the gilt-trimmed and betasselled card, and as she did so, Alexa noticed her very discreetly flick up the tablecloth so it was spread across both of their laps. After a few moments, she saw that Beatrice was running the perfectly manicured forefinger of her left hand down the extensive list of dishes, while her right hand had suddenly disappeared.

Oh no! thought Alexa frantically, realising that D'Aronville's 'arrangement' was already set in motion. A second later, she felt a slender hand – Beatrice's right one – on her thigh, bunching her skirt and making it crawl slowly upwards.

When the pleated cloth lay in rumpled folds at Alexa's hips – just beneath the all-concealing whiteness of the tablecloth – a set of warm, inquisitive fingertips begin to glide over the delicate welts of her stockings. Wanting to look especially well-groomed, and aware that her tan was fading a little, she'd decided against bare legs for this crucial appointment.

'Well, Alexa, what do you think?' enquired D'Aronville suddenly, making Alexa jump and almost squeak out aloud. 'The chef here does a particularly good sole dish.' The concealed fingers were moving again as he spoke, and as he reached over and indicated the item in question on the menu, the exploration beneath the tablecloth moved forward. 'It's very tender.' She felt a

'What I'd like to do', said Beatrice softly from the other side, as she started pinching Alexa's burning clitoris, 'is to have you face down, bare-arsed across this table. Then stick a vibrator inside your beautiful bottom, and drink more champagne while everybody in the room gathers around to watch you climax uncontrollably.'

That was it. Too much. The catalyst. With her memories of Siddig still resonating, the single word 'bottom' made Alexa immediately lose control. She jerked on the banquette, gnawing at her lip in her attempt not to cry out. Her hands clasped convulsively into fists, almost tearing the tablecloth and making glassware move and teeter precariously. Between her legs there was chaos; a wet, pulsating inferno, her juices drenching both the hands that plagued her as her flesh leaped in deep spasms of pure bliss.

As the orgasm raged on, she tasted blood in her mouth, but still couldn't keep herself quiet. She must have made some kind of sound, because the golden-eyed youth looked her way again, as did a slight, bespectacled, rather studious-looking man at another table, who then grinned and whispered to his dining companion.

Everybody's looking at me! thought Alexa again. This time, she wanted to kick and thrash on the banquette, and thrust her pelvis against the hands that still pleasured her. She wanted to scream, tear open her blouse, and massage her aching breasts; not for Sacha's sake but purely for her own.

It seemed like the longest orgasm she'd ever had, but in reality it was over in seconds, leaving her mind disoriented, her limbs weak and her crotch soaking. As she slumped in her seat, a wave of giddiness came over her – a reaction to the unbearable tensions – and when the head waiter solicitously enquired about her welfare, his mention of a faint was nearly accurate.

'Oh no, she'll be fine,' said Beatrice smoothly, both hands on show now as she tipped a little water from the carafe on to her napkin, then dabbed lightly at Alexa's sweaty brow. 'It's just a little over-excitement. Don't worry. I'm a doctor, I'll take care of her.'

'Would you like a little more champagne, Alexa?' enquired D'Aronville after a moment, lifting the bottle with the hand that was now free.

'Yes! Yes, please!' said Alexa, appalled at how croaky her voice sounded. She felt as if she'd been put through a mangle, yet the pit of her belly was still molten. When Sacha handed her a fresh, foaming flute full of newly chilled champagne, she drank the lot, then held her glass out for another.

'So you enjoy our little games?' he said, as the bubbly wine cascaded anew. 'I knew you would, when I looked into your eyes last night. While I was punishing Beatrice . . .' He flashed a look at the doctor which indicated the event would be soon repeated. 'I can see you're going to adore paying your debts.'

His narrow, sculpted lips curved slightly as he spoke, and Alexa knew that what he said was right. Being fondled to climax, right here in this exclusive restaurant, had scared her but also thrilled her to the core. Adrenalin was pounding through her bloodstream, and, looking at first at D'Aronville's hand, then Beatrice's, she wished they were still working between her legs.

She imagined herself on her back on the table in front of them, her crotch bare, and her legs spread wide. One after another, taking turns, every man – and woman – in the restaurant would move between her thighs, and either kiss, stroke or fuck her, depending on their preference; while she, their victim and their goddess, would simply climax again and again and again. Until the cloth beneath her bottom was soaked through with her juices, and her throat was dry and parched from her shrieks of pleasure.

A finger-click broke into her fantasy.

'Hey. Where were you?' asked Beatrice gently, then nodded towards where the waiter was standing, order-pad in hand.

Alexa gulped down more wine, then studied the menu that had lain forgotten before her. With all that had happened, with her orgasms and her terror, she'd quite forgotten that they hadn't eaten yet.

'That!' she said wildly, pointing to the infamous chef's special; then heard first Beatrice, then D'Aronville start to laugh.

Chapter Thirteen

The Debt Goes South

*A*lexa thought about that laughter a lot over the next few days, and she still seemed to hear it now, as she sat in her first-class seat aboard a jet descending towards Nice.

She hadn't expected to be travelling to France alone, but it seemed appropriate somehow. She'd ventured forth to Barbados on her own, and her life had changed completely. Who could tell how this trip might affect her? The words 'Côte d'Azur' had a legendary quality, almost, and those who dwelt there, or even simply stayed there from time to time, had the same half-mythical lustre. Well, at least the ones she'd met so far did.

D'Aronville's 'few days in France' had come about with far less hassle than she'd feared. Realising there was no way she could refuse the offer, she still hadn't anticipated it being easy to sell Tom the idea.

But it had been.

She'd spoken enthusiastically of a contact made in Barbados and followed up over a business lunch, and then, when she'd quoted big numbers to him – the extraordinary 'retainer' she'd been offered by D'Aronville – he'd grudgingly agreed that she should go to France to discuss details with the client.

If only you knew, Tom, she thought now. If only you knew what those details entailed. She was about to surrender her body, her will, even; and the thought of being helpless, an object of pure sex, made her head spin and her belly cramp with lust. What had happened in 'Selene's Kitchen' had been just as Sacha said – a beginning. A taster. And since then, Alexa couldn't remember a single instant when she hadn't been aroused.

She'd even made love again with Tom.

When she'd returned – half cut on champagne and orgasms – from her lunch with Beatrice and Sacha, she'd pulled the plug on her fiancé's wrath by announcing the new contract she'd just secured. A projected redesign of Société Financière D'Aronville's internal budgeting system. She'd sensed some objections brewing, but the sums of money involved had squashed those.

That night, in bed, he'd responded vigorously, albeit silently, when Alexa had reached out and started to caress him. It had taken just seconds to harden his cock; and his forcefulness, as he'd entered her, had been as satisfying as it had unexpected.

The plane ticket had arrived the next day, and not long after the clothes had turned up, too. 'An outfit to travel in', the cryptic note had said, in stark, elegant handwriting. 'Wear this, but bring nothing else. Everything you need will be provided.'

'This' was a designer suit in a colour halfway between royal blue and navy. It was trickily but beautifully cut, with a bottom-grabbing skirt, and a severe 'feature' jacket. The fit was precision-tailored, without a millimetre of play, but it was obviously meant to be that way.

Along with the suit were several other parcels, all from exclusive shops, as well as a package from Circe. There were shoes in navy patent, with the highest heels

Alexa had ever seen; a matching bag, complete with make-up and all the other usual feminine paraphernalia, plus a surprisingly old-fashioned wooden-backed hairbrush; and exactly the kind of underwear she'd expected.

The black bra pushed her breasts upwards and inwards with underwiring, yet covered virtually nothing with its skimpy lace cups; the suspender belt that matched it was little more than a few strands of lace and ribbon; and the blue-black stockings were silk, six denier and seamed. There weren't any panties.

Dressed in it all, and wearing vivid make-up, as specified, Alexa had felt like a high-class call-girl. Every man aboard the flight had ogled her at one time or another, and sitting down in the so-tight skirt entailed exhibiting almost all of her legs. There was only an inch or so of coverage between the hem and her pubis, and it was impossible not to show her stocking welts. As she stirred in her seat, she caught a whiff of the faint musky odour of her vagina, and imagined it floating in the air all around her. Without knickers, there was no way to contain it, and she was getting wetter with every minute that passed. In mid-flight, locked in the plane's toilet, she'd found herself masturbating almost without realising it. She'd wanted to come – fingering herself furiously, with her shaking legs braced against the wall – but D'Aronville's note had also said 'Do not touch yourself. No orgasms until I grant permission.'

As the 'No smoking' sign flashed on, she clipped her seat-belt across her lap, gritting her teeth as the movement made her lace bra chafe her breasts. She was so aroused that even the slightest pressure anywhere made her sex start pulsing. The vibrations of the plane's descent made her moan.

The slow glide towards the earth seemed to take an age; and behind closed eyelids Alexa saw visions . . .

The first was of herself, standing in the aisle, leaning over with her face pressed against the seat, while a unknown man handled her bare buttocks. Then it was

Sacha D'Aronville, sitting opposite her, dragging her painfully by her hair into the space between the seats, so she could suck on his naked, swollen penis. The plane banked a little and there was Beatrice standing beside her, reaching down into the cleavage of the beautiful blue jacket, and letting a silver clamp close cruelly on her nipple . . .

Alexa cried out, orgasming lightly as the plane kissed the ground. She was aware that several fellow-passengers were staring at her curiously, but she couldn't summon the energy to be embarrassed. Let them think what they would; they meant nothing. She was the one who'd been summoned, called to service; their petty little standards were no longer hers.

As she disembarked, Alexa struggled dreamily with her awkward skirt and her difficult high heels. She'd had a glass of champagne on the flight, but she knew it wasn't alcohol that was affecting her. It was sex that was making her dizzy, and destiny.

Shielding her eyes, she walked across the airfield, squinting up at the Côte d'Azur sky, suddenly glad to be alive and in this place. It wasn't all that long since she'd been in the Caribbean, but somehow the sun in the south of France seemed far hotter. The buildings of the terminal were bathed in a light that was golden and decadent, and even the scents in the air seemed voluptuous. The perfumes of pine, and of herbs and other heady greenery, were detectable even amongst the reek of jet fuel and tarmac.

Smiling brilliantly at the good-looking young customs official, Alexa felt his desire reach out and touch her. Her special sense seemed tuned to a pitch of almost painful acuity, making her surroundings – one of the most hedonistic pleasure-loving places in the world – a rich source of unfiltered stimuli. Everyone in her immediate vicinity seemed to thinking about and anticipating sex, and their lust only made hers seem all the keener.

When she saw a familiar face – and an equally familiar

body – beyond the barrier, she could have cried because she wanted him so much.

Drew was as unsuitably dressed for the sun as she was. The last time she'd seen him, he'd been almost naked, in skimpy white shorts that hid nothing; but now he was clad from head to foot in unrelieved black. A silky polo sweater covered his powerful torso, and he wore heavy denim jeans tucked into slouch-top soft leather boots. With his eyes hidden by Ray-Ban Wayfarers, he looked like a minder for some sinister secret society; and with a frisson of foreboding as delicious as it was terrifying, Alexa realised that might well be the truth.

His smile, however, was everything it had been in Barbados. White, uncomplicated and beautiful.

'Welcome to Nice, Alexa,' he said as she reached him, his voice as warm and deep as ever. It seemed like only minutes ago that they'd been lying in her cabana beneath the slowly turning fan, with his cock buried deep inside her body.

'I . . . I didn't expect to see you here,' she stammered, shaken by both image and reality. If Drew was here, it meant Beatrice was also; though she should have expected it, the thought was alarming. Sacha D'Aronville was manipulative enough on his own, but Beatrice's presence meant additional complexities.

'Oh, I get around,' replied Drew, as Alexa hovered, and wondered how to greet him. They'd been lovers in the Caribbean. He'd fucked her, and she'd wept with pleasure in his arms, yet their parting – in Beatrice's presence – had been studiedly casual. The way he was standing now, looking so straight and workmanlike in his forbidding black clothing, seemed to suggest that a handshake was in order, even though Alexa's libido screamed out for much, much more.

She wanted to cling to his body like a limpet to a rock, clamp her open mouth to his, and let her hands travel freely as they kissed. She wanted him to touch

200

her as he had done in Barbados, his penis hardening as she pressed her tongue to his.

While she was still dithering, Drew took the initiative, grasping her upper arm, and escorting her quickly and forcefully from the terminal.

'They're waiting,' he said calmly, when she tried to protest, then simply smiled and steered her to the car park.

Alexa would have liked to dawdle, and take in more of the sights and sounds and smells of this region she'd never before visited, but Drew, it seemed, had different ideas. His manner was polite, almost gentle, but Alexa had the distinct impression she was being frogmarched. 'They' – presumably Sacha and Beatrice – were waiting . . .

In the car park, Alexa got another shock. She'd foreseen a special car to transport her to Sacha D'Aronville: a Bentley, perhaps, a Mercedes or a Roller. But instead, Drew stopped before a much less comfortable vehicle; a low, red beast that could only be a Ferrari.

'You can't seriously expect me to get into that,' Alexa protested, looking down at her abbreviated skirt, and thinking of her stockings and her hidden sexual nakedness.

'It's either that, or walk,' Drew answered, an exciting note of steel in his voice. 'You're honoured really. D'Aronville doesn't normally send the Ferrari for his guests.'

His faint emphasis on the word 'guests' told Alexa that he was fully aware of her status, and that he knew that for the duration of the next few days she had no rights and no say in what was done to her. Beneath her short skirt, her shame made her liquid.

Tottering on her heels, Alexa let herself be almost manhandled into the low, fearsome car. As she swung her hips, and settled her bottom into the bucket seat, her skirt rose up her thighs just as she'd expected, and her naked pubis was exposed to all the world. She heard the hiss of Drew's in-drawn breath, but his face remained stonelike beneath his shades. She was vaguely aware, too, of stares and exclamations from a group of young men who were standing beside an adjacent vehicle, but before they could really react, she was sealed like a forbidden princess in the Ferrari, and Drew was striding around to the driver's side.

Safe behind the tinted glass, Alexa slid deep into the seat as Drew gunned the car, and they roared away from the scene of her display. Her skirt was well up her thighs again, and her stocking-tops were on show to him, but somehow she no longer seemed to care. He'd seen all of her before anyway, so why should he not see her treasure once again? Surreptitiously, she began shuffling further down.

'Are you trying to expose yourself to me?' he enquired, as they swung out on to a wide coastal road.

Trapped by her own urges, Alexa blushed, feeling sweat trickling in her armpits and her cleavage. The close-fitting suit seemed to hug her like a corset, and the fact that she'd been trying to do exactly what he'd accused her of made her whole body seem to glow with humiliation. Glancing down, she saw the dark bands of her stocking-tops, her thin, ribbon-trimmed suspenders, and a few tiny tufts of her black pubic hair where it peeked beneath the hem of her skirt. She couldn't answer because the deed was almost done.

'Well, do the job properly then,' Drew continued, nodding in the direction of her crotch as he negotiated a broad sweeping turn that overlooked rock-strewn cliffs and the sea. The Mediterranean was a mysterious, almost crystalline blue beneath them, and the sunlight danced across it like fireflies.

Looking out across a shallow bay, Alexa pretended to study a passing yacht while she put her hands on her skirt and slid it up. Uncovered, she moaned softly, feeling arousal sweep over her in waves. She was half naked. Vulnerable. The very slut that Sacha D'Aronville intended . . . As she had in the aeroplane, she felt precariously close to coming, and her fingers, spread across the edge of the leather seat beneath her, seemed to tingle with the need to touch her sex.

'Don't do it,' said Drew, his voice suddenly cool. 'He says "no". You're not to come until he says so.'

'Who says "no"?' demanded Alexa, for form's sake. She was wriggling now, dying to reach between her thighs and stimulate herself, her sex lips swollen and her clitoris on fire.

'You know,' Drew answered. He seemed calm and detached behind the mask of his Ray-Bans, but his black-clad groin was bulging. 'You've already gone too far.'

Alexa flexed her thighs, and felt her vulva gape. The skirt was up around her waist now, and her belly gleamed golden in the tint-filtered light. As she reached down, wiggling a fingertip through her sopping black curls, she felt rather than saw Drew smile. She expected him to rebuke her, but instead he decelerated the car rather sharply, then pulled off the main coast road to a chorus of protesting horns from the drivers he'd forced to brake behind him.

Alexa froze, the pad of her forefinger just millimetres from her clitoris, as Drew negotiated a series of twists and curves, turning off on to ever-narrower and more-dilapidated side-roads, until finally they were bumping along over what was more or less a track in the middle of a myrtle grove.

'Get out, please,' he said quietly as the car drifted to a halt, adding 'and don't worry about your skirt' as Alexa began fiddling for her hem.

There was no one about; nevertheless, she felt embarrassed to step out on to the hard-packed dirt with a bare bottom and her pubis on show. This wasn't the handsome, gentle Drew who'd made love to her so skilfully in Barbados. This was a new Drew Kendrick, an emotionless custodian, the servant of Beatrice and Sacha. He would do their will, and probably enjoy it; because their will was to enjoy their new toy.

'What are you going to do?' she asked tightly, backing away from him as he came towards her.

'Just following instructions,' he said, reaching out to take her arm. 'Situation normal.'

There was a touch of irony in his voice that cut through Alexa's arousal. It reminded her of other instructions he'd followed so efficiently.

'Just the way you were following instructions in Barbados, I suppose,' she taunted, trying to shake him off, but achieving nothing. He was turning her now, pushing her face down over the warm, red bonnet of the car, with her bare buttocks presented to the sun.

'Naturally,' he said, his voice calm, almost silken. 'Although I can't say I found it a chore.'

'You beast! You f – '

The flat of his hand across her naked bottom cheek shocked the outrage and profanity from her lips. It was the first time a man had ever struck her, and she couldn't believe how much the impact hurt. The whole of one firm lobe seemed to have been kissed by fire, and she imagined she could feel the flesh swelling. As she started to get up, Drew placed his other hand squarely on the small of her back, then commenced a steady sequence of smacks.

It was like a dream. She could hardly comprehend what was happening to her. She was bare-arsed and squirming over the bonnet of a Ferrari, somewhere in the back of the Provençal beyond. She was being spanked, very painfully and efficiently, because a man she'd met just twice had forbidden her to masturbate.

And Drew was really hurting her, the swine! Drew, who she'd believed was gentle and kind; Drew who she'd hoped might really care for her. A little . . .

'What is it with you?' she demanded, snivelling now from the brisk treatment her bottom was receiving. 'Why are you doing this?'

'Instructions,' he repeated, landing a wallop on the tender underhang of Alexa's left buttock, and making her squeal and reach blindly behind her, trying to soften or deflect the next blow. With frightening speed and deftness, he caught the hand, then the other, and pinioned them both with his left one, while he continued to smack with his right.

'And y . . . you just do everything they tell you?' demanded Alexa, before yowling shrilly beneath another well-aimed stroke.

'Like I told you,' continued Drew, almost wearily, 'I owe Beatrice. I owe her a lot. And she owes D'Aronville . . . It's a chain of obligation. Don't you understand that?' he demanded in return, adding emphasis with a particularly hard smack.

Alexa just sobbed for a while, her spirit wilting as the spanking continued. There was something exquisitely weakening and sensual about lying there having her bottom belaboured. Ceding her pride was every bit as erotic as she'd imagined, and the hot pain was producing powerful effects.

Her arousal had died briefly, from shock and from anger, but as Drew worked on, it began to mass in her belly once again. Alexa found herself drifting as she suffered. She saw Beatrice's face the other night while she was being caned; heard her shouts of pain, and then her hoarse screams of pleasure. She remembered how she'd wanted – desperately – to understand what the doctor was feeling, and she realised now that she did understand. Without thinking she wriggled and spread her thighs.

'Oh no, you don't,' said Drew softly, releasing her hands then lifting her bodily from the Ferrari's gleaming bonnet. 'That's exactly what you've been forbidden, too. Come on, let's have you back in the car.'

Alexa was almost too shocked to be angry, but when she slid back into the low-slung passenger seat, she groaned loudly and swore through her teeth. The smooth leather upholstery was cool against her fieriness, but the pure contrast only made the pain seem worse. Her skirt was rucked up around her groin still, and the thought of struggling with it didn't bear considering. She simply sat where she was, with her sex still on show, and let Drew drive her to wherever they were going.

Their destination, it seemed, was the Villa Isis, which Drew informed her was D'Aronville's summer home. Her travel instructions had been vague – deliberately so, she suspected – and she'd had little idea what to expect once in France.

Sacha's hideaway, however, was magnificent. The Villa Isis stood in a huge semitropical garden which was surrounded by its own high, white walls. Electric gates admitted the Ferrari, then closed when the car had purred through them. Whatever Sacha D'Aronville was planning for her was hidden safely from the eyes of casual tourists . . .

As they wound their way up a drive lined by tall pines, Drew turned towards Alexa and smiled. 'Scared?' he asked, his eyes twinkling as he peered at her momentarily, over the top of his Ray-Bans.

'No! Not in the slightest!' she spat back defiantly, although inside she was profoundly afraid.

'Well, you should be,' he replied. 'Monsieur le Maître has some pretty sophisticated appetites. What I did would be nothing to him.'

'Bollocks! You're only trying to put the wind up me.' Alexa sat straight, though it hurt her, and lifted her chin in a show of bravado. 'And anyway, I might not be as naïve as you think!'

Drew laughed and let the car coast to a halt.

The courtyard at Villa Isis was as beautiful as it was imposing. Tall, pale stone columns formed a classical portico, and before the doorway, in the centre of a huge oval area of raked gravel, was an ornamental pond complete with goldfish and a fountain. Alexa would have loved to leap out of the car, lean over the side and dabble her fingers in the water, but she was all too aware of her lower body on show, and the sizzling red state of her bottom. If there'd been nobody else around she might actually have dared to do it, but at the top of the steps, standing by the imposing double-fronted doorway, was Camilla Fox, observing their arrival.

'Well then, Ms Bold and True, let's have you out of the car, shall we?' said Drew cheerfully as Alexa hesitated.

Wincing, she managed to slide down her skirt a little way, but she was still acutely conscious of her exposed condition. Straightening up, she smoothed ineffectually at her skirt, irritated that both Drew and Sly were grinning. The nurse skipped lightly down the villa steps and ran towards them, her white uniform almost dazzling in the sun.

'It's good to see you again, Alexa,' she murmured as she reached them, then leaned close, obviously intending to give Alexa a kiss. Expecting a peck on the cheek, Alexa turned her head accordingly – only to have her face cupped firmly in both Sly's hands and her mouth swiftly but comprehensively possessed.

When she was released, Alexa was shaking. She stood by numbly as Sly removed an immaculate handkerchief from the pocket of her dress, and blotted herself neatly around the edges of her lips. Then, as if mysteriously knowing that her mouth was once again faultlessly pristine, the nurse slid her hankie back safely into her pocket, without any mention of cleaning Alexa up, too.

Another ploy, thought Alexa grimly, as she followed Sly into a surprisingly large entrance hall. My suit's rumpled, my lipstick's smeared, and my hair's probably a bird's nest. I look like a streetwalker. And I smell, too, she added in silence, catching the scent of her own aroused quim.

'Come along. Hurry up. We mustn't keep them waiting,' urged Sly, striding briskly across the hall. Alexa followed, unstable on her heels, and hating their sharp clatter on the tiles. The room they were crossing was ineffably beautiful, and filled with antique treasures that demanded inspection, but now was not the moment to admire them. Her masters were impatient to receive her, it seemed; and, given what she'd seen at the party, and just now experienced, their slightest displeasure would be expressed upon her body.

Passing through another superbly decorated vestibule, and thence through a smaller room filled with books, they finally came out on to a veranda – a broad, white stone-flagged patio half shaded at one end by an awning. Safe in the beneficent shadow of this canopy stood a huge, richly upholstered couch, which was strewn with cushions and a black velvet throw. On it were two familiar figures.

Sacha D'Aronville was sitting relaxedly at one end, his long denim-clad legs crossed as he sipped a drink and read a leather-covered book. He looked rested and far younger than his years, and wore faded jeans and a tight white T-shirt.

Beatrice, however, did not look relaxed, at least what Alexa could see of her. The doctor was kneeling at the other end of the sofa, her head cradled in her arms, and her face buried in the cushions. Her brilliant hair was spread over her upper back and shoulders, but otherwise, apart from a black lace G-string and a pair of needle-heeled mules, she was completely naked. Her bottom, which was raised as if she were a bitch about to be serviced, was bisected by three lurid red weals. A yellow cane lay on the seat by Sacha's thigh.

At the sound of Alexa's steps, the Frenchman looked up from his reading. He smiled immediately, his blue eyes dancing, then put both his book and his glass of wine aside.

'Alexa. At last,' he said as if he'd been waiting an age for her; then, rising lithely to his feet, he strode across the flags in her direction.

'Cherie,' he murmured, taking both her hands in his, then kissing both her cheeks; the quintessential Frenchman. 'Welcome to the Villa Isis. You're going to be happy here . . . if not always comfortable.' Releasing her hands, he looked back towards Beatrice, then smiled again and quirked his strongly arched brows.

'Beatrice, get up and greet our guest. Your cul is beautiful, mon ange, but I'm sure she'd prefer to see your face.'

The doctor rose to her feet with surprising grace, her pale face not betraying any hint of the marks on her bottom. Shrugging on a robe as she walked – the same kimono she'd worn in Barbados, Alexa noticed – she almost glided across the patio towards them, her elevated heels causing her no problem whatsoever.

'My dear,' she said, then she, too, kissed Alexa, her lips a little moister and more lingering than Sacha's. 'I can smell your sex, you naughty girl,' she whispered in Alexa's ear, then kissed her again. 'Have you been wicked in the car with my Drew?'

'N . . . no,' stammered Alexa, colouring furiously.

'You don't sound so sure,' Beatrice teased, running the backs of her fingers lightly down Alexa's shaking body.

'Not *in* the car,' added Alexa, very conscious of Sacha, his crossed arms, and his elegant, watchful face.

'Ah, so you *have* been bad!' cried Beatrice triumphantly.

'No! No, I haven't!'

'Oh dear, contradiction is such a grievous error,' said Beatrice, swaying slightly on her heels, her kimono billowing around the creaminess of her body. 'What else has she been up to, my love? What crimes have been committed?' she enquired of Drew, who, Alexa suddenly realised, was standing right behind her.

'Licentious talk. Exposing herself. Making free with her own body,' he intoned, his voice solemn yet resonant.

'In that case, we have our work cut out,' said Beatrice, suddenly businesslike. She spun around quickly, and returned to the daybed, with Sacha D'Aronville accompanying her. 'You may prepare her, Drew,' she said quietly, waiting for a moment as her companion took his seat, then carefully lowering her sore bottom on to his lap. Sacha settled the doctor more comfortably into place, then slid one long hand directly between her legs.

Astonished by the eroticism of the sight before her, Alexa jumped when Drew took hold of her. With a deft but violent action, he jerked open the neckline of her expensive suit, then reached in and took hold of her breasts. Lifting them free of the deeply plunging bra, he let the two soft globes rest, exposed, in the ruined opening of her jacket, then rubbed his fingers across the tips of her nipples. The contact was ephemeral, and Alexa couldn't stop herself pushing forward to try and increase it. As she did so, Drew removed his hands and turned his attention to her skirt. This, he yanked upwards with the same exciting force he'd used on her jacket, and left it bunched in ruched folds around her waist.

'Turn her,' said D'Aronville, while his hand worked steadily on Beatrice. Alexa watched numbly, as what looked like four of his fingers pistoned steadily in and out between the doctor's scissoring thighs, while at an angle his thumb mashed against her clitoris.

'Ah,' he murmured, when Drew had taken Alexa by the shoulders and positioned her. 'A red bottom. That wasn't in my instructions either.'

'But it was him!' cried Alexa, twisting back around and pointing at Drew, who stood to one side, his arms crossed as D'Aronville's had been. 'He spanked me . . . across the car.'

'Against my Ferrari?' It was Sacha's turn to grin now, and he seemed to be enjoying Alexa's discomfiture just as much as he was relishing Beatrice's wriggling. The doctor was moaning now, her mouth slack with passion as her hips jerked and her pale thighs quivered. 'And you just let him?' the Frenchman continued, his blue eyes glinting like fire.

There was no answer, Alexa realised, that could get her out of this. Whatever she said would be twisted to accuse her; she was going to get a thrashing either way. Reluctantly, she turned away from the sight of Beatrice being masturbated, and studied the shaded stone wall of the villa.

'Will you bring Alexa's handbag, Camilla?' said Sacha as Beatrice continued to whimper like a baby and Alexa almost felt her pleasure. 'There's an item inside it that we need.'

Oh God, not the hairbrush! It was so . . . so solid!

Why is this happening to me? she pondered in the seemingly endless wait. How could I let it happen? It's not even sex! It's shame. Pain. Degradation. How can I be wet? How can I be swollen and want to come?

When Sly's light footsteps sounded behind her on the stones, Alexa felt her juices start sliding down her leg. It was going to happen now, any moment, and it was going to hurt far more than Drew's hand.

There were small movement sounds somewhere, but Alexa just stared at the wall. She imagined her handbag being opened, and the brush taken out. She saw Drew hefting it, assessing its weight and the degree of force that would be required to wield it. She saw his fingers gliding slowly over the honey-coloured wood, then drifting across her flesh with a commensurate care. In God's name, why had she assumed that only Sacha was an expert disciplinarian?

'A chair, Sly, please,' said the Frenchman suddenly, with the very slightest of catches in his voice. Was what he was doing to Beatrice finally affecting him, too? The doctor's groans were almost pitiful now; as if even she had reached the limits of her endurance.

There was the noise of something heavy being dragged across the flags; without thinking, Alexa turned round. Aware that both Drew and Sacha were eyeing her warningly – she'd moved without permission again, hadn't she? – she studied the very plain, maple-wood kitchen chair that had been placed in the middle of the patio just a few feet away from the couple on the couch.

The chair was simple and sturdy, not a priceless antique or modern collectable. It was clearly specially chosen for its purpose. After a few moments, Drew walked across and sat down on it, his tanned face a smooth impassive mask. Clearly acting in some kind of acolytical role on this occasion, Sly moved to stand before him, holding out his normal gold-rimmed spectacles, which he soberly exchanged for his shades. When this little piece of business was satisfactorily dealt with, the nurse walked away again, then returned with the brush.

'Well, Alexa,' said Sacha, his hand stilling against Beatrice's gleaming crotch. 'Do you know what to do next? Have you ever been across a man's lap?'

Across a Ferrari, yes, she thought, but not a lap. She answered 'no' in a very small voice.

'Then step forward, and put yourself across Drew's knees. Don't worry, he knows what to do.'

I'll bet he does, thought Alexa, obeying like an automaton. With a naturalness that astonished her, she went forward, lay across Drew's denimed thighs, and somehow seemed to find the right position. He adjusted his legs, and she slid a little further over, and suddenly it was as if she'd been doing this thing her whole life. In spite of her fear, in spite of her shame over her naked pink bottom on show to everyone, in spite of her intense, almost agonising arousal, it dawned on her that she felt somehow 'at home'. And the sound she made, when Drew finally touched her, was more of happiness than of terror or oppression.

'Good,' murmured Sacha D'Aronville, as if he understood her feelings precisely. 'The brush please, Camilla,' he instructed, and Alexa sensed the nurse stepping close, handing across the hated object, then returning to her station by the couch. 'In your own time, Drew, if you please,' the Frenchman urged softly, just as Beatrice's cries once again began to soar.

What's he doing to her for pity's sake? thought Alexa, unable to see anything now but Drew's boots and the patio's stone floor. In her mind she saw visions of Beatrice's splayed thighs, and wet red sex, then saw

212

nothing. Nothing at all but pure flaming white, as the hairbrush crashed down on her bottom.

It was a like a three-dimensional slab of sensation, pure pain for just one second, and her surprised shriek temporarily drowned out the groaning Beatrice. Purely on reflex, Alexa's hand shot back to the sight of her injury, but was immediately caught easily by Drew.

'No. You mustn't do that,' he whispered. It was the first time he'd spoken for a while, and his voice was ragged and far less cool than it had been.

Alexa obeyed him, but couldn't stop the frantic writhing of her hips. The single stroke seemed to pulsate like a demon in her flesh, its heat melting through her bottom to her sex. The need both to clutch the pain and to massage her clitoris were equal, and so powerful she found herself sobbing.

Oh God help me, she thought. It's only the first blow . . .

Chapter Fourteen

Scenes from a Bad Girl's Dream

*L*ying in her cool, scented room, with the breeze playing softly amongst the thin net curtains, Alexa could still feel that first blow . . .

Like all the ones after it, it had sent her half delirious, yet at the same time sharpened her perceptions. She could almost analyse the quality of the pain – solid and breathtaking – and marvel at how an experience, a sensation so hideous could make her body burn and rouse so completely. Just the thought of it – a dense, unyielding slab of wood slamming down on to her already hurting bottom, driven by the power of Drew's strong arm – made her poor quim twitch and moisten now, hours later, as she lay face down and secured to her bed.

Except for the steady flap of the curtains, and the ever-present hum of the cicadas in the gardens outside, Alexa's room was quite silent. A perfect receptacle for the sounds she remembered. The terrifying whack of the hairbrush as it hit her bottom; her shrill pathetic yowls, begging for the mercy she'd known she wouldn't receive; Beatrice's guttural grunts and gasps as Sacha had wrung climax after climax from flesh that had already come too much . . .

What's happening to Beatrice now? thought Alexa. She imagined the doctor lying on a bed, too, one rather like her own. Beatrice would be face up, though; her long, elegant thighs supported on cushions, and spread so the breeze could cool her quim. She'd be naked, or perhaps have a shawl or something draped across her shoulders and her breasts, and Sly would have taken care of her, too. The gentle nurse would have ministered to her beloved employer in just the same way she had to Alexa, only in Beatrice's case, the silky healing gel would have been feathered across her inflamed and irritated genital tissue as well as her maltreated buttocks.

Alexa tossed her head against the pillows, troubled even more by the lushness of the picture. She imagined the succulent redness of Beatrice's open vulva, and felt an overpowering desire to kiss it.

'I'm going insane,' she said to herself, stirring uneasily. Then she smiled, wondering if the fact that she was talking to herself confirmed it. I've been thrashed and humiliated, made to do things that I'd never have dreamed of even thinking about a month ago, and all I can do is want more.

What would it be like to be on that other bed now, crouched between those long, pale legs like an animal devouring a feast? For such a treat there would have to be payment.

Perhaps she'd be molested while she enjoyed? She imagined Sacha pressing his fingers to her bottom, then attacking it with his cane; Drew parting the flaming, pain-filled cheeks so he could push the head of his penis inside her.

No, no, no! Too much! She squirmed violently against her bonds, trying to angle her hips. Her loins felt weighted, engorged, her clitoris was aching. If only she could move a little, tilt herself, and then she could rub herself off against the bed.

Sly! For God's sake, please come back! she thought

passionately, thinking of the nurse's sweet kindness towards her earlier.

It had been Sly who'd supported her as she'd climbed awkwardly off Drew's lap. Sly who'd helped her down on to her knees, then guided her tearful face towards Drew's bulging crotch. As Alexa's tormentor had parted his strong thighs, it had been the nurse who'd unzipped him, eased aside his black nylon briefs, then brought his swollen cock out into the open.

Staring numbly at the member before her, Alexa had opened her lips automatically. Drew was a big man, in every sense; as he grabbed her head, and forced himself forwards into her mouth, her throat gagged and she felt herself choke. But only for a second . . .

As his swollen glans butted at her tongue and the soft membranes of her palate, she felt a new relaxation take her over. There suddenly seemed more space for him, more saliva sloshing around to ease his thrusts, and without thinking, she slid her arms around his torso, then caressed his back as he jerked between her lips.

'Good girl,' said Sly somewhere beside her, and Alexa felt a soft hand begin to stroke her exposed neck.

Confusing emotions overwhelmed her, and she sobbed helplessly around the obstruction in her mouth. She wanted to embrace the gentle nurse just as much as she was embracing Drew. She wanted to be a part of the pleasure she could sense all around her, and yet the very experience of extreme frustration – the huge devouring need that was gnawing at her quim from within – was almost a kind of pleasure in itself. She felt herself rising up, yet staying still, passing into an altered state, turning to a pure flame of unsatisfied lust that was only stoked by the suffering in her bottom.

Just when she was sure she could bear no more, Drew gasped and exploded into orgasm, his hot semen jetting heavily into her mouth. His fingers dug into her scalp as his cock leaped against her tongue, and somehow his release seemed to quieten her. She swallowed

216

his emission like an esoteric tranquilliser, then allowed herself to be drawn away and off his sex. With the greatest of discomfort in both her bottom and her vulva, she stood up, swaying on her silly high heels, and allowed Sly to begin escorting her from the room.

The last things she saw were a series of bizarre but crystal-sharp freeze-frames.

Drew, slumped back on his simple wooden chair, his arms dangling nervelessly at his sides, and his softening cock gleaming with her spittle. Then Beatrice, still on D'Aronville's lap, her creamy thighs spread obscenely wide, and her G-string around her ankles like a tether. Her blue-eyed French lover was still plaguing her wet sex, and now pushing a foreign object inside it – a long, immensely thick alabaster faux penis that made the doctor's eyes widen as it slowly impaled her.

'No! Oh yes, yes, yes . . .' were the last words Alexa remembered as she stumbled her way from the patio.

Sacha D'Aronville's Villa Isis was a sublimely beautiful, an almost Elysian haven, but Alexa couldn't seem to focus on its wonders. Like an obedient lamb, she let Sly lead her through the hall, and on up a huge sweeping stairway, but as she ascended her perceptions were internal. Each tottering step brought a jolt: discomfort in the well-chastised globes of her bottom, and between her legs a different kind of ache. By the time the nurse paused before a four-panelled door, Alexa was biting her lips and fighting a flood of tears.

'Don't worry, sweetheart,' murmured Sly when they were inside. 'Don't fret, I'm going to see to you now.'

And she did, thought Alexa, coming back to the present as she lay fastened to her comfortable white bed. What Sly had meant by 'see to you' was to slip her long nimble fingers between Alexa's streaming labia, and bring her immediately to orgasm where she stood.

The relief had been so longed for, and the ecstasy so enormous, that she would have collapsed if not for the nurse. As if perfectly accustomed to having climaxing

217

patients falling over on her, Sly had taken Alexa's weight with no discernible effort, and held her upright until the spasms were over. After that, she'd led her to the luxurious en-suite bathroom, and got on with the process of looking after her.

Alexa had been stripped, bathed, and had a dozen intimate tasks performed for her. The quietly efficient nurse had done everything. cleaned Alexa's teeth, smoothed moisturiser on her skin, even supervised her using of the toilet. This last had made Alexa protest at first, but once sitting on the seat – wincing at the pressure on her buttocks – she'd found the whole process peculiarly exciting. Especially having her crotch dabbed and wiped . . .

'That's a good girl,' Sly had said encouragingly when the ablutions were over. 'And now we're going to put you down for your rest.'

The nursery connotations had lulled Alexa with a sweet sense of being cared for, but she soon realised that things weren't that simple. When Sly had dressed her in a truly lovely nightgown – a frilly voluminous swathe of Victorian style pin-tucked white voile – she'd been made to lie face down on the bed and, to her astonishment, been put into fetters. The old-fashioned bedstead had brass rails at its head and foot, and she'd been secured spread-eagled between them. The restraints were very amenable ones – soft, felt-lined leather cuffs attached to white cords – but even so, she was virtually immobilised. Sly had placed a thin cotton-covered pillow beneath her head, and another, thicker one beneath her hips, then meticulously turned back her nightdress, leaving her still-reddened buttocks displayed.

After that, the nurse had very delicately and painstakingly massaged a clear, soothing balm into Alexa's naked bottom, then slipped dainty, knitted bedsocks on her feet.

'There. All nice and ready,' Sly had whispered, then,

kissing Alexa's forehead like an affectionate governess, she'd left the room and closed the big door behind her.

'Ready for what?' Alexa muttered, feeling the slow fires burn again in her loins.

Would it be punishment? Or pleasure? And inflicted by whom? She was here to pay off Sacha for saving her business – but so far, since she'd arrived, he'd done nothing more than kiss her on the cheek. He must want her – even though, strangely, she still couldn't read him sexually – yet he almost seemed reluctant to touch her. He was content to let others do that. All and sundry, in fact. She'd been handled by everybody she'd seen in the household so far, but what if there were others still waiting?

Anybody could come in now. And do anything. Her bottom was bare; her sex was available; she was helpless. She thought of Beatrice and the white stone dildo. What if Sacha wanted to push the thing inside her instead this time? And not necessarily into her –

Oh God! Alexa shuffled furiously, her clitoris twitching at the obscenity of the image. What was it about her bottom – and the things people wanted to do to it – that suddenly so acutely aroused her? She'd never felt this way before the changes.

Lying here was making her mind do strange things. How long had it been since Sly had left? It seemed like an age, and yet, apart from the ache of her spankings, and the deeper ache between her thighs, she felt oddly contented. There was a sense of acceptance building inside her. The submission, she supposed, that Beatrice had hinted at. A surrender to her own nature as much as to any outside agency. She had a sudden strong feeling that if she asked to be released, now, from both her bonds and her agreement, she'd be allowed to walk away freely. And perhaps even still get the 'payment' she'd been promised?

But she didn't want to walk away. The thought made her unimaginably sad. The prospect of more punishment terrified her, but somehow that terror also had a quality of rightness. Of fate. Of being 'her'.

In the midst of her musings came a sound – the faint, sliding creak of a big door moving slowly on its hinges.

Then there were footsteps . . .

Who is it? Who are you? thought Alexa, her heart leaping. She felt unable to speak, and from where she lay, it was impossible to crane her head enough to see. The unknown visitor was soft-footed, so it could be a man or a woman, and she sensed a hesitation, a deliberate holding back. Not from any kind of fear or doubt, but from an urge to tease her and arouse her. She tried to reach out with her mind, to connect with a desire that matched hers – and met nothing.

The very blankness gave her visitor away, and as if he'd perceived he'd already been rumbled, Sacha stepped into Alexa's field of view.

'How do you feel, cherie?' he murmured, squatting down beside the bed, his knees bent and his thighs taut beneath his jeans. His blue eyes bored into her, and for a moment, she almost choked on the force of her lust for him. His face was so elegant, so intent, his expression so comprehensively knowing. His white hair made him seem like an ice-god; not old, not young, but frozen for ever at the peak of his strength and intelligence. Alexa's tongue felt like lead in her mouth, but she longed to plead that he use her in any way he chose.

'Cherie?' he repeated coaxingly, tipping forward on to his knees and reaching out to touch the side of her face.

'I'm frightened,' she said, her voice almost a child's.

'Not of me, surely?' he said, his thumb gliding across her lower lip, then pressing down on it to open her mouth. Leaning forward, he pressed his pointed tongue into the breach he'd created, then licked at Alexa's own tongue. The moment was so evocative, so very much like another kind of licking, that her hips swayed lewdly

220

on the pillow, and she sobbed as he withdrew and sat back on his haunches.

Laughing softly, he cocked his head on one side. 'What is it you want, Alexa?' he asked, his cool eyes darkening as if he, too, felt the same surge of lust.

'I don't know,' she whispered. 'I . . . I just want something.'

'Well, if you leave it in my hands, ma petite,' His cultured voice sounded almost wistful. 'I'm afraid we must do what I want.'

Standing up, he stepped closer to the bed and looked down at her. His fingers settled on the curve of her bottom.

'Do you want that?' he murmured in her ear as he leaned over her, letting his hand curve around her glowing rump. 'Your bottom is magnificent, Alexa. So fresh, so exquisitely tempting. It deserves nothing less than the severest of treatment.'

'But why?' she gasped, as his fingers stirred and tormented her.

'Why not?' he countered, beginning to squeeze, to palpate. 'A *cul* like this should always be fiery. Always a rose-red delight to the eye.'

Alexa fought against her bonds. The heat was flaring through her belly again, massing low and ponderously in her sex. She circled her hips against the pillow, and felt Sacha's gripping hand ride the movement, his fingertips brushing her cleft.

'Let me prepare you, cherie,' he said quietly, sitting down half-sideways on the bed beside her but not relinquishing his hold on her bottom. Leaning over her back, he began kissing the nape of her neck: touching his lips lightly to the sensitive skin there, then blowing on it and delicately nibbling.

'You're superb, Alexa,' he said, ruffling the wayward black fronds of her hair. 'I'd love to whip your naked bottom until you can't stop crying. Then have you . . . Fuck you while you're still wailing, and listen to the change in your screams.'

221

As he sat up again, steadying himself, she felt his free hand slide in beneath her midriff, then adjust upwards until he was cupping her breast. His finger and thumb grasped her nipple, then tweaked it through the stuff of her nightdress. Alexa moaned again. Struggled. With her senses so focused on her bottom and her vulva, she hadn't realised how her breasts craved his touch.

'Please,' she sobbed, 'Oh please . . .'

'Please what?' demanded Sacha, his voice edged with fierceness.

'I don't know,' she said again, distraught, lying, because she did know now what she wanted. Or at least what she wanted first of all.

'You're lying, *ma petite*,' he purred, circling her reddened bottom cheek with his palm. 'This is what you want!' He squeezed again, making her tingle infernally. 'You want me to smack this. Beat it. Make it burn. Don't you?'

She whimpered, and he bent over and kissed the line of her jaw.

'Don't be afraid, Alexa. Admit what you want. What you need. And I'll give it to you in the fullest of measures.' His fingers flexed, gripping the muscle of her buttock, while his mouth gently caressed her sweating brow. 'Tell me!' he hissed, his breath like a truth drug against her skin.

'Pl . . . Please. I . . . I want you to spank me,' she whispered brokenly, not really knowing what she was saying, except on the very deepest and barely conscious level. Her buttocks were still hurting from the last time, so why in God's name was she asking – no, begging! – for more?

'With the very greatest of pleasure,' he purred against her neck, while his hands worked her bottom and her breast. 'Believe me, you don't know how much.'

Alexa groaned beneath his efforts, anticipating the greater pain ahead. Her hips wove wildly against the pillow, and she could feel the cloth beneath her crotch becoming moist.

But as Sacha straightened up, abandoning her, she seemed to feel a sudden chill in the air, a coolness and withdrawal to his demeanour. 'You're so eager, Alexa,' he said almost primly. 'So wanton. The way you waggle your body is crude. You do realise this requires a harder lesson?'

It's a form of words, thought Alexa, trying to still herself. It's the reason, the arbitrary, chosen justification of all this. There has to be a ritual, a procedure. 'Cause and effect', she suddenly heard in another voice, and realised how right those words had been.

'Alexa!'

'Yes, I understand,' she said quietly through gritted teeth, wanting the ordeal to begin, knowing it would tax her yet bring her to fulfilment.

'Bon,' said Sacha crisply. 'And I believe here is the perfect implement.' He reached down, out of Alexa's line of sight, then straightened up again, holding a slipper in his hand, one of a backless, thin-soled leather pair she'd noticed set neatly beside the bed. In her innocence, she'd thought that they'd been left for her to wear, but obviously they had another use.

'*La pantoufle*,' he said, swishing it whimsically, his eyes glittering as he bent down to show it to her. 'Strong yet flexible . . . *Formidable*. And I believe you must have fifty strokes to begin with.' He paused, seemed to ruminate. '*Oui. Cinquante* . . . but with the option of more.'

With that he dropped the slipper back on the bed again, and slid his arm underneath her belly. Lifting her up, his sleeve just brushing her pubis, he rearranged the pillow, then the angle of her body. 'Much better,' he said almost to himself as he let her settle down again. 'Now I can smack the undercurve with far more precision.'

It seemed so cold, so calculating, yet conversely so hot and exciting. Alexa quivered as he backed away for a moment and seemed to study the dynamics of the situation. Out of the corner of her eye, she watched him hefting the slipper, twisting it this way and that, as if calculating patterns of force. She groaned involuntarily as he moved to her side again, his denim-clad loins so close to her. He was erect, she could see; a huge bulge was pushing out his buttoned fly. Even as she watched, he touched himself briefly, then returned his cool attention to her plight.

'This will hurt, Alexa. Hurt a lot,' he said evenly. Then, just as she began to shiver with the deepest and most abject fear, he leaned close, kissed her throat and whispered, 'Don't be frightened, cherie. I'm here. Don't be frightened.'

It didn't make sense. *He* was the danger that terrified her. But there was no more time to debate such absurdities, for almost as he spoke, he started spanking her.

The pain was intense. Doubly dreadful on a pre-punished bottom that was still sore from the hand and the brush. Through a hot red blur of growing agony, Alexa realised Monsieur le Maître was counting. Marking out her strokes very evenly and softly in French. She understood a little of the language, but soon couldn't follow him at all. Whatever number he'd reached was too much . . .

She was writhing again, and crying, marking the strokes herself with a yell at each one. The slipper seemed extraordinarily powerful as it impacted upon her, and each smack made her fight against her bonds. After one particularly fierce blow, that made her hips fly up a clear foot from the pillow, and made her yelping shrill up to a scream, Sacha stopped, temporarily, and crouched down once again beside her.

'Please try not to cry out, cherie,' he said quietly, as if her reactions were out of all proportion, and she was making a childish fuss over nothing. 'Beatrice is sleeping, and if she wakes up and hears you screaming, she may need me.'

Through her haze of desire and anguish, Alexa could

almost imagine the doctor's feelings. What if Beatrice were tied up, too? What if she heard these sounds – the slap of leather, and the cries of a woman being punished – and became unbearably aroused? Then couldn't touch herself to relieve the sweet ache?

'She's bound and gagged, so she can't call out for Camilla,' said Sacha softly, confirming Alexa's strange visions. 'Shall I gag you, too?' he asked, reaching down to stroke her wet, tear-stained face, then letting her suck on his thumb like a soother.

Alexa nodded, still suckling. The fire in her bottom was still raging, but it was another, more potent sensation which would not let her lie there in silence.

Opening a drawer in one of the vanity cupboards beside the bed, Sacha drew out a fine black silk scarf. This he knotted efficiently around her lower face, in between her teeth, in an arrangement that was snug, yet strangely unnerving. Even so, Alexa felt an odd sense of peace to feel the thing in her mouth, a feeling that she could relax more, and completely surrender to his will. He could spank her as hard as he liked now, without either of them worrying about the noise.

The slippering continued, and Alexa bucked and fought against her bonds. With her mouth stopped, Sacha seemed freed to achieve a new artistry, a higher, more distinct level of torment. He worked the slipper's flat sole over every inch of her buttocks, until the whole area was one great throb. Her swollen sex wept, and her cries were muffled grunts – but nothing mattered except the fall of each blow. It was a lifetime since either of them had been counting.

Suddenly, Alexa realised she wasn't being smacked any more. It was the strangest sensation, this absence of punishment. She felt as if her bottom had been tasting hot leather since before the dawn of time, and now – to her astonishment – she missed it. An air of preternatural silence descended on the room like the twilight that was falling outside. The only sounds she could hear were the crickets chirping incessantly in the garden outside and the sibilant whisper of the breeze in the curtains.

After a few moments of intent listening, Alexa imagined she could hear another sound too. The thump thump of blood pounding in her bottom. On the back of that, she suddenly heard something else, something very close and not of her making – the steady rasp of a man's ragged breathing. Sacha's breathing, deepened by exertion – or perhaps by something else?

Turning her head, and lifting her damp, tear-blurred eyes, Alexa looked up at him. Then felt a sudden surge of female exultation. Monsieur le Maître was no longer quite so glacial, so controlled. His handsome face was flushed, and his eyes were exceptionally, almost maniacally, bright. His smooth silver hair was attractively dishevelled, and he was pressing one pale hand against his groin. It was the first time his perfect poise had been disturbed.

'Pauvre petite,' he murmured, looming over her again, and pushing his hands beneath her nightdress at the front. He fondled her breasts roughly for a second or two, then withdrew and started pulling at his belt.

For one ghastly instant, Alexa quailed, wondering if she could possibly take a strapping on top of a slippering, but then she saw him fling the belt to the floor, step out of his shoes, then – barefoot – begin unbuttoning his jeans.

He was nude under the denim, and his circumcised erection jutted hugely from beneath the hem of his T-shirt. It brushed her arm as he moved close again, and unfastened the cuff that held her left wrist. In silence he moved to the four corners of the bed, and set each of her limbs loose in turn, without once touching the flaming redness of her bottom.

'You're beautiful, Alexa,' he gasped finally, climbing on to the bed beside her, and slipping a hand beneath each of her armpits. 'Come up on to your knees,' he commanded, and Alexa groaned as he lifted her bodily, the jerky movement jagging the tenderness of her rear.

He's going to have me now, she observed dreamily, crouching like an animal before him and imagining her crimson posterior glowing like an obscene, bifurcated target. He's going to fuck me, or bugger me, or both, she thought, thrusting her flaming haunches upwards to welcome him, and biting her lips at the resulting flash of pain.

'Yes!' she hissed as the slippery tip of his penis made contact, and butted blindly against her punished inner cheeks. She tried to relax and pout her anus open to receive him, then yelped as he gripped a smarting lobe in each of his hands and pulled wide the dark furrow in between them.

Expecting penetration at any second, she was surprised, then chagrined when he didn't enter her. Instead, and causing her to wail again at the distress it caused her, he laid his penis in the channel between her buttocks, then pressed the raging flesh inwards and upwards so he was trapped by the very heat he'd created.

The humiliation was so overpowering, and so grotesquely delicious, that Alexa almost climaxed there and then. Sacha was masturbating himself with her ruby-red, mortified bottom cheeks; sliding roughly to and fro against her pain. She could feel his balls slapping against the soft undercurve of her rump and his pre-ejaculate fluid oozing out on to the small of her back. With a sudden great cry, he jerked wildly above her, and then, as his fingertips grabbed and gouged at her cruelly treated buttocks, she felt his shaft leap and buck against her anus. Warm, liquid silkiness jetted out on to her back as she sobbed and howled at the fury in her bottom.

Mercifully, Sacha's recovery was rapid.

'Forgive me,' he murmured, levering his body off hers, then turning her over, and enfolding her in his arms. She groaned anew as her tenderised backside was pressed against the bedding, then felt her cries being smothered by his lips. Collapsing into the cradle

227

of his hold, she stoked her own pain by squirming like an elver and pushing her crotch against his warm and naked thigh.

'Patience, cherie, patience,' he whispered against her lips and her jaw as he deftly rearranged their sweating bodies. She felt him raise his hand to his mouth for a moment, pause, then with a sure grace, slide it between her thighs. When his moistened finger touched her clitoris, she climaxed instantaneously, and shouted his name as her pleasure rolled and tumbled.

What seemed a long time later, Alexa surfaced from a peculiar, tangled dream. Her bottom still felt terribly painful, but it had metamorphosed into a brilliant, luscious inferno that seemed to fill her loins and belly entirely. Every so often, Sacha would reach down and fondle her soreness, making her groan, and then kiss her face and hiss with joy.

'You're magnificent . . . *magnifique*,' he whispered, kneading her left buttock with one hand and rubbing her sex with the heel of the other. Orgasm fluttered again, and she nipped at his throat as she spasmed, then kissed him more lingeringly as it faded. 'So fresh . . . So quick to learn. So unafraid to accept what you need.'

She didn't know what to say. 'Thank you' seemed mundane, naïve. Extending the kiss, she pressed her body against his, sealing herself against him with their combined perspiration. Her thin nightie was bunched beneath her arms now, and his T-shirt had ridden up, too. She could feel him all the way from her midriff to her thighs, yet to her surprise, he remained flaccid and relaxed.

What do you really think of me, Monsieur le Maître? she pondered, enjoying the firm lines of his body despite the fact he remained puzzlingly unaroused. He'd desired her a short while ago, that was certain, and he was clearly enraptured by her bottom, and the process of rendering it scarlet and agonised. But his finer feelings remained a total mystery. All she could discover came to her via empirical data. There was no way she could 'read' him or 'sense' him . . . Would she even want to, she wondered, if his shield of ambiguity were ever to come down?

Sacha D'Aronville was certainly a beautiful and desirable man, and as she wriggled against him, she considered the few facts she was sure of.

He was in superb physical condition: he was lean, muscular and lithe, and his skin had a smooth glow of health. His pure silver hair, however, and the nets of faint lines at the corners of his eyes, indicated that his youth had been over many years ago. He had all the irresistible worldliness and sly, erotic gravitas of a man who was well into his fifties, and yet his body could have passed for that of someone much, much younger. In spite of all that had just passed between them, he remained exactly what he'd been when they'd started: an enigma.

'You are a greedy girl, Alexa,' he said suddenly, prising her off him. 'Splendid, but greedy . . . And I need to conserve myself for later.'

'For Beatrice?' she asked impulsively, saying the first thing that came into her head.

His answer was a soft laugh and a quick, hard pinch of her bottom. She cried out, and felt tears pop into her eyes, but fearlessly she held his blue gaze.

'Are you jealous, ma petite? Envious of the pleasure I share with her?'

Was she? Still fuzzed by the stinging in her rear, she examined her feelings about Beatrice, and 'Beatrice and Sacha'. She was fascinated by both of them, and excited by both of them; the idea of the doctor and this strange, multifaceted Frenchman together excited and entranced her beyond measure. Suddenly she longed to see them in bed with each other, their bodies twining in elaborate, extended lovemaking. Sacha's long, patrician penis sliding deep into Beatrice's sex.

'No, I'm not jealous,' she said finally. 'But I would like to watch you together. Making love, that is, not

229

just . . . Well, not just you caning her or masturbating her.'

The request was both outrageous and presumptuous. Yet, as he pulled back from her, Sacha was smiling – the most honest, uncomplicated and youthful expression she'd yet seen on his face.

'Beatrice . . .' he pronounced the name in the French fashion, '. . . is as magnificent and adorable as you are, my lovely Alexa. But the difference is that she knows it far too well.' A slightly calculating look appeared in his eyes that made Alexa's blood run cold, then immediately turn hot. 'She's proud and wilful and she needs a firm hand to keep her in line. She has a tendency to take too much from people. More than she has a right to.'

Alexa felt bound to defend the doctor, who, after all, had opened her eyes to an amazing new world. 'She's a little manipulative, granted,' she said steadily. 'But her heart's in the right place. I'm sure of it!'

'You're right,' said Sacha more gently, 'and I suspect you find her arousing, too?' He smiled again, letting his fingertips drift across her breast. 'Have you made love with her yet?'

'Well, not exactly,' replied Alexa, remembering her 'examination'. It seemed like a lifetime ago now, but it still had the power to stir her. She imagined herself back on the red leather couch with the doctor's long fingers sliding over her.

'Ah . . .' murmured Sacha, as if he, too, could see the memory. 'I understand. But would you like to enjoy her more completely?'

Alexa could only nod now, then gasp. His warm hand had slid between her legs again, wreaking havoc as her mind filled with Beatrice.

Chapter Fifteen

Unexpected Pleasures

*I*t had been twilight by the time Sacha left her, and
though she'd half expected to be summoned downstairs by a dinner gong, Alexa was happier when a
young maid, in a plain grey dress and starched apron,
arrived with what was obviously a supper tray.

It was a surprise to encounter an ordinary household
servant in Sacha's palace of debauchery, but logic suggested that a vast establishment like Villa Isis needed a
whole army of help to maintain it. Alexa could only
assume that Sacha's staff had been especially selected
for their discretion and an ability to remain unshocked,
regardless of what they saw or heard. Certainly the girl
who brought her meal was smiling and exquisitely
polite, and seemed totally untroubled by Alexa's
creased nightgown and tousled hair, the disordered
condition of the bed, and the very marked smell of
semen in the air. The maid asked a question in French,
and though her knowledge of the language was nomi-
nal, and her brain still half doped by sex, Alexa gathered
she was being asked whether she wanted a bath.

'*Non!* Er . . . *Merci*,' she answered, thinking of her
punished bottom, and how lying against a hard, por-

celain bath might feel. *'Je prends une douche,'* she added doubtfully, not quite sure if she'd chosen the right words.

It seemed she had, though, because the rather personable little maid smiled again, murmured *'Bien sûr, Ma'm'selle,'* and began – with quiet, unassuming efficiency – to set out fresh nightclothes for Alexa, and then strip the rumpled sheets from the bed.

At a loss, Alexa left her to it. Moving very slowly and carefully, she took her shower, then, even more carefully, she dried herself. Sniffing dubiously, she opened the container of herbal cooling gel that Sly had used on her earlier. Then holding her breath and gritting her teeth, she applied it. The procedure was one of the most unpleasant things she'd ever had to do to herself, but when it was over she was amazed by the rapid improvement. Her buttocks were still tender, and still quite hot, but after what had been inflicted on them, the gel's effect was miraculous.

The maid was gone when Alexa emerged into the bathroom, but the bed was made and the whole room had been tidied. The patio doors which led on to the balcony had been opened a little wider, and she noticed that the rich pot-pourri de Grasse – which was spread around in small terracotta bowls – had been stirred to refresh its pungent fragrance. She could no longer smell Sacha or sweat.

Her supper was simple but delicious. Sliced charcuterie and cheeses, served with wedges of succulent tomato and pepper. Kneeling on the bed, with her tray beside her, Alexa discovered a hunger that she hadn't been aware of. She devoured most of the tasty food with her fingers, along with several large hunks of fresh bread. There was a small carafe of wine on the tray, too, along with a pretty, bell-shaped glass. Alexa poured some experimentally, never having been a fan of red wine, but when she tasted she was pleasantly surprised. The ruby-coloured fluid was superbly light and very soft on the palate, and its mellow strength hit her belly like a glow.

Having drunk more than she'd meant to, and feeling cheerfully full, Alexa lay down sideways on the bed.

What a completely peculiar day it'd been. What a wonderful one . . . So full of wildness and such unexpected pleasures. Gingerly, she touched her bottom through the voile of her delicate nightie, and considered the elation that her punishments had brought her.

'You're not the girl you thought you were, Alexa old love,' she whispered to herself, remembering her protestations of feminism and personal freedom. In the orbit of a special kind of man, it seemed perfectly acceptable – no, appropriate – to surrender one's will to his whim. Pain was still pain. Everything that had been done to her had hurt like fury, but somehow been a key to something else. A special state, a sublime higher realm. A domain of sexuality where the rules that governed ordinary mortals didn't apply. With a feeling of both wistfulness and a weird sort of thankfulness, she realised her old life was over. Her engagement to Tom would have to end.

But he's a good man, she thought, straightening up, still on her side, and reaching for the last of the wine. A good man who would be a marvellous husband for some other kind of woman. A woman who didn't have strange needs.

As she finished her wine, Alexa heard a noise from the garden. Female laughter, and the low, quiet teasing of a separate, distinctly masculine voice. Curious, she slid gingerly off the bed, and padded on bare feet to the window, where she stood by the opening, but shrouded by the curtains.

Two figures were playing some sort of mock fighting game on an area of lawn just below. Two entirely naked figures tussling and batting at each other with towels, their perfect bodies silhouetted in the moonlight. After a second they paused for a brief kiss, but it was really nothing more than a simple brushing of lips, with very little hint of sex.

The nude frolickers were Drew and Sly. Drew's strong body looked impressive and familiar, but the handsome nurse looked quite different without her prim uniform and with her blonde hair flying loose.

For a moment, Alexa thought of rushing down on to the lawn to join them. She had a feeling that she might be welcome. There was an aura of amiable sensuality about the laughing, naked couple, as if they just might end up having sex together, but more in friendship than anything. And they certainly wouldn't turn away another . . .

Any combination of bodies and sexes was probably acceptable at Villa Isis, but Alexa suddenly felt too new to enter this one. Especially without an invitation. When all was said and done, Drew had spanked her today, hadn't he? And beaten her bottom with a hairbrush. It might be an infringement of some arcane disciplinary protocol to rush up to him and ask him to be her lover.

While Alexa was still pondering, a soft cry rang out across the garden. It was a woman's voice, and from the way Sly and Drew looked up, in a direction somewhere to the left of where Alexa stood concealed, it was clear it had come from another bedroom.

Beatrice's bedroom?

Dear heaven, what's he doing to her now? Alexa wondered. Another cry floated out into the night, but this time it was more recognisable, more definable. Whatever was happening, Beatrice was clearly in paradise. Her outpourings continued, grew almost savage, until finally they spiralled up to a clear, very beautiful wail that quite triumphantly announced her orgasm. There was a fainter, more male cry then, too.

Below, on the lawn, Drew and Sly exchanged knowing smiles. Then, picking up their towels from where they'd dropped them, they began strolling arm in arm down the garden, towards the path that led to the beach.

For a moment Alexa felt jealousy, then realised it was a pointless emotion. Drew and Sly had been colleagues, and probably friends and lovers, long before she'd come on the scene. Why shouldn't they take a moonlight swim together? She was far too tired to join them anyway. Her eyelids were already drooping.

Putting aside her tray, she went into the bathroom to clean her teeth. But when she returned and lay down to sleep, her mind instantly filled again with images. Sacha and Beatrice, their bodies contiguous as they writhed on a silk-sheeted bed. She could almost hear the endearments, the sweet nothings whispered in French. What if they were talking about her? Sacha might be describing how he'd beaten his little English girl, then enjoyed himself between the cheeks of her petit cul – Beatrice would just love to hear that!

Beatrice's bottom could be just as red as mine though, thought Alexa, rolling on to her back and feeling her buttocks start to throb. He'll be holding her there as he thrusts himself into her, digging his fingers in like he did with me. Oh God, it's no wonder she was screaming!

As Alexa reached behind to touch her rump, her quim heaved in a long, liquid surge. Placing her other hand between her legs, she paraded more images through her head. She saw Beatrice, naked but for elbow-length gloves and a Wehrmacht cap, being licked between her legs, by first Sacha, then Drew, then Sly . . . Sacha, bare-chested, in leather trousers whose saucy cut-outs revealed his male bottom. Sly, stretched face down across an altar of some kind, blindfolded and with a white penitent's robe folded up to reveal her smooth buttocks and thighs.

As the last image arrived, so did her orgasm. While her clitoris danced, Alexa pictured Drew entering Sly, their naked bodies thrashing on the sand as gentle foam-capped waves rolled over them.

* * *

Alexa awoke with a start, sensing a foreign presence in the room. Lifting her head, she opened her eyes in the warm, scented darkness and tried to make sense of what might lie in the shadows.

About to speak, she felt an uncoiling awareness of power and maleness, and saw a tall, broad form rise from her dressing chair in the corner and approach silently across the polished boards and the rug.

Not Sacha, she thought, shaking off the last remnant of sleep. A dark head inclined towards her, and a large hand fell gently across her mouth. 'In silence,' a familiar voice hissed, then the hand was gone. She felt the sheet being thrown aside, then her thin gown being pushed upwards to expose her. Unyielding fingers gripped her hips, and dragged her bodily across the mattress, punishing her tender buttocks in the process. Her legs flopped over the side of the bed, then were pushed apart so her moist, musky sex was laid open. Trembling with the anticipation, she looked up into Drew's face, but found it unreadable in the darkness, apart from the sharp glint of his glasses. She felt lashed by a huge blast of desire, both his and her own, and as a zipper buzzed, and a hand tested her, fingertips paddling in her channel, she experienced no surprise at being dripping and ready.

You've wanted to do this all along, she thought, gnawing her lip as he raised her up and his penis pushed into her like a bludgeon. All that smacking, and sucking, it was a substitute. An elaborate precursor to this.

He gave her simple, rough sex; uncomplicated, but supremely blissful. She made a small sound of protest when he reached forward, took her hand, then pressed it against her pubis; but another command, this time almost telepathic, made her dig through her curls and find her clitoris. He wanted her to masturbate as he took her, and suddenly it was what she wanted, too. She got down to her task with enthusiasm.

Once she was rubbing, Drew took her securely by the

hips and began sliding into her fiercely but evenly. It was difficult not to cry out, and once or twice she moaned, but in the main, she obeyed him and stayed silent. Within moments she was climaxing around him, her legs waving on either side of him as he continued to pursue his own agenda. Her spasms seemed to have little effect on him, and his thrusts remained long, deep and smooth. It was only after he'd been shafting her for a good ten minutes, and she'd come herself again and again, that he finally showed signs of being close. She felt his fingers flex, and dig into her, and right at the very depth of his in-stroke, he froze, and threw back his dark head.

'Dear God,' he cried, his voice hoarse, yet astonishingly distinct, and his flesh rippled and leaped deep inside her.

'Drew!' she gasped, defying him right at the peak. Blindly, she curled forward, grabbed his thigh and squeezed it in a makeshift caress. Drew in turn abandoned his hold on her, then, reaching for her free hand, took it and gripped it. Their fingers entwined as they shared the supreme moment.

When it was over, he was all silence again. Withdrawing precisely, he eased her backwards on the bed to stop her sliding off it, then fastened up the zip of his jeans. A tall, gleaming figure in the darkness, he lifted her with no discernible effort and laid her gently back against the pillows. Leaning across, he placed a single, fleeting kiss on the damply matted curls of her pubis, then re-covered her with her nightie and the sheet.

Before she could speak, or even move, he was gone.

Was that what was called a mercy fuck, I wonder? she thought dreamily, as sleep swept in from the Mediterranean to claim her. And if it was one, was it for my benefit – or his?

Strangely enough, Drew was merciful the next night. And at the same time every night after . . .

In the velvet darkness of the small hours, he would

237

pad quietly into her bedroom, then make love to her thoroughly and silently – inducing orgasms that were both lingering and precious.

That first night, as she sweated and twisted against him, Alexa wondered if anyone else knew Drew was with her. She was supposed to be Sacha's plaything for the duration, and maybe, by extension, Beatrice's. And yet her stolen, poignant couplings with their strong-limbed masseur would provide no amusement for either Monsieur le Maître or Madame la Maîtresse. Especially as the sex was so straight.

No hairbrushes, no spanking, no humiliation. Just plain, honest, normal lovemaking, performed with power, imagination and tenderness. An oasis of straightforward pleasure within an interlude that was becoming increasingly involved.

When the first morning came, Alexa was surprised that she was allowed to sleep in. A tiny noise had broken into her sleep and woken her, but by the time she'd struggled up to full consciousness, its source had clearly been and gone. Last night's supper tray had been replaced by another bearing breakfast: a plate piled with fresh-baked croissants, plus butter curls and conserve, and a pair of tall sterling silver pots – one filled with dark fragrant coffee and the other with hot creamy milk.

Alexa ate one croissant straight away, then immediately reached for another, feeling greedy, but squashing the guilt. The coffee too was superior . . . For the first time ever, she found its taste matched its smell; strong but not bitter, its powerful aromatic flavour perfectly balanced by the bland richness of the milk.

As she first enjoyed her sybaritic breakfast, then embarked on a leisurely toilette, Alexa considered what the day ahead might hold. Erotic discipline was clearly Sacha's predilection, but somehow now it was one of hers, too.

But why? she thought, smoothing moisturiser into her face after her shower as she revisited her reflections of last night. Letting a man dictate to her, by thrashing her naked bottom, ran counter to every self-determinist ideal she'd ever believed in. Thinking of what she'd gone through yesterday, she hardly recognised herself as the competent, assertive Alexa of KL Systems, and the fiancée who'd mostly got her way.

She was still pondering when the door swung open, and Sly walked in briskly into the room, her sensible heels tapping on the boards.

'Come along, sleepyhead, you're wanted,' she said cheerfully, dropping a number of strange objects on the bedspread, then taking Alexa firmly by the arm.

It must be any kind of dominance that gets to me, thought Alexa, standing up at the pretty nurse's urging. She could feel her body responding already, excited by Sly's verve and her air of assurance, and the business-like way she got down to things. In a flash, her robe was peeled off and she was naked.

'Monsieur le Maître is having a massage,' announced Sly matter-of-factly, tossing the robe aside. 'And he requires your attendance. So we'd better look lively and have you ready.'

'But I can't do massage,' Alexa protested, thinking immediately of Drew, in the night. Had he returned to Sly's bed after hers?

'Of course you can't,' said Sly, first cupping Alexa's breasts, then slipping her hand, sideways on, into her crotch. 'It's dear Drew who does the massaging. You'll just be there to keep Sacha entertained. Come on, now, turn around . . . I want to check the condition of your bottom.'

Her heart pounding, Alexa turned around, then felt Sly's gentle hands on her rump, palpating it for indications of injury. There was some residual tenderness and she made a small sound of discomfort as the nurse pressed harder, but to her surprise, when she looked over her shoulder, Alexa saw her flesh was barely marked. Only a faint veil of pinkness remained.

'Good. Excellent,' murmured Sly. 'Now, over you go so I can examine you inside.'

'Wha . . . What?'

'Now, now,' soothed Sly, resting her hand on Alexa's naked back. 'Don't be difficult. I don't want to have to report any reluctance. It's only a simple rectal inspection.'

Another part of the game, thought Alexa excitedly, leaning forward across the bed, and resting her face against her folded arms. Another humbling, but in disguise. She could feel moisture welling in her vulva.

'Spread your legs, darling,' said Sly gently, moving around Alexa's side to reach for something she'd dropped on the bedspread. Alexa wanted to sway towards the nurse, clasp her hips and then hug her. She wondered if Sly would perhaps lift up her snowy white skirt . . .

Snapping free of her fancies, Alexa set her feet apart and thrust out her bottom, well aware that the action would display her shining labia. She wanted Sly to touch her now, wanted it quite desperately, and when the nurse's hand settled on her delicately glowing bottom cheek, she whimpered with delicious expectation.

'You're so keen, sweetheart, aren't you?' said Sly with some amusement. 'I've never known a woman get so wet so soon.' She paused, and her fingers flexed meticulously. 'Except Bea, of course, but she's a special case.'

Alexa waited – her thighs quivering, her nipples hard, her sex awash. Closing her eyes to contain the gorgeous tension, she listened to the nurse's preparations. She heard the snap of rubber gloves, the tiny slurp of something oozing from a tube.

'Relax, Alexa love,' whispered Sly in her ear, and then the invasion of her modesty began.

'Oh no . . . Oh no . . .' crooned Alexa, as her bottom tried to fight the probing finger. A fleeting picture of

Siddig appeared behind her eyelids, and the association made her sphincter yield and give.

'There. That's better,' encouraged Sly. 'You can take that, can't you?' The finger wiggled gently back and forth. 'It's nice having something in there, isn't it? You know you like it. You liked it well enough in Beatrice's surgery. And you certainly liked it with our pretty Sudanese friends, didn't you?'

Dear heaven, these people know everything, thought Alexa, her body rocking as Sly's finger swirled and pushed. She supposed now that there had been a camera in that opulent London bedroom; it certainly wouldn't have been difficult to hide. She imagined Sacha, Beatrice, Lord alone knew who else, all watching as she'd been lowered oh-so-slowly on to Siddig's hard penis, then had the pleasure of Yusuf's tongue upon her sex.

Groaning, she pushed back on to Sly's finger, then sobbed when the nurse pulled away.

'Oh no, no, no,' the other woman chided. 'You've to wait for all that . . . I have specific instructions not to let you come until you're in the presence of Monsieur le Maître.'

Alexa shook, but held the pose, feeling the stickiness of the lubricant in her groove. She could hear Sly sorting through her paraphernalia again, and wondered what would be inflicted on her next.

'Now then, we just have to put a little harness on you, darling, and then we're ready,' said Sly encouragingly, picking up something that jingled. 'Relax again. Everywhere this time. He wants something put in both your naughty places, I'm afraid. To remind you why you're here, and whose you are.'

Almost before she'd had time to absorb what the nurse was saying, Alexa felt her bottom being invaded again. Something round, very large, and smooth was being pushed inside her rectum, and in a blind, hot panic she felt an awful urge to void herself.

'Easy . . . Take it easy,' coaxed Sly, reaching beneath

Alexa's belly to massage away the cramps. 'You're all right. You're clean as a whistle. Nothing'll happen.'

Alexa fought hard to believe her, and after a moment, her insides began to calm. A couple of seconds later, the sensations changed again and became pleasant; and then, as Sly inserted a second obstruction – into her vagina this time – Alexa's panting turned to soft, delighted moans. She could feel straps of some kind being secured around her waist, and realised the jingling sound had been several sets of buckles.

'Let's get you fastened up then,' said Sly, as she encouraged Alexa to stand up. Something seemed to be dangling and tickling her knees now; so, for the first time in several minutes Alexa opened her eyes, and looked down towards what hung around her legs.

As she watched in a blend of awe and horror, she saw that a harness had been fitted around her loins. A black leather strap – which was somehow attached to both the objects inside her – was pulled up between her buttocks at the back and this was clipped, as far as she could tell, to a narrow leather belt around her waist. There was still another strip of leather dangling down at the front, but this Sly quickly looped up, then slid between Alexa's swollen labia. The final touch was to fasten the crotch strap to the belt at the front.

As the nurse tightened the array, paused to consider, then tightened it again, Alexa realised that the strip of leather traversing her vulva was thickly padded, and that against her clitoris there was an added protrusion. A stiff little leather-covered roll.

'Oh God,' she whimpered, when Sly tugged lightly and the objects lodged inside her jostled.

'Nice, eh?' observed the nurse, running her tongue along her lip as she peeled off her sticky gloves. 'Well, I like it when I have to wear one.'

The image of Sly in a harness was almost too much for Alexa. The nurse was extraordinarily beautiful when naked, as last night in the moonlight had shown, and the thought of that slender, pristine body being so intimately constrained and abused was as shocking as it was exciting.

'Now, just a couple more touches,' said Sly, picking up another item from the bed – an-inch wide black velvet choker which she fastened around Alexa's neck. 'Voilà,' she exclaimed, sliding the press stud around to the back. 'And now these . . .'

'These' came from a tissue-padded box, and were a pair of black patent stiletto pumps with heels that looked every bit of four inches high.

'I don't think I can wear those,' said Alexa, admiring the beauty of the shiny black shoes but dubious about their extreme height.

'Oh, you can!' proclaimed Sly, bending down to slip the left one on Alexa's bare foot, offering her back for Alexa to rest on as she did so. 'You'll be fine. And it's not as if you're going on a route march.' She straightened up, reached for the other shoe, then the process was repeated, leaving Alexa feeling as if she was suddenly on stilts.

The sensation was precarious and giddying, and when she tried to take a step, she almost fainted. Each tottering movement joggled the dildos in their niches and rubbed the little leather roll against her clitoris.

'I can't . . . I can't do this,' she gasped, swaying.

'Now, now,' the nurse chided, backing away and then holding out her hands. 'Come on . . . Walk towards me. You can do it!'

Alexa complied, gnawing her lip and clenching fists. Every tiny motion seemed to work the harness deeper into her vulva; even breathing was a subtle stimulation. Her intimate orifices were both sealed and possessed. She was invaded, and demeaned by the invasion, because her violators were mindless chunks of rubber that could remain in her body indefinitely: immune, inanimate, unstirred. A finger or a penis seemed less shaming.

'Just a few final touches. Stand still.'

Alexa stood very still, as much as she could, while

Sly added a few well-chosen cosmetics. A little dark eyeliner, some mascara, and crimson lipstick on both her mouth and her nipples. She applied the lipstick to Alexa's sex, too, rubbing it in, beneath the strap, until she moaned and her belly began to spasm.

'You're too runny for this really,' commented the nurse as she eyed her pink-stained fingers, then cleaned herself meticulously with tissues.

The walk that followed was agonising – five long, seemingly endless minutes of crawling along the edge of an orgasm. Every step was an exquisite assault on her wet, beleaguered sex; every turn of a corner brought a surge of almost choking apprehension. What if some servant, or some as yet unmet guest should be waiting beyond it, and see her bound and paraded like a barbarian's naked love prize? She was gasping like a bellows when Sly opened the last door and led her into a long airy salon, flanked by open French windows, that had a massage table set right at its centre.

'Ah, cherie, we've been waiting,' said Sacha D'Aronville as they approached. His cool eyes flicked quickly to Alexa's crotch – and the harness – and he favoured her with a narrow, knowing smile. 'How do you like your little adornment?'

He was lying stretched out on the massage couch, his body already oiled, and with a small towel draped strategically across his loins. Behind him stood Drew, looking massive when compared with the slim Frenchman, and wearing a black cutaway vest and brief shorts. His grey eyes regarded her expressionlessly, slightly masked by the tinted lenses of his glasses.

'Well?' prompted Sacha, coming up on to his elbow, then brushing his fingers through his bright, silvery hair. 'Are you enjoying it? Are you being stimulated? Do you feel as if you might have an orgasm?'

'Yes. Yes, I do,' she said tightly, the very word itself almost triggering her.

'Well, try to hold on . . . I'll be disappointed if you give in to it too soon.'

'Oh no!' she keened, weaving on her feet and almost falling against Sly.

'Oh yes. You must wait,' he said softly, lying down again. 'If you come before I do, you'll be sorry . . .' With that, he settled himself comfortably on his back, spreading his thighs a little. The tiny towel slid an inch or two sideways. 'When you're ready, Drew,' he said pleasantly, then he nodded to the waiting masseur.

What followed was pure torment. Drew began working on Sacha's arms and shoulders; seeking out tensions with his fingers and his thumbs, then digging deep and kneading to dispel them. Alexa remembered Barbados, and those strong hands kneading her shoulders, then last night and that strong body making love to her. She wished passionately that she was on the table, being manipulated, the swelling stresses in her vulva being relieved. She imagined Drew unbuckling the harness with great gentleness, then replacing the rubber inside her body with his flesh.

As she watched, the obstructions in her vagina and her rectum seemed to enlarge and caress her inner membranes. They pressed on every part of her; there was no way to get relief. She could feel herself engorging, getting hotter and hotter, wetter and wetter. She took a step, set her feet a little further apart, to try and alleviate the stress, then whimpered pathetically as her sex began to pulse.

'Are you coming, Alexa?' enquired Sacha, stirring on the table. His eyes were closed, yet he seemed to sense what was happening inside her, as if he, too, had a sexual sixth sense.

'No!' she cried, digging her nails into the palms of her hands, and wishing she dared to clasp her crotch and jam the harness against her clitoris. She was only half a heartbeat away from exploding, and too far gone now to observe Sacha's dictum.

'I think we'll need the cuffs soon, Camilla,' said the Frenchman quietly, as Drew slapped him on the shoulder in a signal to turn over. Deliberately tantalising her, Sacha clasped his towel to his body, and slid over without revealing his genitals.

So beautiful, she thought, gazing at the lightly tanned rounds of Sacha's rump. His backside was firm and perfectly muscled; not too flat, not too rounded, the furrow very deep and well defined. Just right for spanking, observed Alexa suddenly, imagining a whip or a belt in her hand. For an instant, she pictured Drew restraining Sacha instead of oiling and massaging him, while she slashed down a thin cane without mercy. She could even abuse his anus with a dildo too, fill him as he'd ordered her filled.

The last image destroyed all her resistance. Without thinking, she grabbed the girdle that circled her belly and yanked it where it met the descending crotch strap.

Pleasure attacked her immediately. Her clitoris leaped, her vagina pumped, and even her rectum made a grab at its intruder. A weird, inhuman cry seemed to be wrenched from the very heart of her, and she would have fallen – orgasming convulsively – if Sly hadn't stepped close to support her.

'Oh baby, now you've done it,' whispered the nurse as she first steadied Alexa's waverings, then took her by the wrists and secured them in handcuffs.

Alexa sobbed, and began to struggle against her bonds. Her hands were immobilised, pinned together at the small of her back, just when her sex and her breasts ached for contact. The climax she'd just experienced was shallow and inconclusive – simply an appetiser for the release her body craved.

'Please . . . oh please,' she whispered to no one in particular.

Sacha adjusted himself on the massage couch, and turned towards her, his head resting sideways on his arms. 'Naughty girl,' he murmured, 'I told you not to come.' He grinned at her, his eyelids drooping sleepily. 'And you took pleasure without permission last night, too,' he continued, with the most infinitesimal indication towards Drew.

246

Bastard! thought Alexa, staring ferociously at the tall masseur. He'd given her away, the swine, to his master . . . or whatever the hell his relationship to Sacha was. As if sensing her scrutiny, or perhaps even her silent cry of rage, Drew looked up from his efforts – the ruthless pummelling of Sacha's gleaming backside – and met her gaze, his own eyes remote.

Suddenly, for one instant, Alexa's sexual awareness gained a brand new dimension. Somewhere in Drew's unruffled demeanour, right at the very centre of it, she sensed remorse and a bleak, powerless anger. He was as much a pawn in this as she was, she realised, and obligated to Sacha D'Aronville by the debt he owed to Beatrice. He'd probably been sent last night, ordered to her room to make love to her.

Maybe Drew's being punished as well?

The thought popped into her head like a bolt from the blue, and as it did, she surveyed him more intently. Perhaps he had come to her bed simply because he wanted to, and having her displayed here before him, with her body in bondage, was an indirect way of chastising him, too?

'*Mon Dieu . . . C'est merveilleux*,' murmured Sacha suddenly, his hips squirming under Drew's ministrations. He was rubbing himself unashamedly against the white-sheeted couch, and purring with contentment like a cat. When the masseur's long fingers dug deep, then flexed and palpated, the Frenchman groaned and pushed his bottom towards the pressure.

'*Je vous en prie!*' he said roughly, then almost whined when Drew's thumbs slid neatly inside him. From where she stood, teetering and swaying on her heels, Alexa saw Sacha's tight opening being stretched and dilated and his blue eyes roll up in pure bliss. Drew was crouched right over him now, working the puckered hole remorselessly, and almost fucking his moaning Master with his hands.

The penetration went on for several minutes, then Sacha shook his head and panted, 'Enough!'

247

Drew stopped as ordered, and withdrew. Sacha rolled on to his back then sat up, his erection pointing upwards like a shining reddened prong.

'Alexa. Cherie,' he said softly. 'Come here and give me your mouth.' He spread his legs on the table and patted the space he'd made between them, then reached down to jiggle his rigid member.

The massage couch was large, and there was plenty of room for Alexa to get on it and kneel between his knees, but actually getting there made her catch her breath and whimper. With her hands bound in the cuffs, her every movement was clumsy, and she jerked and faltered even with Sly's guiding help. As she climbed into position, the dildos shifted and rolled into an entirely different configuration, their infernal contours working on new areas of congestion. Crouched between Sacha's tanned legs, she could feel her tormented sex weeping around the harness, her silky juices sliding freely down her thighs. She came again as her lips opened on Sacha's cock.

Crying, and slobbering over the stiff organ against her tongue, she felt a profound sense of helpless subjugation. Her French Master had covered every angle; asserted control over not only her body but her mind and her emotions. He was filling her mouth with his hot living flesh, just as he'd ordered her orifices to be stopped up with cold rubber. He'd made her powerless to resist her own pleasure and orgasms, and made her behave like an animal, almost, before a man who she suspected admired her.

Gulping furiously, she craned her neck to look up towards Drew, who now stood like a graven image by Sacha's shoulder. She tried to flash an expression of empathy towards the tall masseur, and make contact with the grim, detached mind behind his glasses; but before she could, Sacha somehow seemed to intercept her silent message.

The Frenchman smiled at her; a slow, cool smile of blue-eyed triumph which degraded quickly into a raw orgasmic snarl. His slim hips jerked violently, and his cock jabbed her palate, just as he reached out and dragged Drew's face towards his.

And then, while Sacha ejaculated heavily and filled her mouth with semen, she was forced to watch him savagely kiss a man.

Chapter Sixteen

No Way Back

*A*lexa didn't see the two men kiss again, although what they did together when she wasn't with them continued to intrigue her even now.

His pleasure over, Sacha had risen from the couch invigorated. He'd called for a robe and a glass of wine, and when Sly had supplied both, he'd settled down to watch Drew punish Alexa.

It had been a short session, but profoundly intense. She'd been spread over a trestle, still cuffed and bunged, and had her buttocks soundly whipped with a switch. Then, sobbing and wriggling, she'd been divested of her harness, but not her cuffs, shoes and choker; and, at Sacha's order, Drew had stepped behind her, gripped her hips – and fucked her. She'd been so wet, she remembered, that her juiciness had been embarrassingly audible; she'd been able to hear Drew's thrusts as well as feel them. After about a minute, she'd climaxed hugely and looked up into Sacha's eyes as she spasmed. He'd smiled at her, then walked across and kissed her.

And that sort of crystallises everything, I suppose, she thought now, in her flat, back in London. Every encounter, every scene, every act of sex in every combination; they'd all been both deviant and tender. She'd been subjected to a dozen different humiliations, but there had always been a certain kindness about them too. A word. A gesture. A look. One gem of gentleness to assuage the deepest hurt.

She'd been spanked and played with by Beatrice and by Sly. She'd been taken, in every orifice, by Sacha, and by Drew at Sacha's behest. She'd been tied up, strapped down, and clad in the most constricting and peculiar of garments. Leather basques, rubber hoods, panties with holes and protuberances in the most intimate of places.

But each weird act had brought her closer to her tormentors – if you could call them that when the dynamics were variable. One minute she was chained, naked, to the balustrade on the patio, having her haunches alternately smacked and fondled. The next, she was in bed between Beatrice and Sacha, and was being pleasured by both of them in turn.

And every night, of course, there had been the silent episodes with Drew, sometimes fierce, sometimes lyrical, but always comfortingly 'straight'. The only strange thing was that neither he or she referred to them afterwards.

But now she was back home, where the air was cooler, there was no scent of pines, and everything seemed depressingly normal.

'Pull yourself together, Alexa,' she told herself. 'Everybody's had what they want. The fee's paid. The game's over.' She looked around at the luggage she'd acquired while in France, which formed part of her 'fee', she supposed. Sacha had lavished scores of gifts on her; her Gucci suitcases contained revealing clothes, filmy lingerie, expensive cosmetics, as well as other items far more practical.

A banker's draft for a ridiculous amount of money, given to her with a Gallic kiss on the hand and a grave, cool-eyed assurance that her obligations were now discharged in full. A slim folder, filled with names and addresses, and a set of brief but telling letters – in which *Société Financière D'Aronville* endorsed KL Systems with its highest recommendation. There were even a number of letters containing plaudits for her personally, as a systems analyst, although Alexa had suspicions about the content of some of these. Certain phrases might conceal crucial double meanings.

Whatever the letters said, one thing was for certain. Life from now on would be different. There was no way back. At least, not to her relationship with Thomas. What she'd felt in France wasn't just restlessness inspired by exotic surroundings. She'd changed so much that to go on wouldn't be fair to either of them, and she had a gut feeling that he'd probably agree with her.

In a reflective moment, she looked down at her left hand. It was prophetic, somehow, that they'd never actually gone out and bought a ring.

So, if there was no looking back, she had to look forward. How would things be from now on? Could she still work for him? Be with him every day, even if they didn't share their nights? It would be tricky. And so would working with Quentin, after what had happened in the washroom.

Maybe she ought to work for herself now instead, as Sacha seemed to be suggesting with his glowing letters of reference? She had contacts of her own aplenty, and probably funds too, after she'd ironed out the details of the *Société Financière D'Aronville* payment with Tom. She could strike out, both professionally and personally, get a new place, a new routine, new friends. A circle that might begin with her doctor . . .

Beatrice had promised to get in touch, in the next day or so, when she returned to England after a couple of nights' stopover in Paris. She'd tried to persuade Alexa to travel with her – cajoling and coaxing with all the considerable guile at her disposal – but Alexa had declined. It seemed fairer to fly straight home. And face Tom.

The flat was empty, but his message on the answer-phone told her he'd be coming home later. She listened carefully to the tone of his voice, trying to gauge his mood, his thinking, but the short recording was perplexingly neutral.

As evening wore on, Alexa took a shower, then studied her body as she dried herself. Sacha hadn't used a cane on her as he had on Beatrice; he'd hinted that he was 'saving' it. There were a couple of faint, fading bruises across the crown of her left buttock, but otherwise she was smooth and unmarked. It was disappointing, really, that there was so little to show for her ecstasy. With a sigh, she slid into one of her new items of lingerie: a simple floor-length nightgown, in off-white bias-cut silk. She sprayed herself with perfume, also new – a light jasmine-based blend that she knew cost a fortune – and rubbed a little French moisturiser into her face and her throat. Running her fingers through her hair, she fluffed out its soft natural curl.

What is this, Lavelle? she enquired of herself, looking at her face in the mirror, as if her motives might be written there. The instinct to make herself look desirable, eroticise even, had become automatic now, but should she really be following it now?

Is this the set-up for one last seduction? she thought. Was that the way to tell him? While he was mellow, pleasured; inside her, perhaps?

It seemed preposterous, but was any other way any kinder? Still not sure, she poured a large glass of wine.

The feeling of a body in the bed disturbed her sleep. The shifting of weight, and the unmistakable presence of a man. Even drowsy and hardly able to think, Alexa sensed desire all around her.

'Drew?' she queried, her questing fingers encountering a bare flank, then a firm male thigh.

'Is that his name, then?' said Tom quietly, his voice strangely calm.

Instantly awake, Alexa tried to sit up and lunge for

the light-switch, but Tom twisted across her and restrained her.

'No! It's OK. This is better in the dark.' He paused, seemed to be searching for words. 'I've known something was wrong since you got back from Barbados. Something serious . . . I've been waiting for you to tell me there was another man. There had to be a reason for the spending, and the hair and everything.'

Now it was Alexa's turn to think carefully about her words. She couldn't stay with Tom any more, because she didn't love him or want to live with him, but she didn't want to hurt him either. There was a lot of her that still cared, still felt fond of him.

'It's hard to explain,' she said cautiously, reaching for his hand, and feeling relief when it curved comfortably around hers. 'But I would like to try . . . As best I can. You deserve it.'

Tom was silent for a while, his fingertip moving against her palm in a way that had always aroused her.

'OK, I'm listening,' he said at length, sounding resigned but also half intrigued.

'Something happened to me in Barbados.' she began hesitantly. 'It wasn't to do with a man. Well, not at first. It was me, I changed . . . Or maybe something that was already in me finally got knocked to the surface.'

As she recounted the story of her bump on the head, and the peculiar set of events that had followed it, the man beside her remained quiet and attentive. Alexa edited the account carefully, to spare his feelings as much as anything, but even so, she could still sense his perfect astonishment, and in some places his horror and alarm. When it was over, he fell into a long, thoughtful silence, his fingers still loosely twined with hers.

'I . . . I can't handle all that,' he said at length, then moved uneasily beside her. 'It's exciting, some of it, but it's not for me. It's too extreme. I couldn't live a life like that. I don't want to . . .'

Alexa could feel the honesty in his voice. And the puzzlement. They were too different now, maybe they always had been. She opened her mouth, to say she knew not what, but Tom spoke up again and pre-empted her.

'It's a relief, really. I've always had a feeling something wasn't quite right, but I thought it would go away. That we'd work through it. Pull together, you know, for the sake of KL and what have you.' He paused, then squeezed her hand in a way that felt distinctly like a caress. 'But that doesn't mean I don't care for you, Lexie. I still do, and in some ways I always will, but I know now it would be a disaster to marry you.' He hesitated again, then laughed and pulled her fingers to his lips for a kiss. 'I'm sorry, that didn't sound right. But I think you know what I mean.'

'I do. And you're right,' she said, experiencing a surge of warm feeling for him now that the truth was out. Some things had, on occasion, been very good for them. And they didn't have to jettison all of their relationship, did they? She rolled a little way across the bed towards him.

'We could still be friends, though,' he offered, pre-empting her a second time. 'Work something out with the business. Have dinner now and again, for old times' sake. Even . . . Well . . . Oh God, I don't know how to say this!' he cried exasperatedly, 'Come on, you're the bloody liberated one, the sexual free spirit. Help me!'

Alexa smiled in the darkness, and placed her hand on his warm, lean hip. He was naked, which was not how he usually came to bed, and her drifting fingers soon encountered what she'd sensed and been expecting.

'We could still go to bed together occasionally? Is that what you're saying?' she suggested. 'As friends, of course,' she added teasingly.

'Yes. Yes, that's it, sort of. I th – ' he broke off then, groaning as she began to caress him with the long, sliding strokes he'd always loved. 'Look. Oh God, Lexie

. . . We're in bed now, and we're friends. Do you think we should start this new relationship of ours now?' He writhed, pumping his hips a little to the rhythm of her hand. 'Just . . . Just the things we've always done. You know? Nothing weird. None of that other stuff. Is that OK?'

'I think so,' she murmured, giving him a delicate squeeze before releasing him, and then falling back against the pillows invitingly. Wriggling, she eased up her silky nightdress, and felt the cool cotton of the sheet against her bottom. Then, letting her thighs fall open, she put her arms out and drew Tom towards her.

His body felt strong, hard and hot. He wasn't a muscle-man like Drew, or aesthetically lean like Sacha, but despite this, Tom had always had his attractions. His penis was rigid where it brushed and bobbed against her, but he did not thrust straight in. Alexa smiled to herself as he began to kiss her neck, and stroked her breasts in slow circles through her bodice. Tom's technique had always been adequate, and even – on occasion – mildly inspired, but she sensed now that he was trying especially hard. He was a man, after all, with an ego; he wanted to look good beside the spectres of others.

She wanted to tell him not to bother, and not to worry, and that she enjoyed the way they'd always made love. It wasn't sex that made them incompatible, it was a way of thinking; their goals; the way she'd changed.

And the way her thoughts, even now, began to wander . . .

As Tom squeezed her nipples through the fabric of her nightgown, she saw a masked woman leaning over her, applying small, elaborately engraved clips to the tips of her breasts.

'Oh yes! Oh yes, harder!' she whispered, and in her fantasy the woman – Beatrice? Sly? Loosie? – tightened the clips by turning tiny silver screws.

Tom complied, and again she sensed his subconscious competitiveness. He pinched her teats, twisted them a little, and then, as she squirmed and whimpered, she felt him free one of them and slide his hand between her legs.

'It really excites you, doesn't it?' he whispered, one hand twisting, one rubbing. 'Pain. Domination. The things you described.'

'Yes,' Alexa gasped as he drew out her firm breast like a cone, stretching it away from her ribcage and tugging and tweaking at the nipple in the process. Her hips began to jerk of their own accord, but Tom's fingertip rode the gyrations, pressing roughly against her hot, aching nexus. She was aware of him looming over her, sitting up, manipulating her like a puppetmaster. The feeling was wonderfully familiar.

For an instant, she thought of Sacha, and how this was so much like something he might do, then she thought of nothing. Nothing at all. She subsumed everything to the demands of her senses as Tom rearranged his assault between her legs, filling her vagina with a fat wedge of his fingers while his thumb mashed and swirled against her clitoris.

'Dear God!' she cried softly as she came.

She'd sucked him then. She'd known it was what he wanted; the perfect reward for the pleasure of his hands. As she'd tasted him, Alexa had felt oddly optimistic, but now, several days later, she wished everything was as clear.

Running her tongue unconsciously over her lips, she let the echo of his flavour distract her, and seemed to hear again his harsh cry of release. He'd cursed her as he came, but there'd been affection in it; a note of fondness even orgasm couldn't mask. Alexa smiled. They could be friends still. They could be lovers occasionally, even. Who knows, she thought, maybe even one day he'll be able to handle the 'other' things?

But for the moment, they couldn't continue living together, and, as this was Tom's home, it was she who had to leave. He'd tactfully arranged another out-of-town visit, to Wales this time, leaving Alexa with free time to up and leave.

If only it was that easy, she thought, picking up her coffee cup, and sipping as she prowled around the flat. She was saying goodbye, she realised, bidding her farewells to their better times together.

It took a while, and left her almost tearful, but it didn't make her doubt her decision. She had a new vision, new needs, a new life, but what she didn't know was exactly where to begin it.

One option had presented itself just an hour ago. A long, intimate letter had arrived by courier, from France, an approach she'd been more than half expecting.

Live with me, Sacha urged, in a written English as compelling as his voice. Travel with me. We can explore everything we began at Villa Isis, then go further . . . I've been thinking of your naked body, Alexa. Your breasts. Your sex. I've been thinking about your cul, imagining you under the cane. Hearing your screams, tasting your wetness. I want you, Alexa, cherie. Your pleasure. Your pain. And I can show you another side of me too. A side I think you might enjoy . . .

It was a tempting offer. Almost irresistible. And the idea of a new Sacha intrigued her. It was clear to her what he was offering, what those words meant. She'd touched the paper and imagined a reversal of their roles. Herself severe, in leather perhaps; Sacha abject, naked before her, waiting for a blow. The thought excited her, but she knew she wasn't ready. There was much to learn before she saw Sacha D'Aronville again. She needed total confidence before she could control him as he'd controlled her. Her new dealings with Thomas might give her some practice, but her instincts told her he wasn't a true test.

When her bag was packed – with just a few things she immediately needed – she still hadn't decided where to go. Her few long-standing female friends were also Tom's friends, and she didn't think any of them would understand her now. Her new persona wasn't the Alexa they'd always known, in their conventional eyes she'd probably seem a monster.

She could, of course, take a room in a hotel for a while – she had the money now. But it wasn't until she was in her car, and driving south through the City, that she realised exactly where she was going. A destination that should have been blindingly obvious all along . . .

It was Drew who answered the black-painted door, even though it had been Beatrice's bell that she'd pushed. He stood facing her across the threshold, his handsome face smiling a welcome, his muscular body an even greater invitation, clad only in running shorts and T-shirt.

'Come in,' he said, reaching for her bag. 'Beatrice has been expecting you.' He paused, their fingers in contact on the handle. 'We all have . . .'

Alexa baulked. Was he gloating? Were he and his mistress so sure of their hold on her? She tightened her grip on her suitcase and tried to prise it free.

'Hey! Don't be like that,' he said, the case remaining immovable in his hand. 'You're wanted here. But nobody's going to take you for granted. It's your choice to stay.' His mastery of her bag suddenly yielded.

'I'm not Beatrice's puppet, you know,' proclaimed Alexa stubbornly, belying her own words by stepping forward into the hall as Drew backed up.

'Neither am I,' said Drew quietly. 'Come on . . . I'll show you to your room. Beatrice had it made up on the off chance.'

Alexa eyed him narrowly, and suddenly he stopped in the middle of the hall, and shrugged. 'OK . . . I owe her. We both know I have obligations. But there's a difference between that and being her plaything. Believe me.'

'If you say so,' replied Alexa, making her voice wry, but in actual fact accepting what he said. Even in the service of others, there was something that stayed untamed about him. It was the quality she admired most, a steely core that was both noble and arousing. He'd obeyed Sacha D'Aronville's orders, performed every perverted task like the perfect subordinate, yet remained unsullied for all that. She wondered how busy he was this morning, and found herself staring at him, studying the sheen on the skin of his arms, the contours of his strong, bare legs.

'So, where is the good doctor?' she enquired, as Drew began walking again, in the direction of the steps. 'If she was so sure I'd turn up, why isn't she here to greet me?'

Drew turned for a moment, his foot on the first step. 'She's busy. Catching up after last week's little "jaunt" . . . She does actually have patients, you know,' he answered with a grin, his eyes twinkling behind his glasses. 'I know she's not . . . Well, she's not your average family practitioner, but she does sometimes treat the sick and dispense medicine.' He shrugged his broad shoulders and started up the stairs, his movements almost balletic for a man so tall and solid. 'At least some of the time.'

'Of course,' murmured Alexa, thinking of her own 'treatment'. She could almost feel the red leather beneath her back again, and the gossamer touch of a woman's stroking hand.

As she followed Drew up to the second floor, passing the now-familiar paintings, furniture and bric-à-brac, Alexa was washed by a deluge of eroticism. This house, this lovely ornate house, seemed imbued by its owner's personality. She could sense Beatrice nearby – even, she imagined, faintly hear her voice somewhere along the corridor – almost taste her and touch her in the air. The doctor's possessions were all around her: the sensual images on the romantic Victorian pictures, the lushness and richness of the furnishings. Even the walls themselves seemed to hold echoes. Beatrice's teasing laugh, and her husky moans of pleasure. Alexa faltered as her mind flicked back to France, and the sensation of a breast beneath her tongue.

'Are you OK?' enquired Drew, making her snap back to the present, and the door that stood before them.

'Er, yes,' said Alexa quickly. 'It must be rushing up all those stairs. I'm not as fit as you, you know. I spend most of my life at a keyboard.'

'Well, maybe we can do something about that,' replied Drew archly, opening the door and letting it swing open. 'When you're settled in, we'll start work on you. I'll make out a programme . . . Exercises, diet, massage. That sort of thing.'

'I can imagine,' said Alexa pointedly, passing into the pretty and very feminine bedroom. Under any other circumstances she would have paused to admire her new surroundings, but the man with her commandeered her attention. She remembered the first time Drew had massaged her, by her cabana in Barbados. It had set everything that had happened since in motion.

He chose, it seemed, not to rise to the bait, but simply set her case on the bed. 'I'll leave you to it, then. If you need anything – coffee, something to eat, whatever – Beatrice's housekeeper is in the kitchen, on the ground floor. You can reach her by dialling "2" on the housephone.' He nodded to the slim white receiver on the bedside table. 'And if there's anything else . . .' He shrugged, as if he didn't quite know what that might be, 'I'll be out in the garden; down at the bottom. You'll be able to see me from here.' He pointed to the lace-curtained window, and beyond it, the doctor's large garden.

'And what am I supposed to want you for?' she observed tartly, feeling stung. Did he assume that she was going to fling herself at him straight away, after she'd only been here a few minutes? That she'd just unpack her belongings and think, 'Hey, I feel randy now, where's Drew?' It was true, she realised, feeling the tension in her belly and her breasts, but it irked her to be considered so predictable.

'I don't know!' he snapped back at her. 'Someone to talk to . . . To be your friend. I just thought you might need some company; Bea's likely to be busy all morning.'

'I'm sorry,' murmured Alexa, ashamed of her assumptions. 'I'm a bit mixed-up. I need time to think.' She offered a nervous smile as her mind filled with images of this man, as he'd been in France, and before that, in Barbados. 'I don't really know what I'm doing here.'

'It's OK,' said Drew softly, taking a step forward. For a moment, Alexa thought he was going to take her in his arms, and her body shivered right at its core. But then he just smiled, his grey eyes strangely gentle behind his glasses, and walked slowly and lithely towards the door. 'Like I said, you know where I am if you need me.'

And with that, he was gone, leaving Alexa feeling adrift and vaguely cheated. She hadn't come to this house, this morning, with a specific act of sex in mind, but now she was here, breathing in an aura of received sensuality, and seeing a beautiful male body so lightly clad, she wanted sex. She wanted Drew, she realised. Specifically, and desperately. And as she faced facts, her memories unfurled.

She saw him naked in Barbados, rising above her in the whiteness of her sun-filled cabana. She saw him in France, all dressed in black and slumped in that chair on the terrace. His penis was exposed, just losing its stiffness, and still wet from its sojourn in her mouth. She saw his shadow, massive but comforting, as she'd seen it when he'd come to her at night and given her a pleasure that she'd thought at first was secret.

Making a sound somewhere between a sigh and a moan of frustration, she opened her case and began unpacking her clothes.

Would it be so wrong to go down now, and make the first move? She threw undies into a drawer, then crossed back to the window and looked out. Drew was there, just where he'd said he'd be, trimming the edge of the lawn with some implement she didn't know the name of. With his T-shirt off, he looked wholesome and straightforwardly male, and Alexa felt her desire for him swell. He wasn't a brainless, two-dimensional stud, she knew that. The games they'd played in France had shown him to be well versed in sophisticated sexuality, but there was simple manly honesty about him, too. That nobility that had so moved her earlier . . .

'Go to him,' said a soft, purring voice from right beside her.

Alexa turned sharply, her heart leaping, and discovered that she wasn't alone. She'd been so absorbed in her ruminations, and in her yearnings for Drew, that she'd never even noticed the arrival of Beatrice. The doctor was standing just a yard away, still in her white coat, with a knowing expression in her brilliant brown eyes. She glanced down towards the garden, then returned her attention to Alexa, her red mouth curving beautifully into a smile.

'I . . . I left Tom,' began Alexa haltingly, suddenly aware of the audacity of just turning up at a house she'd only visited once before. 'I wasn't quite sure where to go. I wondered if you could put me up for a few days. If it's any trouble, I can go to a hotel.'

'The hell you will!' said Beatrice emphatically, taking a step forward and sliding her arm fondly around Alexa. 'You're welcome here.' She squeezed, her long fingers splaying across Alexa's ribs as she put her face close, almost close enough for a kiss. 'You're wanted here . . . I was on the point of suggesting it a hundred times in France, but it seemed wiser to let you make your own decisions.' Her lips gently brushed Alexa's cheek, then she drew back and smiled another of her captivating smiles.

Alexa felt dizzy, and looked away. Beatrice had effortless overpowered her, touched her with far more than just her hand or her arm. Everything about the physician was seductive: the lovely face, the luscious mouth, the thick coils of her brilliant red hair. She was soberly dressed, for once – in a man's waistcoat and trousers beneath her smock, and a pinstripe shirt with a severely knotted tie – but somehow her clothes barely contained her.

Unable to answer, Alexa tried to smile, and was rewarded with another swift kiss.

'This is my house, Alexa. My home,' the doctor said, her brown eyes provocative. 'And as the Spanish would say, Mi casa es su casa; everything that's in it is yours.' With a graceful motion, she nodded towards her garden, and to the half-naked man who was tending it. As she did so, her caressing hand slid downwards and squeezed Alexa's bottom through the fabric of her dress.

The statement was unambiguous. Beatrice was sanctioning Alexa's interest in Drew. She was giving her guest the use of her lover. It was a kind gesture, but magnificently arrogant.

'But he isn't yours to give,' countered Alexa boldly, moving her rump against the slowly fondling fingers.

'True,' accepted Beatrice, her voice light but serious. 'But even if he was, I suspect you could take him. Easily . . . You're young. Intelligent. An individual. If you wanted him, he'd be yours like a shot. And there wouldn't be anything I could do about it.'

'I wouldn't do that! I want him, yes . . . but not at your expense, Beatrice,' Alexa said firmly, looking away from Drew and the garden and deep into her companion's glowing eyes.

'Good!' said the doctor, the tips of her fingers pressing tantalisingly inward and brushing Alexa's sex from the rear, through her clothes. 'We'll share him then. And, as I have to go out, and I had him this morning, I'd say that it's round about your turn . . .'

'Now?' gasped Alexa, leaning backwards on to the delicately probing fingers as she looked out towards the garden below. Drew had paused a moment, and slid off his glasses as he mopped his sweaty brow. The action was so unstudied, yet so sensuous, that Alexa's body grew feverishly moist.

'Oh, yes, my dear, now,' cooed Beatrice, pushing. 'You're hot for him. I can almost feel your wetness through your dress.' Her other hand shimmied slowly down Alexa's belly, then moved inwards, dividing her labia through the thin layers of her clothing.

'Go on, Alexa,' she coaxed. 'Go to him. It's completely secluded in the garden, you can have him there. Over there, on the grass. Imagine it, making love in the sunlight . . . Remember how you loved it in Barbados?'

Alexa swayed, bewitched by Beatrice's words as much as her touch. She twisted spasmodically between the doctor's fondling hands, then stood, shaking and defenceless, as her skirt was lifted and her panties skinned down.

'You won't need these,' said Beatrice, letting Alexa step free of the already sodden garment. Flinging the cotton scrap into the corner of the room, she reached down to the slippery cleft that they'd covered. One finger began to move devilishly, then with a gasp, Beatrice snatched her hand away. 'Goddamnit! You're too tempting, do you know that?' she accused, then pushed Alexa, bemused, away from her, 'Get on down there!' she ordered. 'Go and fuck him. Before I get so hot to have you that I can't break off!'

Alexa almost ran from the room, then paused at the door to glance helplessly at Beatrice.

The doctor grinned lasciviously, and mimed 'Shoo!' Alexa hesitated in the doorway, then obeyed her, just as Beatrice dropped her hand to her own crotch . . .

Drew was kneeling as Alexa approached him. He was tugging at stray weeds along the edge of the lawn now, and tossing them away into a pile. After a moment, he looked up, as if he'd heard her hesitant footsteps, then sat back on his heels as she moved in close.

'Are you OK,' he enquired quietly, his eyes steady.

Alexa realised that after her brush with Beatrice she must look flushed and wild. She pushed her fingers through her hair, feeling harassed and no longer quite as sure of herself as she had on the way down. What was the best way to make the first move? Even now, she couldn't bring herself to ask, outright, in words . . .

Drew grinned. 'It looks as if Beatrice has been after you,' he observed, pulling off the heavy gloves he'd been wearing to tend the garden.

'What on earth do you mean?' Alexa felt her mettle rising quickly; it was infuriating to be 'read' so easily. Especially when that was supposed to be *her* trick.

'Well, it seems to me that Beatrice has started something . . . and then decided she'd like *me* to finish it off.'

'I don't know what you're talking about,' Alexa said airily, preparing to back away.

But before she could move, Drew had a hold on her, his powerful arms folding around her thighs. Hugging her close, he seemed to nuzzle her like a puppy, rubbing his nose and mouth against her belly through her skirt.

Unable to stop herself, Alexa cupped his head and dug her fingers into his silky black hair. She could smell his sharp cologne rising up off his skin, but much stronger than that, the aroma of his sweat. Both in body and in scent, he was every bit as tempting as the woman who employed him; as her head began to spin, Alexa forgot everything and surrendered to his lure. Without thinking she thrust her pelvis forward.

'Oh, yes,' she murmured, as she felt him pull back, then start plucking at the thin cotton skirt of her dress. Even as it brushed her knees, she was parting her legs accommodatingly, and as it was whisked up over her smooth, uncovered hips, she jerked her vulva instinctively towards his face.

As the sun shone down on her back, Alexa was fully aware of how lewd she looked – standing with legs wide, and her sex wet and gaping – but for the life of her, she couldn't give a damn. She was also conscious – regardless of what Beatrice had said about having to go out – that the doctor was still watching from the window . . . and the idea of surveillance made Alexa's body melt.

'Lick me,' she ordered, forgetting her every last qualm as she crushed her quivering flesh against Drew's handsome face, then moaned joyfully as his long tongue dived in. 'Oh yes, more! More!' she growled, clutching up her skirt so he could grip her naked buttocks, and grinding her hips as the pleasure grew and grew.

This is it! This is me . . . It's what I want! thought the new Alexa as the age-old spasms racked her.

And as she climaxed, the devil inside her laughed . . .

Visit the Black Lace website at
www.blacklace-books.co.uk

FIND OUT THE LATEST INFORMATION AND TAKE ADVANTAGE OF OUR FANTASTIC FREE BOOK OFFER! ALSO VISIT THE SITE FOR . . .

- All Black Lace titles currently available and how to order online
- Great new offers
- Writers' guidelines
- Author interviews
- An erotica newsletter
- Features
- Cool links

BLACK LACE – THE LEADING IMPRINT OF WOMEN'S SEXY FICTION

TAKING YOUR EROTIC READING PLEASURE TO NEW HORIZONS

LOOK OUT FOR THE ALL-NEW BLACK LACE BOOKS – AVAILABLE NOW!

All books priced £7.99 in the UK. Please note publication dates apply to the UK only. For other territories, please contact your retailer.

THE ANGELS' SHARE
Maya Hess
ISBN 0 352 34043 6

A derelict cottage on the rugged Manx coast is no place for a young woman to hide out in the middle of winter. But Ailey Callister is on a mission – to find and overthrow the man who has stolen her inheritance. Battling against the elements and her own desire for sexual freedom, she fights ghosts from her past to discover the true identity of Ethan Kinrade, the elusive new owner of the vast, whisky-producing estate that by rights should be hers.

Coming in August

IN PURSUIT OF ANNA
Natasha Rostova
ISBN 0 352 34060 6

Anna Maxwell is a pixie-like bad girl with a penchant for brawny men, determined to prove her innocence when accused of stealing from her father's company. Los Angeles-based bounty hunter Derek Rowland sets off in pursuit of his fugitive, discovering that Anna's resolve is as strong as her libido. Derek's colleague, Freddie James, is convinced that Derek is being taken for a ride – and not the good kind. Freddie, meanwhile, is engaged in her own rather delicious struggle with a new lover. The sexual stakes rise as desires and boundaries are pushed to their limits.

DANCE OF OBSESSION
Olivia Christie
ISBN 0 352 33101 1

Paris, 1935. Devastated by the sudden death of her husband, exotic dancer Georgia d'Essange wants to be left alone to grieve. However, her stepson Dominic has inherited his father's business and demands Georgia's help in running it. The business is *Fleur's* – an exclusive club where women of means can indulge their sexual whims with men of their choice and take advantage of the exotic delights Parisian nightlife has to offer. Dominic is eager to take his father's place in Georgia's bed and passions and tempers run high. Further complications arise when Georgia's first lover, Theo Sands – now a rich, successful artist – appears on the scene. In an atmosphere of increasing sexual tension, can everyone's desires be satisfied?

Coming in September

THE PRIVATE UNDOING OF A PUBLIC SERVANT
Leonie Martell
ISBN 0 352 34066 5

I love the sound of heels on a bathroom floor in the morning. It sounds like . . . Mistress.

Madame K, *femme fatale* and sexual subversive, 38, is an uncompromising deviant. She exacts her pleasures through the disciplinary art of male humiliation, where attention to aesthetic detail is lovingly realised, and punishment is not given lightly.

Simon Charlesworth, cabinet minister, 52, is undergoing a crisis. Party politics, domestic routine and thoughts of mortality have recently begun to crush his soul and he is desperately seeking something. He hungers for authentic experience and excitement – but he doesn't yet know what form this might take.

When these two very different personalities meet by chance one evening in a bar in Victoria Station, London, the wheels are set in motion for a descent into sexual excess and an exploration of the human condition at its most primal. Through a series of humiliating and extreme adventures Charlesworth achieves the divine oblivion of erotic ecstasy. But there is something in Madame K's past that is due to return. Something that could cost Charlesworth everything he owns.

THE MASTER OF SHILDEN
Lucinda Carrington
ISBN O 352 33140 2

When successful interior designer Elise St John is offered a commission at a remote castle, she jumps at the chance to distance herself from a web of sexual and emotional entanglements. Yet, as she sets to work creating rooms in which guests will be able to realise their most erotic fantasies, she finds herself indulging in fantasies of her own, about two very different men.

Blair Devlin – overtly sexy and self-confident – is a local riding instructor. Max Lannsen – the Master of Shilden – is darkly attractive but more remote. All the seem to have in common is their hatred for one another. Then, when Elise's sensual daydreams become reality, she discovers that each man's future depends on a decision she will soon be forced to make. To which of them does she really owe her loyalty?

Black Lace Booklist

Information is correct at time of printing. To avoid disappointment, check availability before ordering. Go to www.blacklace-books.co.uk. All books are priced £6.99 unless another price is given.

BLACK LACE BOOKS WITH A CONTEMPORARY SETTING

☐ ON THE EDGE Laura Hamilton	ISBN O 352 33534 3	£5.99
☐ THE TRANSFORMATION Natasha Rostova	ISBN O 352 33311 1	
☐ SIN.NET Helena Ravenscroft	ISBN O 352 33598 X	
☐ TWO WEEKS IN TANGIER Annabel Lee	ISBN O 352 33599 8	
☐ SYMPHONY X Jasmine Stone	ISBN O 352 33629 3	
☐ A SECRET PLACE Ella Broussard	ISBN O 352 33307 3	
☐ GOING TOO FAR Laura Hamilton	ISBN O 352 33657 9	
☐ RELEASE ME Suki Cunningham	ISBN O 352 33671 4	
☐ SLAVE TO SUCCESS Kimberley Raines	ISBN O 352 33687 0	
☐ SHADOWPLAY Portia Da Costa	ISBN O 352 33313 8	
☐ ARIA APPASSIONATA Julie Hastings	ISBN O 352 33056 2	
☐ A MULTITUDE OF SINS Kit Mason	ISBN O 352 33737 0	
☐ COMING ROUND THE MOUNTAIN Tabitha Flyte	ISBN O 352 33873 3	
☐ FEMININE WILES Karina Moore	ISBN O 352 33235 2	
☐ MIXED SIGNALS Anna Clare	ISBN O 352 33889 X	
☐ BLACK LIPSTICK KISSES Monica Belle	ISBN O 352 33885 7	
☐ GOING DEEP Kimberly Dean	ISBN O 352 33876 8	
☐ PACKING HEAT Karina Moore	ISBN O 352 33356 1	
☐ MIXED DOUBLES Zoe le Verdier	ISBN O 352 33312 X	
☐ UP TO NO GOOD Karen S. Smith	ISBN O 352 33589 0	
☐ CLUB CRÈME Primula Bond	ISBN O 352 33907 1	
☐ BONDED Fleur Reynolds	ISBN O 352 33192 5	
☐ SWITCHING HANDS Alaine Hood	ISBN O 352 33896 2	
☐ EDEN'S FLESH Robyn Russell	ISBN O 352 33923 3	
☐ PEEP SHOW Mathilde Madden	ISBN O 352 33924 1	£7.99
☐ RISKY BUSINESS Lisette Allen	ISBN O 352 33280 8	£7.99
☐ CAMPAIGN HEAT Gabrielle Marcola	ISBN O 352 33941 1	£7.99
☐ MS BEHAVIOUR Mini Lee	ISBN O 352 33962 4	£7.99

BLACK LACE ANTHOLOGIES

BLACK LACE NON-FICTION

To find out the latest information about Black Lace titles, check out the website: www.blacklace-books.co.uk or send for a booklist with complete synopses by writing to:

Black Lace Booklist, Virgin Books Ltd
Thames Wharf Studios
Rainville Road
London W6 9HA

Please include an SAE of decent size. Please note only British stamps are valid.

Our privacy policy
We will not disclose information you supply us to any other parties.
We will not disclose any information which identifies you personally to any person without your express consent.

From time to time we may send out information about Black Lace books and special offers. Please tick here if you do <u>not</u> wish to receive Black Lace information.   ❑

Please send me the books I have ticked above.

Name ....

Address ....

....

....

....

Post Code ....

Send to: Virgin Books Cash Sales, Thames Wharf Studios, Rainville Road, London W6 9HA.

US customers: for prices and details of how to order books for delivery by mail, call 888-330-8477.

Please enclose a cheque or postal order, made payable to Virgin Books Ltd, to the value of the books you have ordered plus postage and packing costs as follows:

UK and BFPO – £1.00 for the first book, 50p for each subsequent book.

Overseas (including Republic of Ireland) – £2.00 for the first book, £1.00 for each subsequent book.

If you would prefer to pay by VISA, ACCESS/MASTERCARD, DINERS CLUB, AMEX or SWITCH, please write your card number and expiry date here:

....

Signature ....

Please allow up to 28 days for delivery.